MAGIC TREE HOUSE®

DINOSAURS BEFORE DARK

MARY POPE OSBORNE'S
MAGIC TREE HOUSE®
DINOSAURS BEFORE DARK

THE GRAPHIC NOVEL

ADAPTED BY
JENNY LAIRD

WITH ART BY
KELLY & NICHOLE MATTHEWS

A STEPPING STONE BOOK™
RANDOM HOUSE 🏠 NEW YORK

Text copyright © 2021 by Mary Pope Osborne
Art copyright © 2021 by Kelly Matthews & Nichole Matthews
Text adapted by Jenny Laird

All rights reserved. Published in the United States by Random House Children's Books, a division
of Penguin Random House LLC, New York. Adapted from *Dinosaurs Before Dark*, published by
Random House Children's Books, a division of Penguin Random House LLC, New York, in 1992.

Random House and the colophon are registered trademarks and A Stepping Stone Book and the colophon
and RH Graphic with the book design are trademarks of Penguin Random House LLC. Magic Tree House
is a registered trademark of Mary Pope Osborne; used under license.

Visit us on the Web!
rhcbooks.com
MagicTreeHouse.com

Educators and librarians, for a variety of teaching tools, visit us at RHTeachersLibrarians.com

Library of Congress Cataloging-in-Publication Data
Names: Laird, Jenny, adapter. | Matthews, Kelly (comic book artist), illustrator. |
Matthews, Nichole, illustrator. | Osborne, Mary Pope. Dinosaurs before dark.
Title: Dinosaurs before dark / Jenny Laird; illustrated by Kelly and Nichole Matthews.
Description: New York: Random House Children's Books, [2021] | Series: Mary Pope Osborne's Magic tree house |
Summary: Retells, in graphic novel form, the tale of eight-year-old Jack and his younger sister, Annie, who find
a magic tree house which whisks them back to an ancient time zone where they see live dinosaurs.
Identifiers: LCCN 2020032698 (print) | LCCN 2020032699 (ebook) |
ISBN 978-0-593-17471-5 (trade paperback) | ISBN 978-0-593-17468-5 (hardcover) |
ISBN 978-0-593-17469-2 (library binding) | ISBN 978-0-593-17470-8 (ebook)
Subjects: LCSH: Graphic novels. | CYAC: Graphic novels. | Dinosaurs—Fiction. |
Time travel—Fiction. | Magic—Fiction. | Tree houses—Fiction.
Classification: LCC PZ7.7.L28 Din 2021 (print) | LCC PZ7.7.L28 (ebook) | DDC 741.5/973—dc23

The artists used Clip Studio Paint to create the illustrations for this book.
The text of this book is set in 13-point Cartoonist Hand Regular.

MANUFACTURED IN CHINA
10 9 8 7 6 5 4 3 2 1
First Graphic Novel Edition

This book has been officially leveled by using the F&P Text Level Gradient™ Leveling System.

For Mallory and Jenna,
two of Jack and Annie's best friends
—M.P.O.

For Quinn, who was born to fly
—J.L.

We dedicate this book to our mother,
a teacher, who taught us to love reading, drawing,
and learning; our brothers, for inspiring us to follow
in their footsteps; and our cats, for never letting
us forget what is truly important (feeding them).
—K.M. & N.M.

CHAPTER ONE
Into the Woods

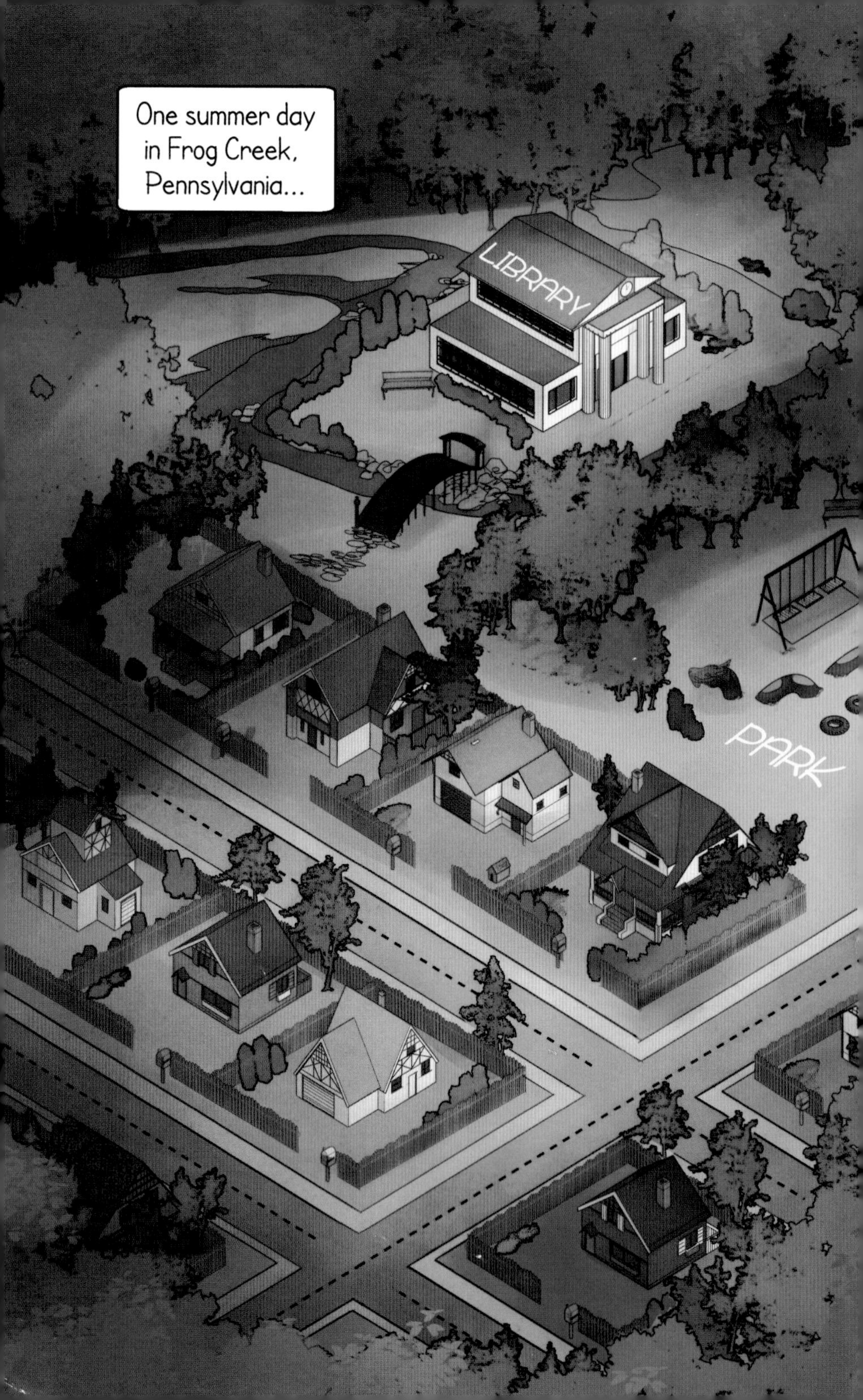
One summer day in Frog Creek, Pennsylvania...
LIBRARY
PARK

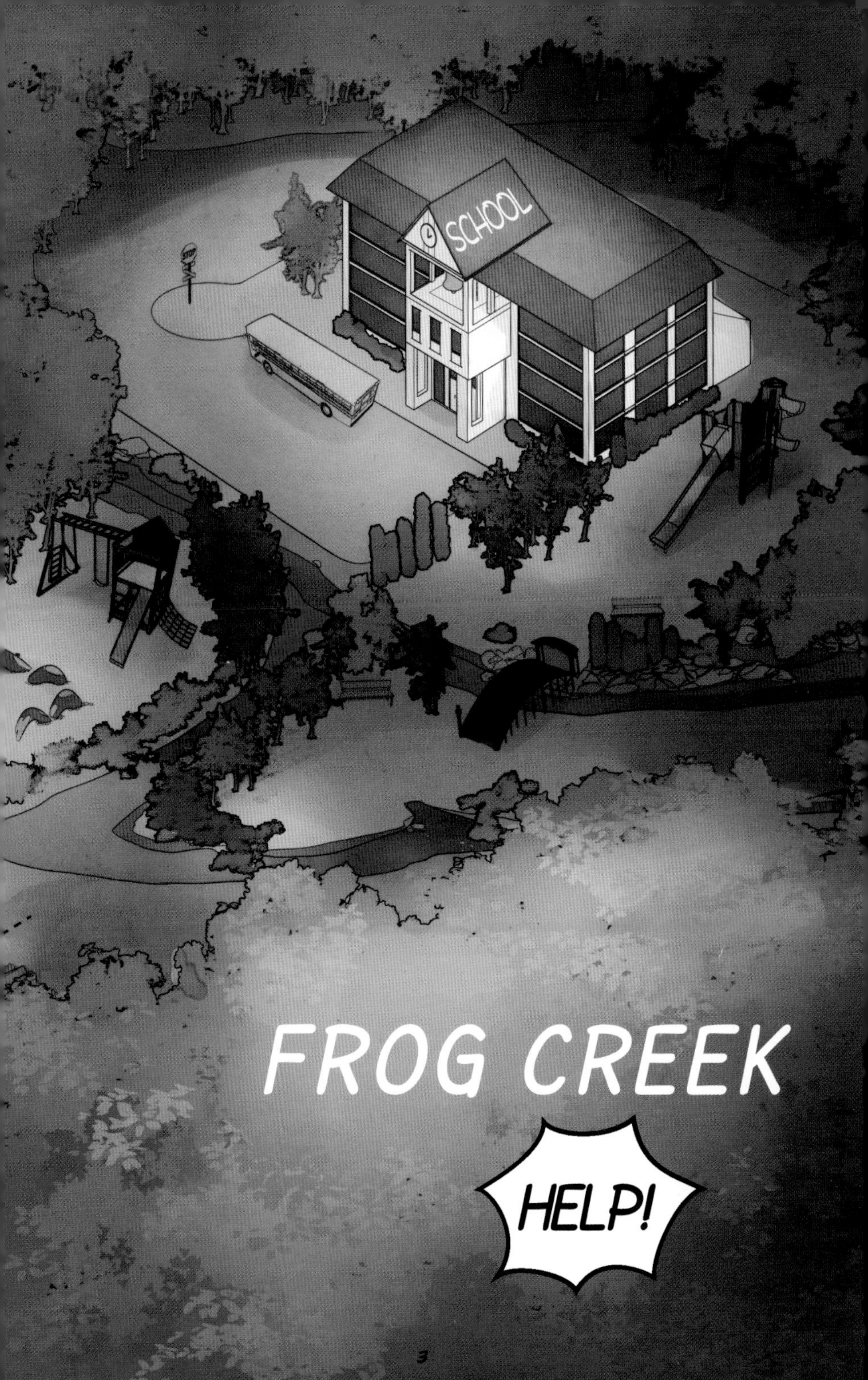
SCHOOL
STOP
FROG CREEK
HELP!

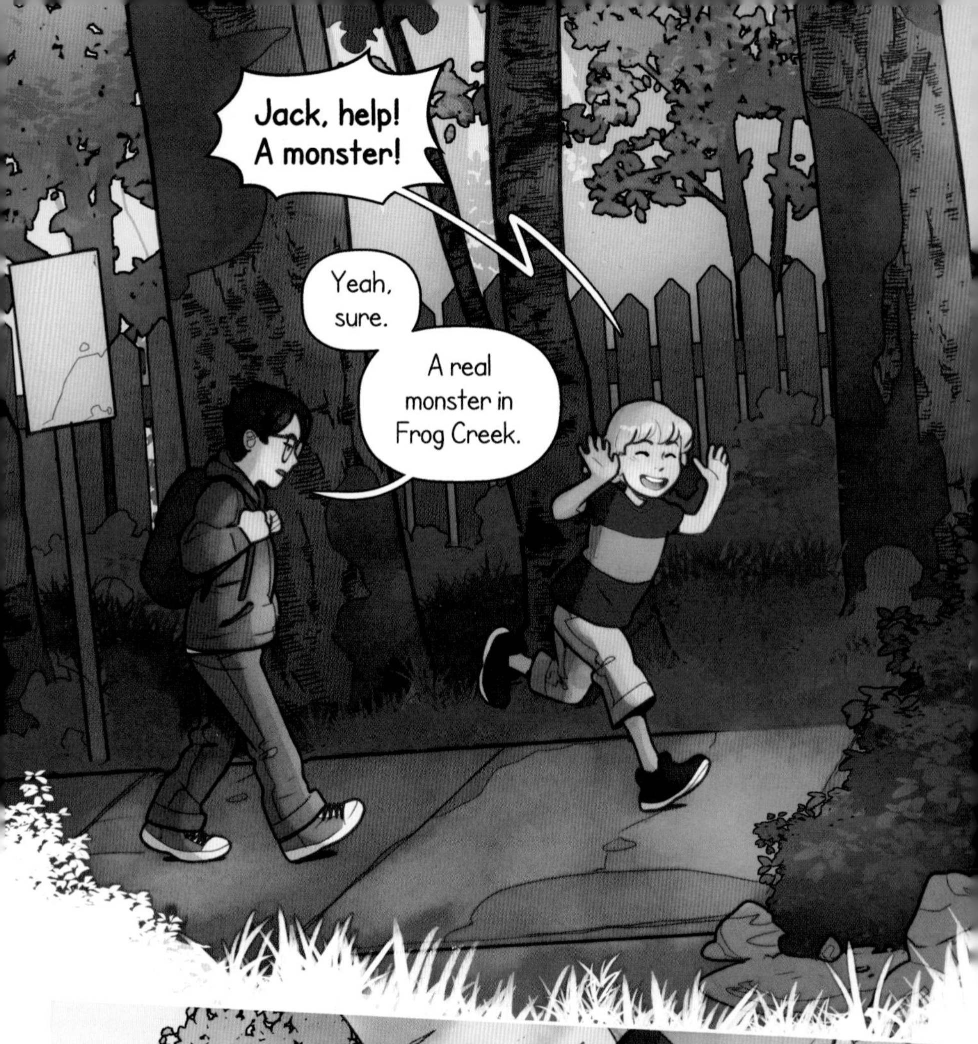
Jack, help! A monster!
Yeah, sure.
A real monster in Frog Creek.

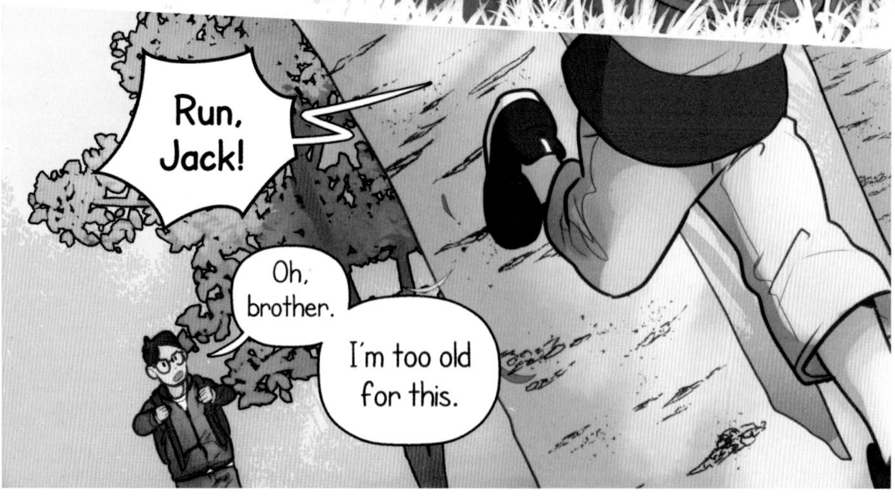
Run, Jack!
Oh, brother.
I'm too old for this.

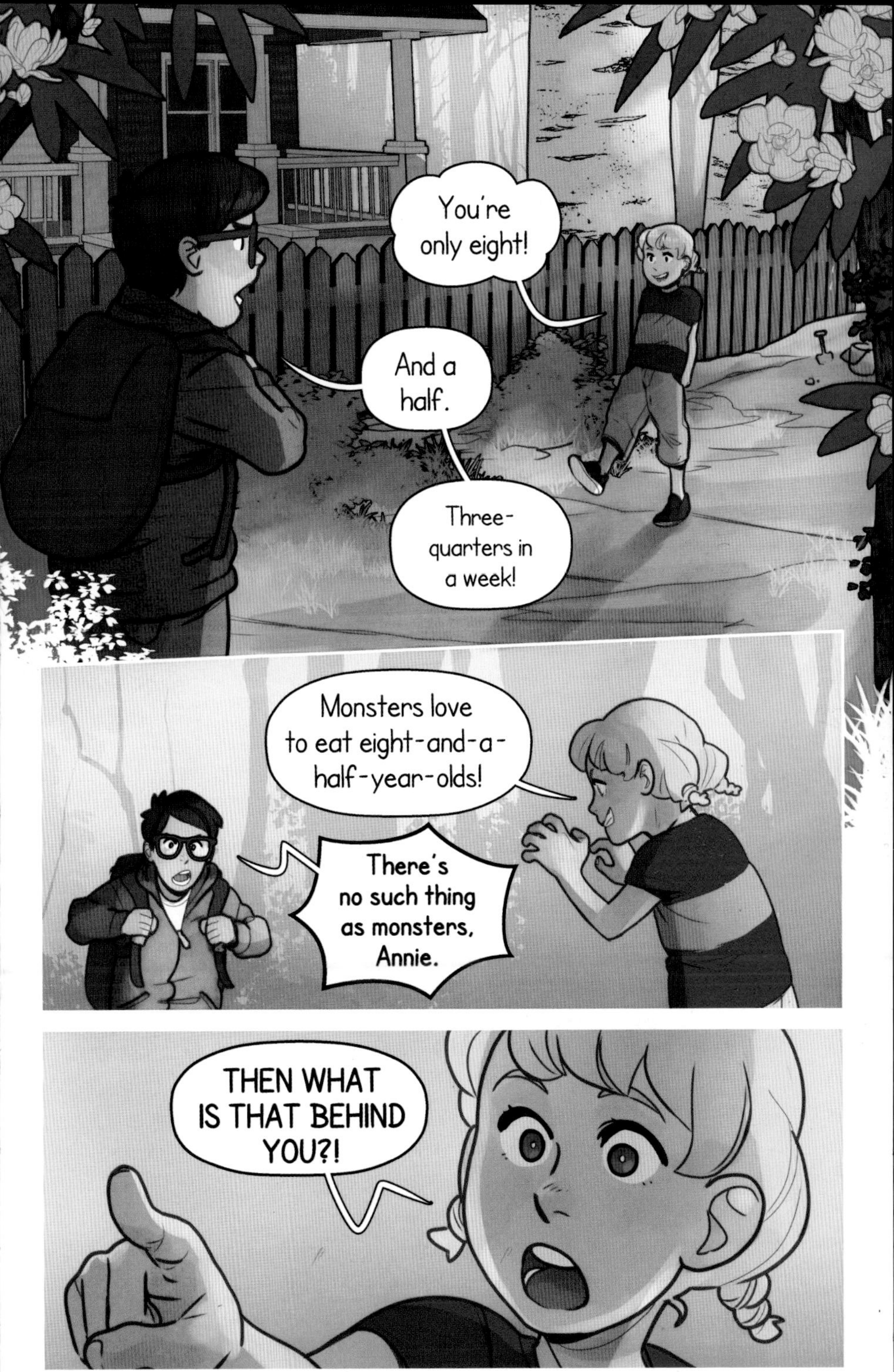
You're only eight!
And a half.
Three-quarters in a week!
Monsters love to eat eight-and-a-half-year-olds!
There's no such thing as monsters, Annie.
THEN WHAT IS THAT BEHIND YOU?!

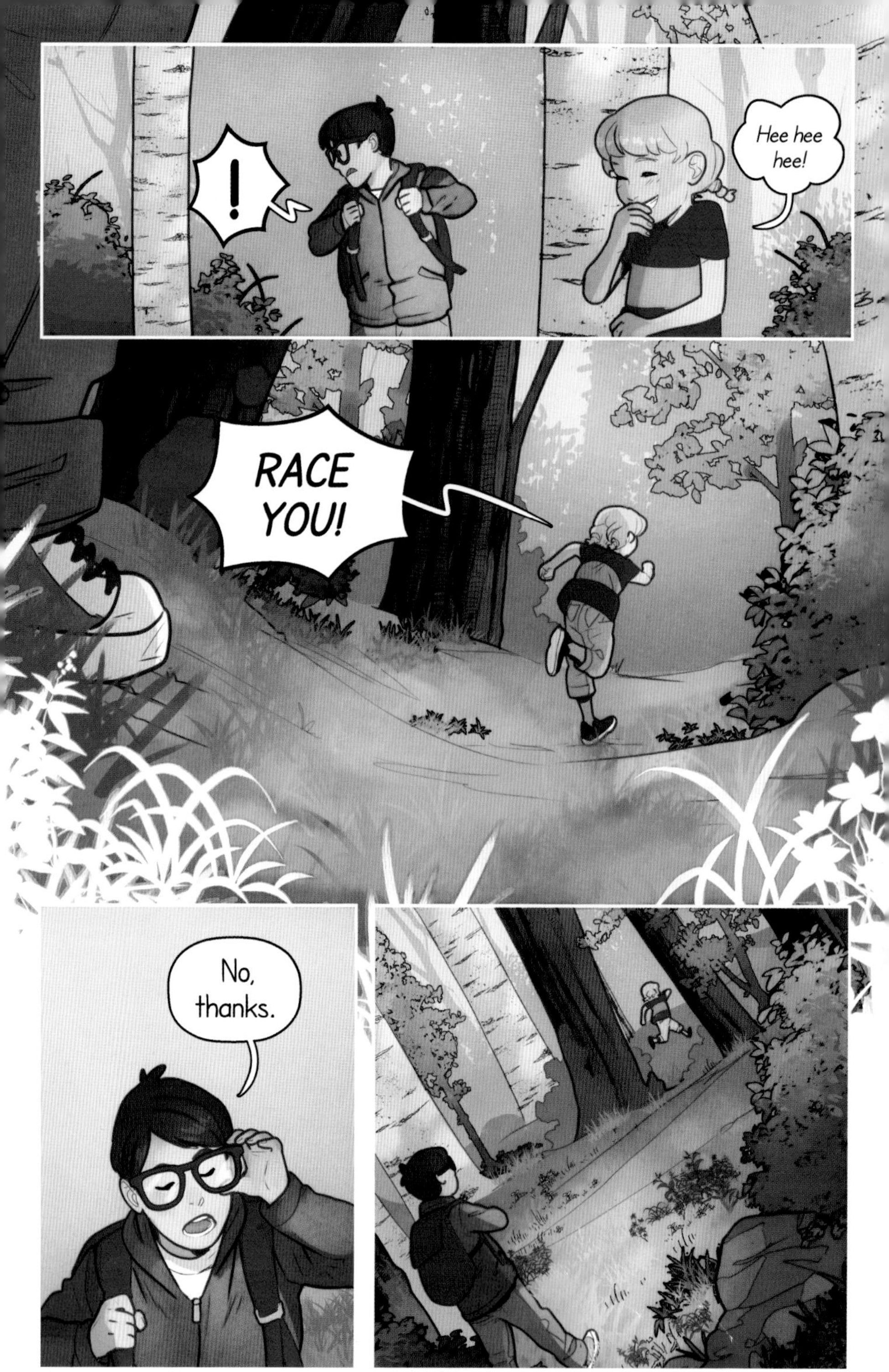
!
Hee hee hee!
RACE YOU!
No, thanks.

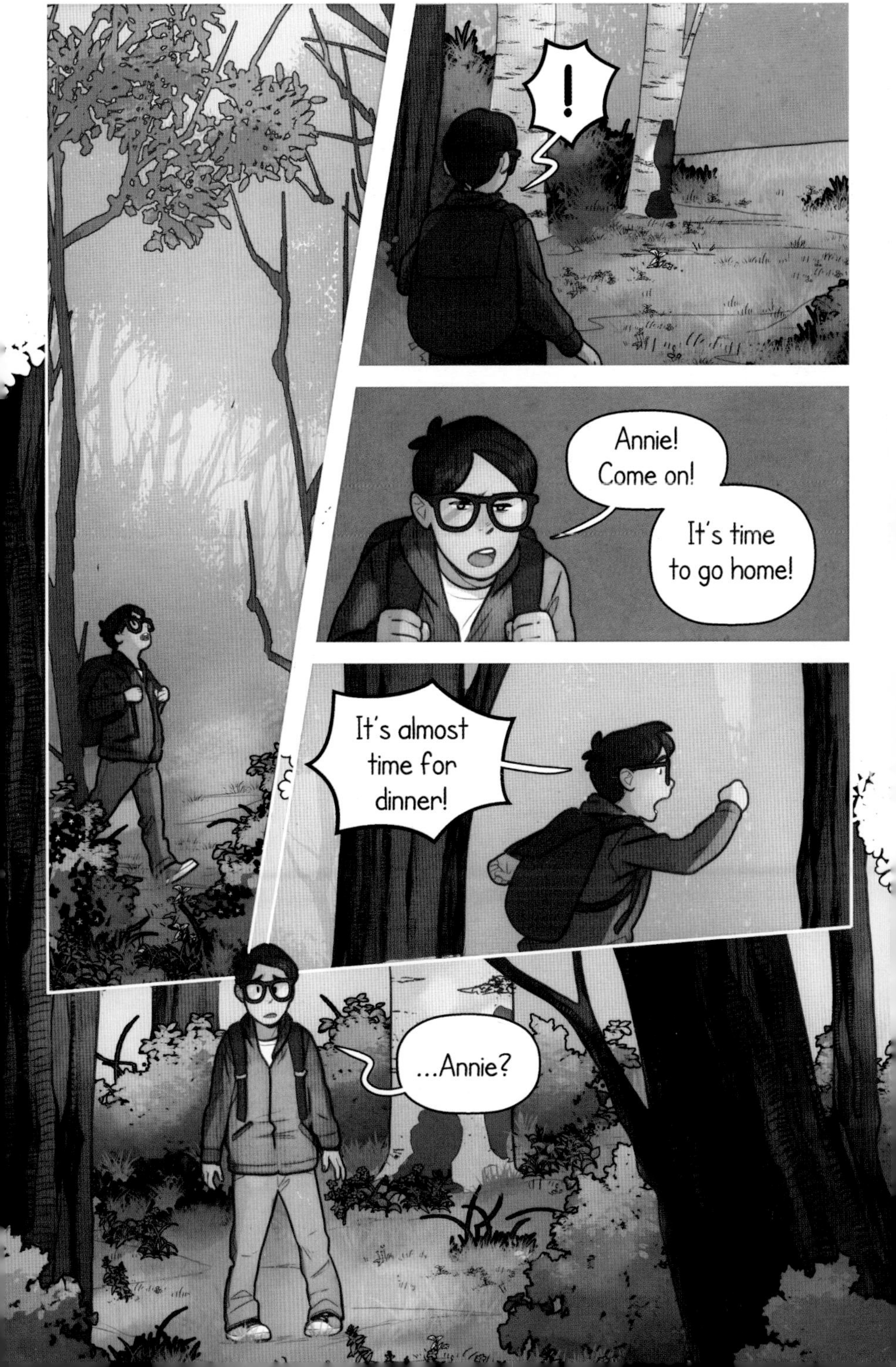
!
Annie!
Come on!
It's time
to go home!
It's almost
time for
dinner!
...Annie?

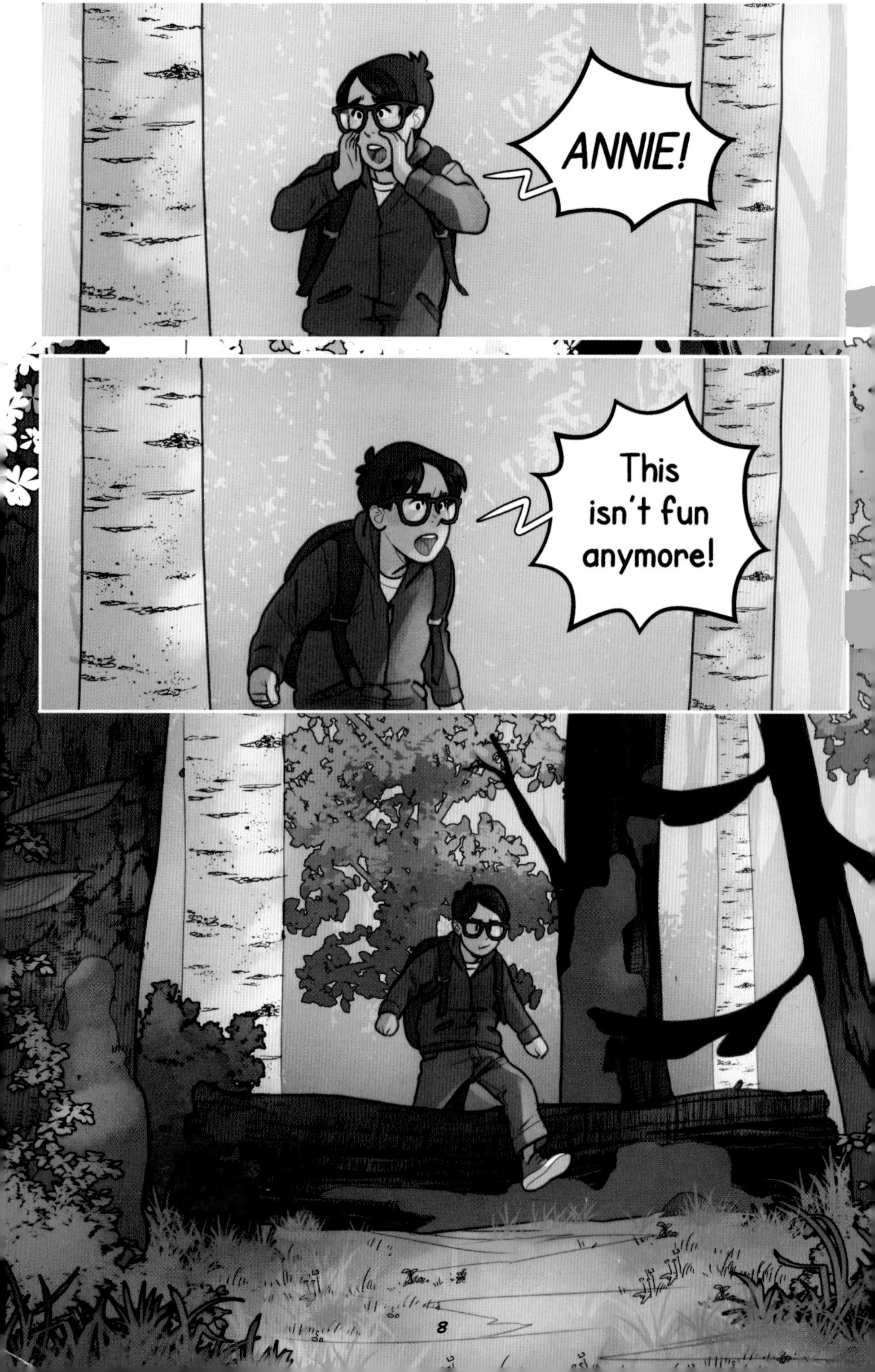
ANNIE!
This isn't fun anymore!

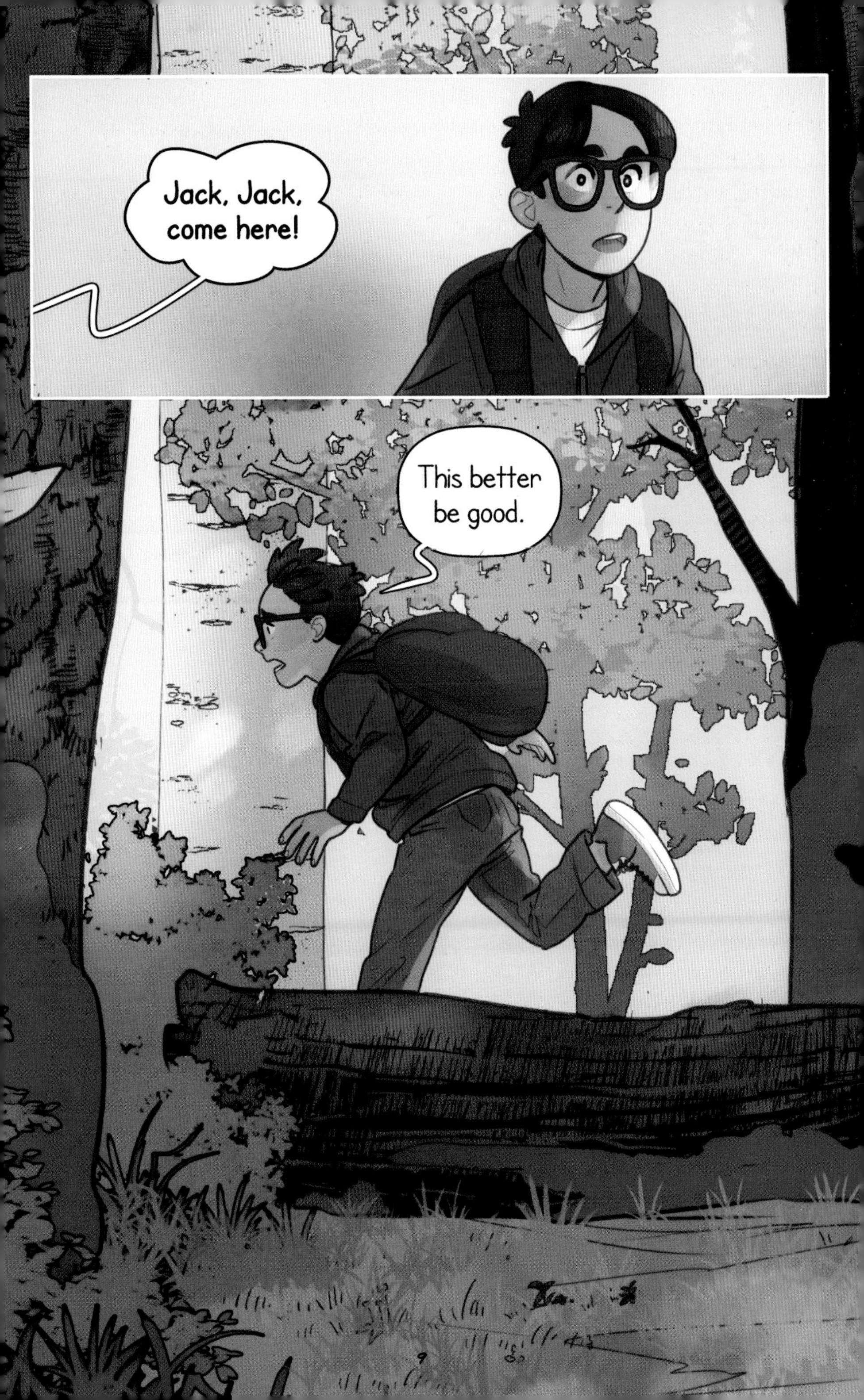
Jack, Jack, come here!
This better be good.

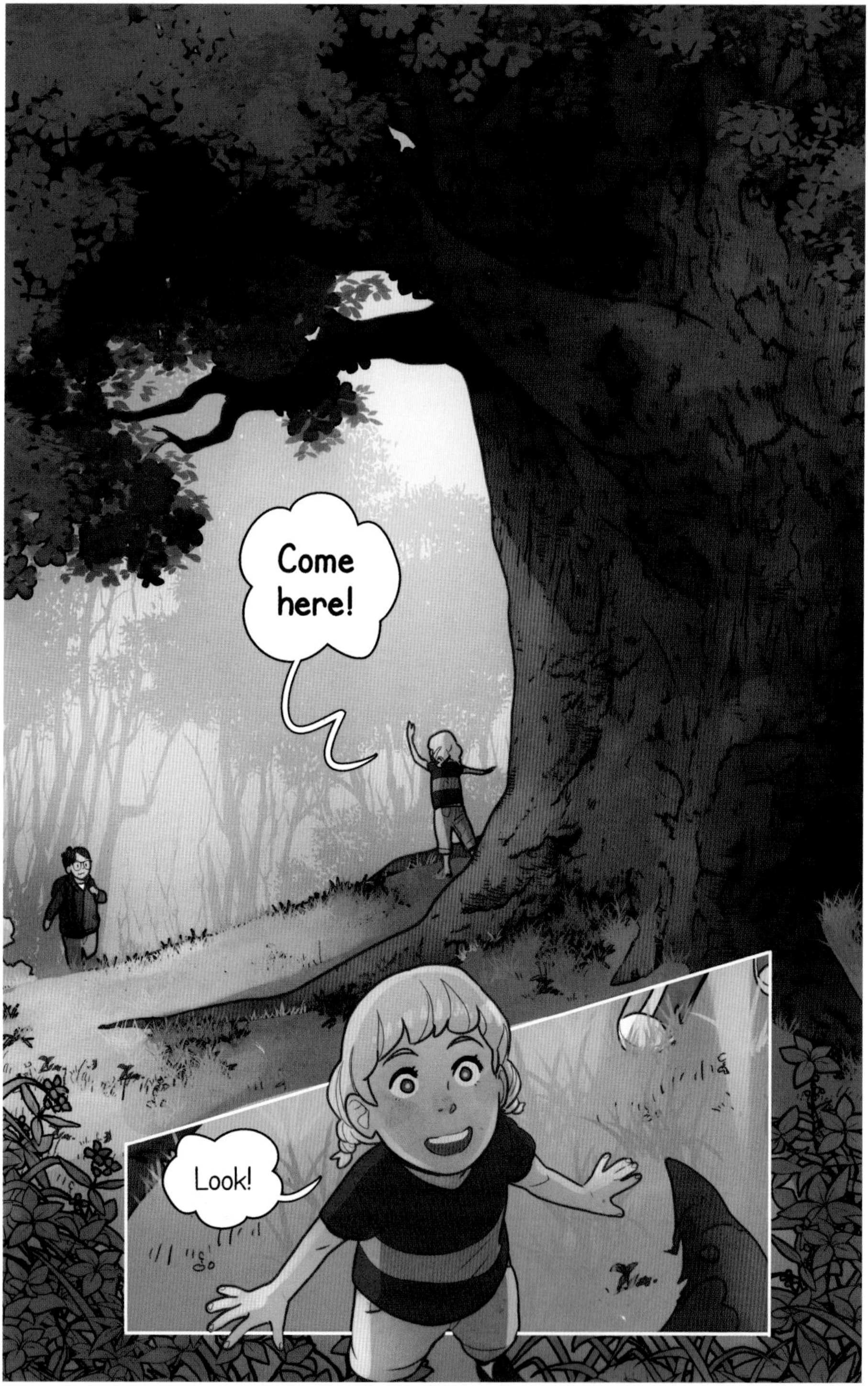
Come here!
Look!

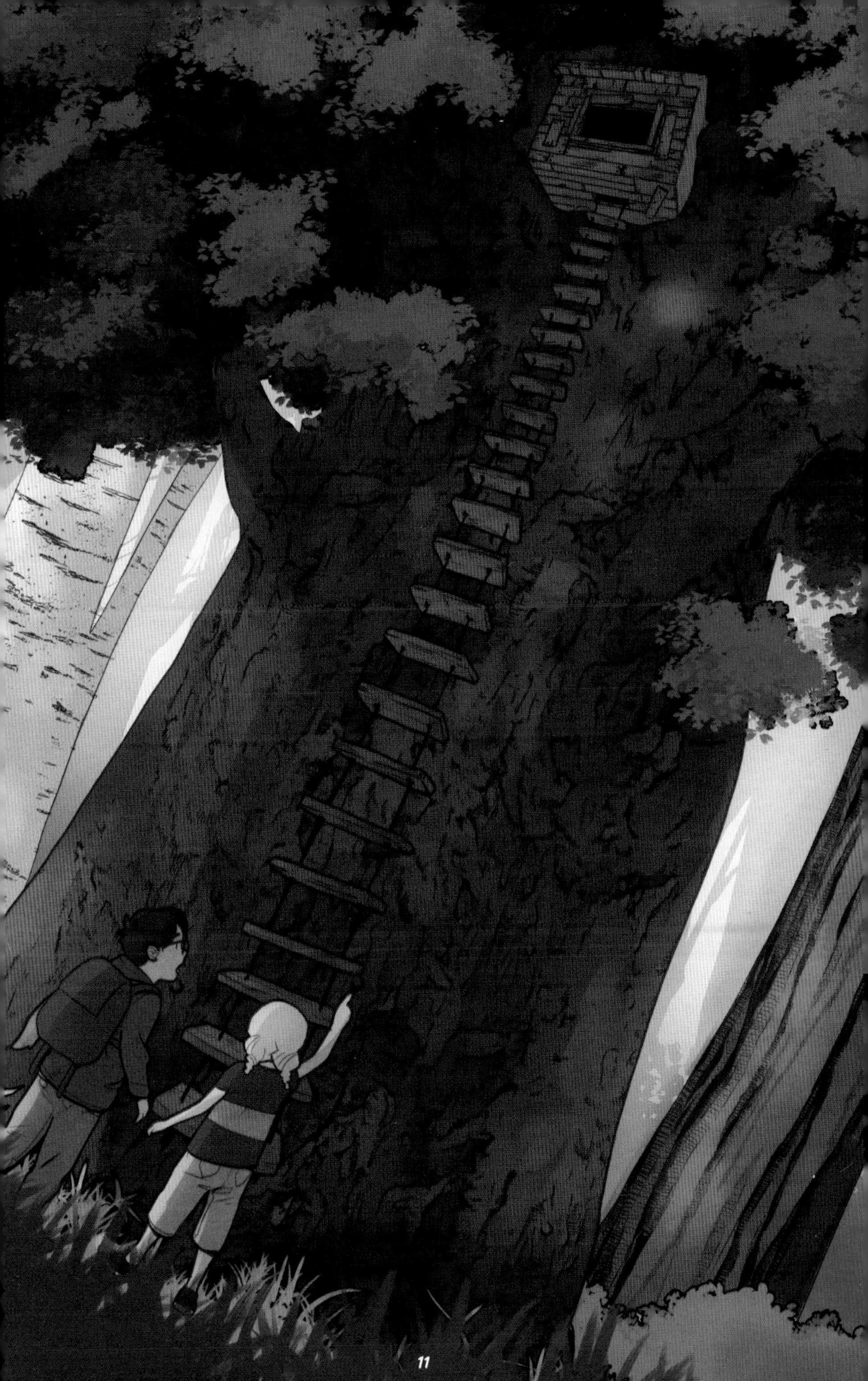

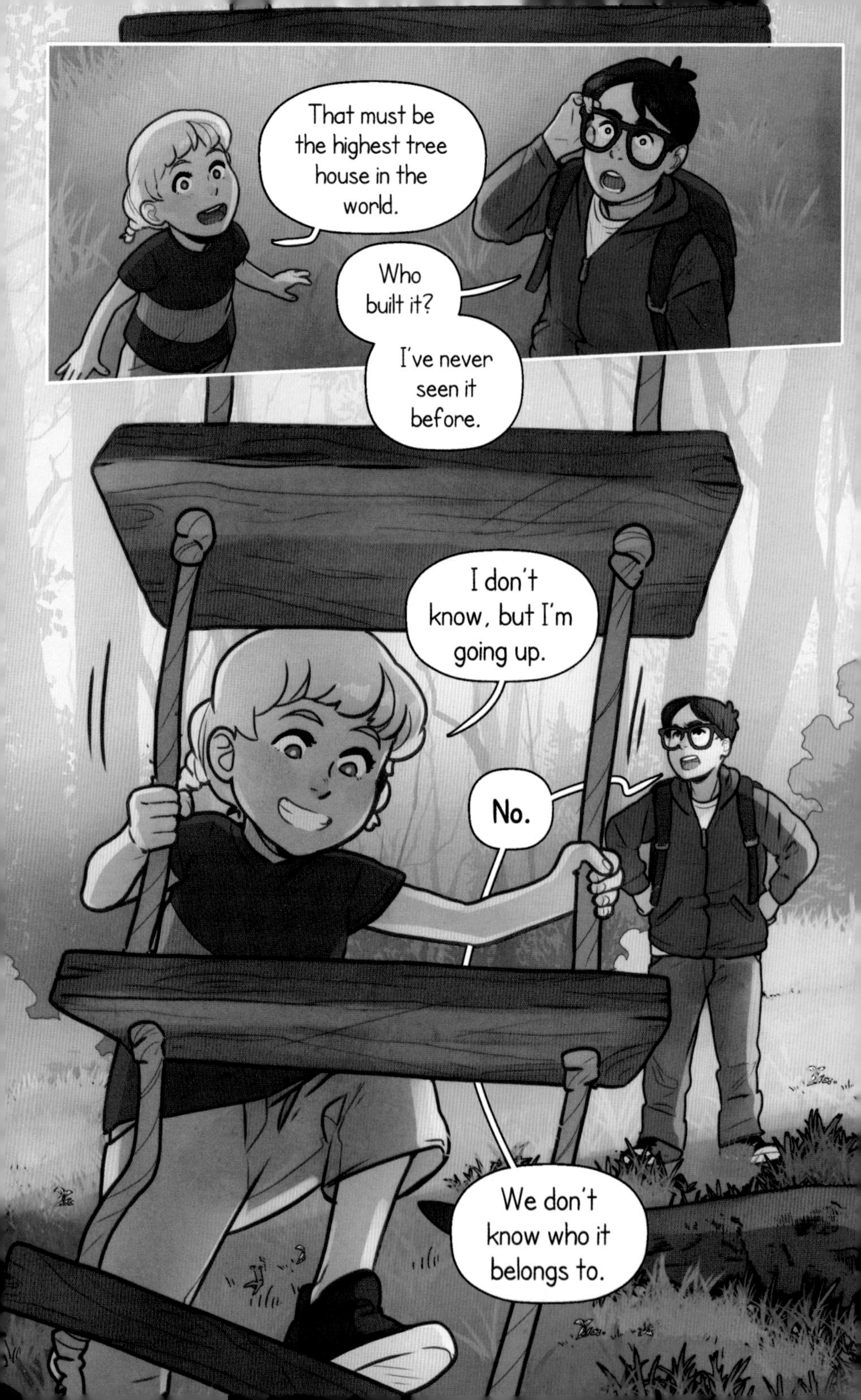
That must be the highest tree house in the world.
Who built it?
I've never seen it before.
I don't know, but I'm going up.
No.
We don't know who it belongs to.

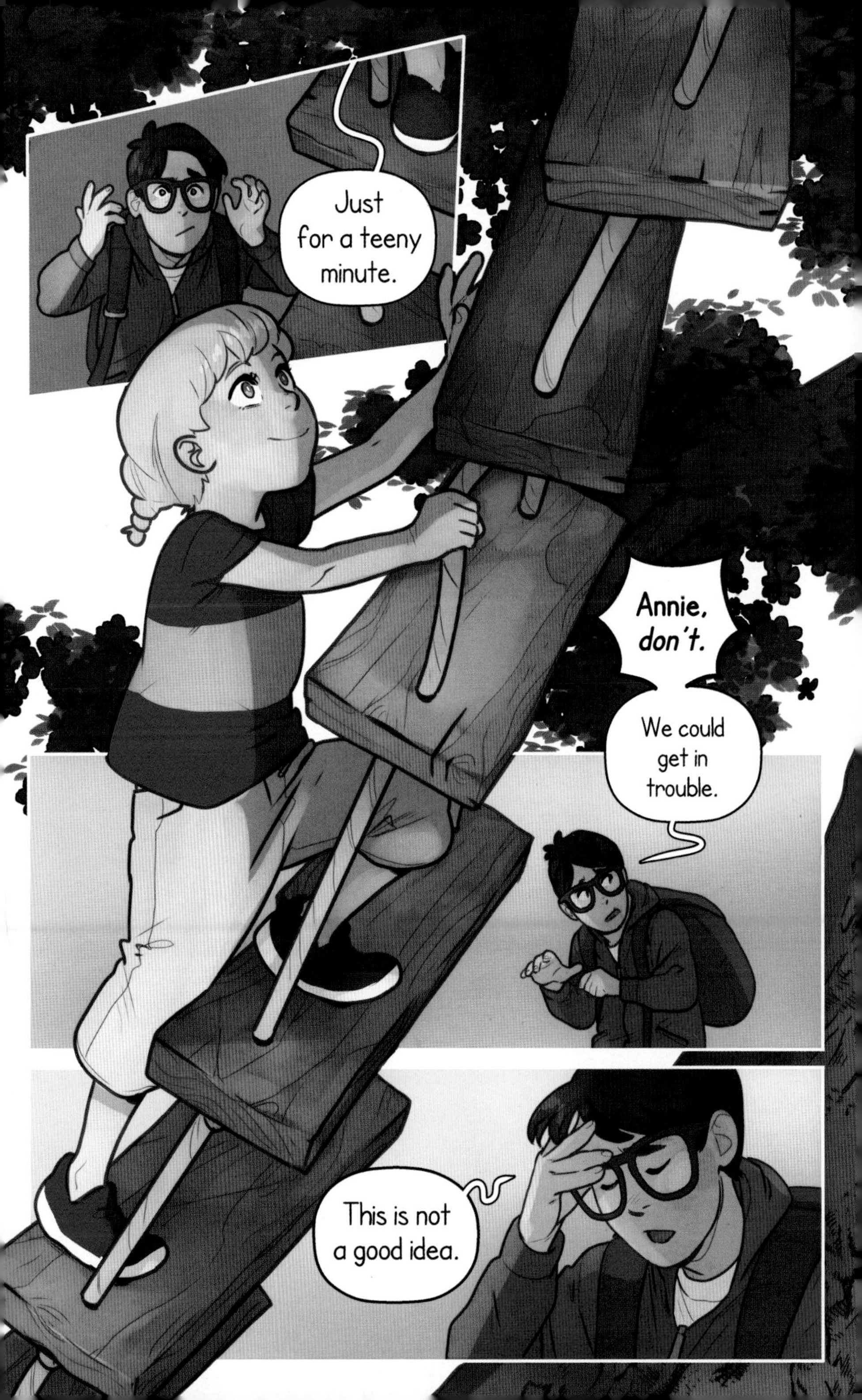
Just for a teeny minute.
Annie, don't.
We could get in trouble.
This is not a good idea.

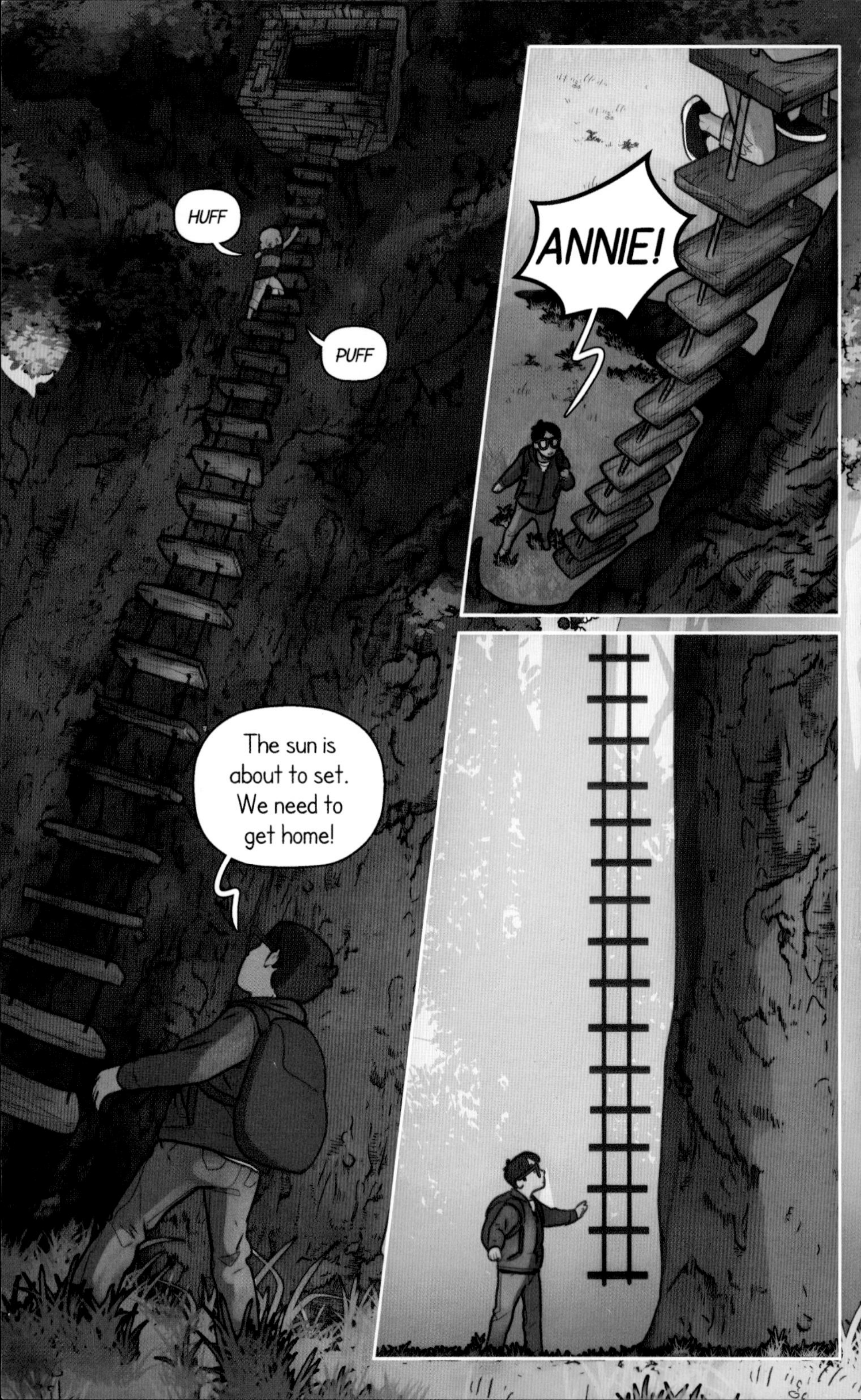
HUFF
PUFF
The sun is about to set. We need to get home!
ANNIE!

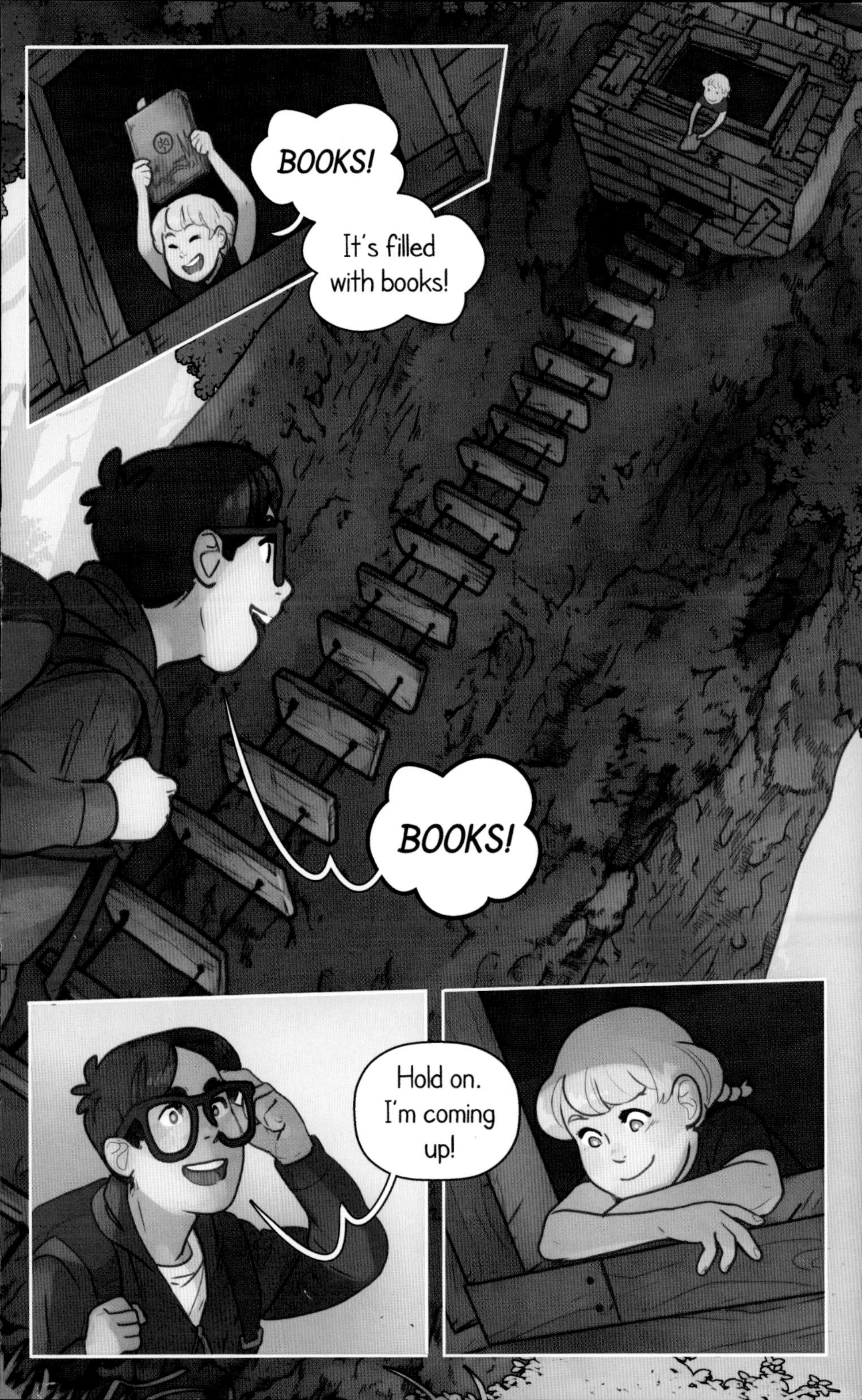

BOOKS!
It's filled with books!
BOOKS!
Hold on. I'm coming up!

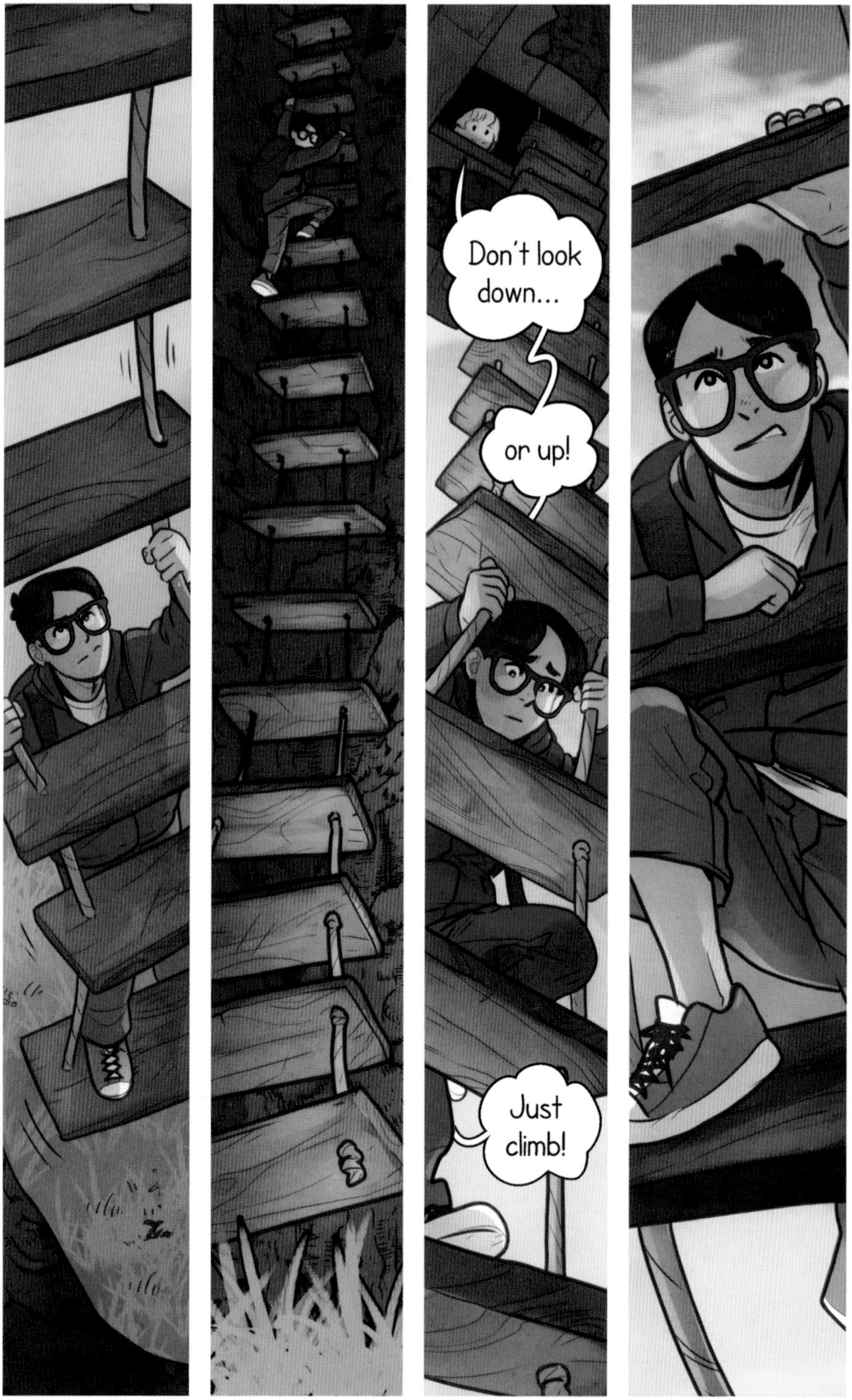
Don't look down...
or up!
Just climb!

CHAPTER TWO

The Wish

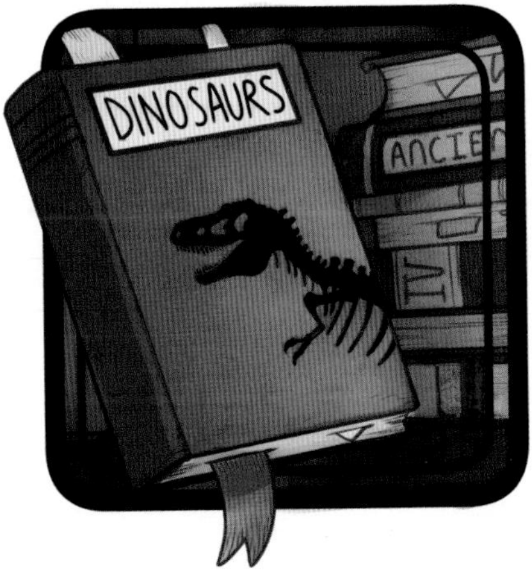
DINOSAURS
ANCIE

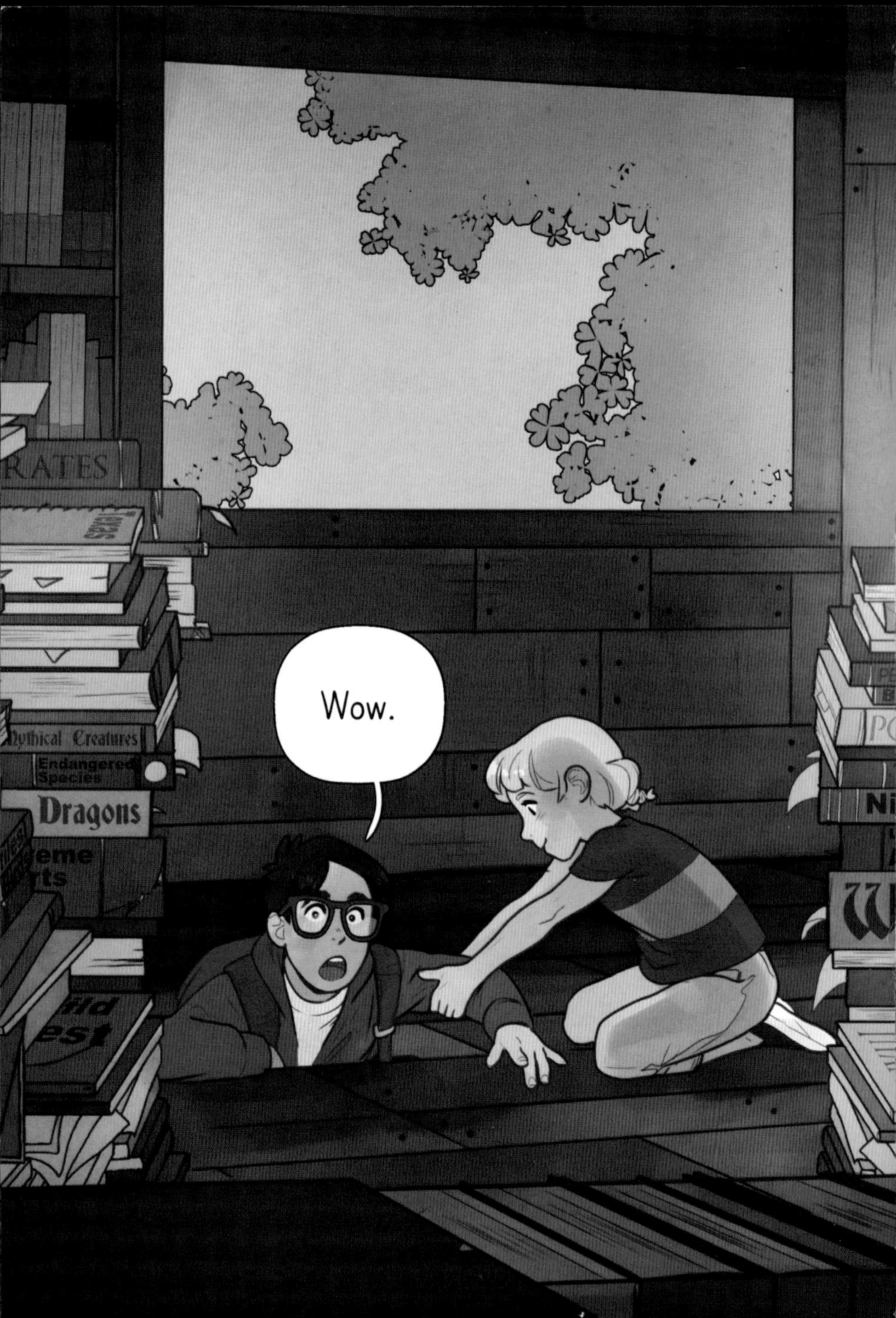
Wow.
Endangered Species
Dragons

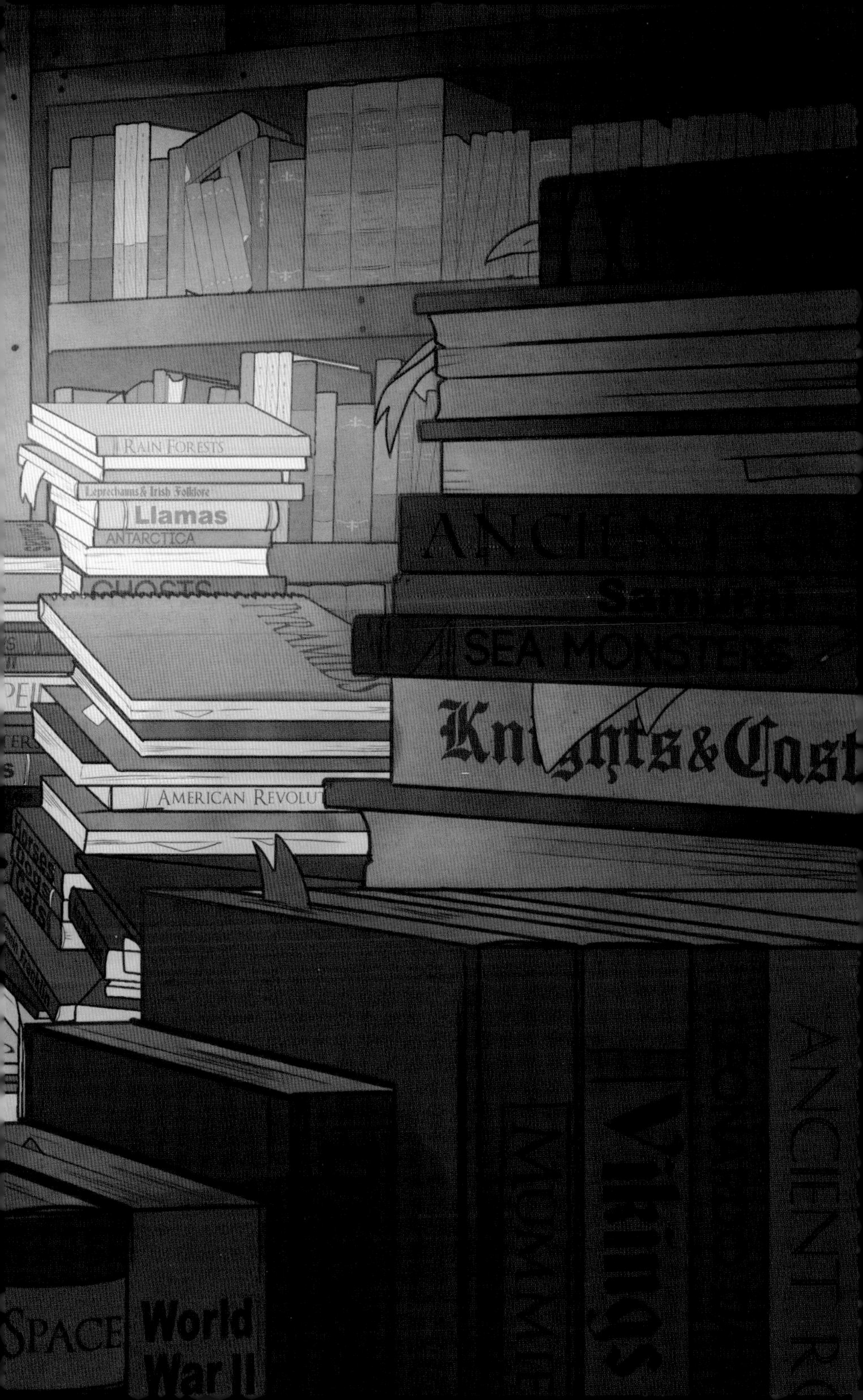
RAIN FORESTS
Leprechauns & Irish Folklore
Llamas
ANTARCTICA
SEA MONSTERS
Horses
Dogs
Cats
SPACE
World War II

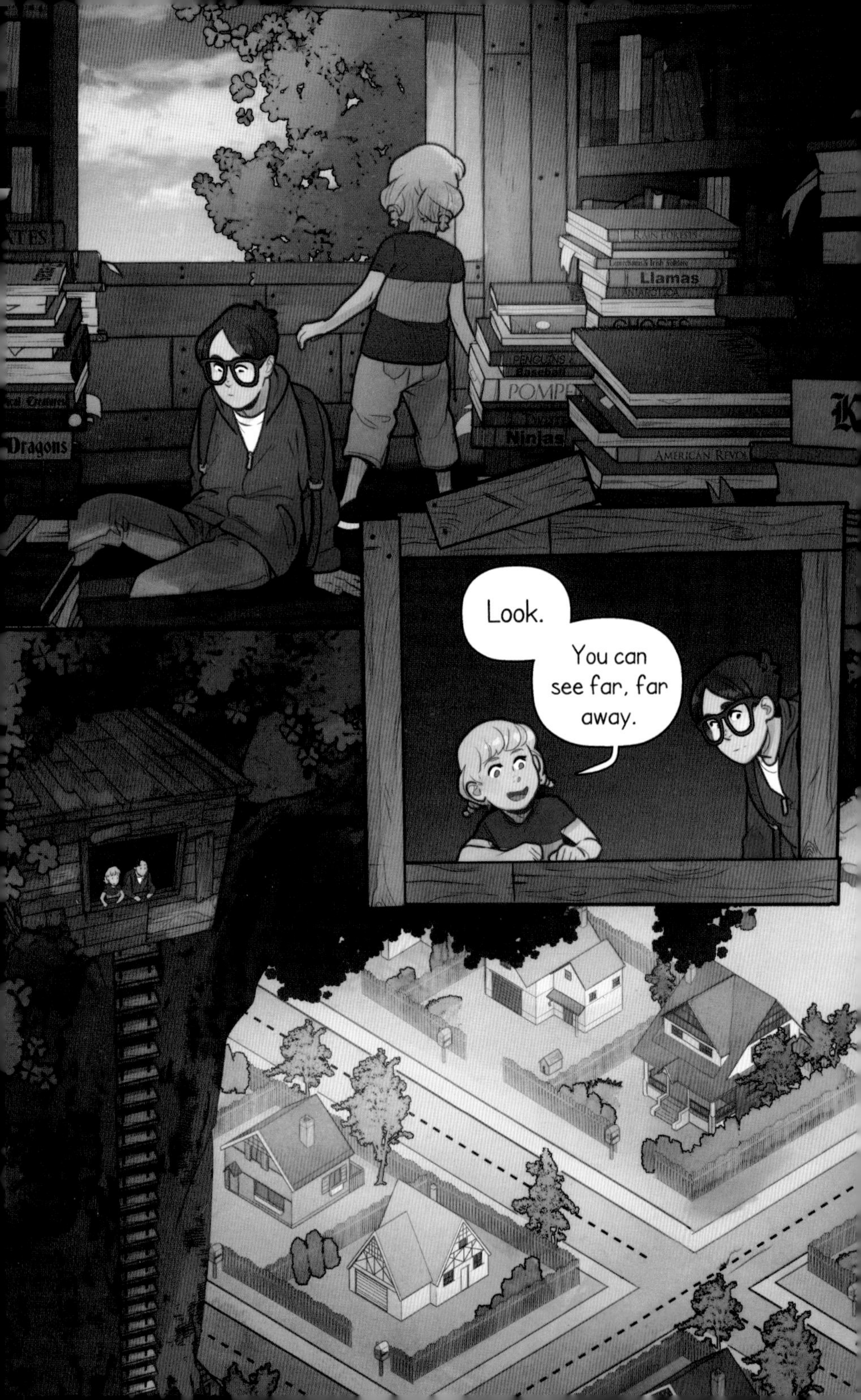

Llamas
Baseball
Ninjas
Dragons
Look.
You can see far, far away.

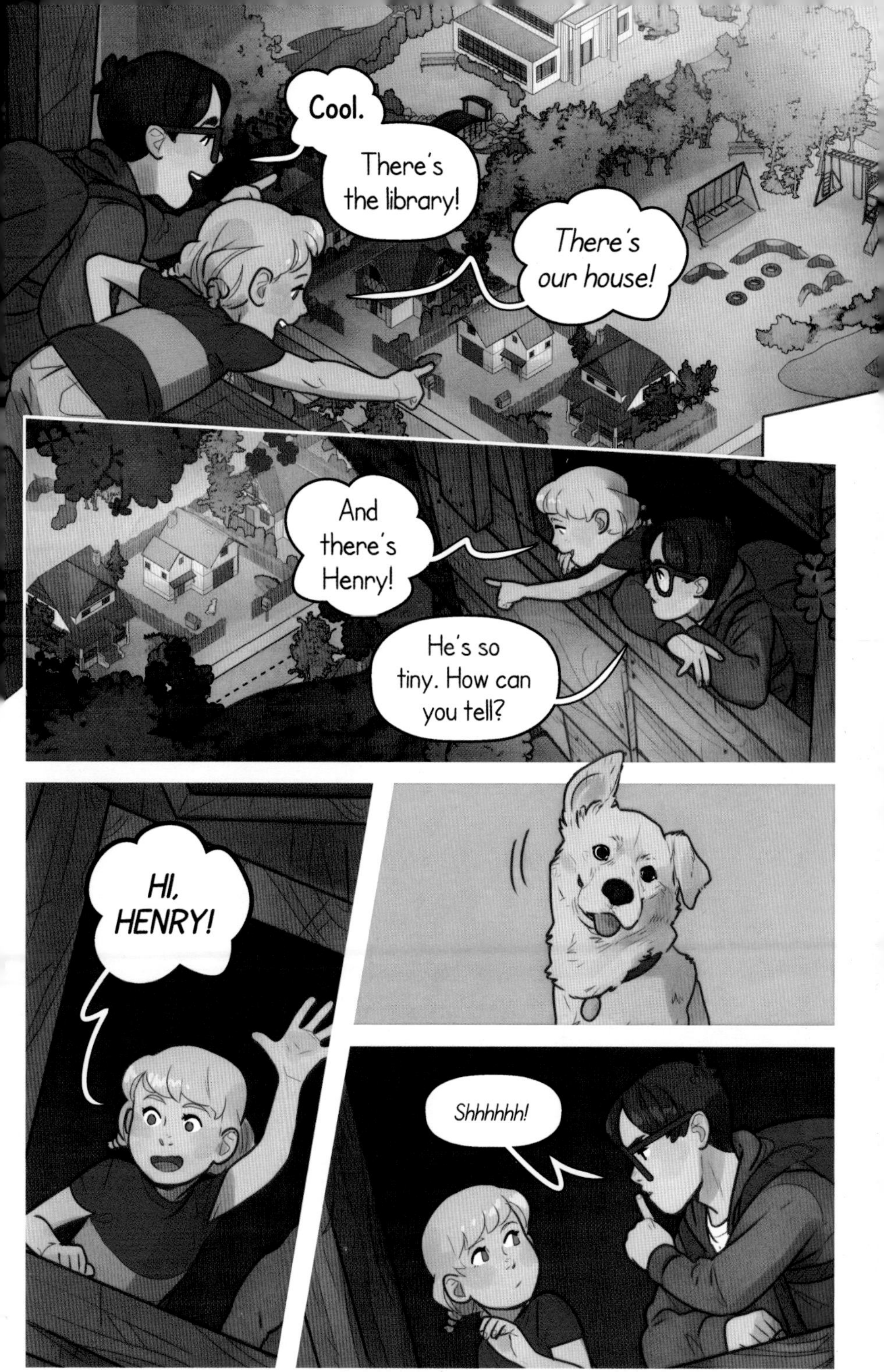
Cool.
There's the library!
There's our house!
And there's Henry!
He's so tiny. How can you tell?
HI, HENRY!
Shhhhhh!

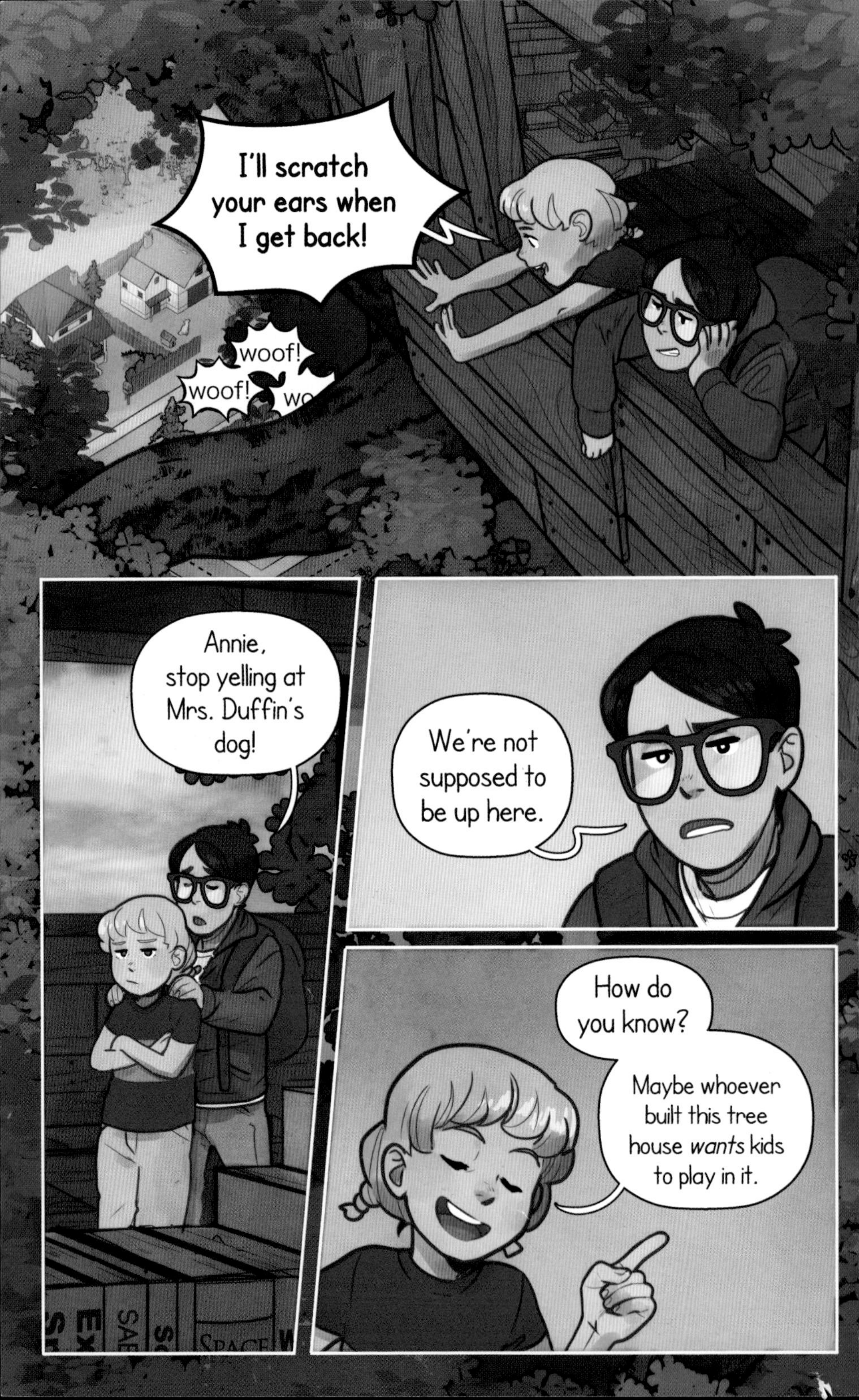

I'll scratch your ears when I get back!
woof!
woof!
wo
Annie, stop yelling at Mrs. Duffin's dog!
We're not supposed to be up here.
How do you know?
Maybe whoever built this tree house *wants* kids to play in it.
SPACE

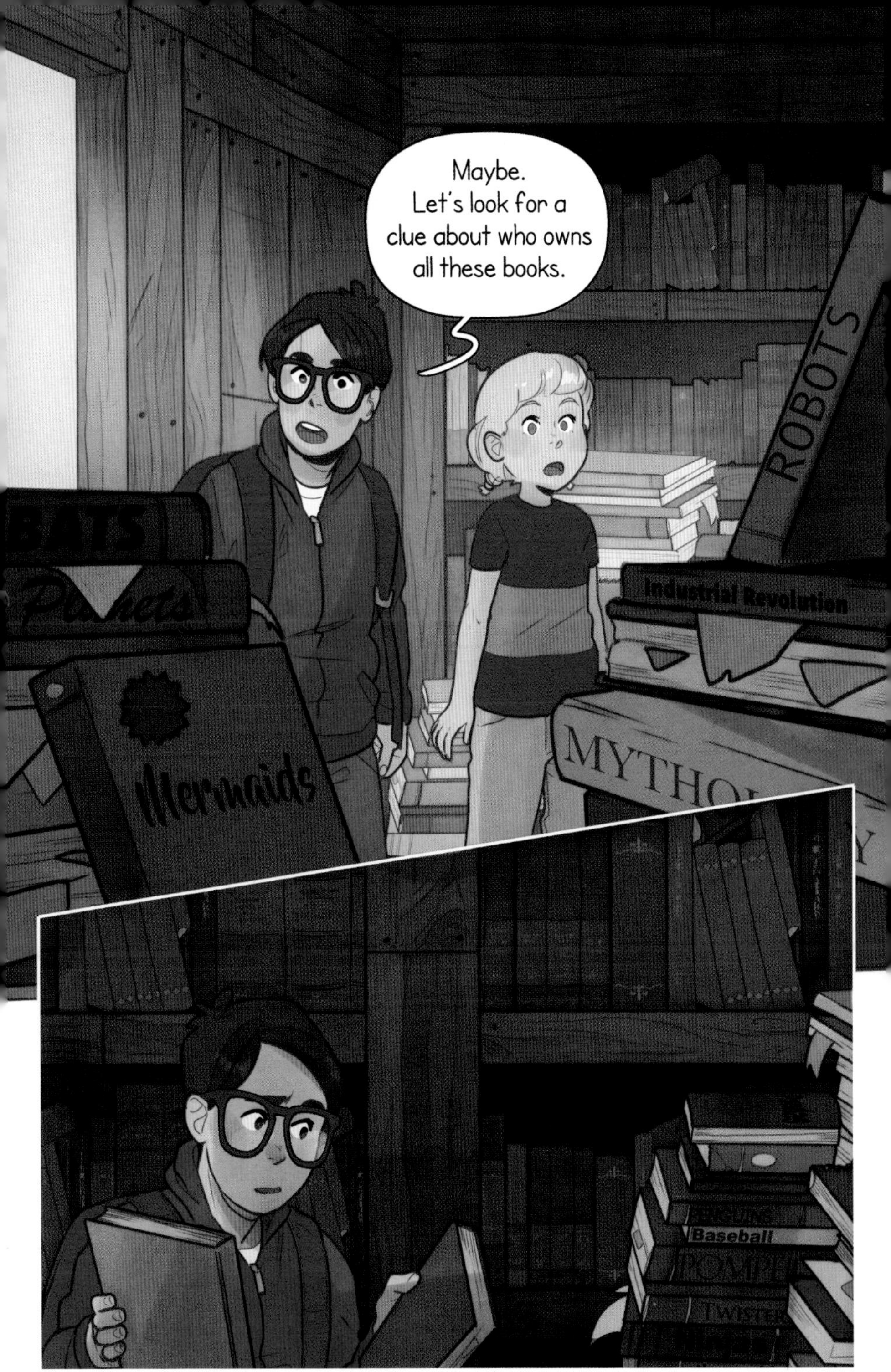
Maybe. Let's look for a clue about who owns all these books.
BATS
ROBOTS
Industrial Revolution
Mermaids
Baseball

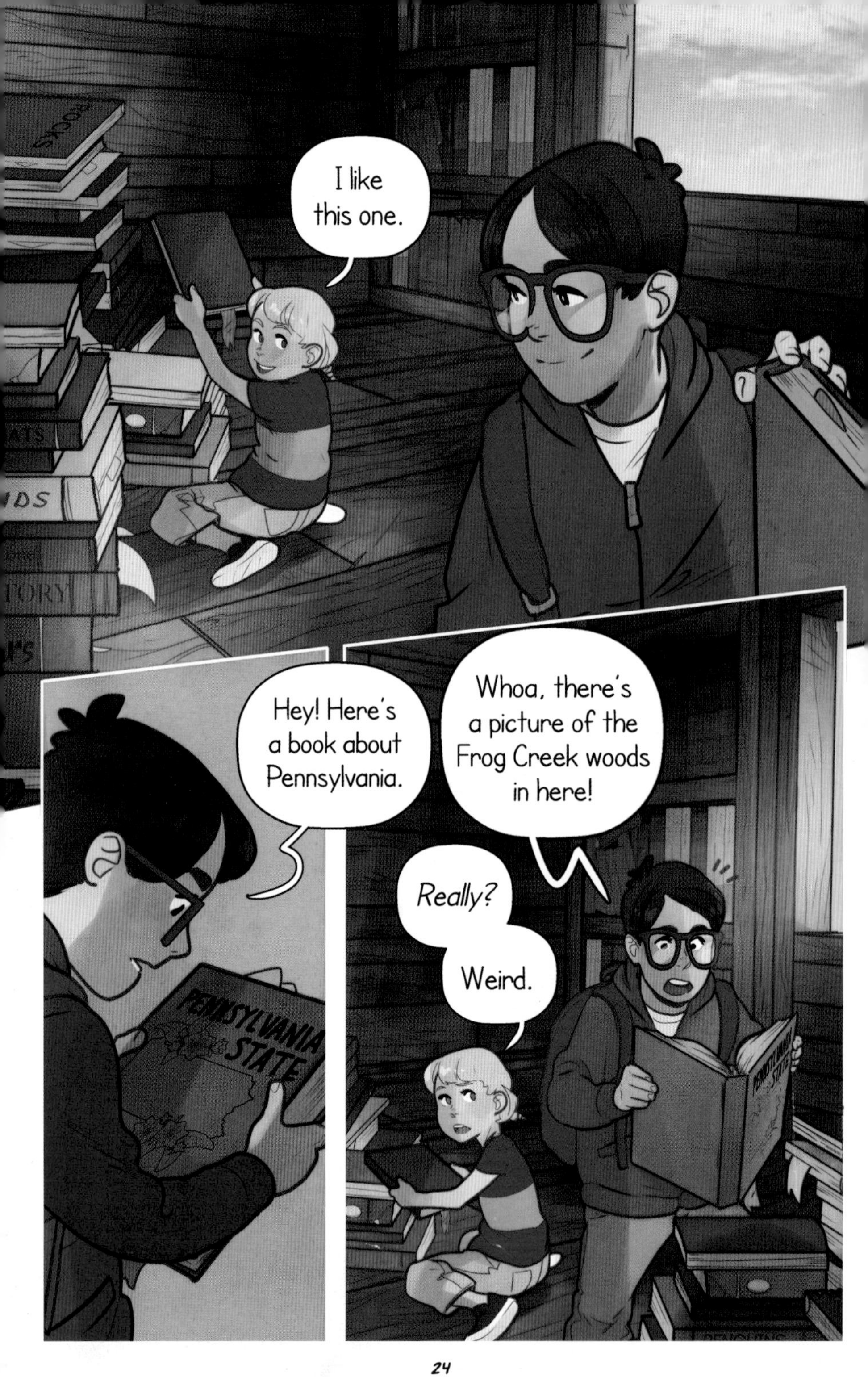
ROCKS
I like this one.
Hey! Here's a book about Pennsylvania.
PENNSYLVANIA STATE
Whoa, there's a picture of the Frog Creek woods in here!
Really?
Weird.

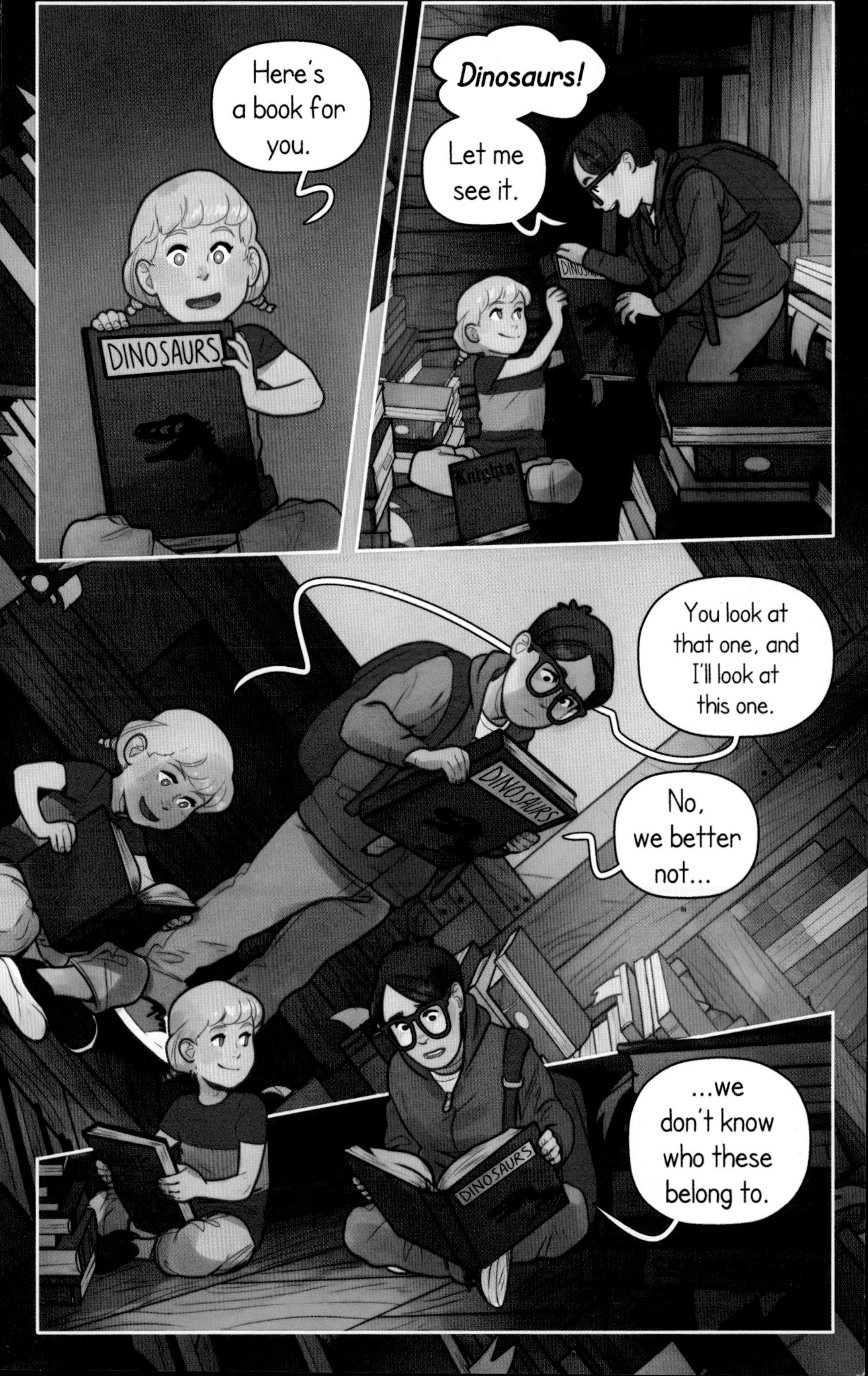
Here's a book for you.
DINOSAURS
Dinosaurs!
Let me see it.
DINOSAURS
Knights
You look at that one, and I'll look at this one.
DINOSAURS
No, we better not...
...we don't know who these belong to.
DINOSAURS

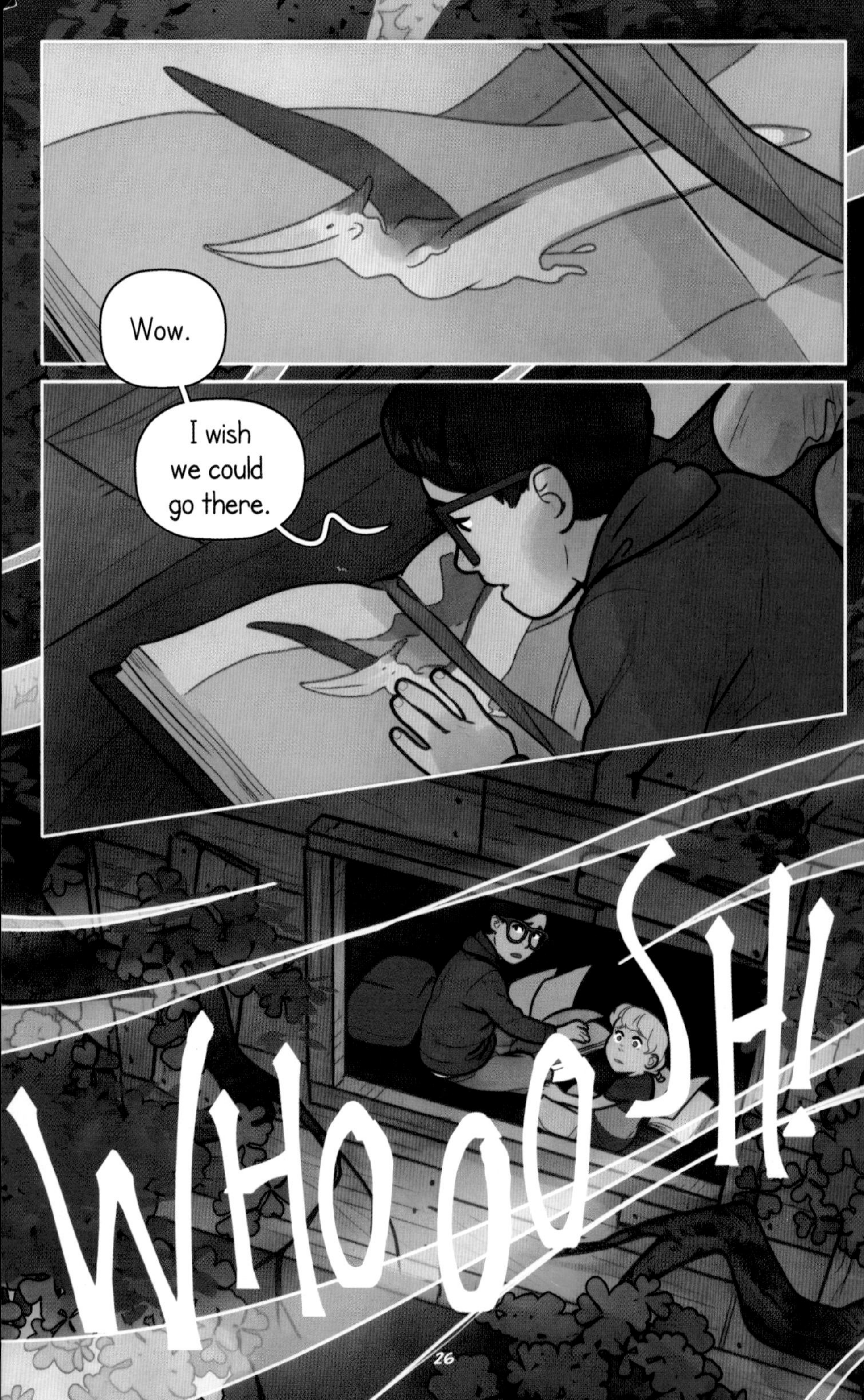

Wow.
I wish we could go there.
WHOOOSH!

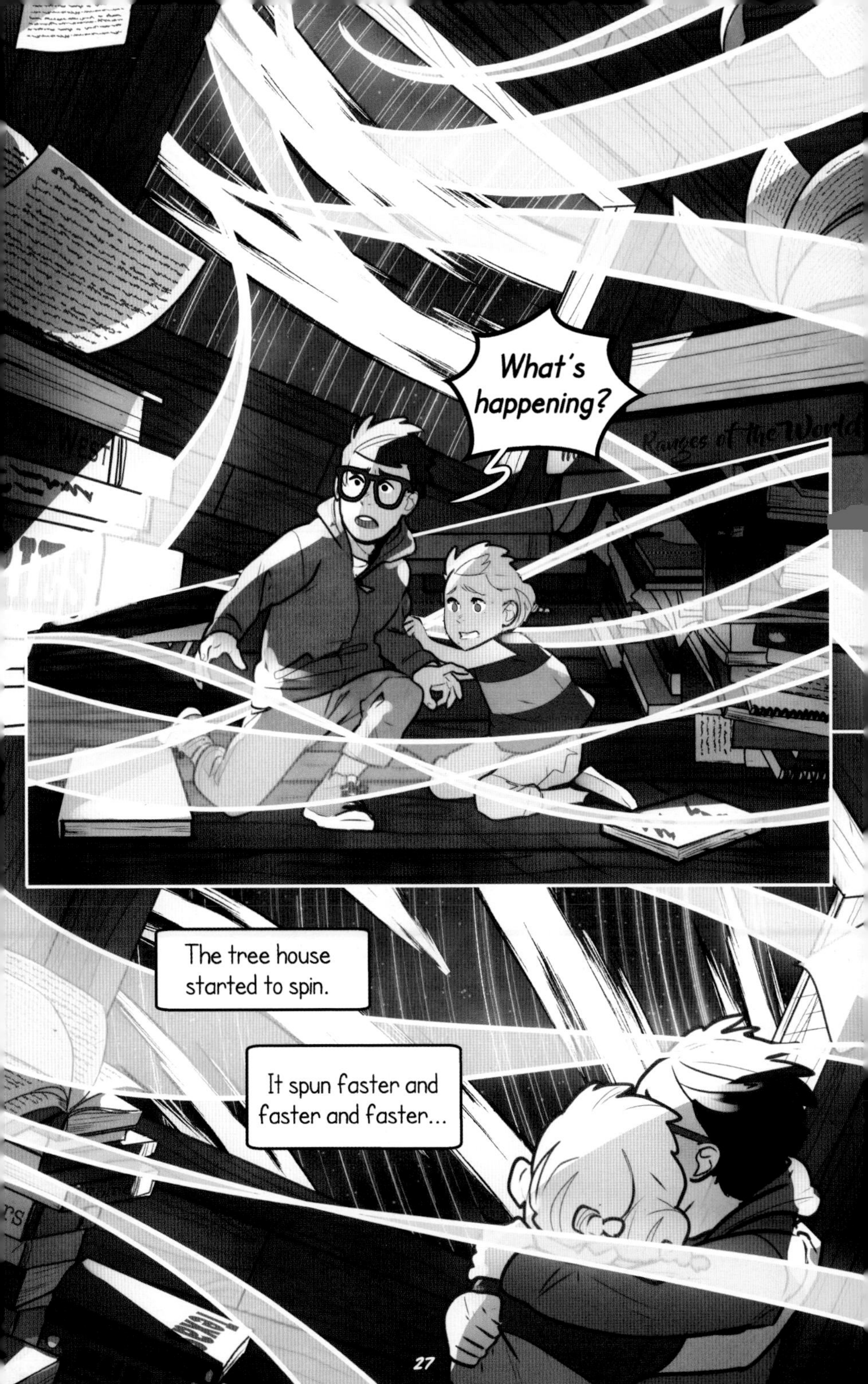
What's happening?
Ranges of the World
The tree house started to spin.
It spun faster and faster and faster...

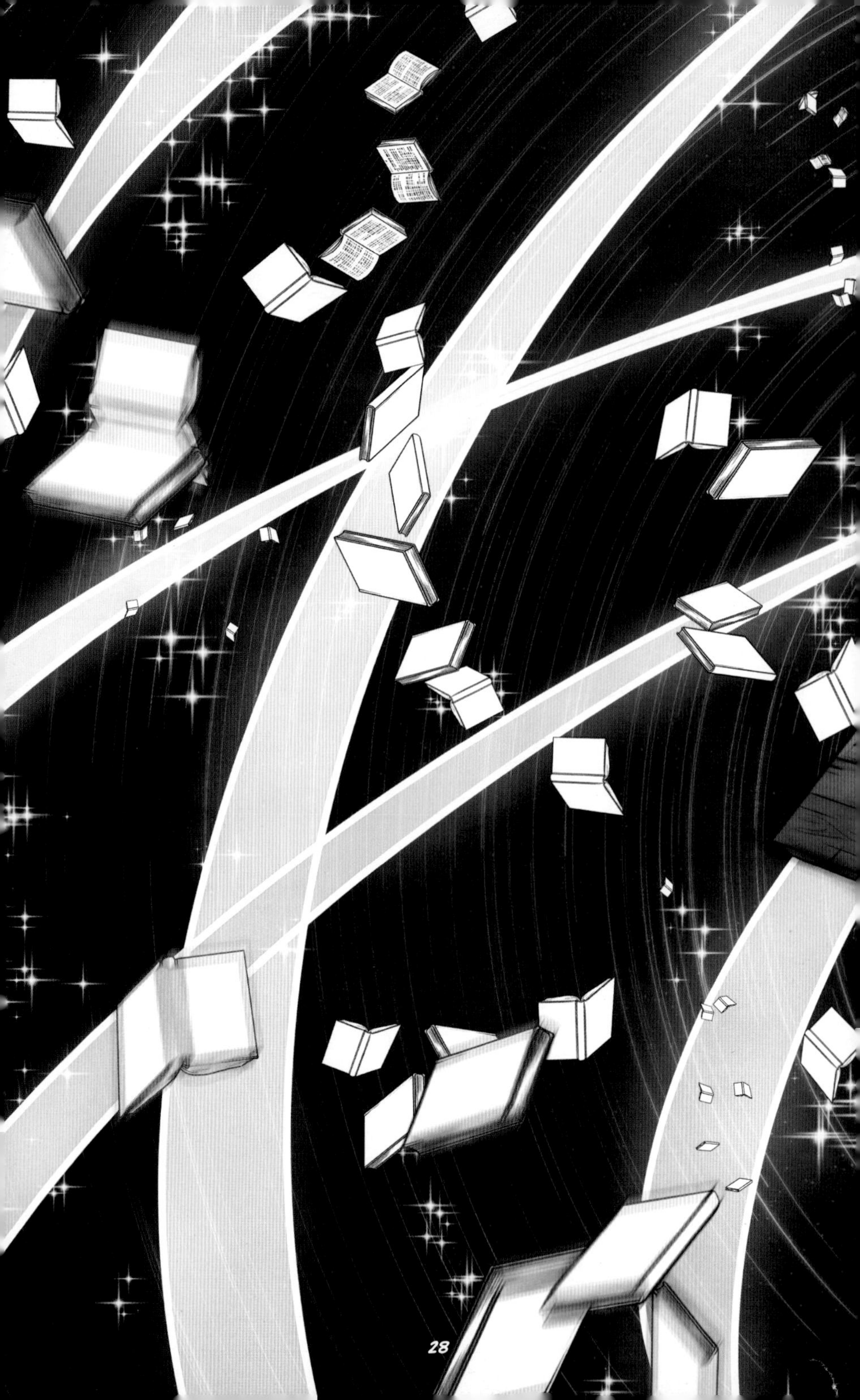

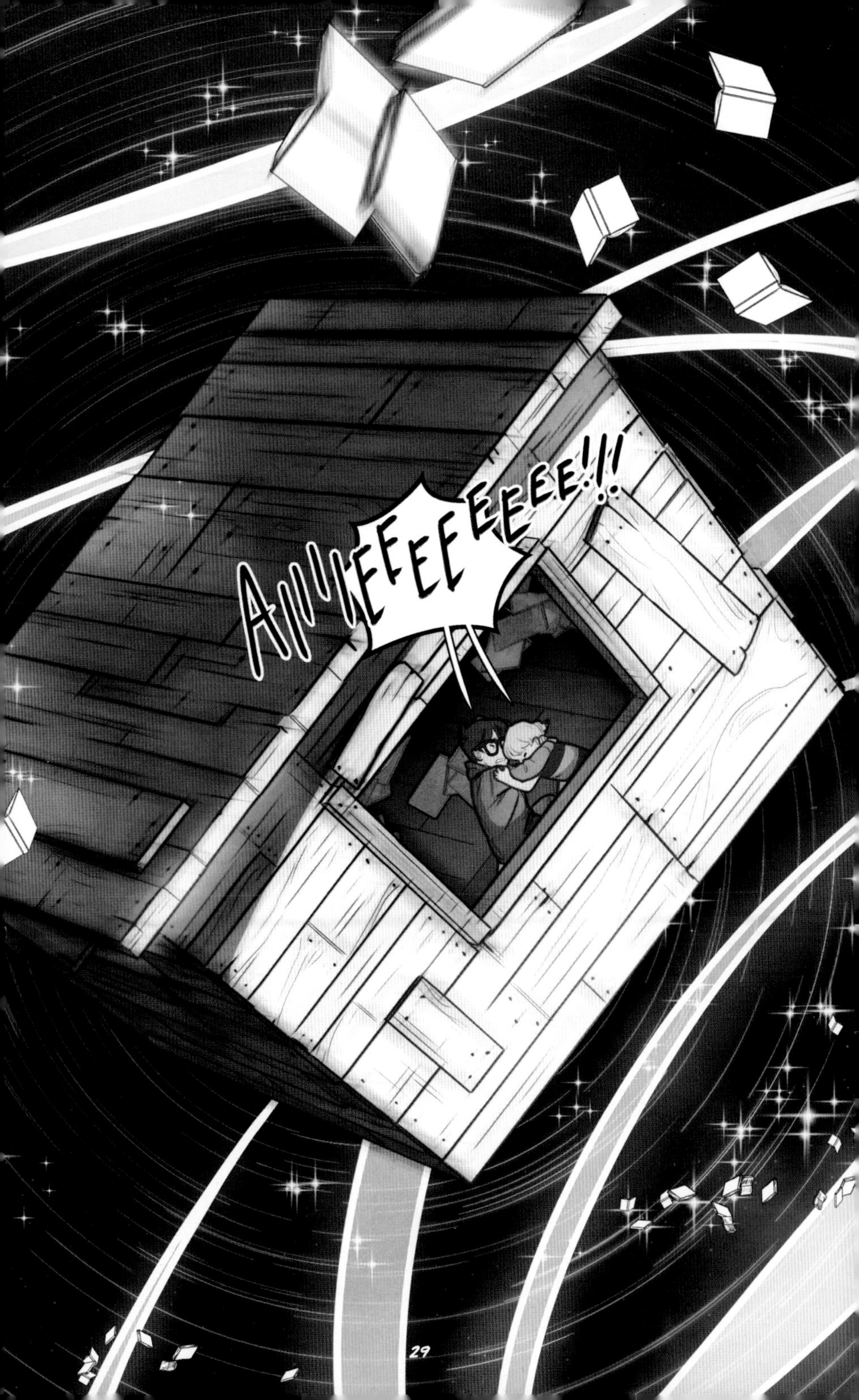
AIIIEEEEEEEEEE!!!

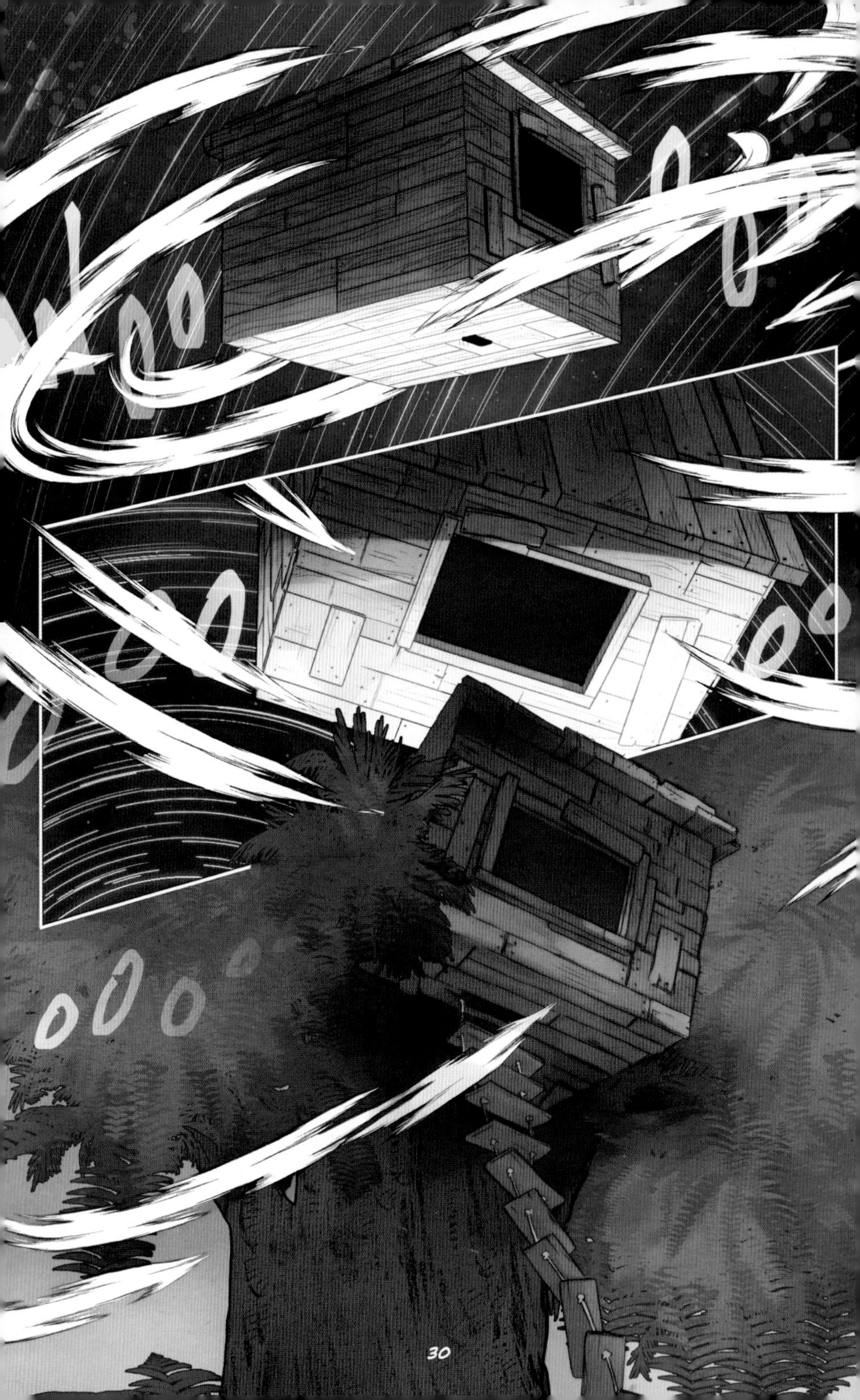

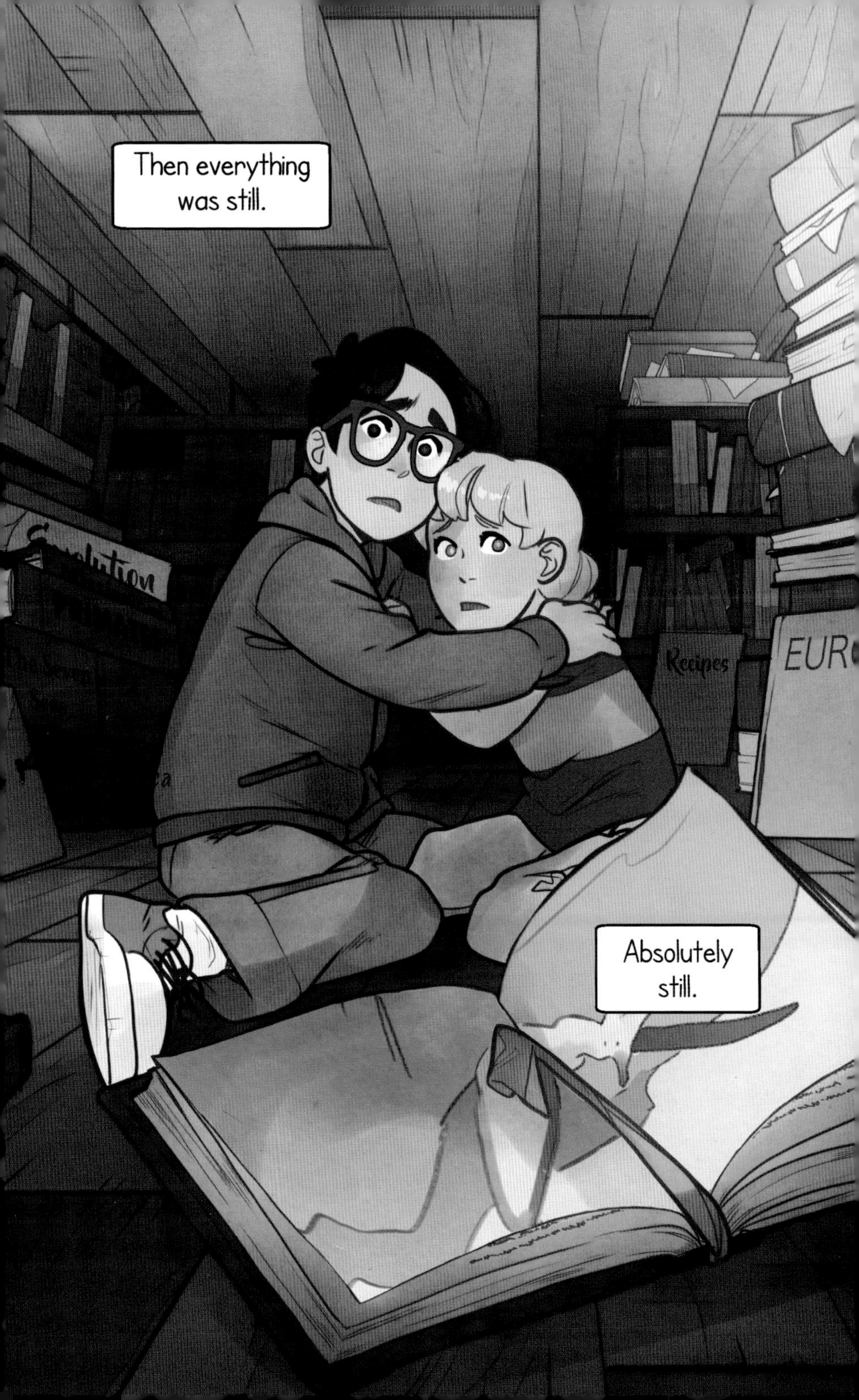
Then everything was still.
Recipes
EUR
Absolutely still.

CHAPTER THREE
Where Is Here?

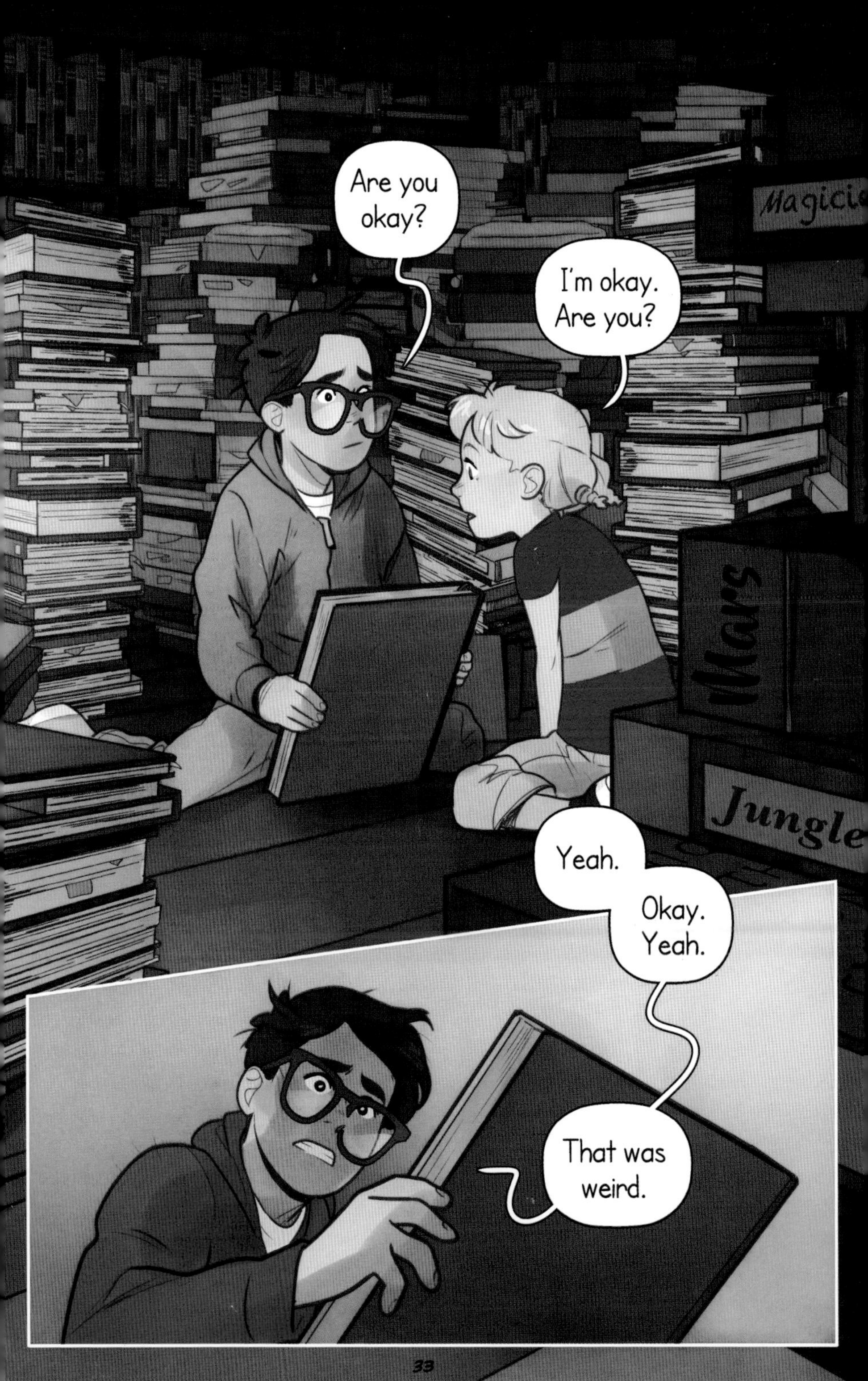
Are you okay?
Magicia
I'm okay. Are you?
Mars
Jungle
Yeah.
Okay. Yeah.
That was weird.

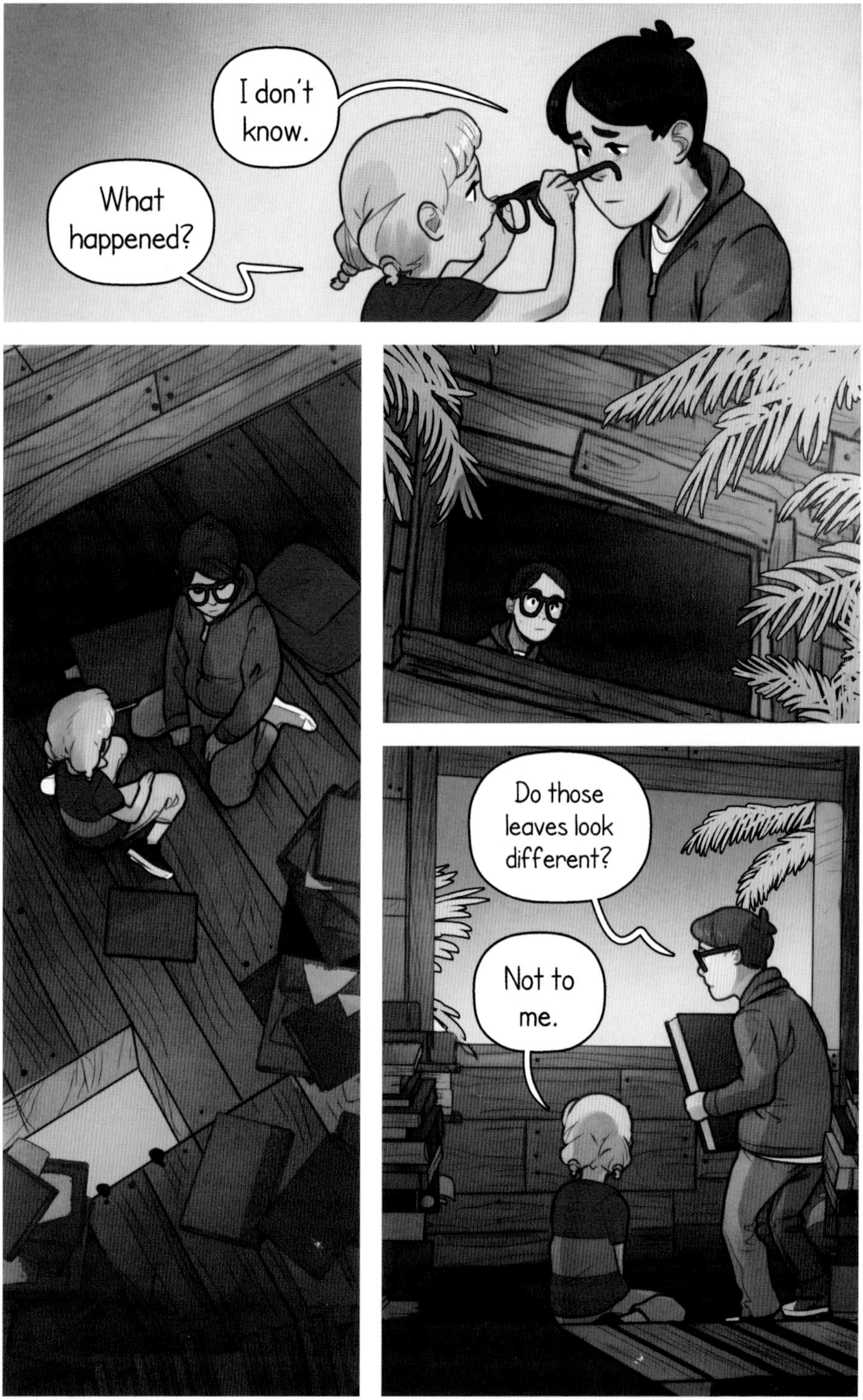
What happened?
I don't know.
Do those leaves look different?
Not to me.

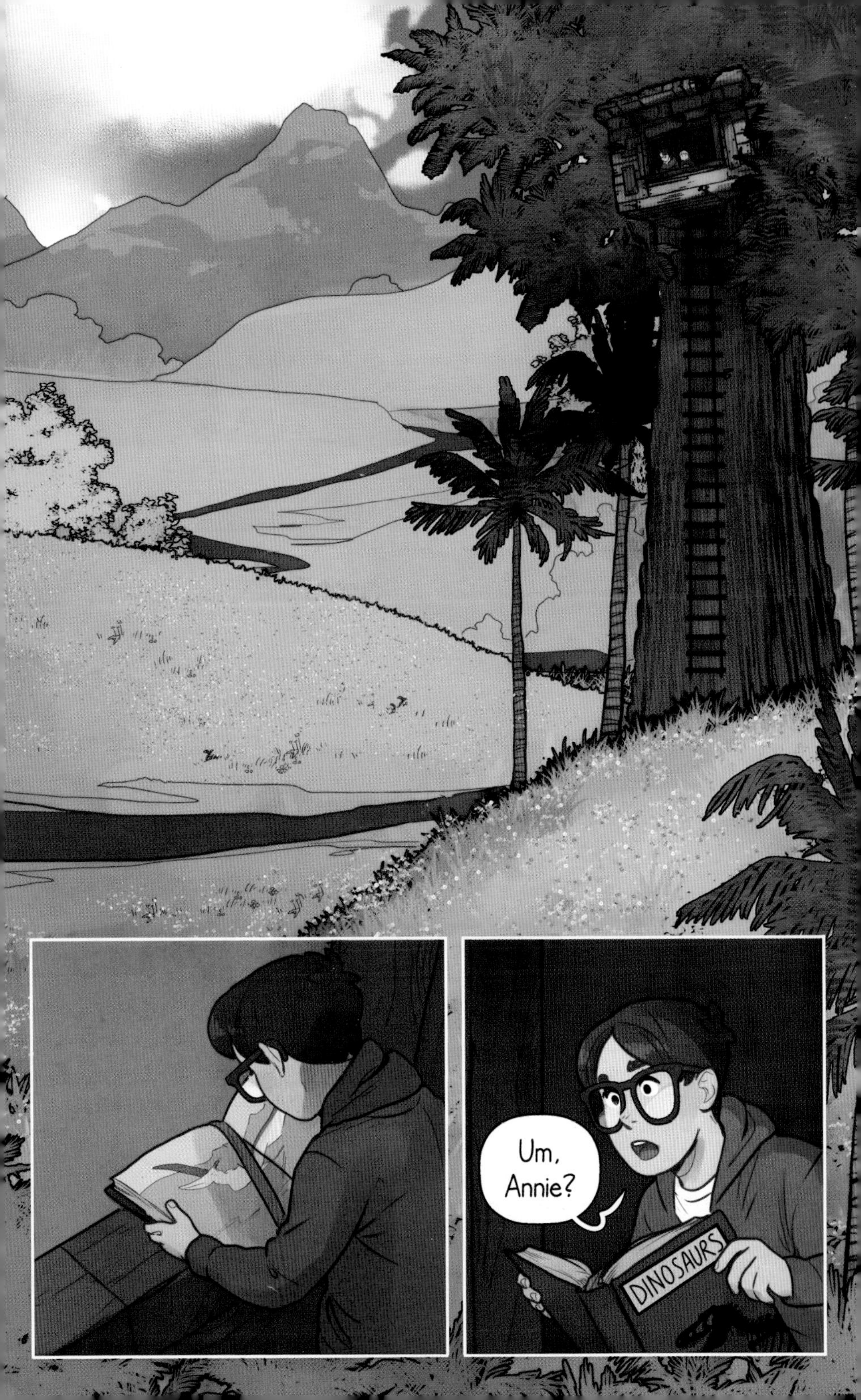
Um, Annie?
DINOSAURS

Where are we?

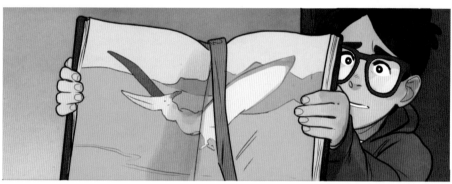

It's the same.

Yeah, exactly the same.

Except real...

and alive.

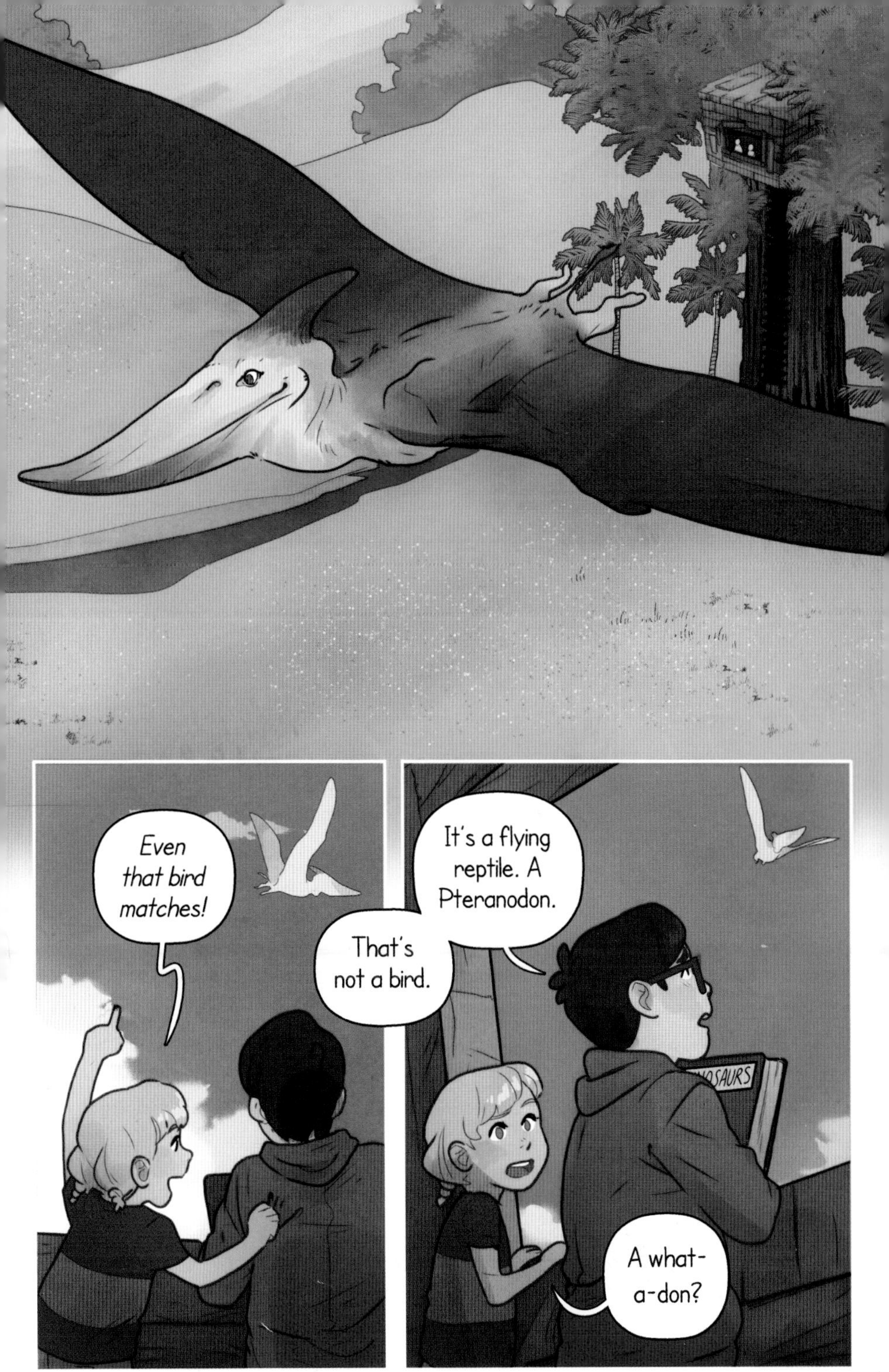
Even that bird matches!
It's a flying reptile. A Pteranodon.
That's not a bird.
A what-a-don?

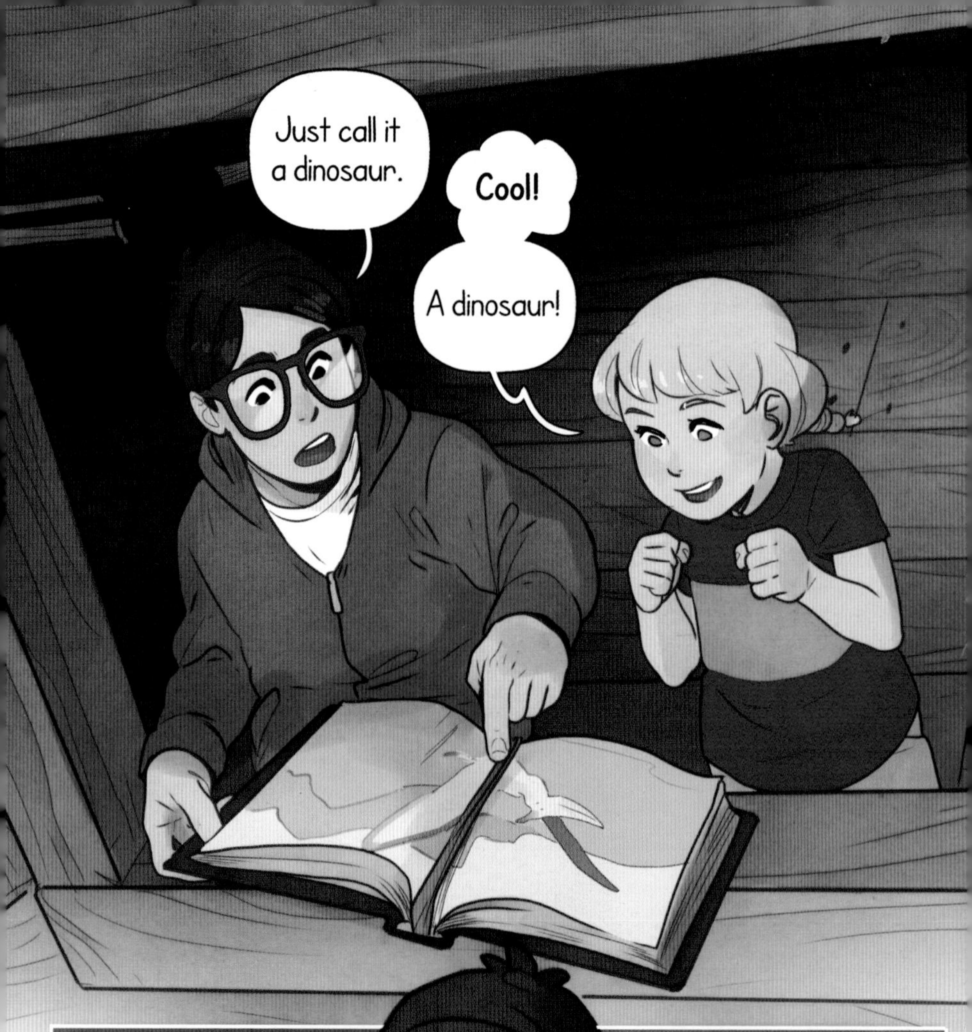
Just call it a dinosaur.
Cool!
A dinosaur!

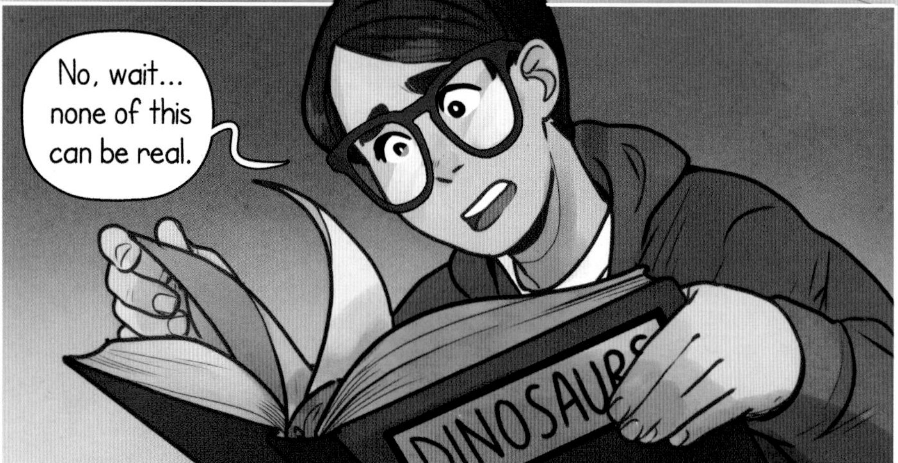
No, wait... none of this can be real.
DINOSAURS

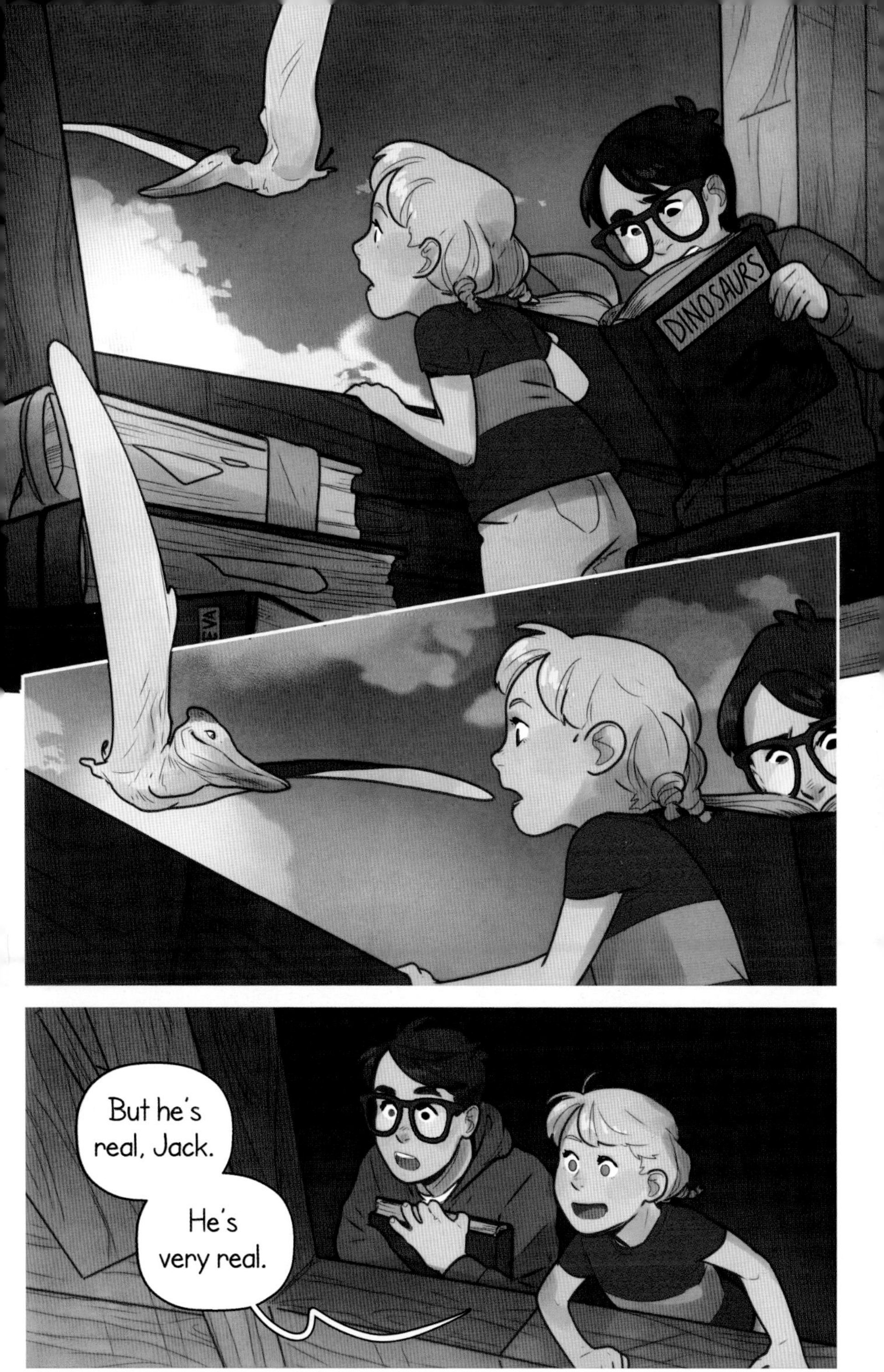
DINOSAURS
EVA
But he's real, Jack.
He's very real.

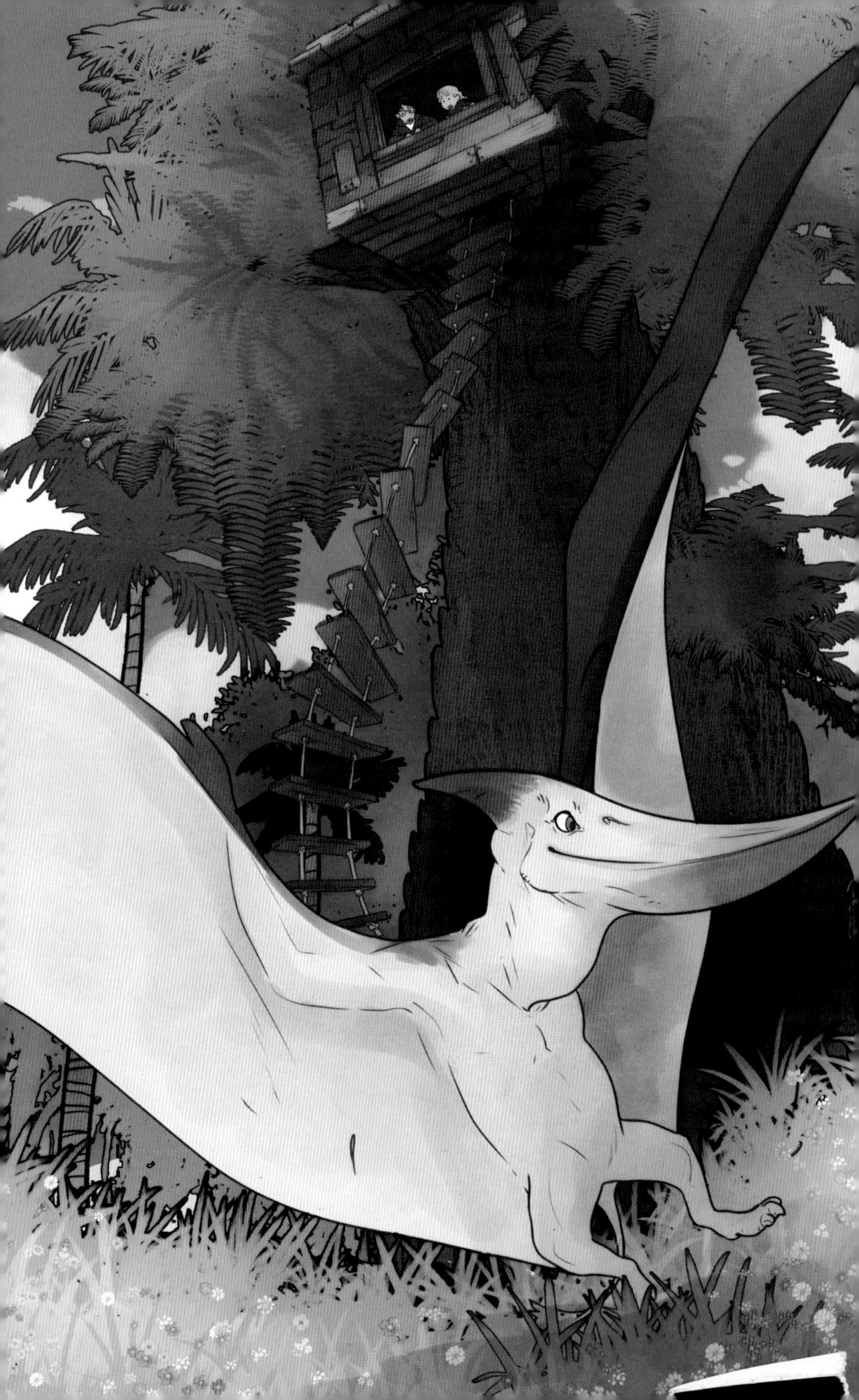

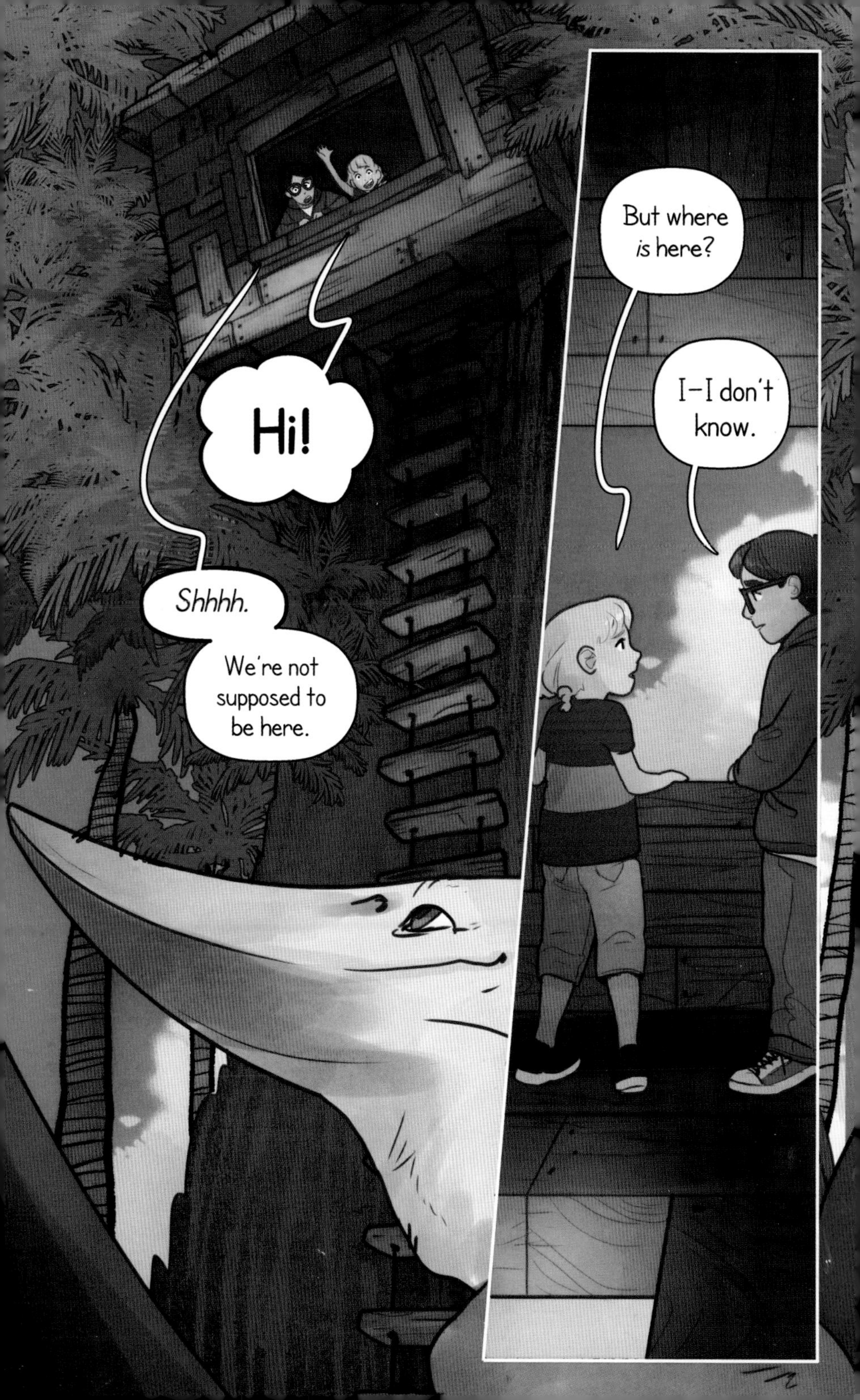
Hi!
Shhhh.
We're not supposed to be here.
But where *is* here?
I–I don't know.

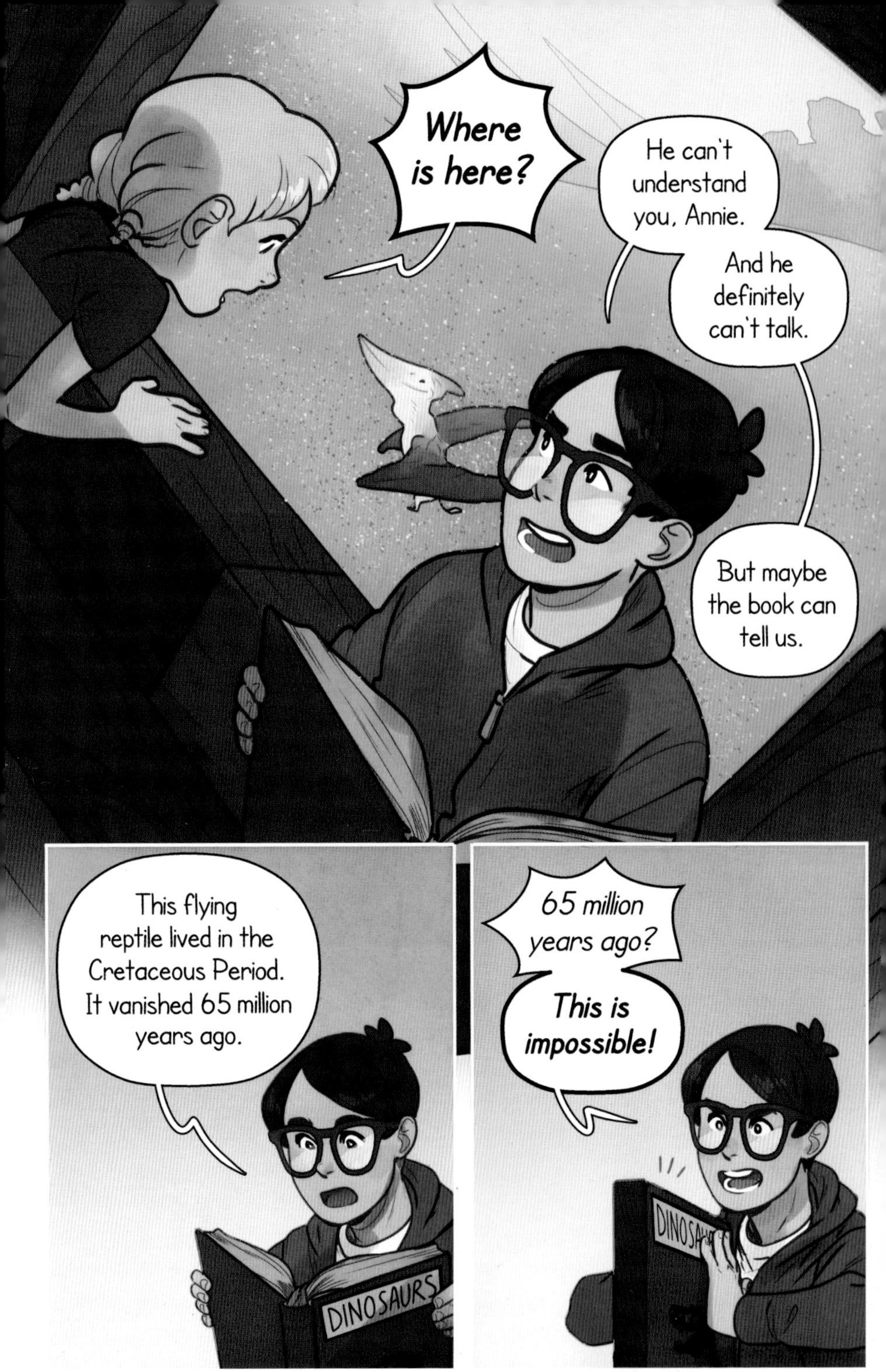
Where is here?
He can't understand you, Annie.
And he definitely can't talk.
But maybe the book can tell us.
This flying reptile lived in the Cretaceous Period. It vanished 65 million years ago.
DINOSAURS
65 million years ago?
This is impossible!

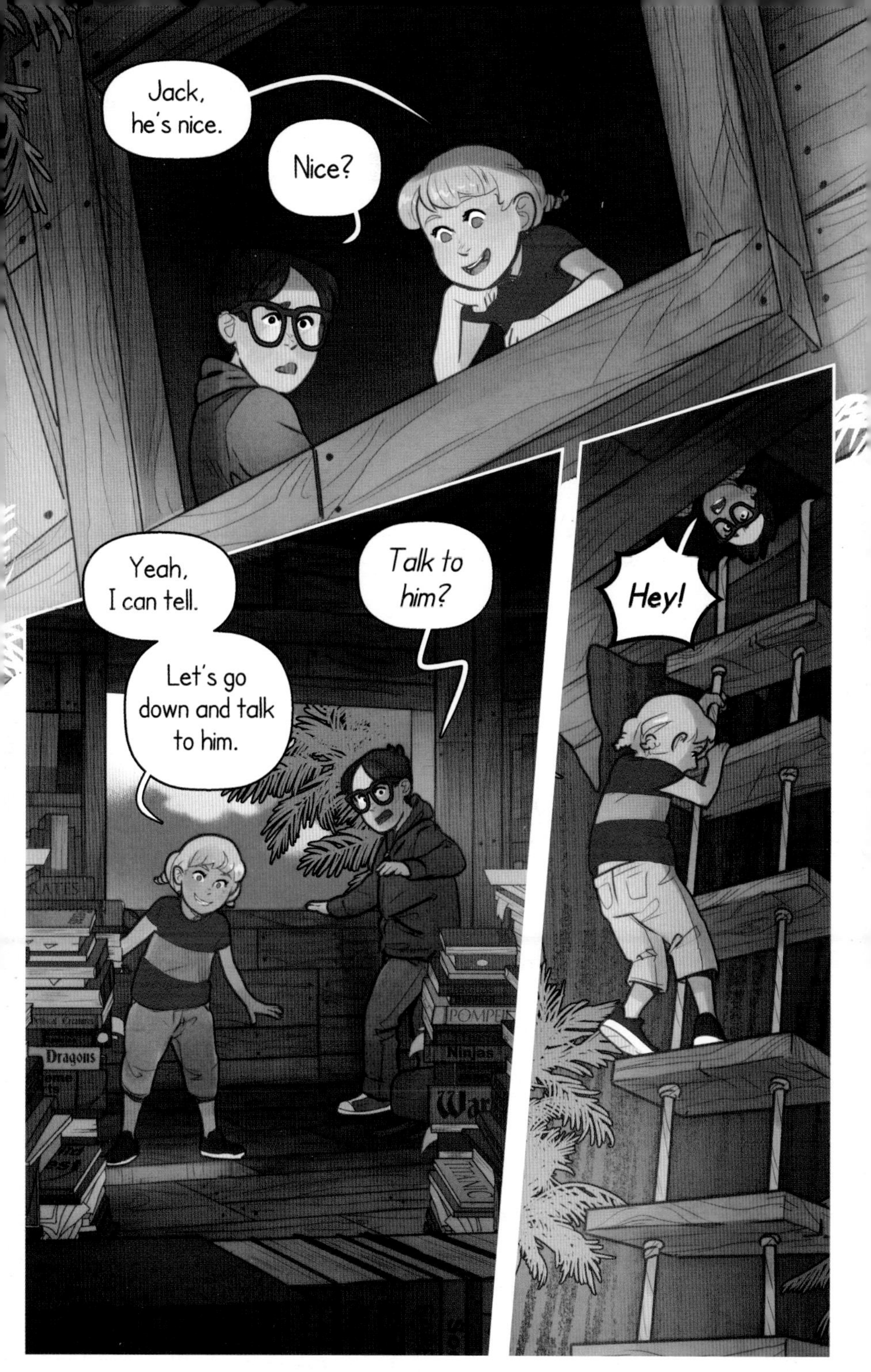
Jack, he's nice.
Nice?
Yeah, I can tell.
Let's go down and talk to him.
Talk to him?
Hey!
Dragons
Ninjas

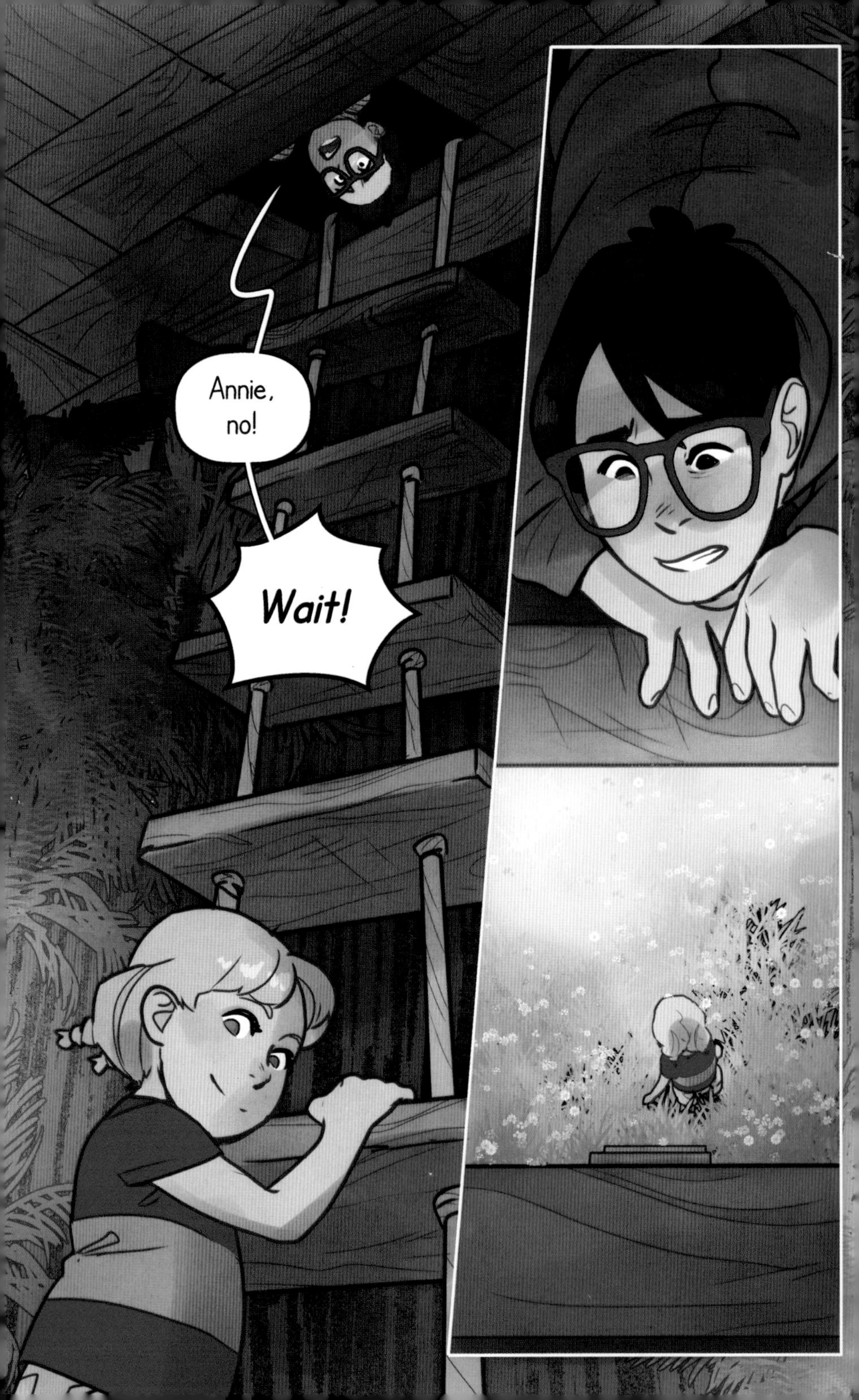
Annie, no!
Wait!

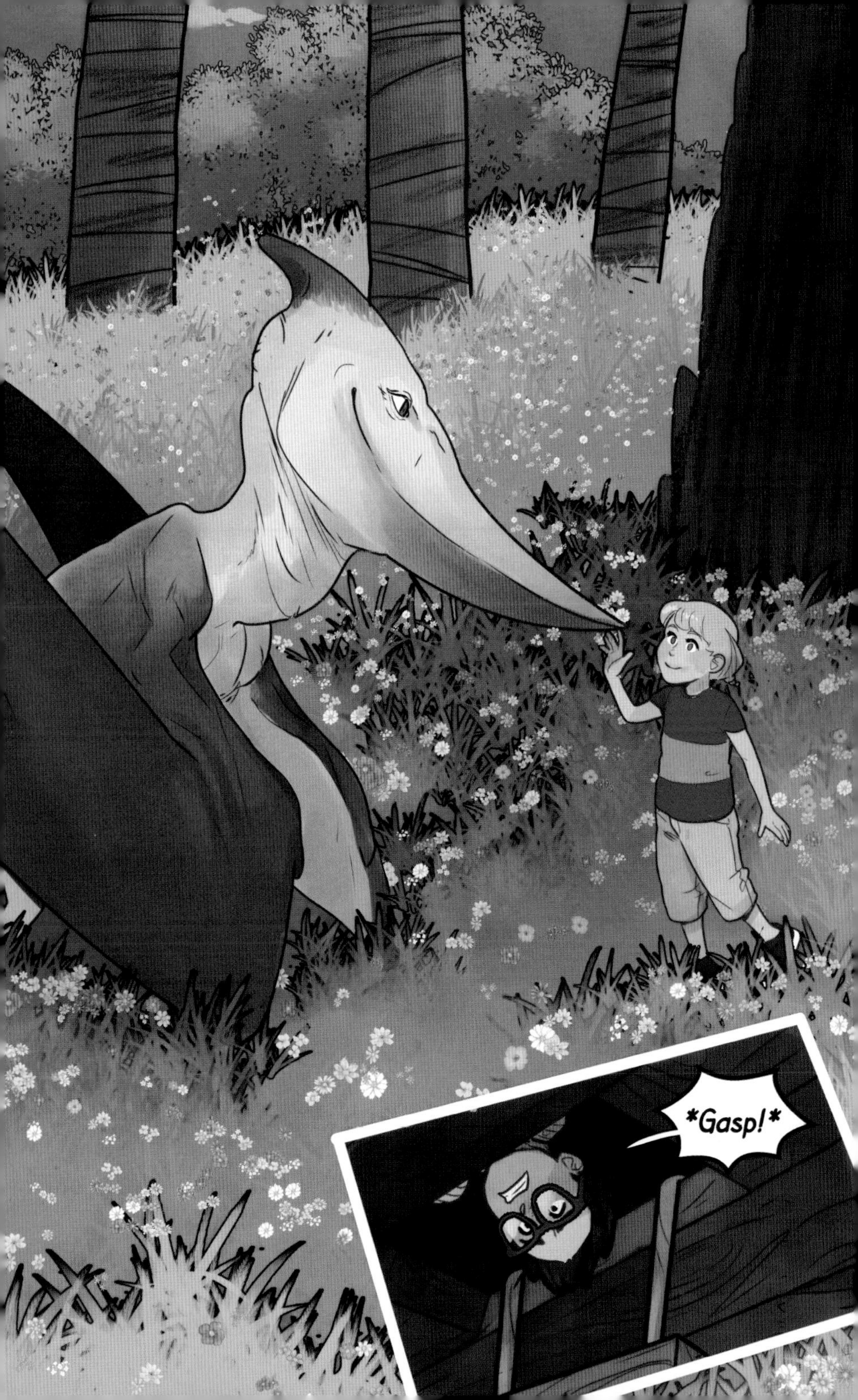
Gasp!

CHAPTER FOUR

Henry

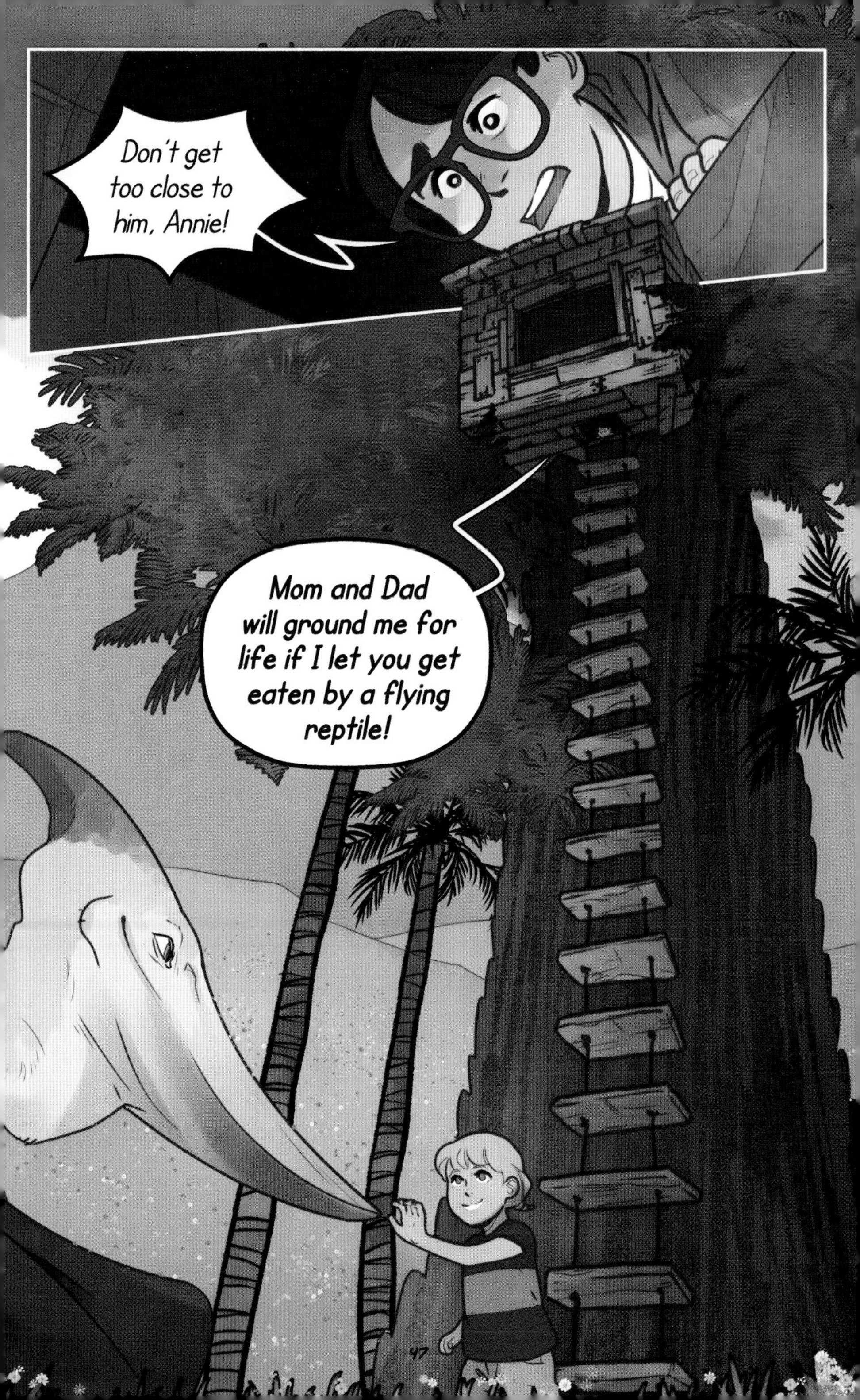
Don't get too close to him, Annie!
Mom and Dad will ground me for life if I let you get eaten by a flying reptile!

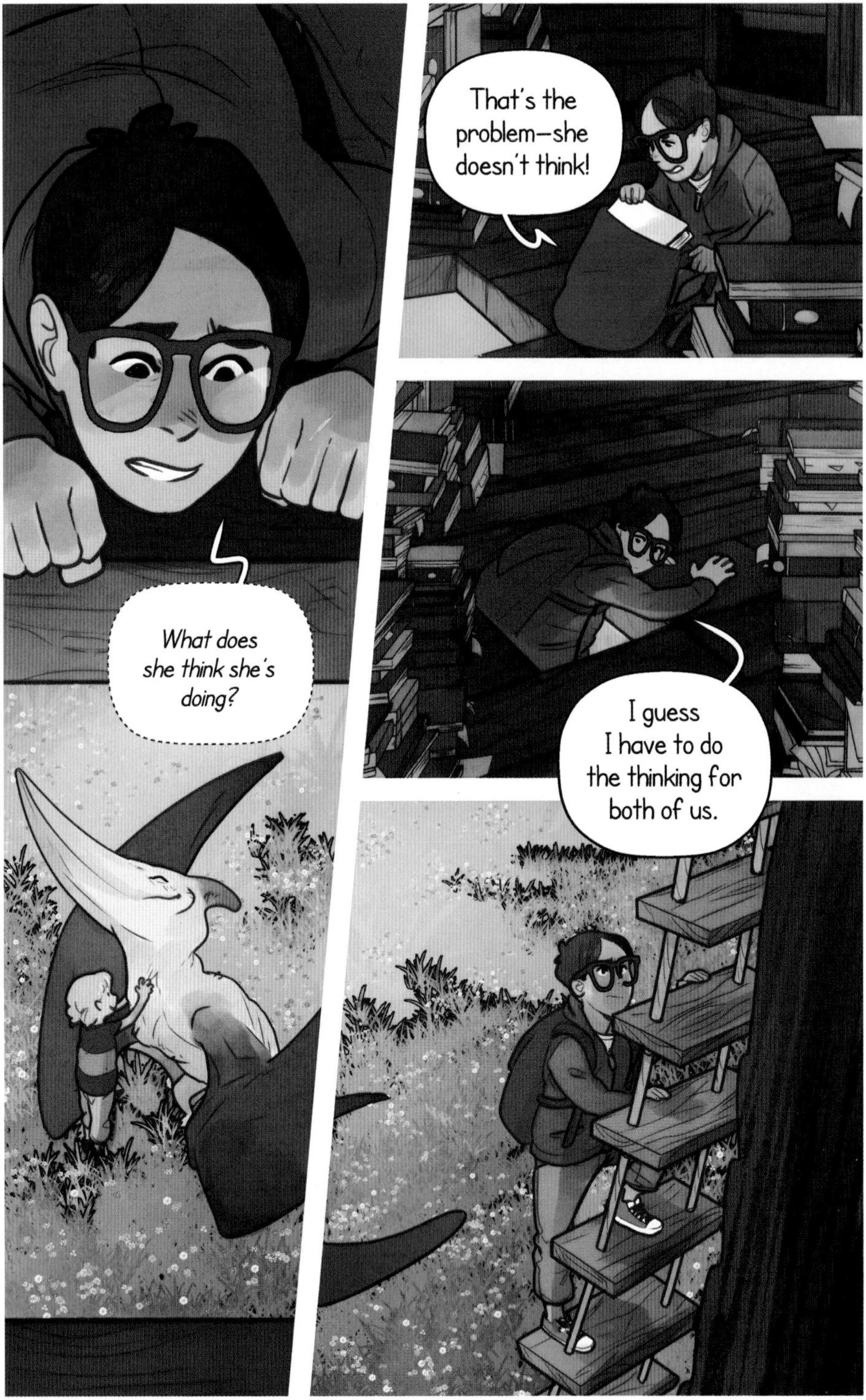
What does she think she's doing?
That's the problem—she doesn't think!
I guess I have to do the thinking for both of us.

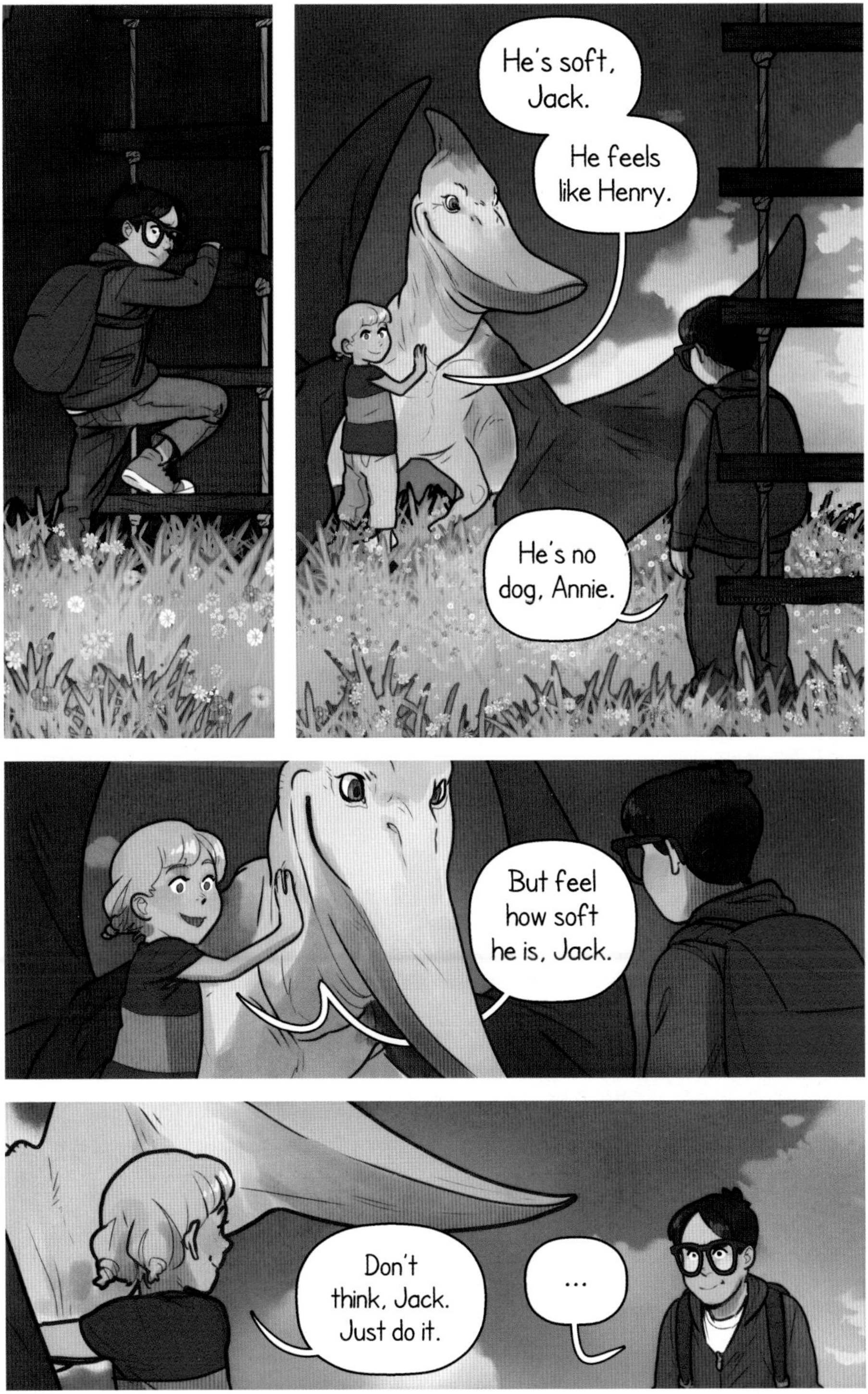
He's soft, Jack.
He feels like Henry.
He's no dog, Annie.
But feel how soft he is, Jack.
Don't think, Jack. Just do it.
...

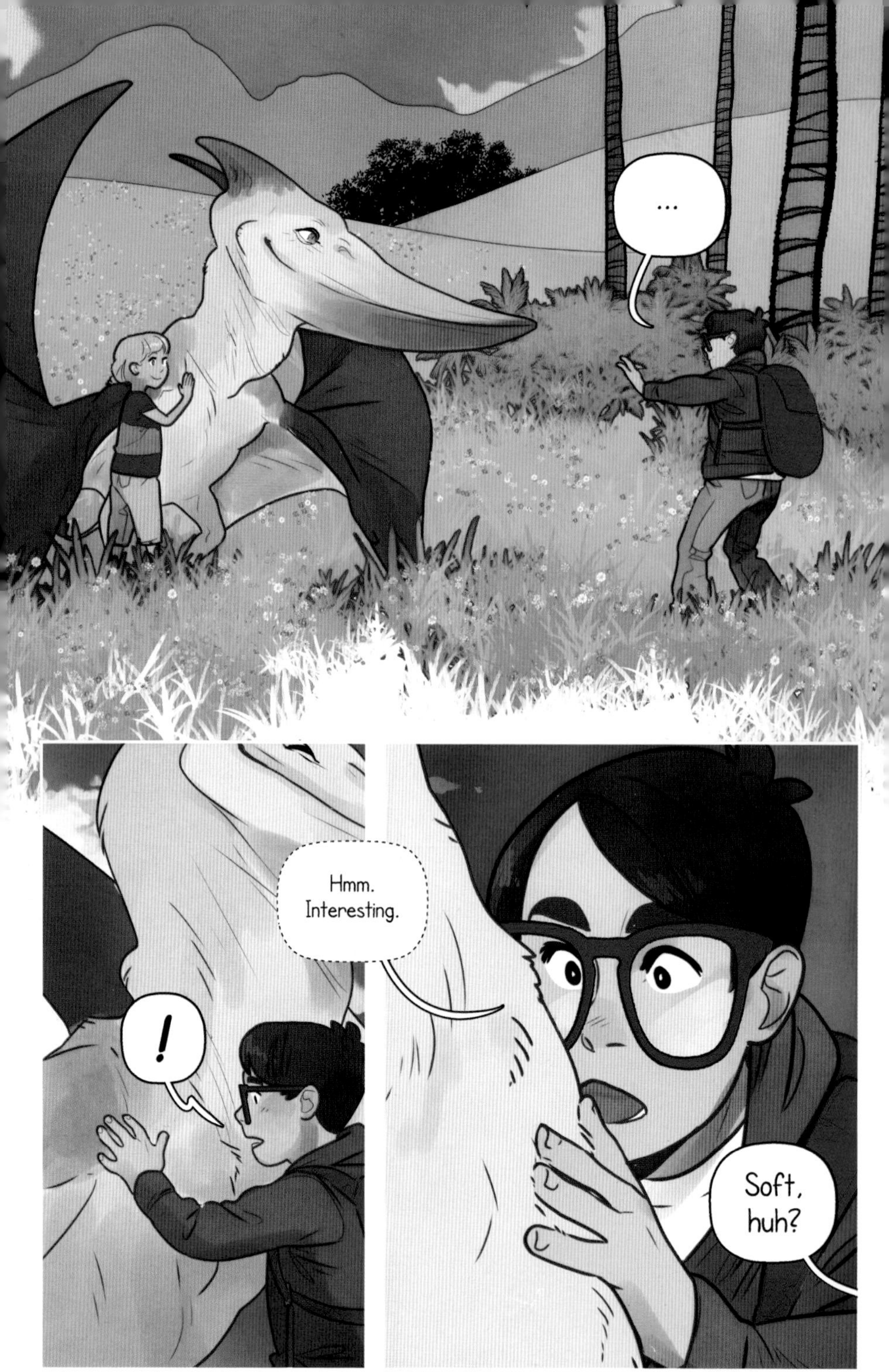
...
Hmm.
Interesting.
!
Soft,
huh?

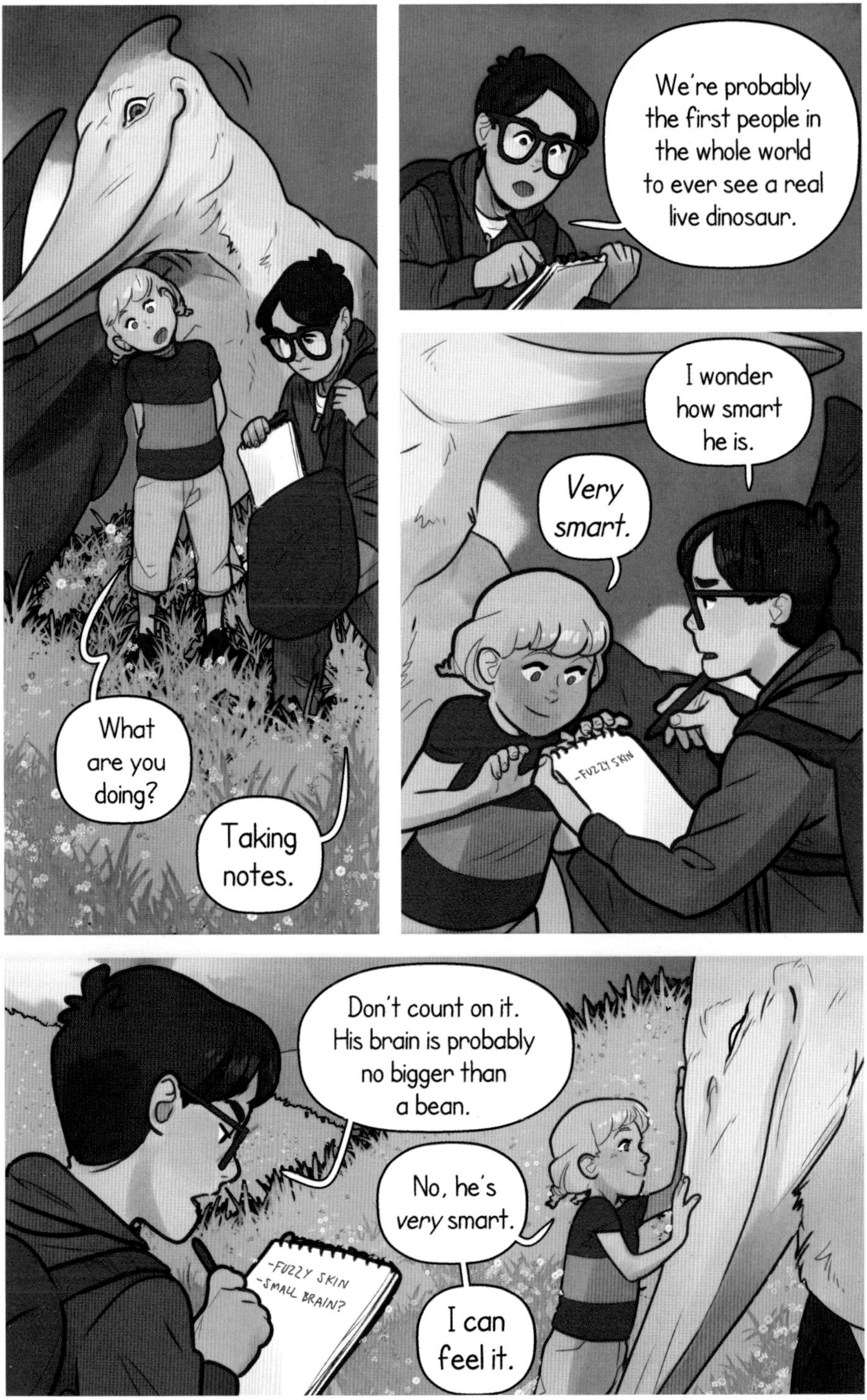
What are you doing?
Taking notes.
We're probably the first people in the whole world to ever see a real live dinosaur.
I wonder how smart he is.
Very smart.
-FUZZY SKIN
Don't count on it. His brain is probably no bigger than a bean.
No, he's very smart.
I can feel it.
-FUZZY SKIN
-SMALL BRAIN?

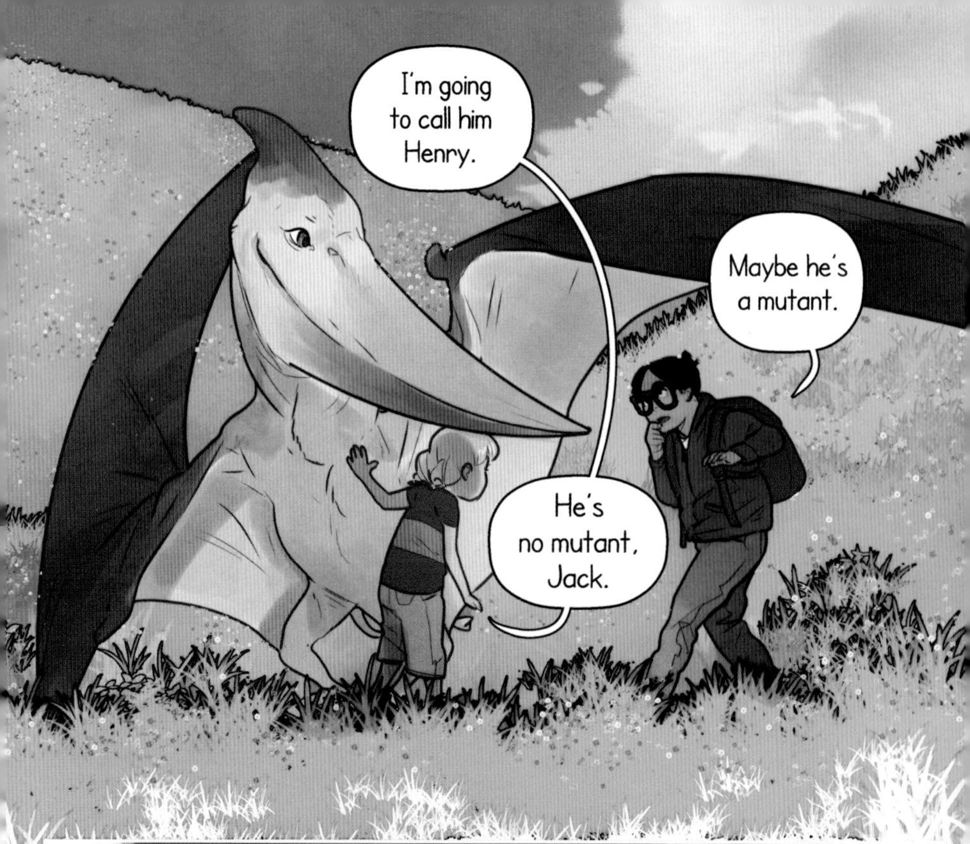
I'm going to call him Henry.
Maybe he's a mutant.
He's no mutant, Jack.

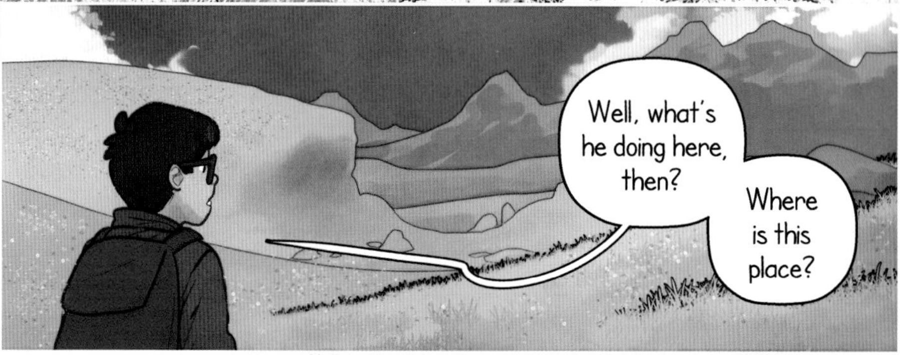
Well, what's he doing here, then?
Where is this place?

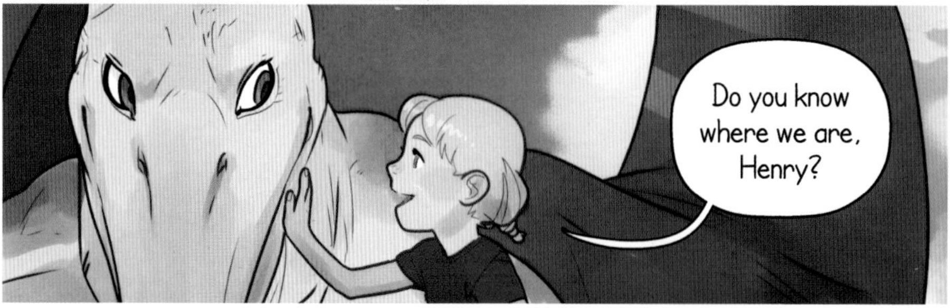
Do you know where we are, Henry?

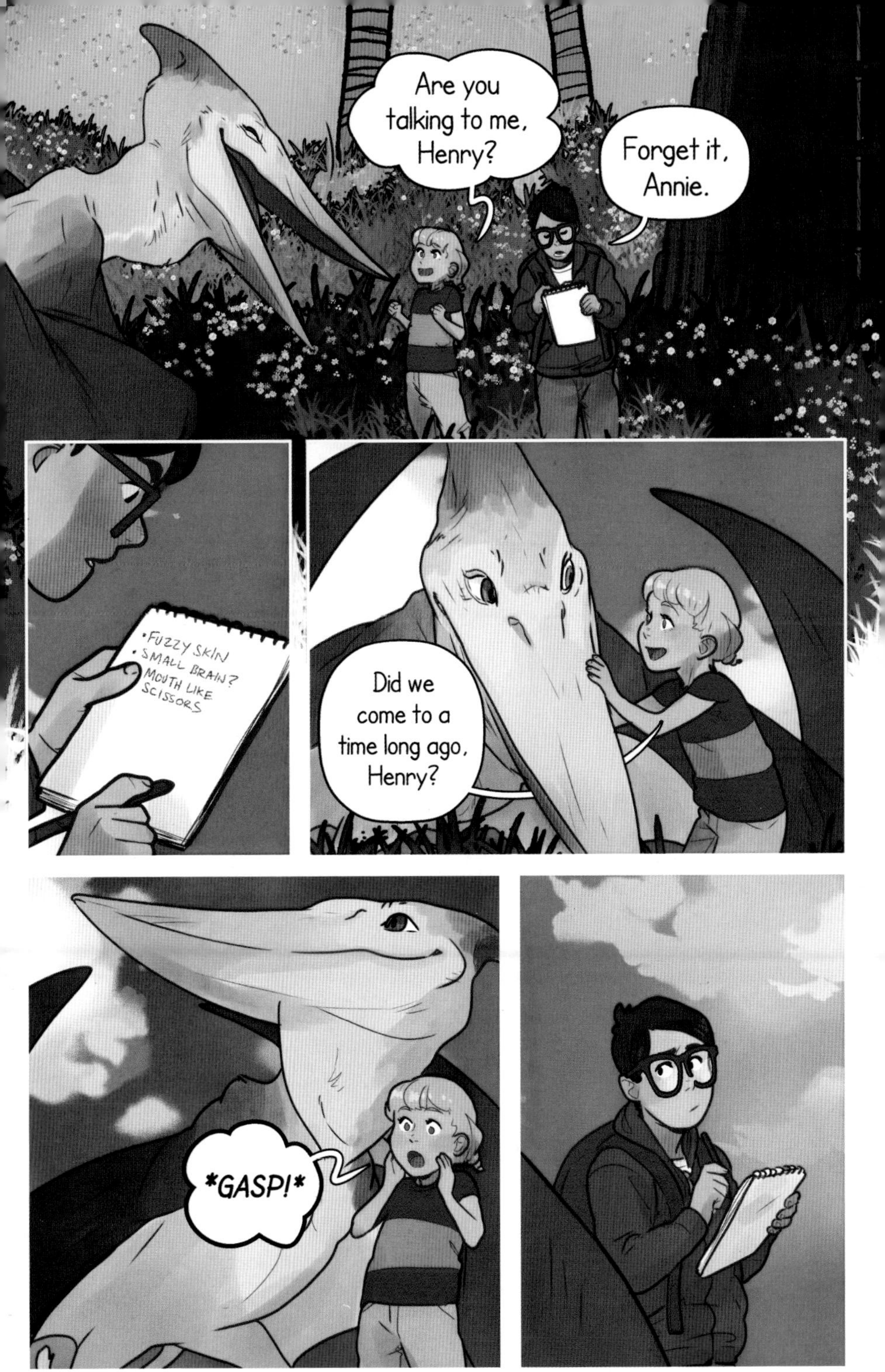

Are you talking to me, Henry?
Forget it, Annie.
• FUZZY SKIN
• SMALL BRAIN?
• MOUTH LIKE SCISSORS
Did we come to a time long ago, Henry?
GASP!

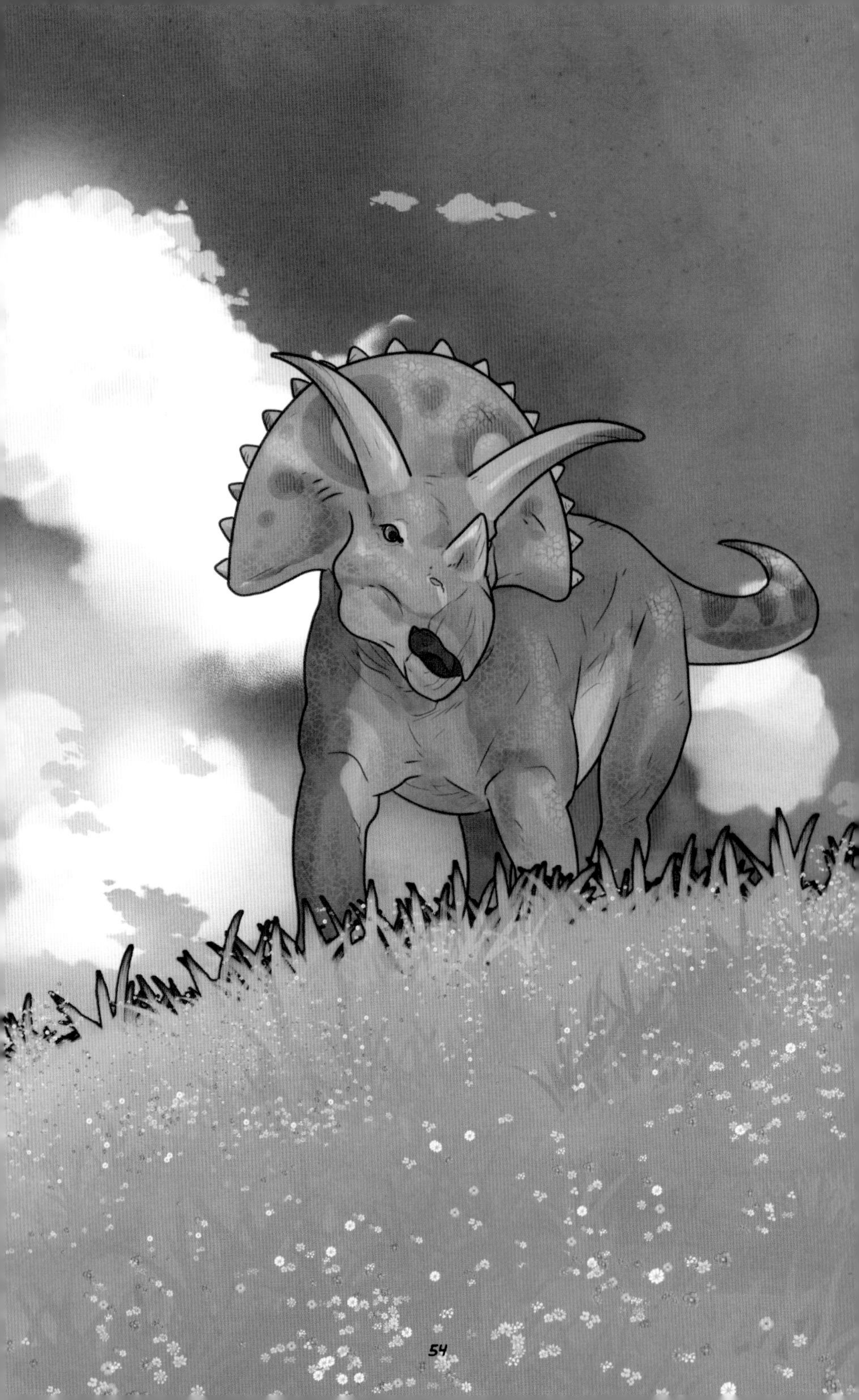

CHAPTER FIVE
Gold in the Grass

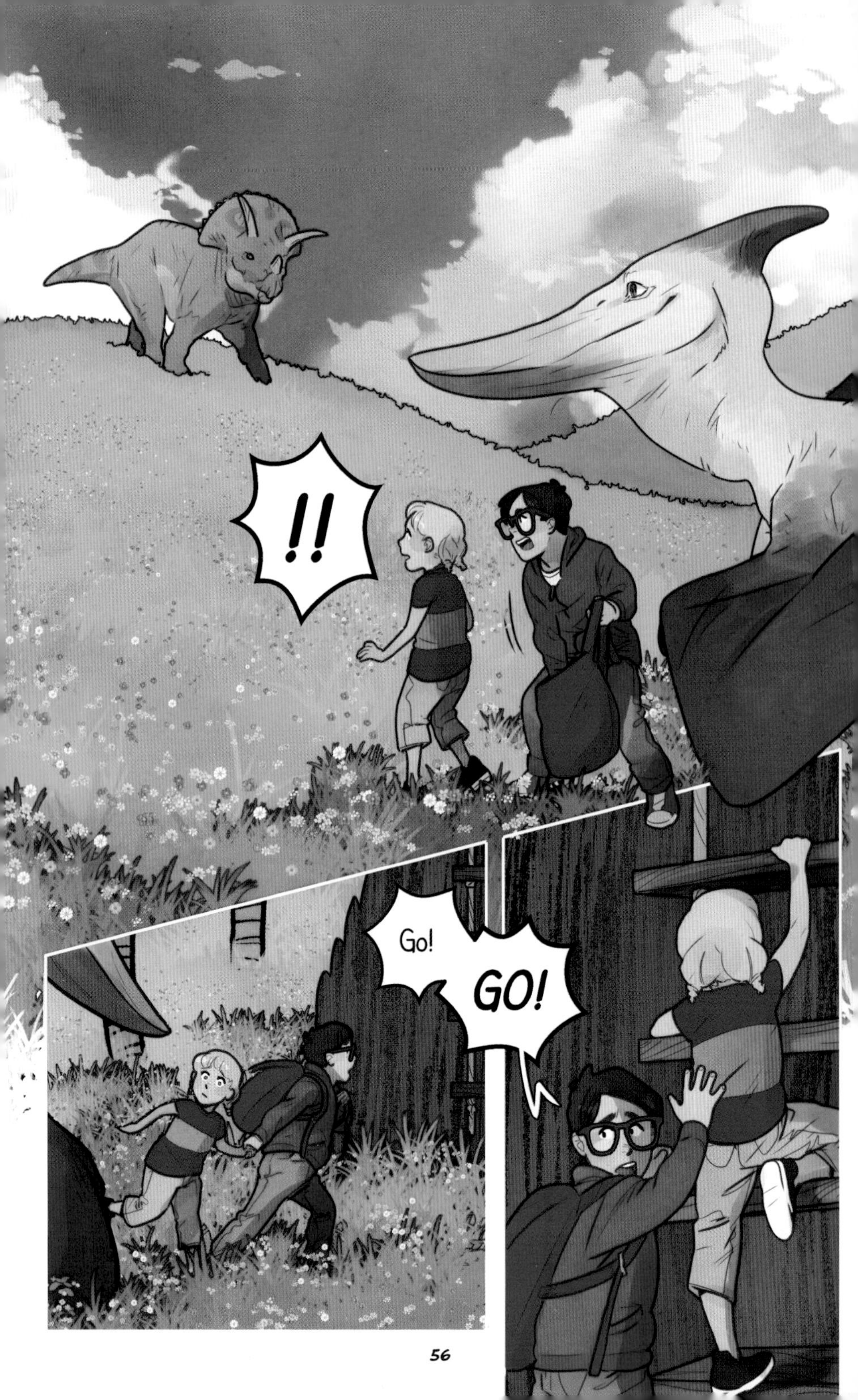
!!
Go!
GO!

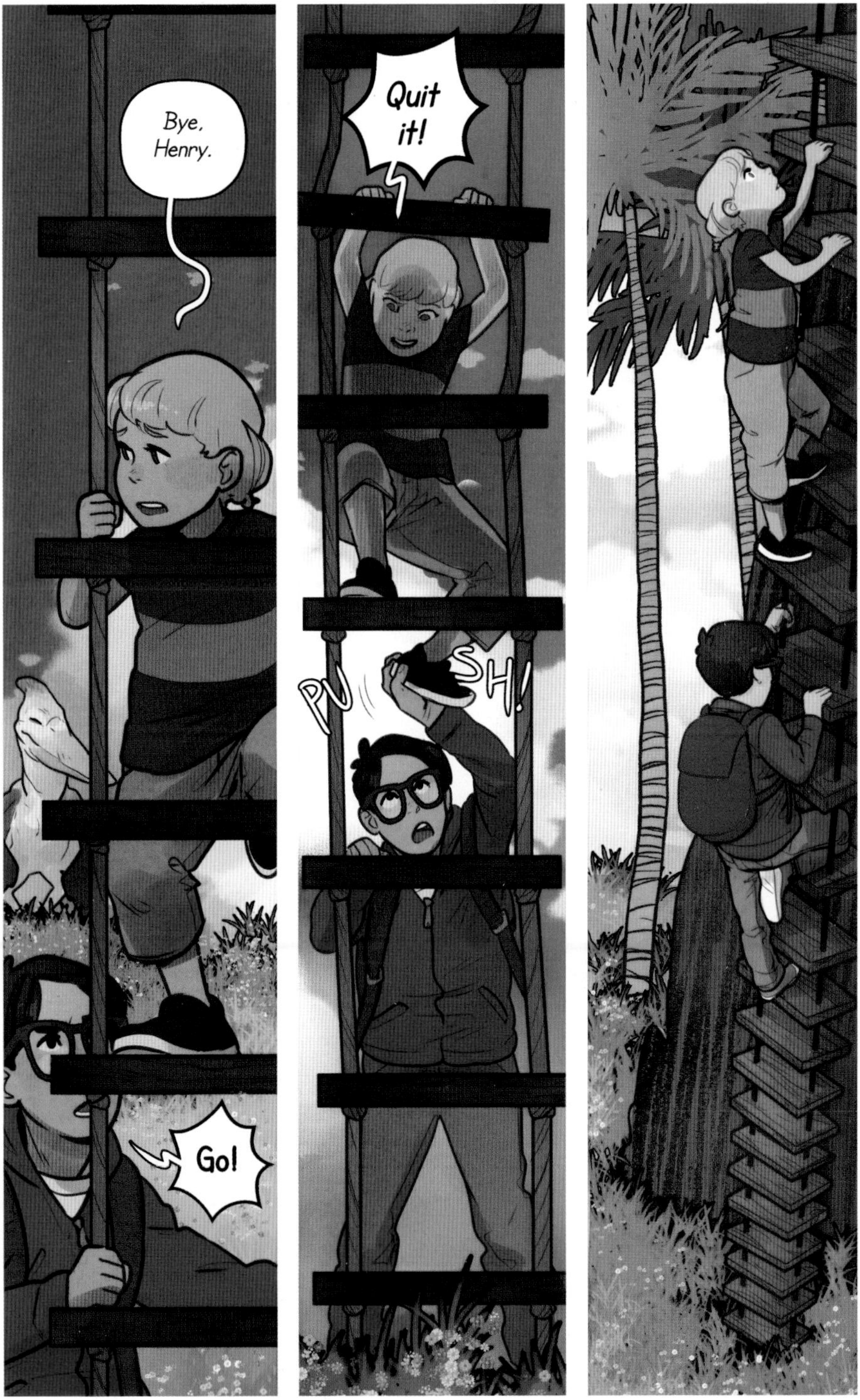
Bye, Henry.
Go!
Quit it!
PUSH!

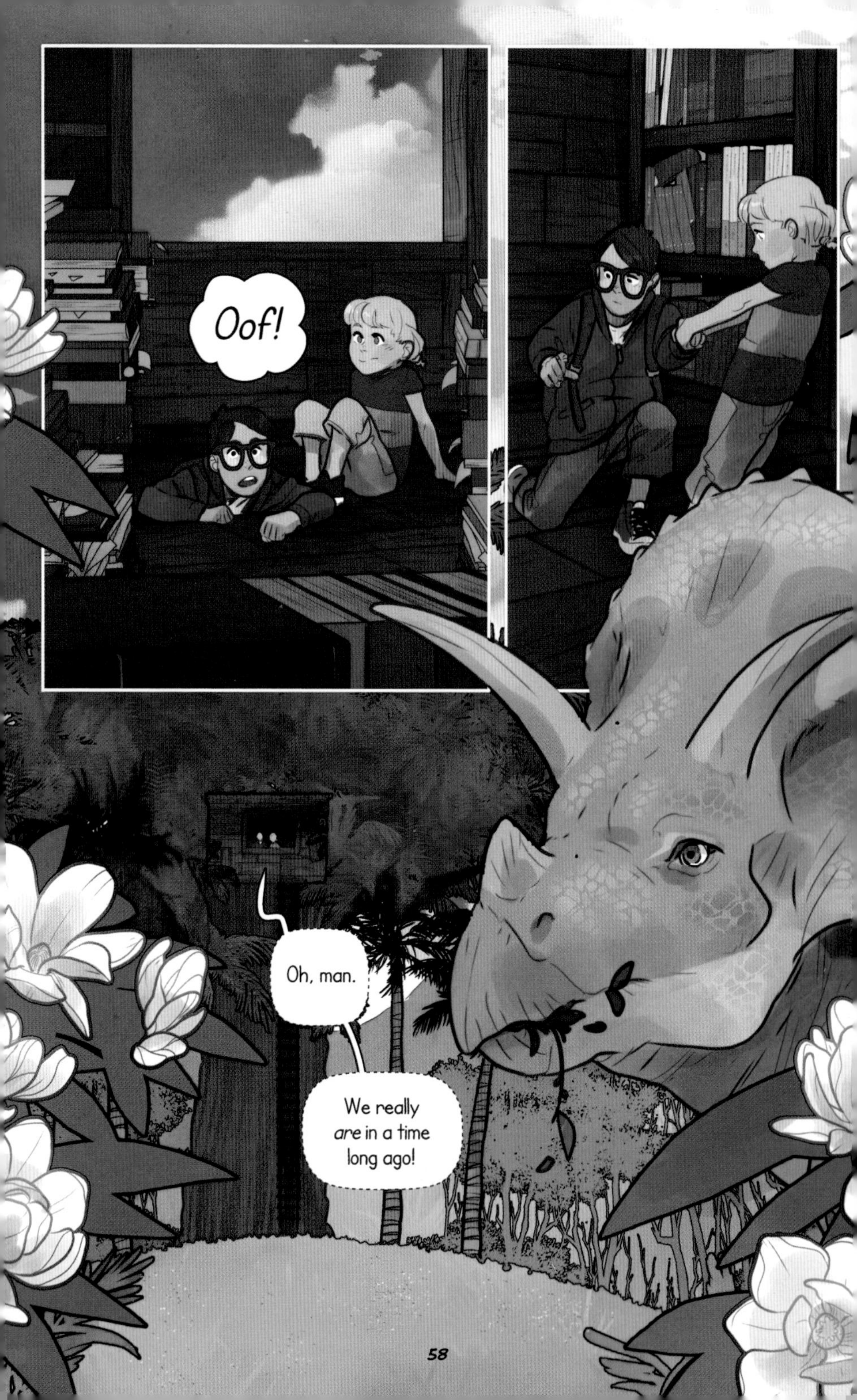
Oof!
Oh, man.
We really *are* in a time long ago!

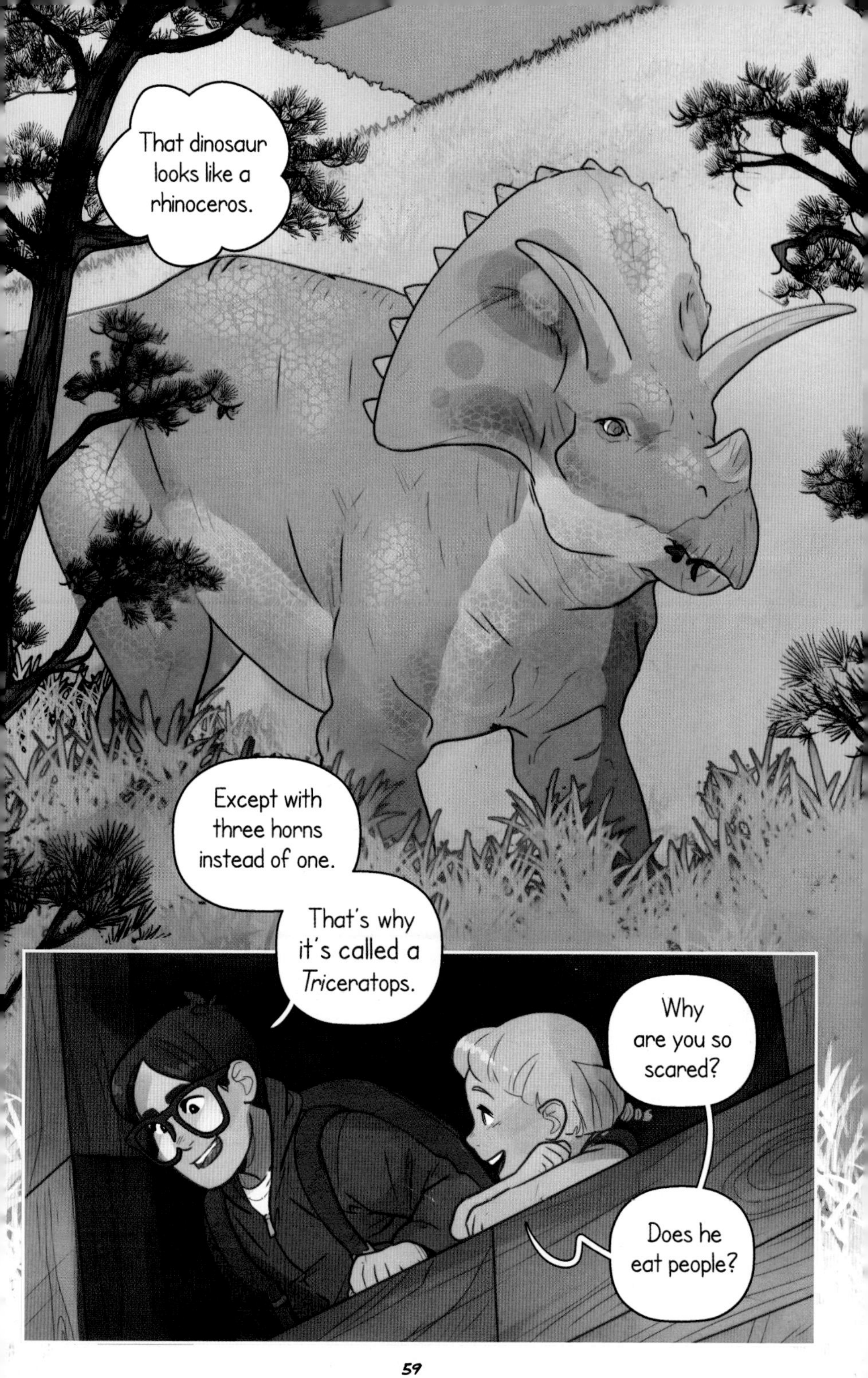
That dinosaur looks like a rhinoceros.
Except with three horns instead of one.
That's why it's called a *Tri*ceratops.
Why are you so scared?
Does he eat people?

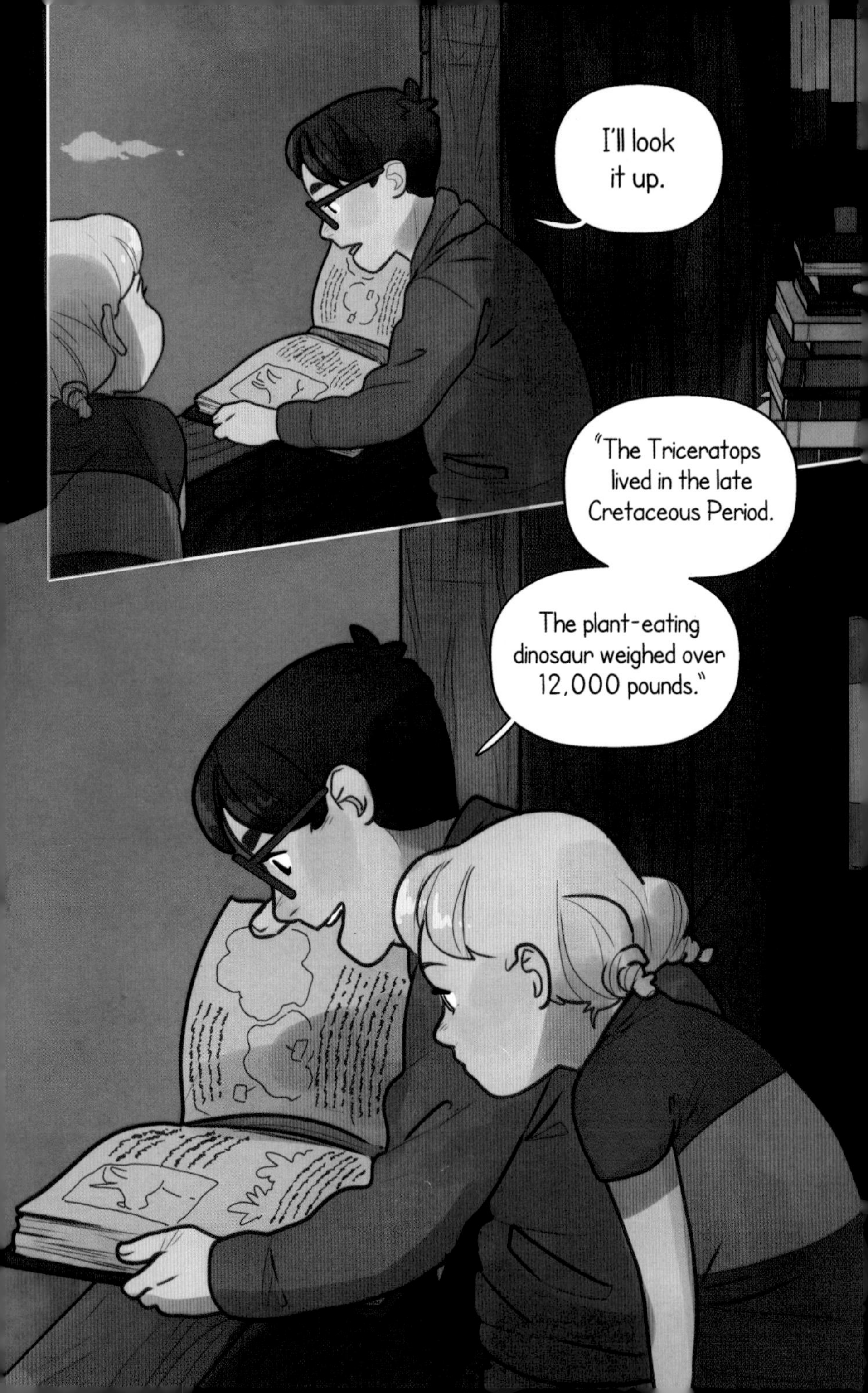
I'll look it up.
"The Triceratops lived in the late Cretaceous Period.
The plant-eating dinosaur weighed over 12,000 pounds."

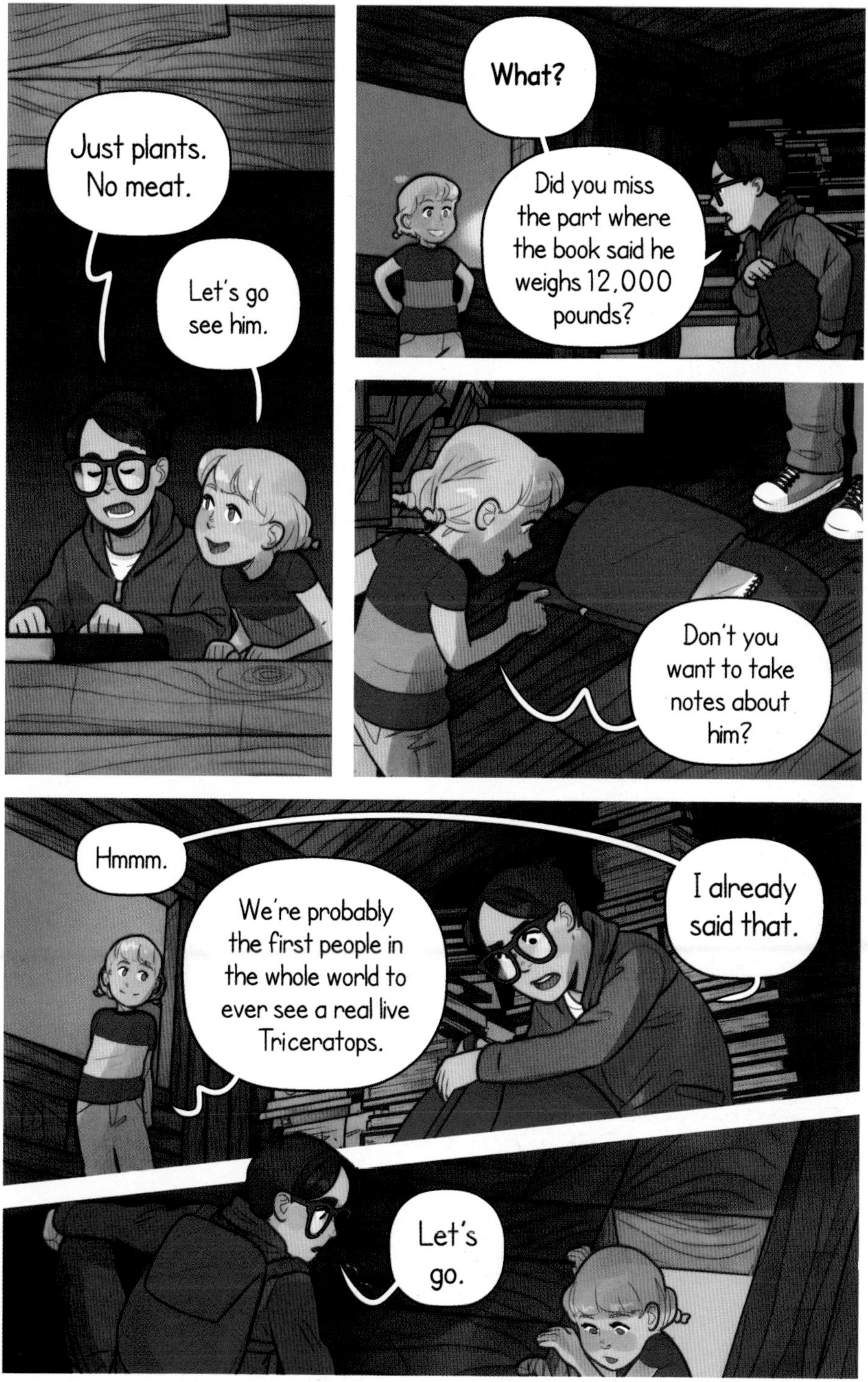
Just plants. No meat.
Let's go see him.
What?
Did you miss the part where the book said he weighs 12,000 pounds?
Don't you want to take notes about him?
Hmmm.
I already said that.
We're probably the first people in the whole world to ever see a real live Triceratops.
Let's go.

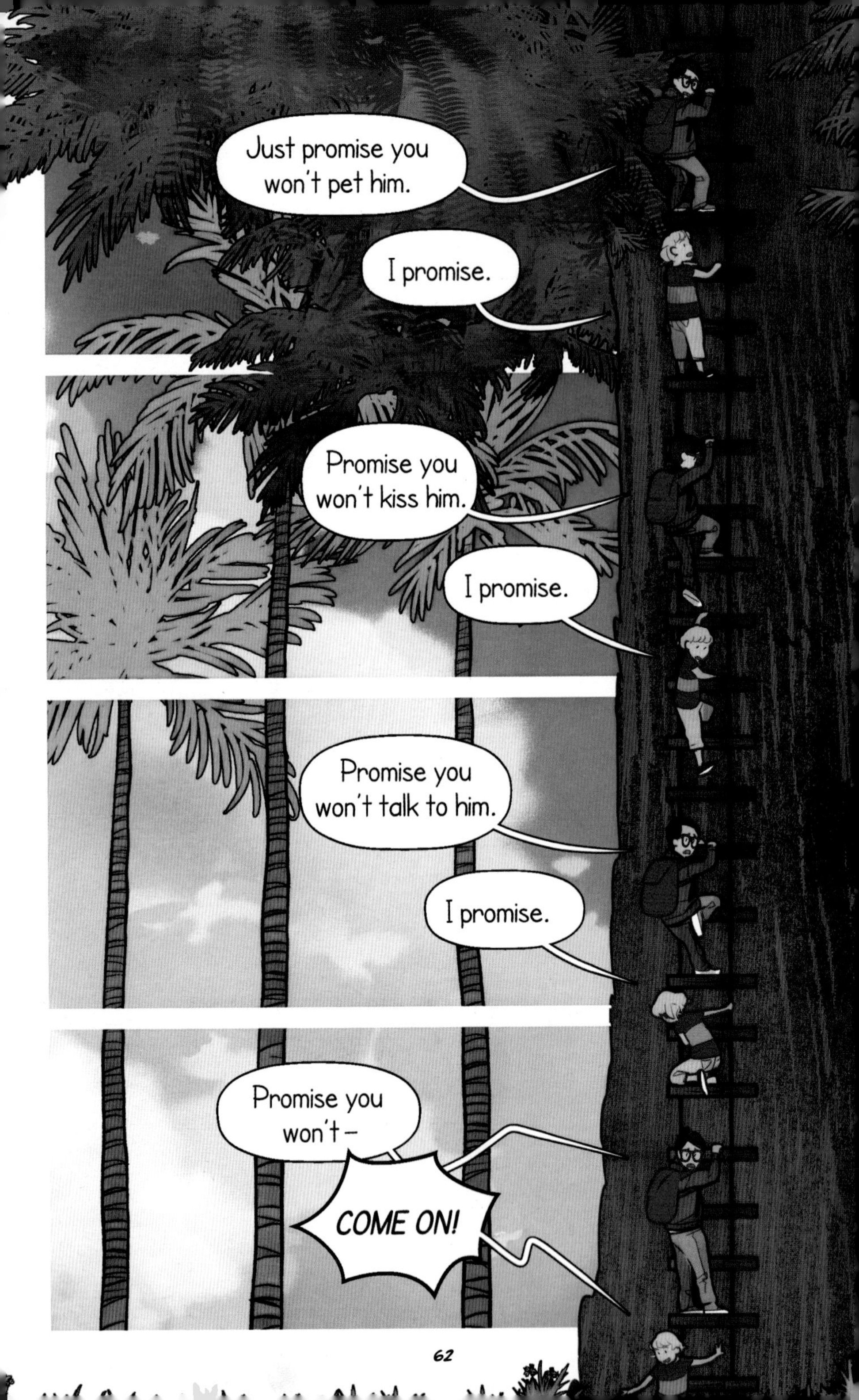
Just promise you won't pet him.
I promise.
Promise you won't kiss him.
I promise.
Promise you won't talk to him.
I promise.
Promise you won't –
COME ON!

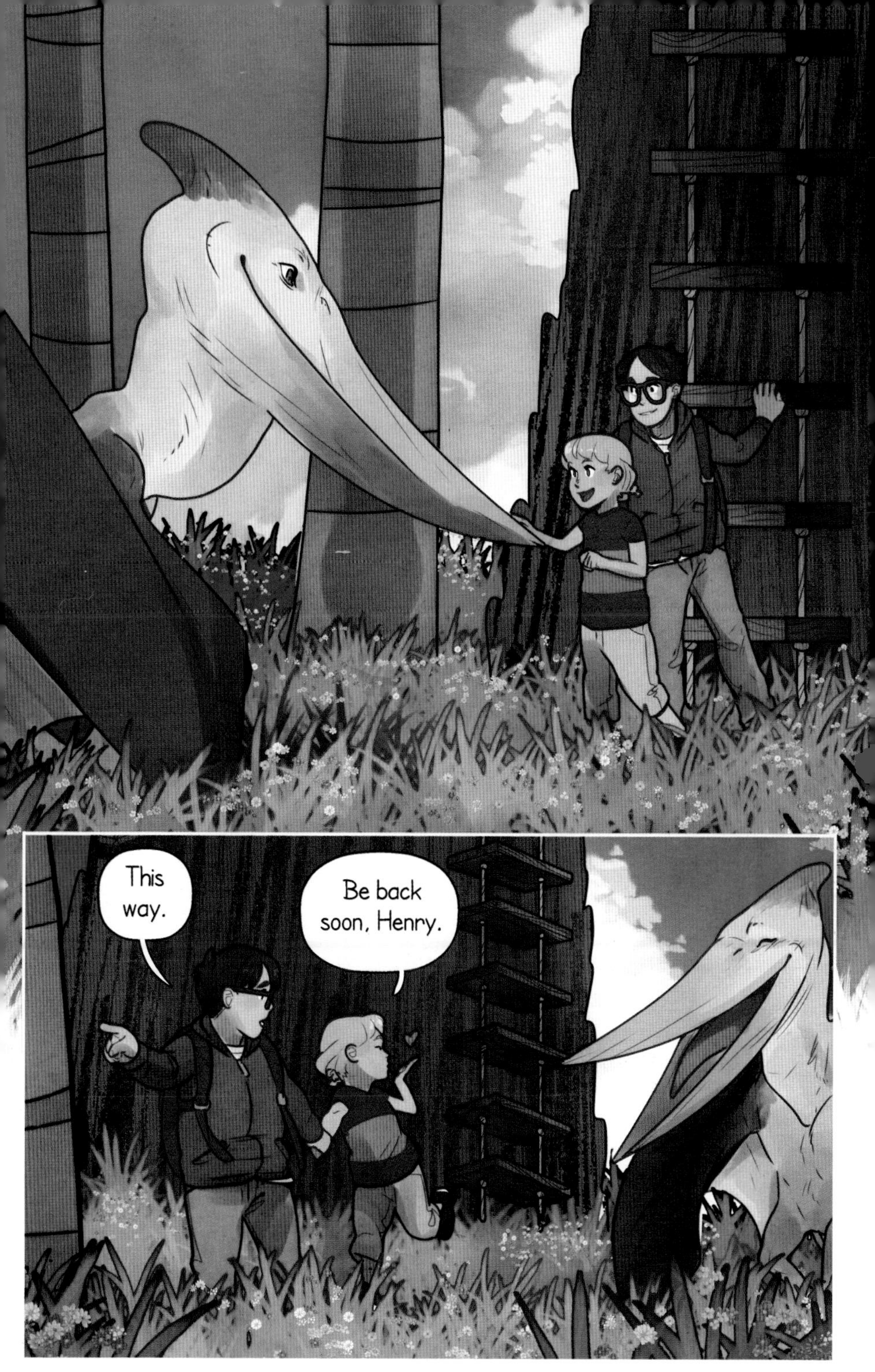
This way.
Be back soon, Henry.

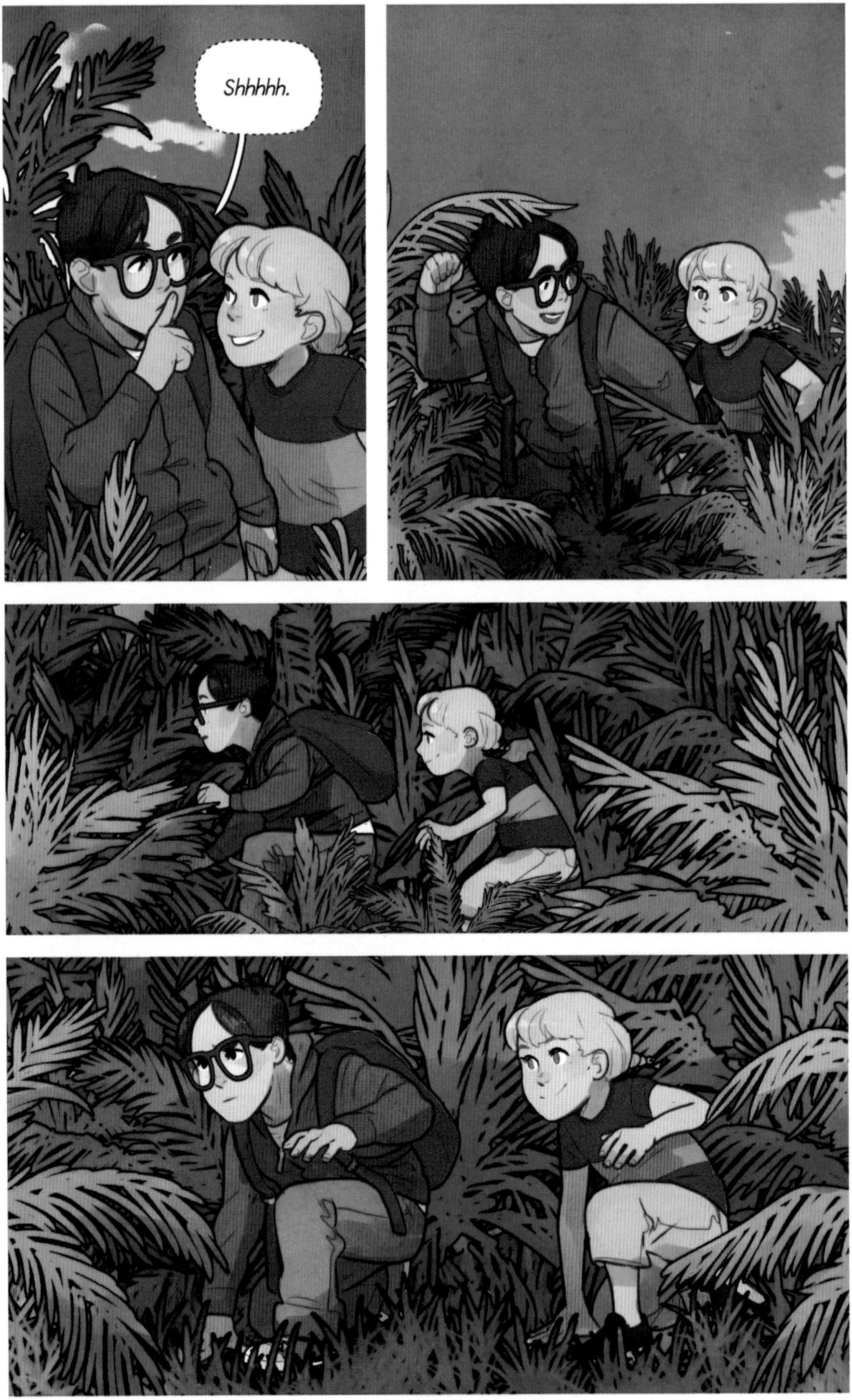
Shhhhh.

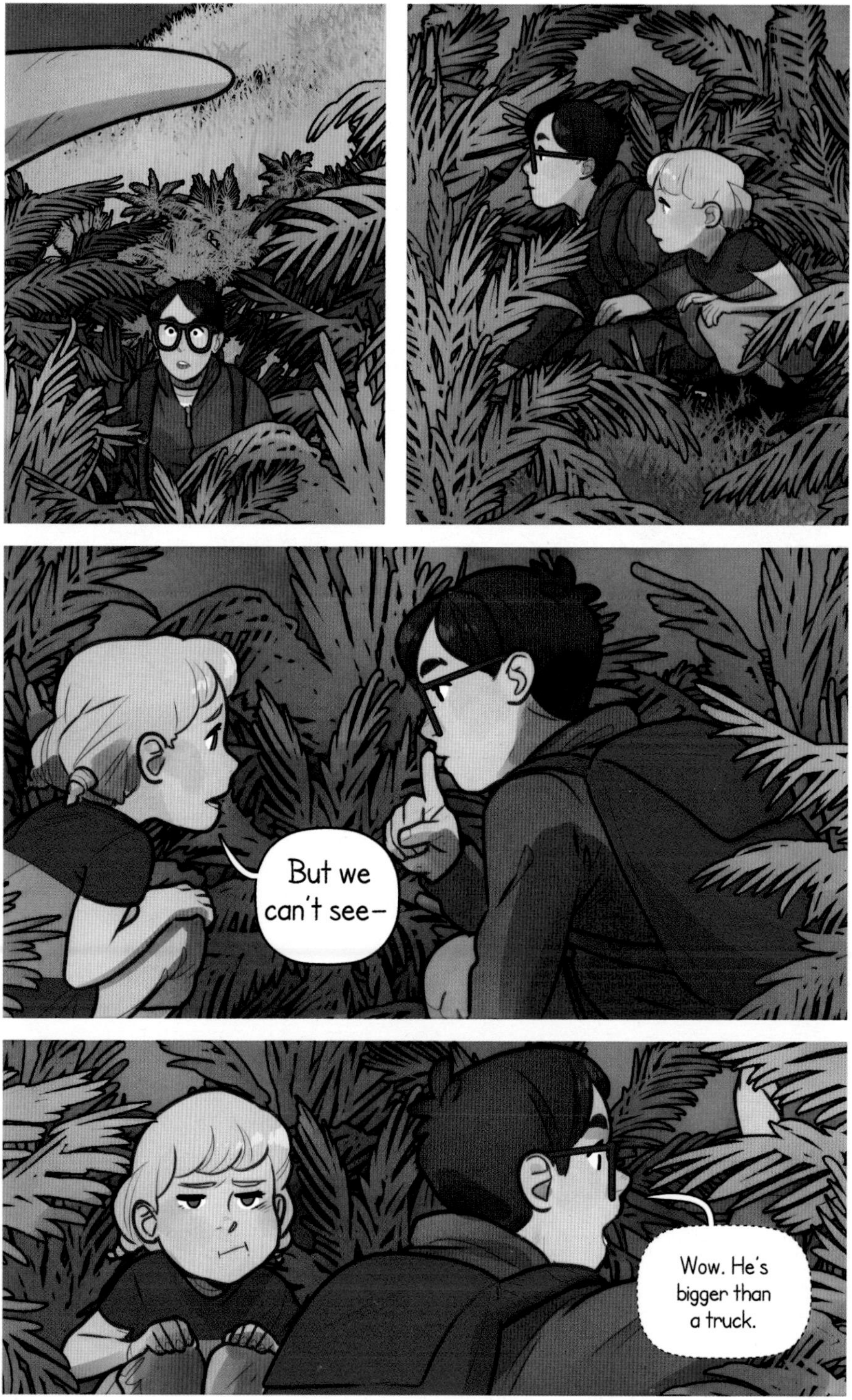
But we can't see–
Wow. He's bigger than a truck.

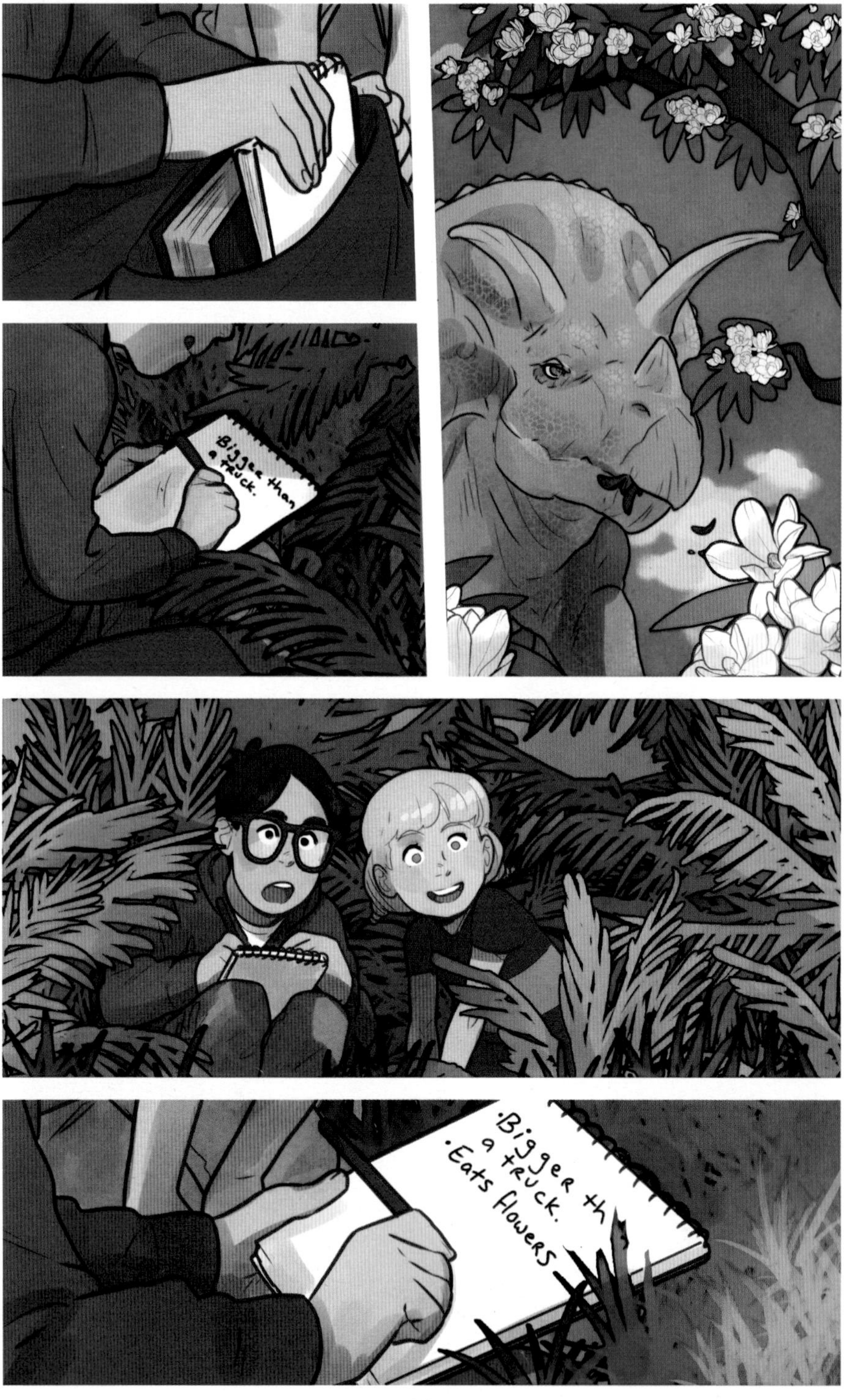
·Bigger than
a truck.
·Bigger th
a truck.
·Eats flowers

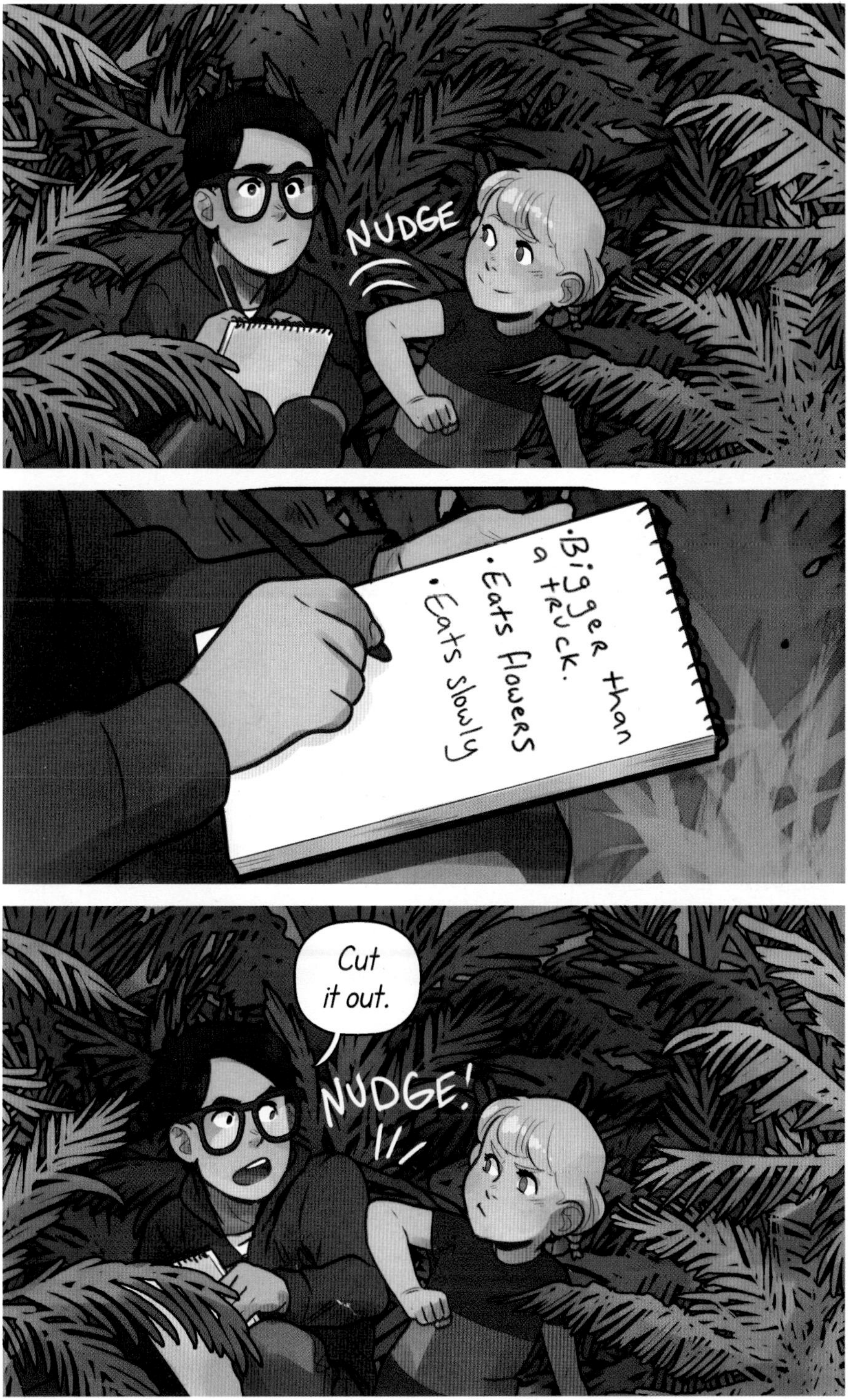
NUDGE
•Bigger than a truck.
•Eats flowers
•Eats slowly
Cut it out.
NUDGE!

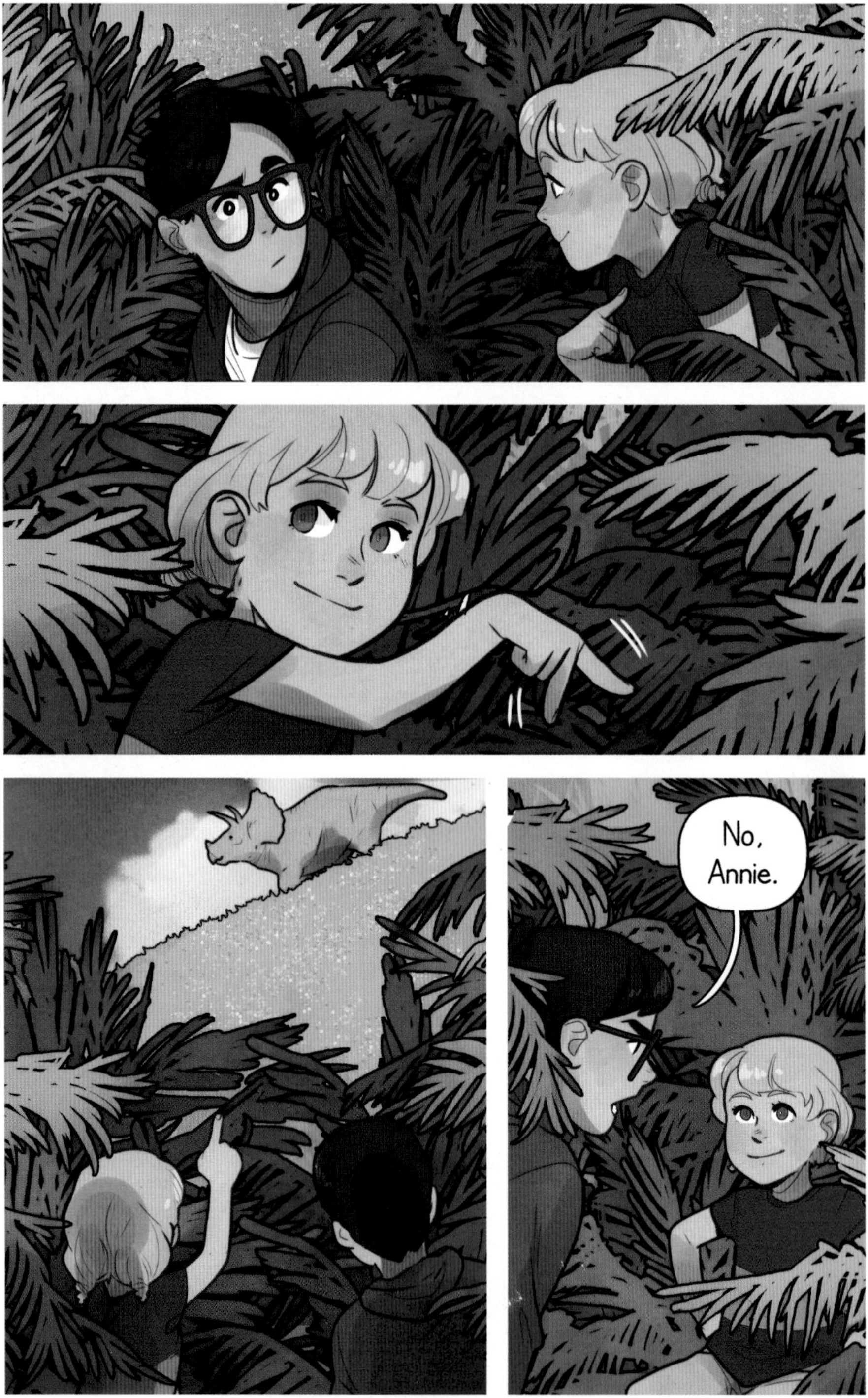
No,
Annie.

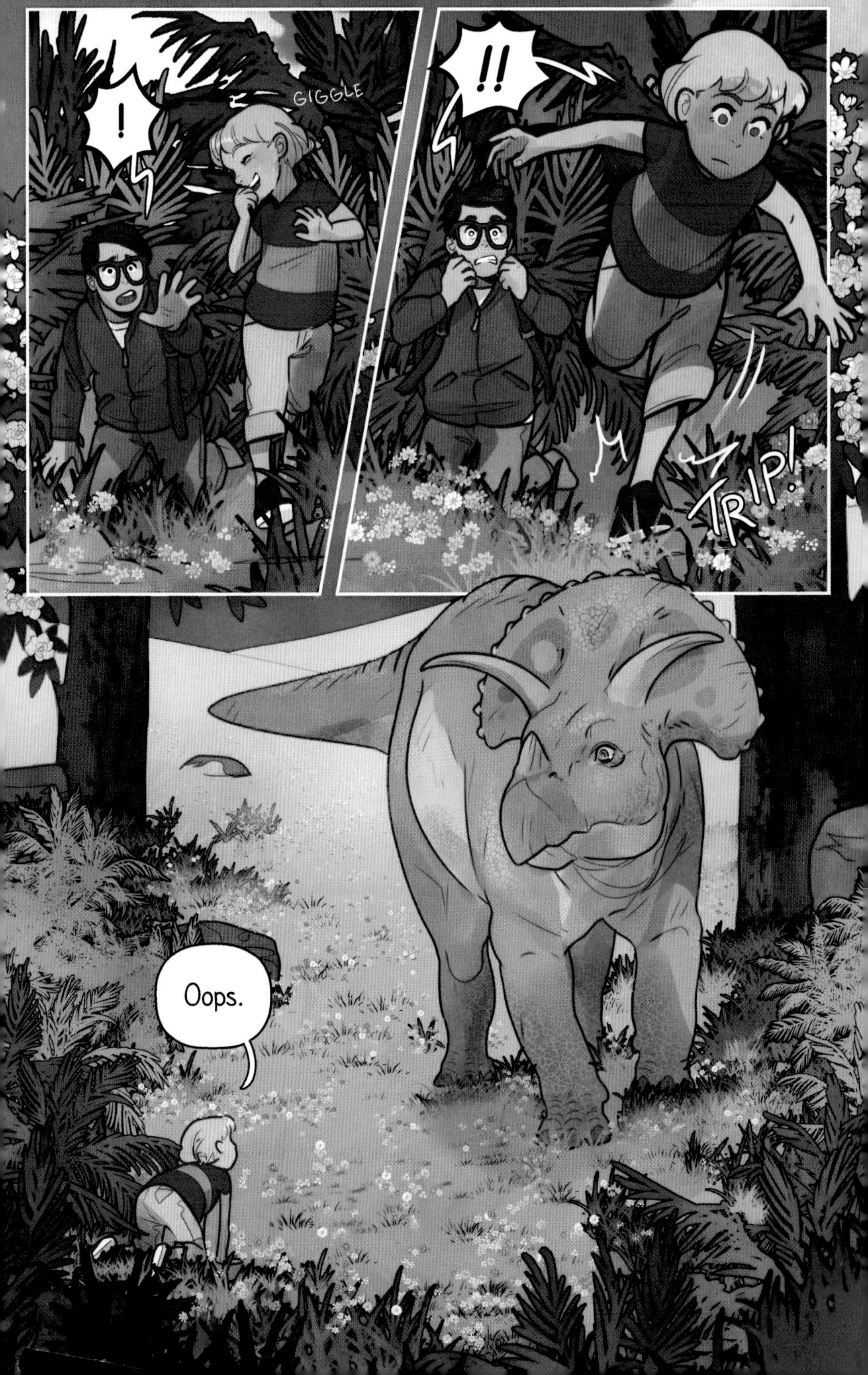
!
GIGGLE
!!
TRIP!
Oops.

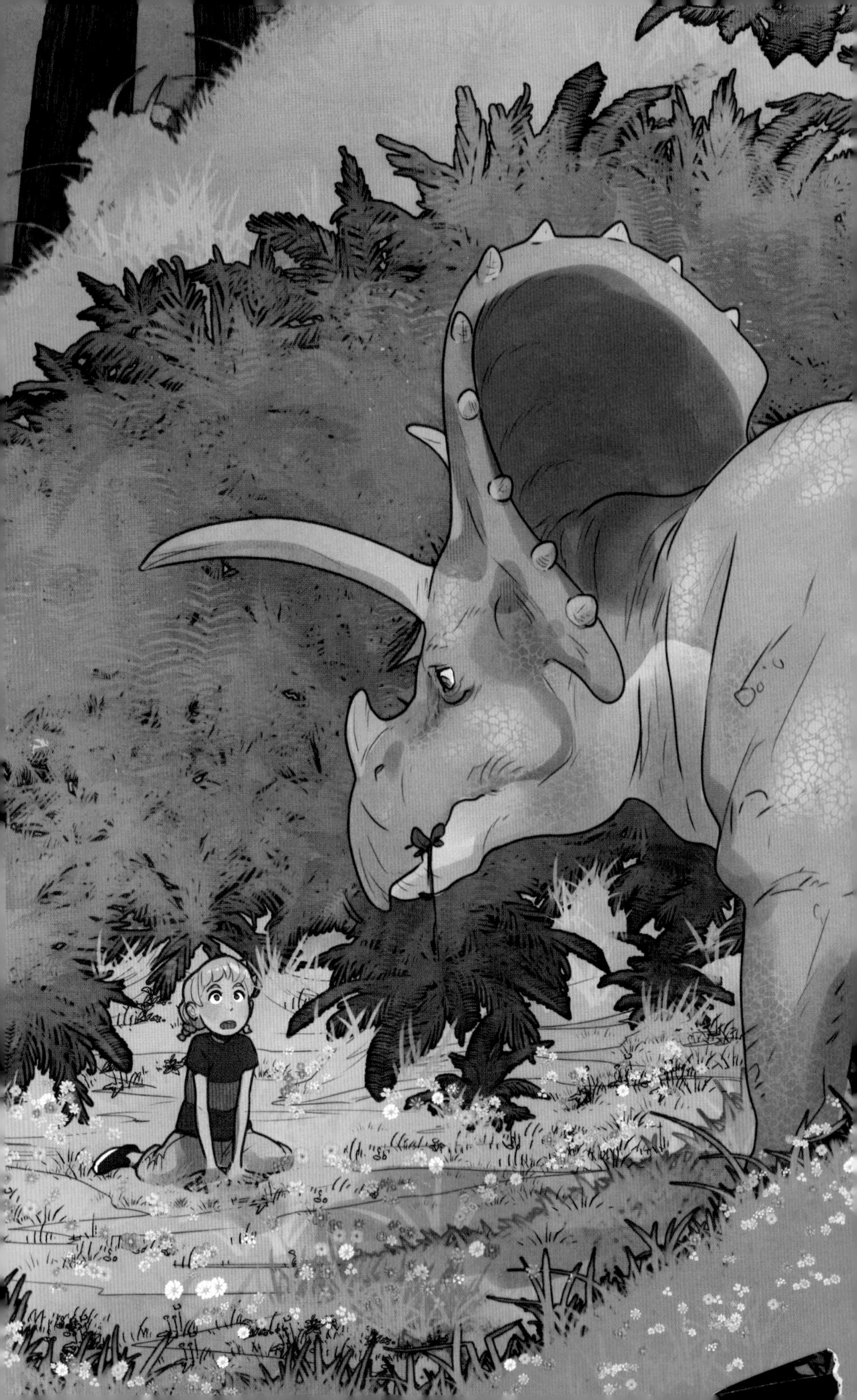

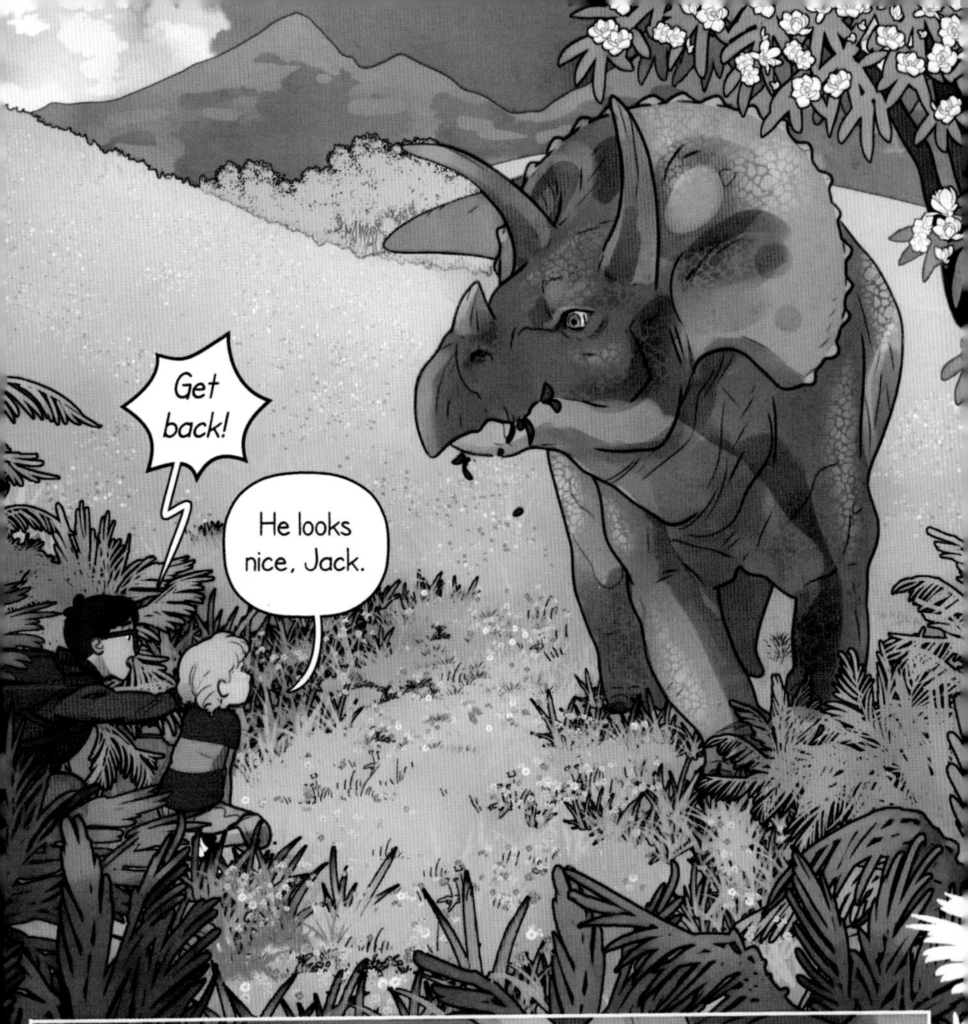
Get back!
He looks nice, Jack.

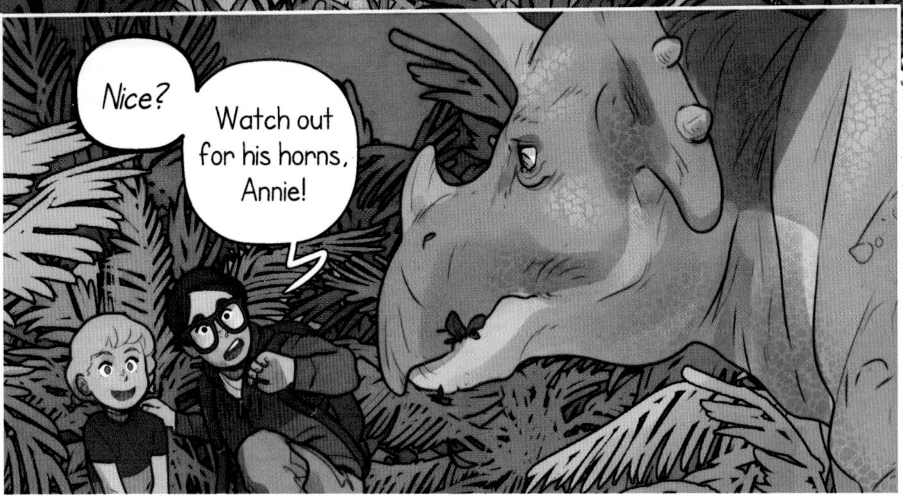
Nice?
Watch out for his horns, Annie!

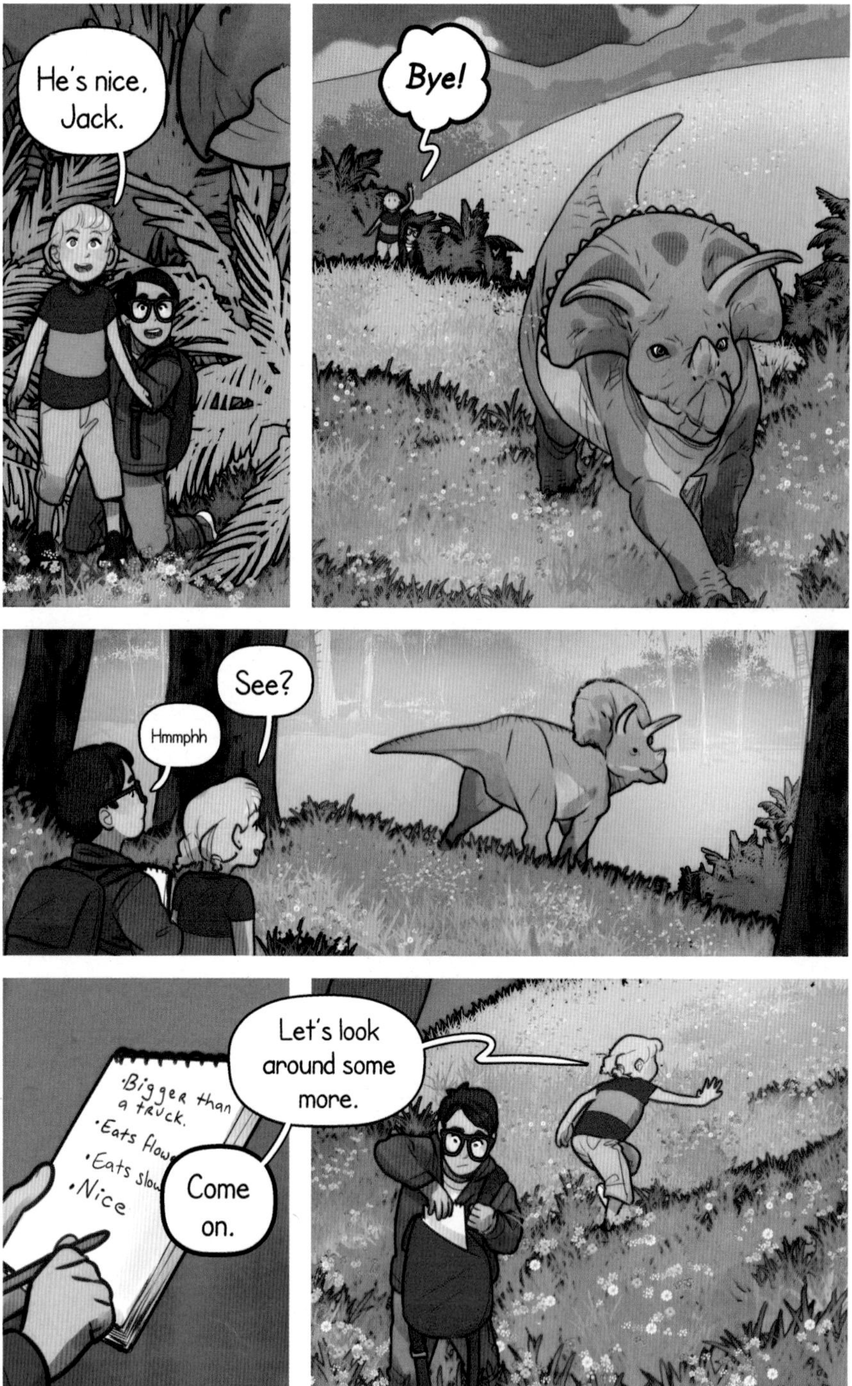
He's nice, Jack.
Bye!
Hmmphh
See?
•Bigger than a truck.
•Nice
Let's look around some more.
Come on.

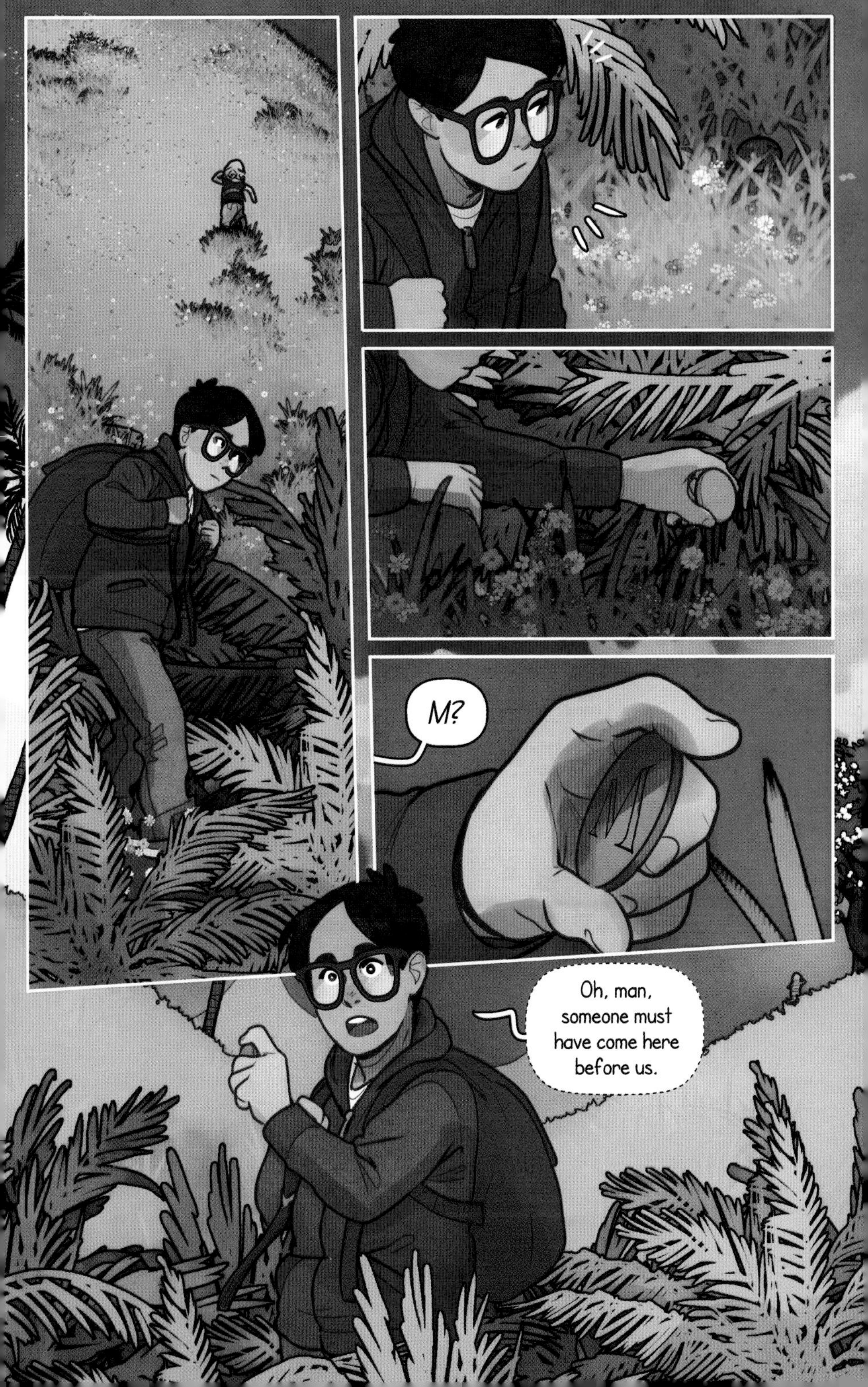
M?
Oh, man, someone must have come here before us.

CHAPTER SIX

Dinosaur Valley

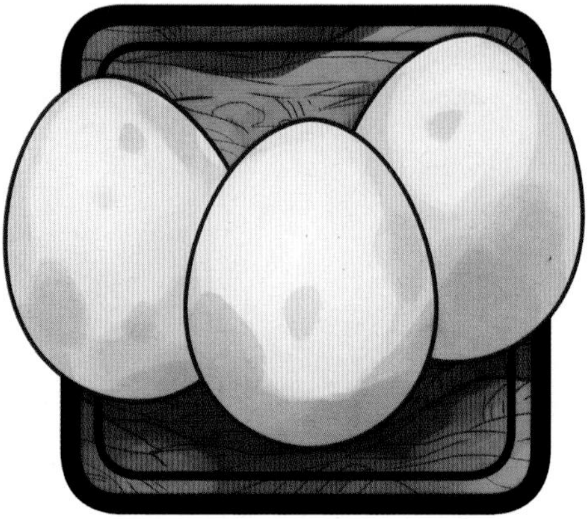

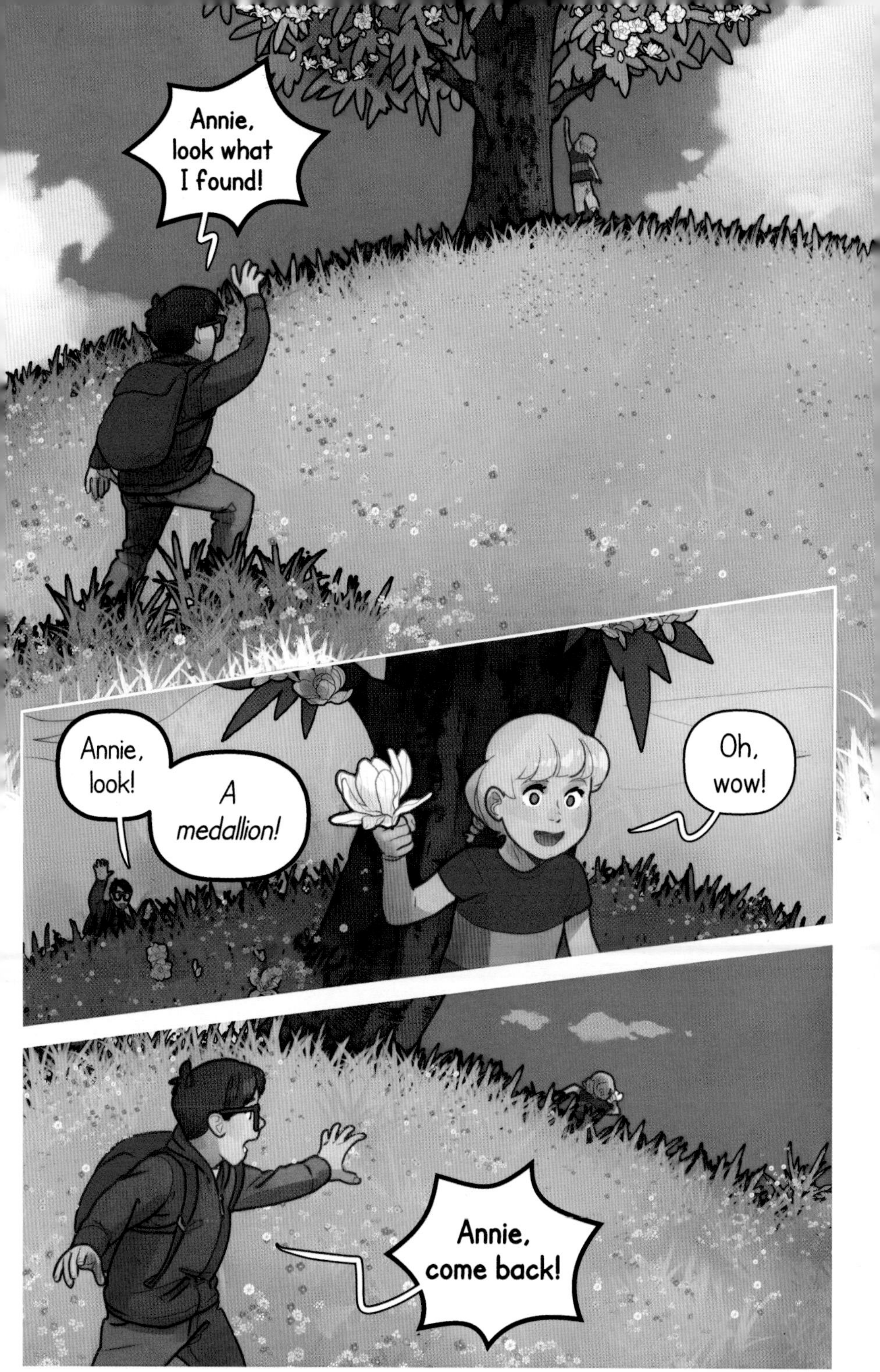
Annie, look what I found!
Annie, look!
A medallion!
Oh, wow!
Annie, come back!

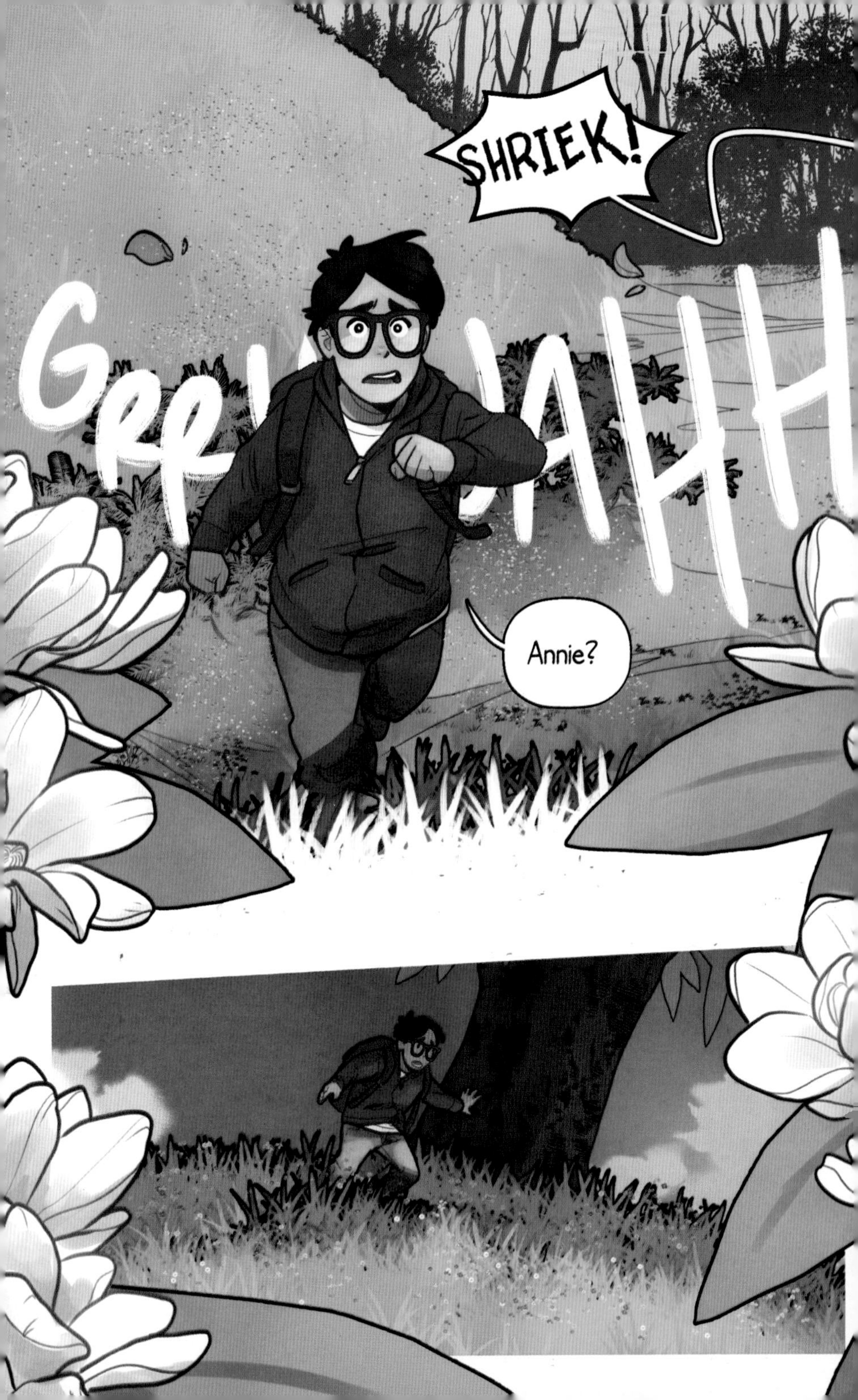
SHRIEK!
Annie?

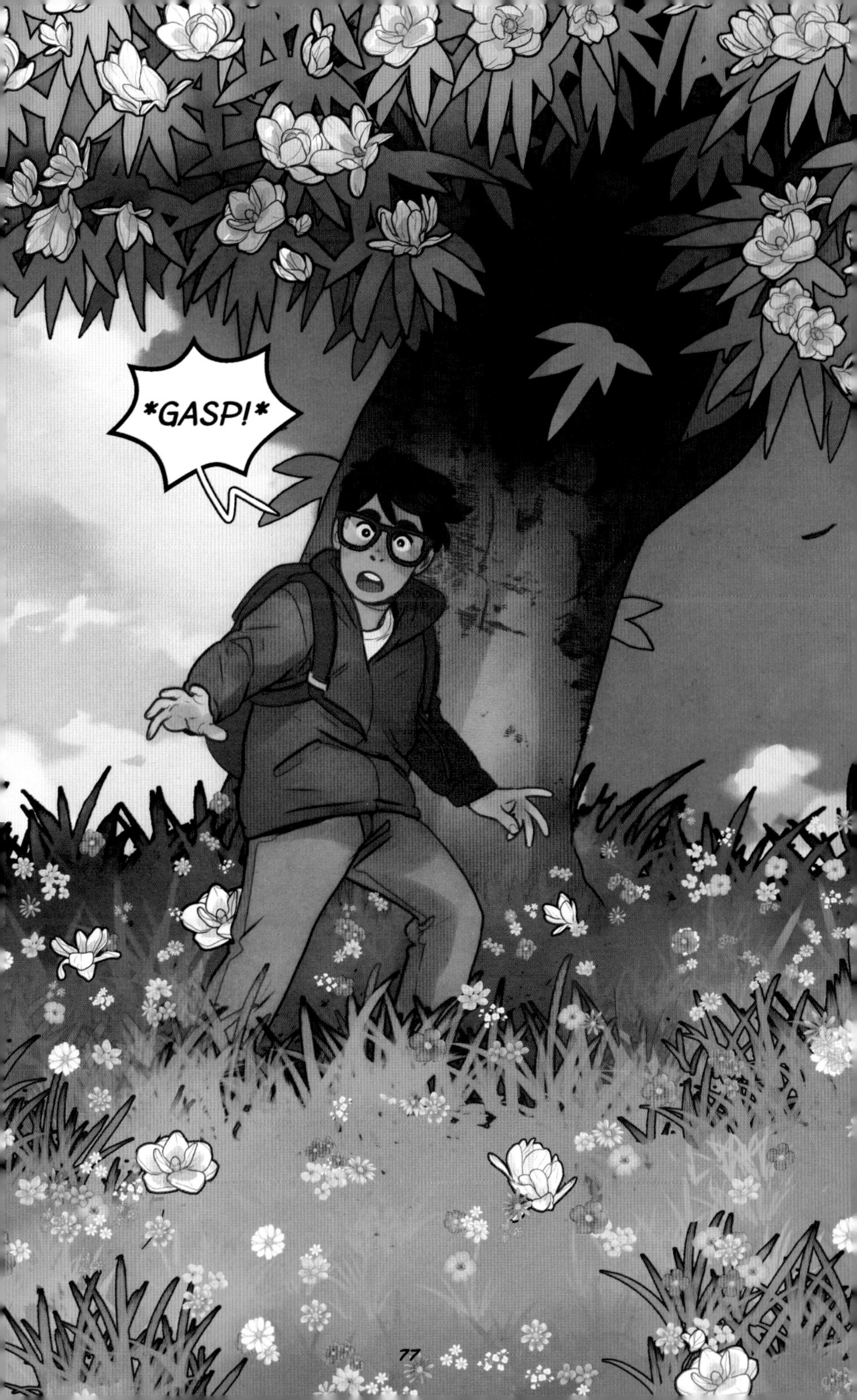
GASP!

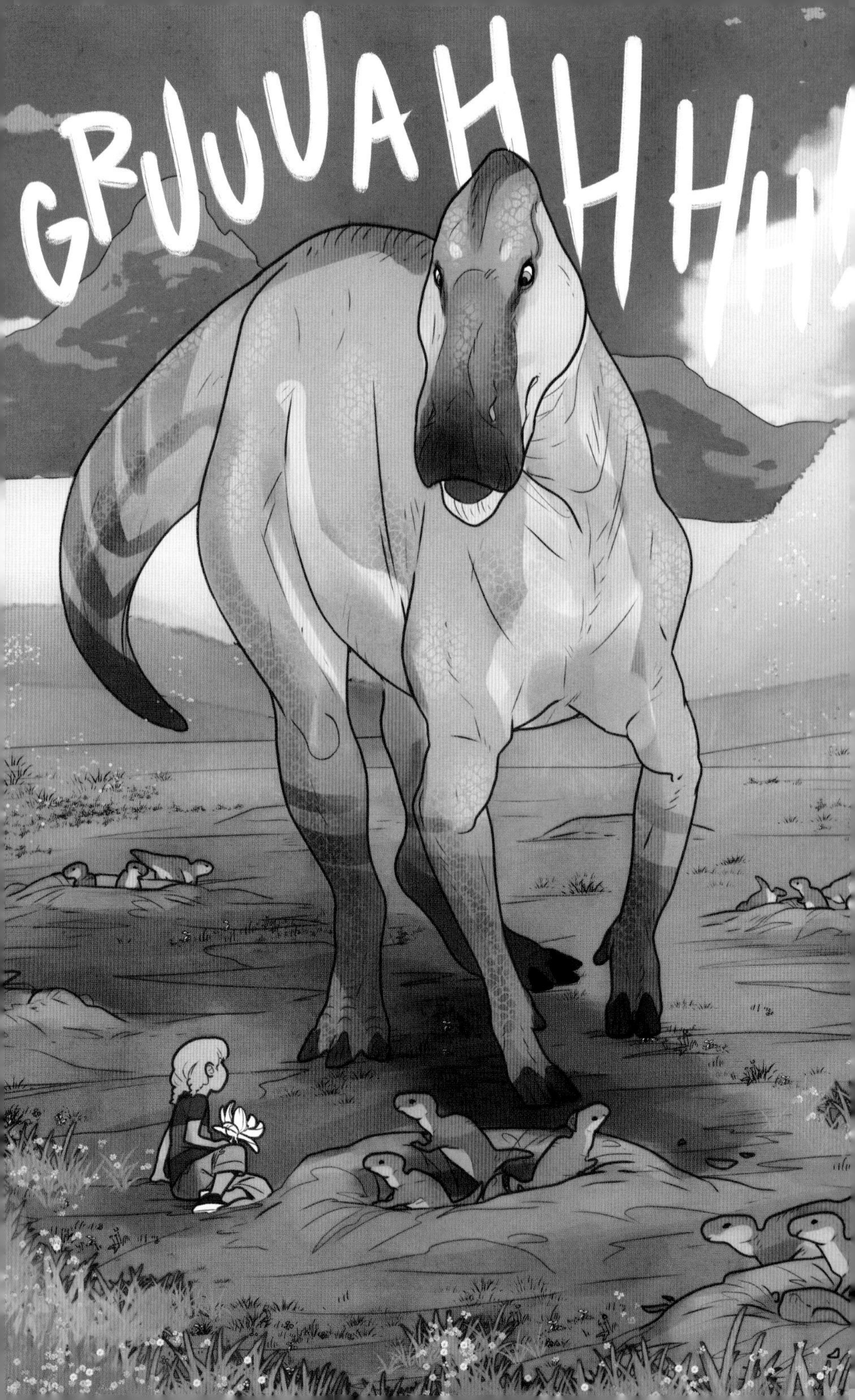
GRUUUAHHHH!

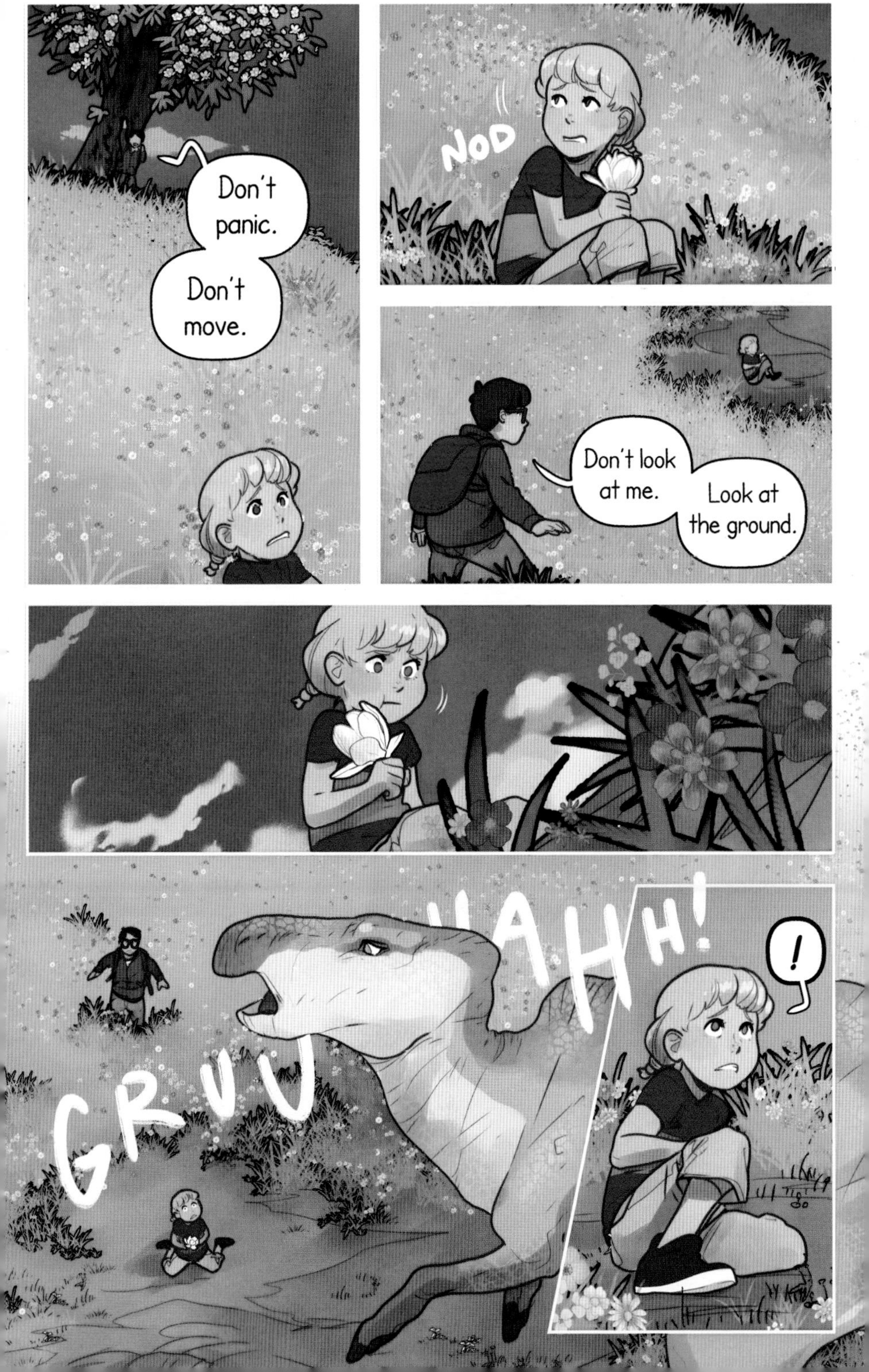
Don't panic.
Don't move.
NOD
Don't look at me.
Look at the ground.
UAHH!
!
GRUU

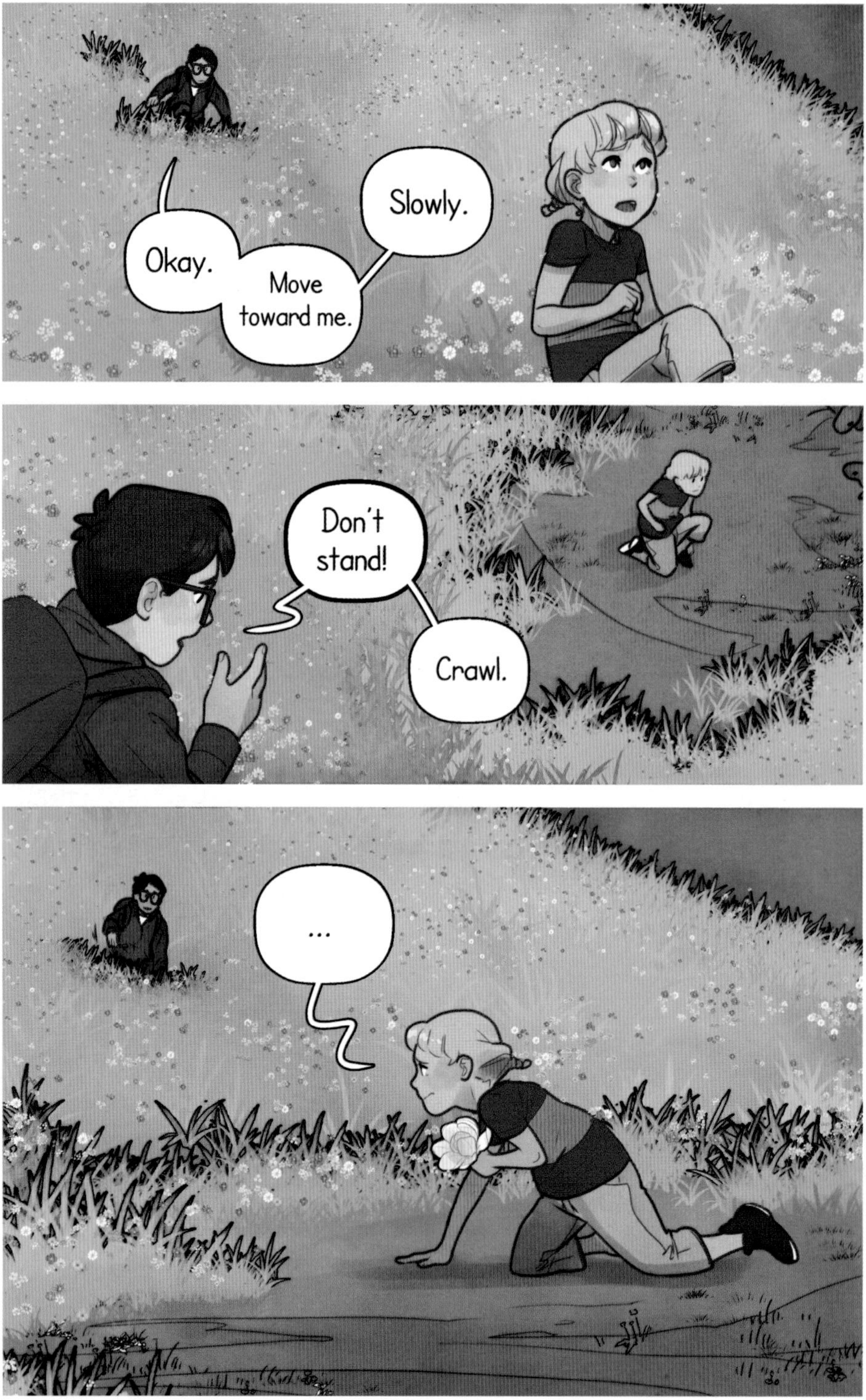

Okay.
Move toward me.
Slowly.
Don't stand!
Crawl.
...

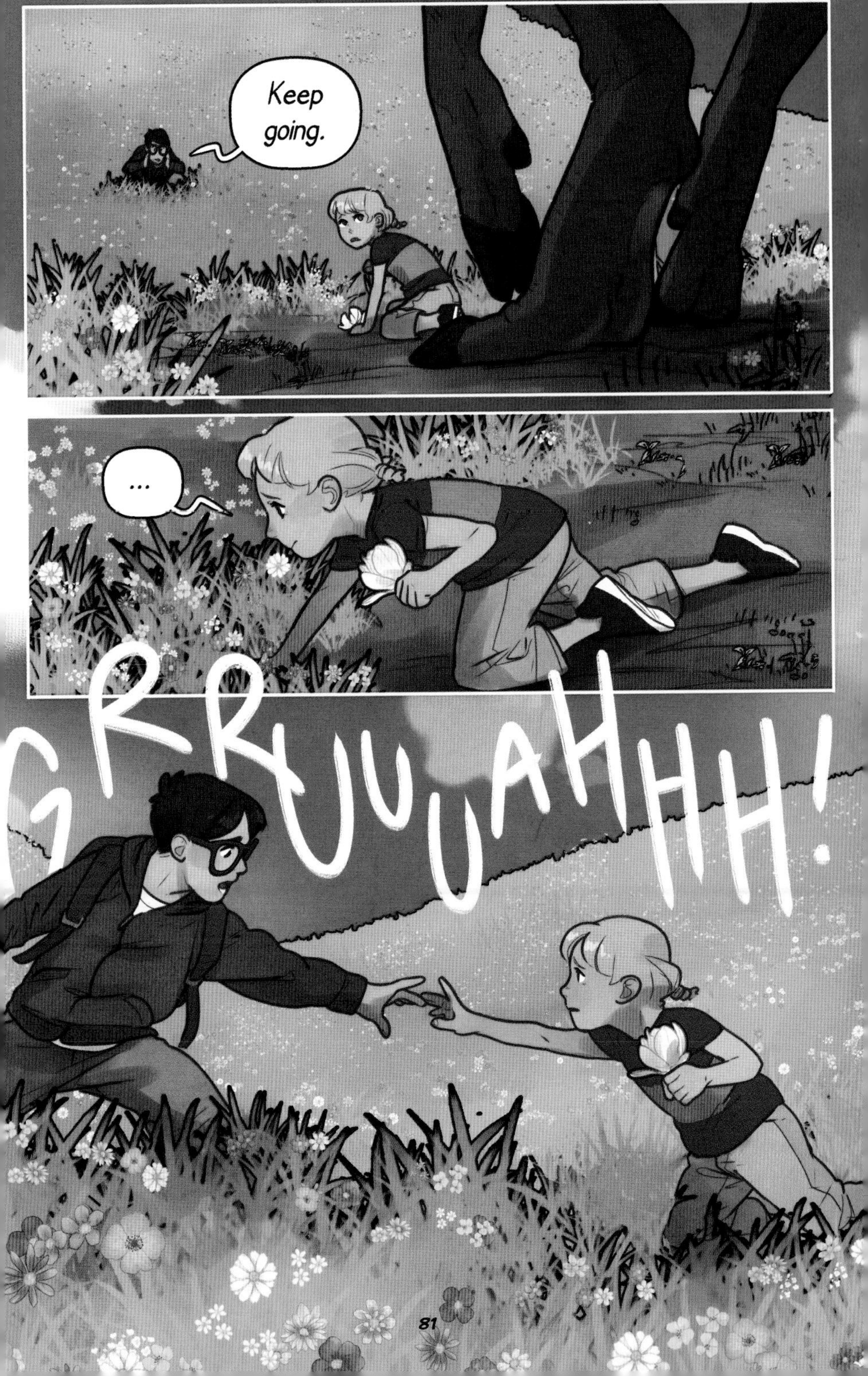
Keep going.
...
GRRUUUAHHHH!

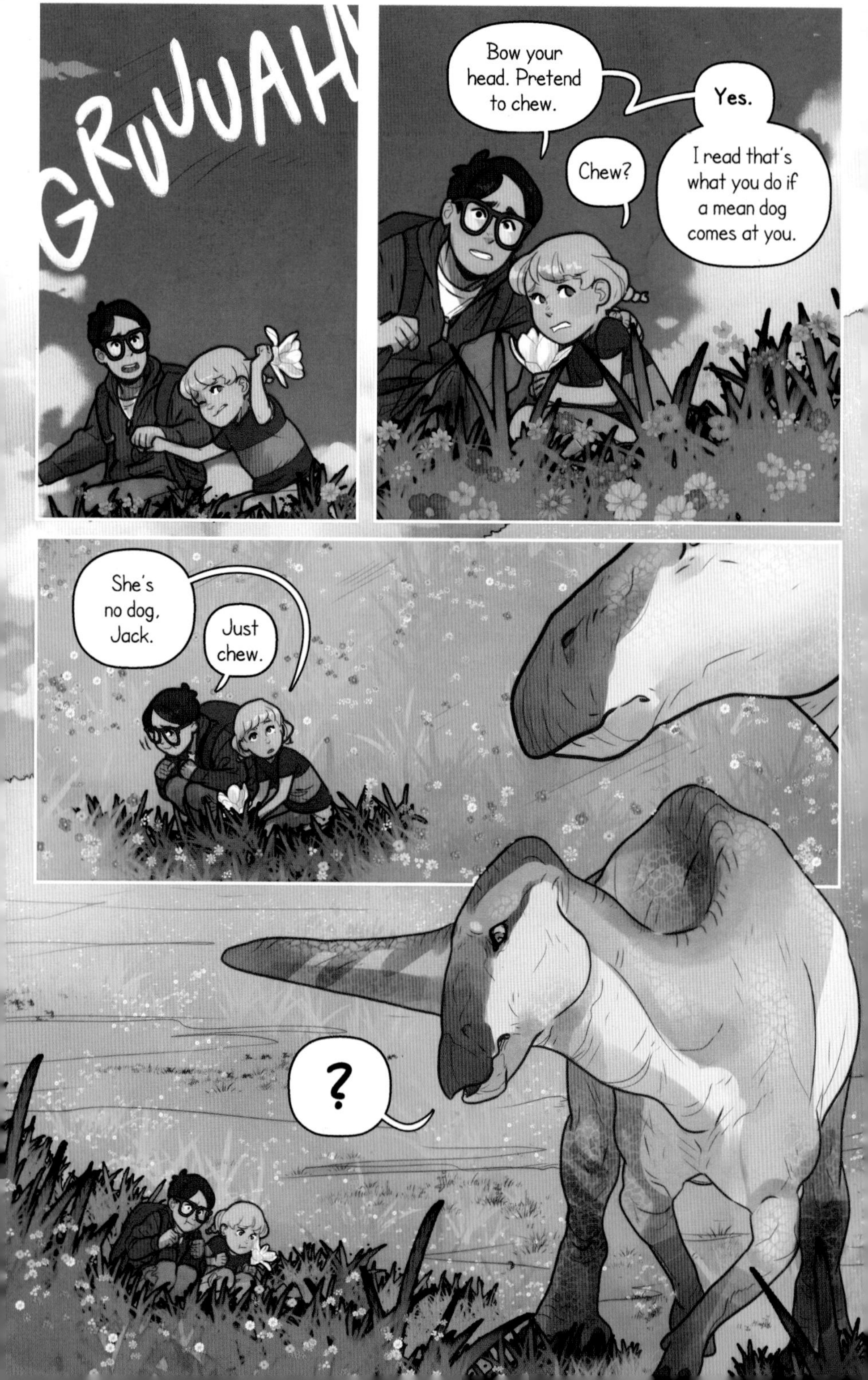
GRUUUAH
Bow your head. Pretend to chew.
Chew?
Yes.
I read that's what you do if a mean dog comes at you.
She's no dog, Jack.
Just chew.
?

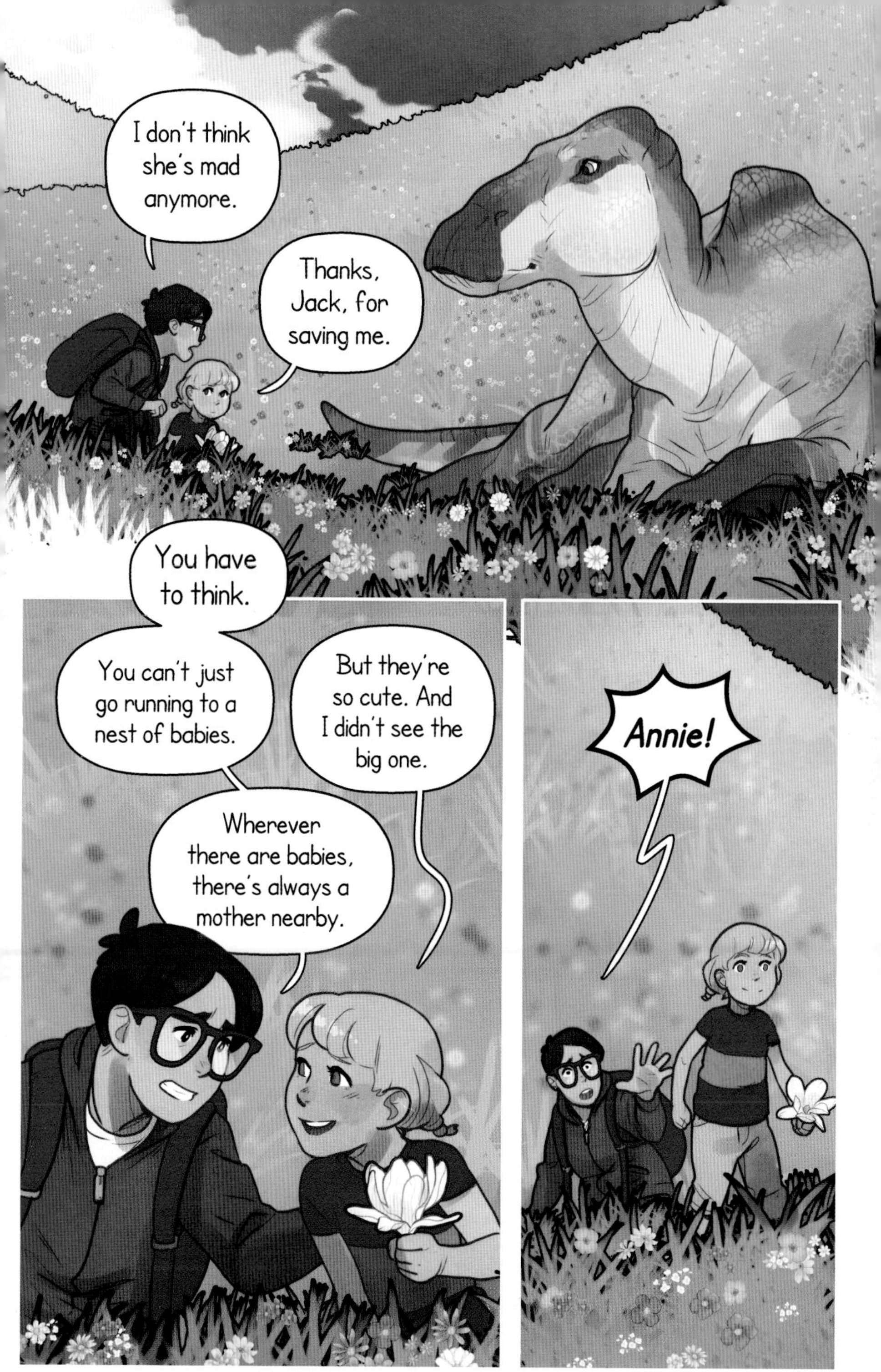
I don't think she's mad anymore.
Thanks, Jack, for saving me.
You have to think.
You can't just go running to a nest of babies.
But they're so cute. And I didn't see the big one.
Wherever there are babies, there's always a mother nearby.
Annie!

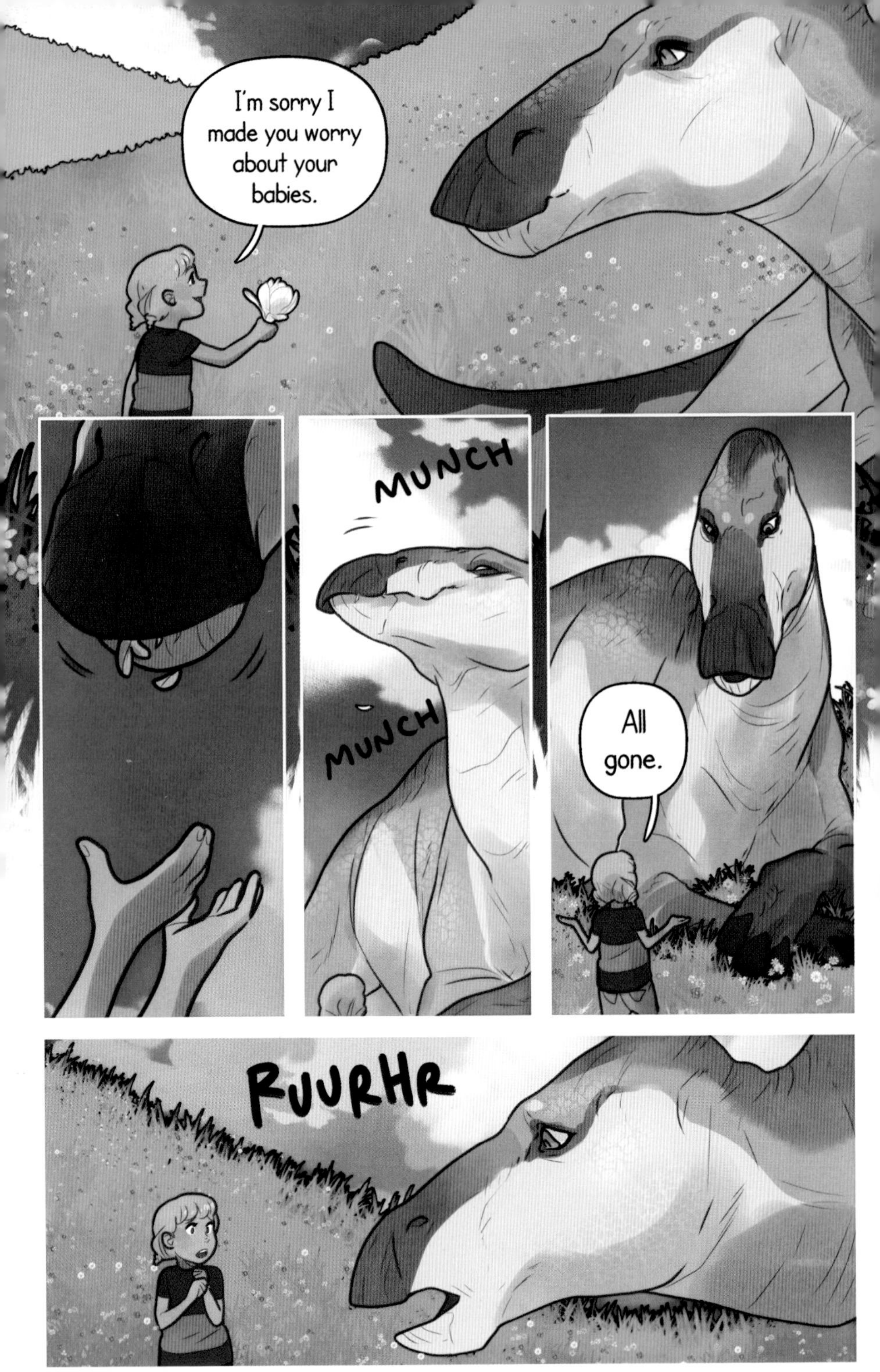
I'm sorry I made you worry about your babies.
MUNCH
MUNCH
All gone.
RUURHR

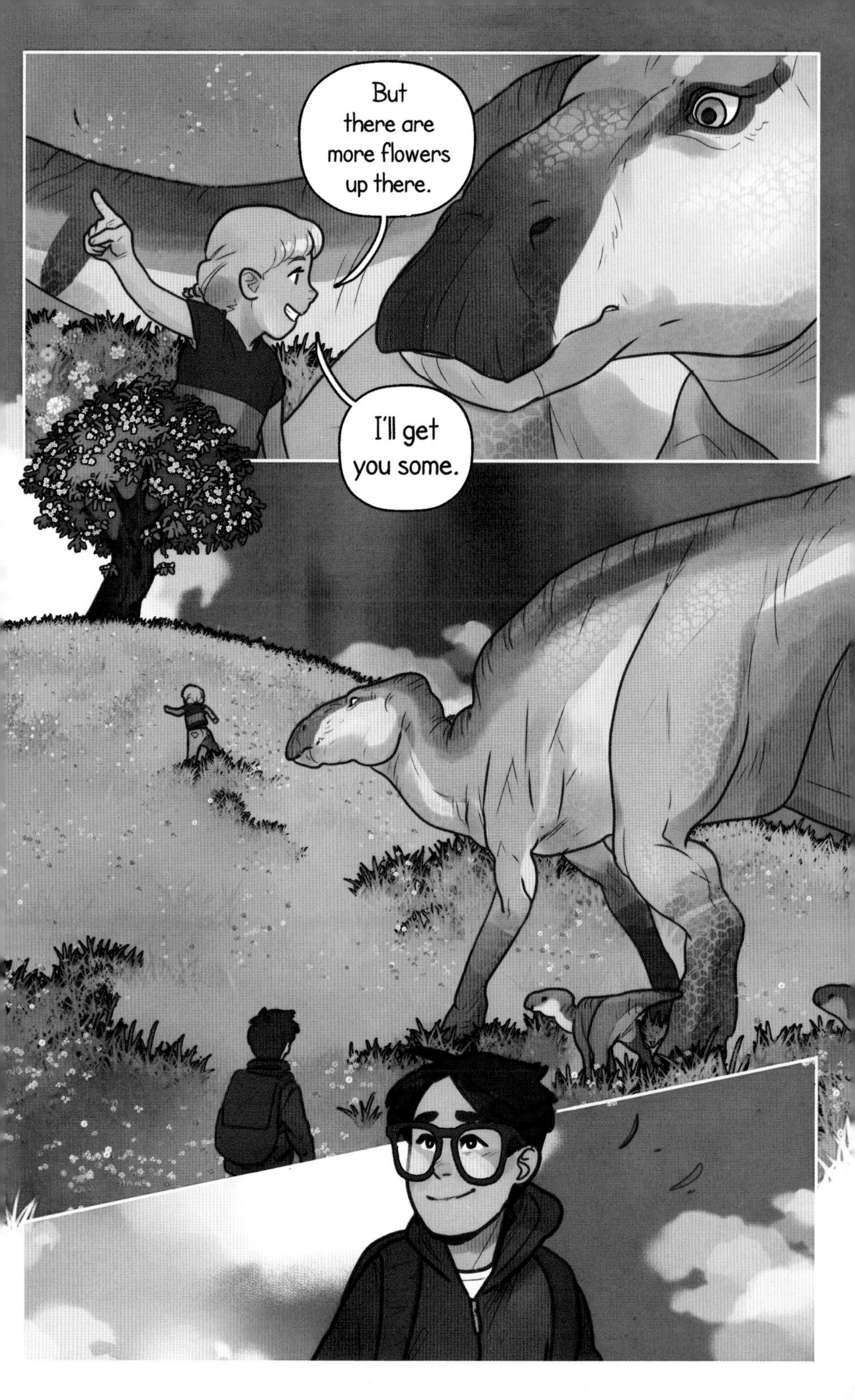
But there are more flowers up there.
I'll get you some.

Hmm, where are the other mothers?

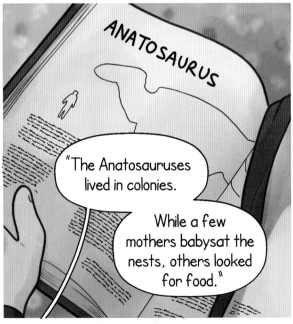

ANATOSAURUS

"The Anatosauruses lived in colonies.

While a few mothers babysat the nests, others looked for food."

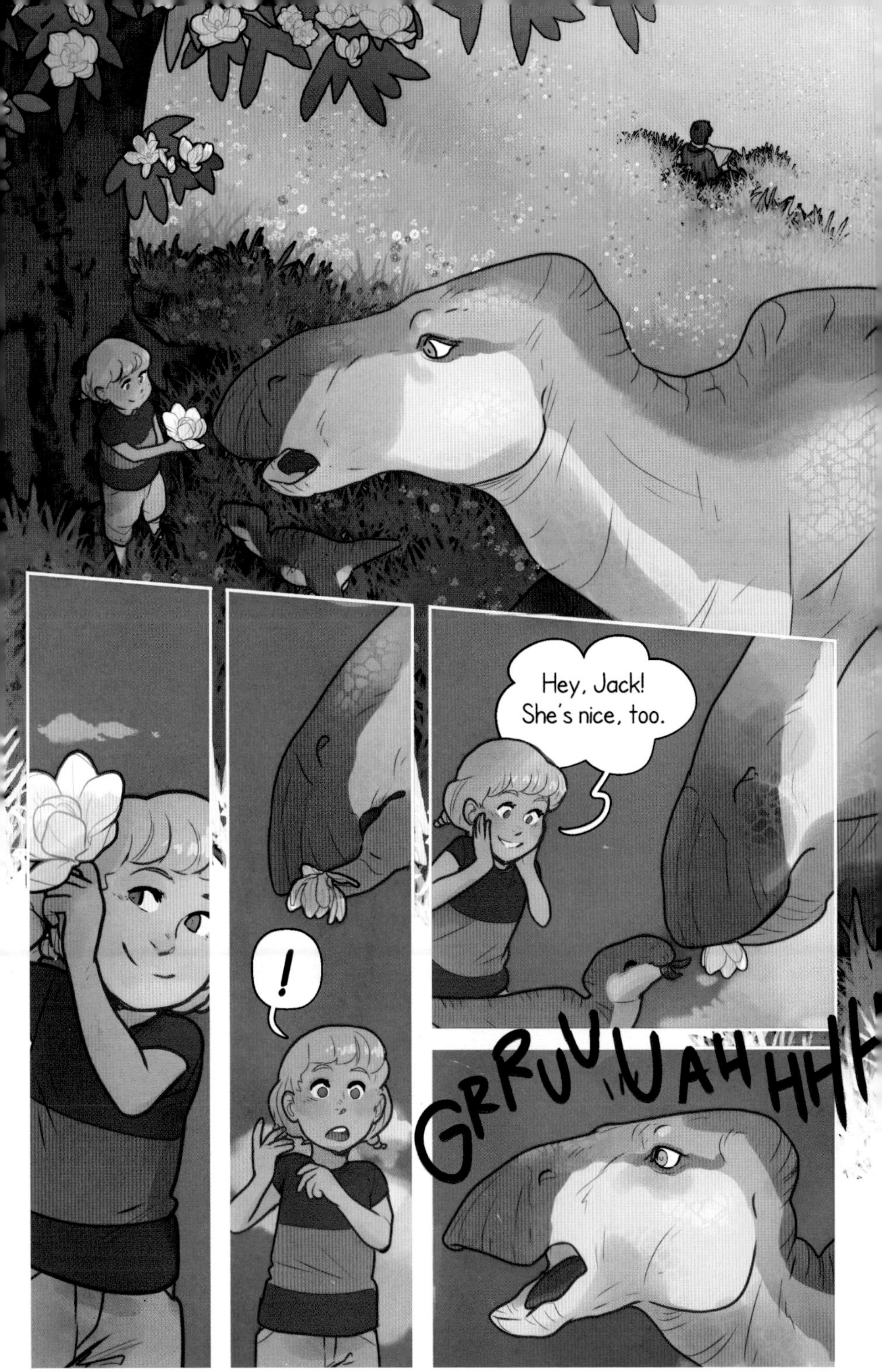
Hey, Jack!
She's nice, too.
!
GRRUUUNAHHHH

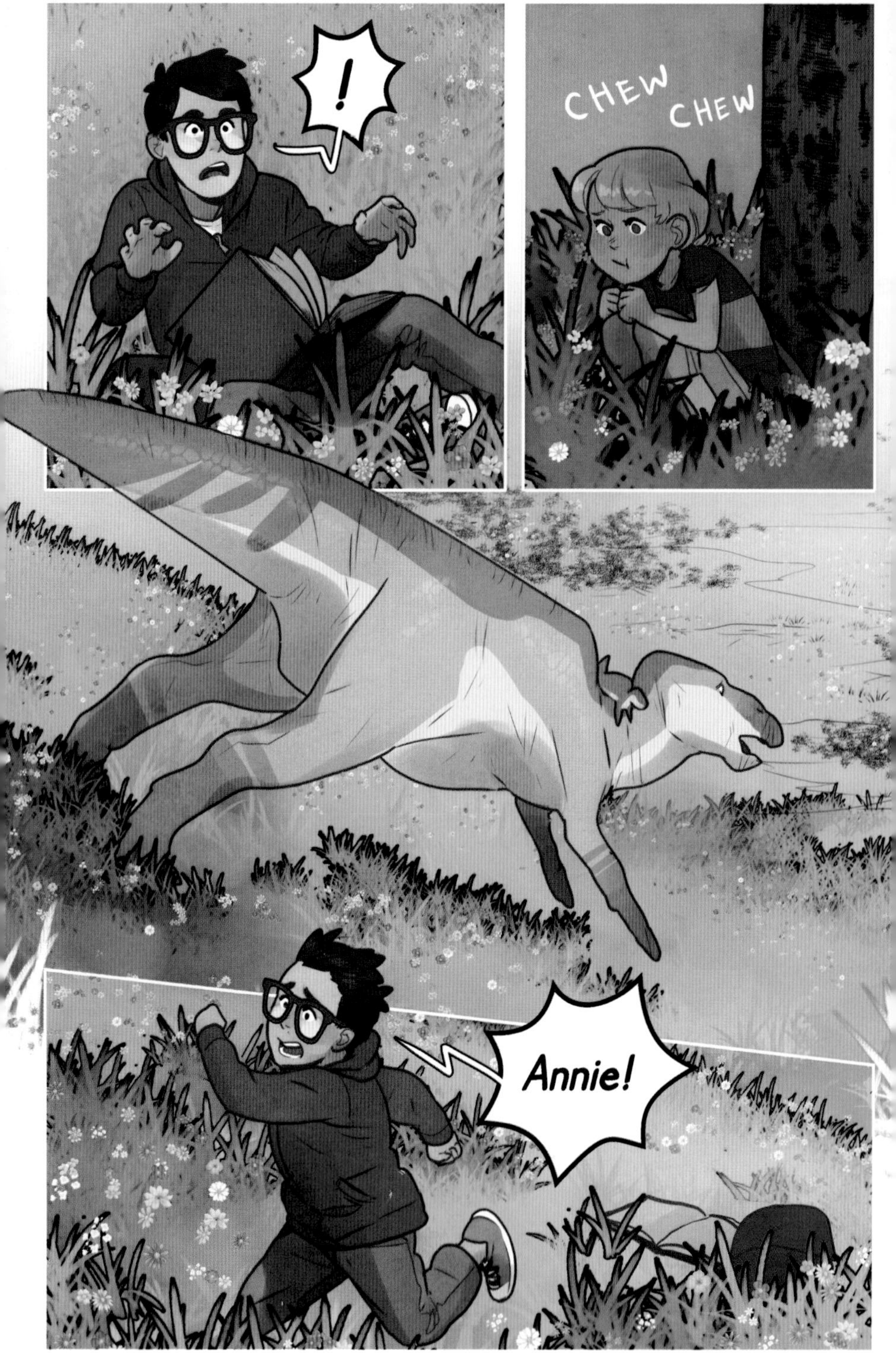
!
CHEW CHEW
Annie!

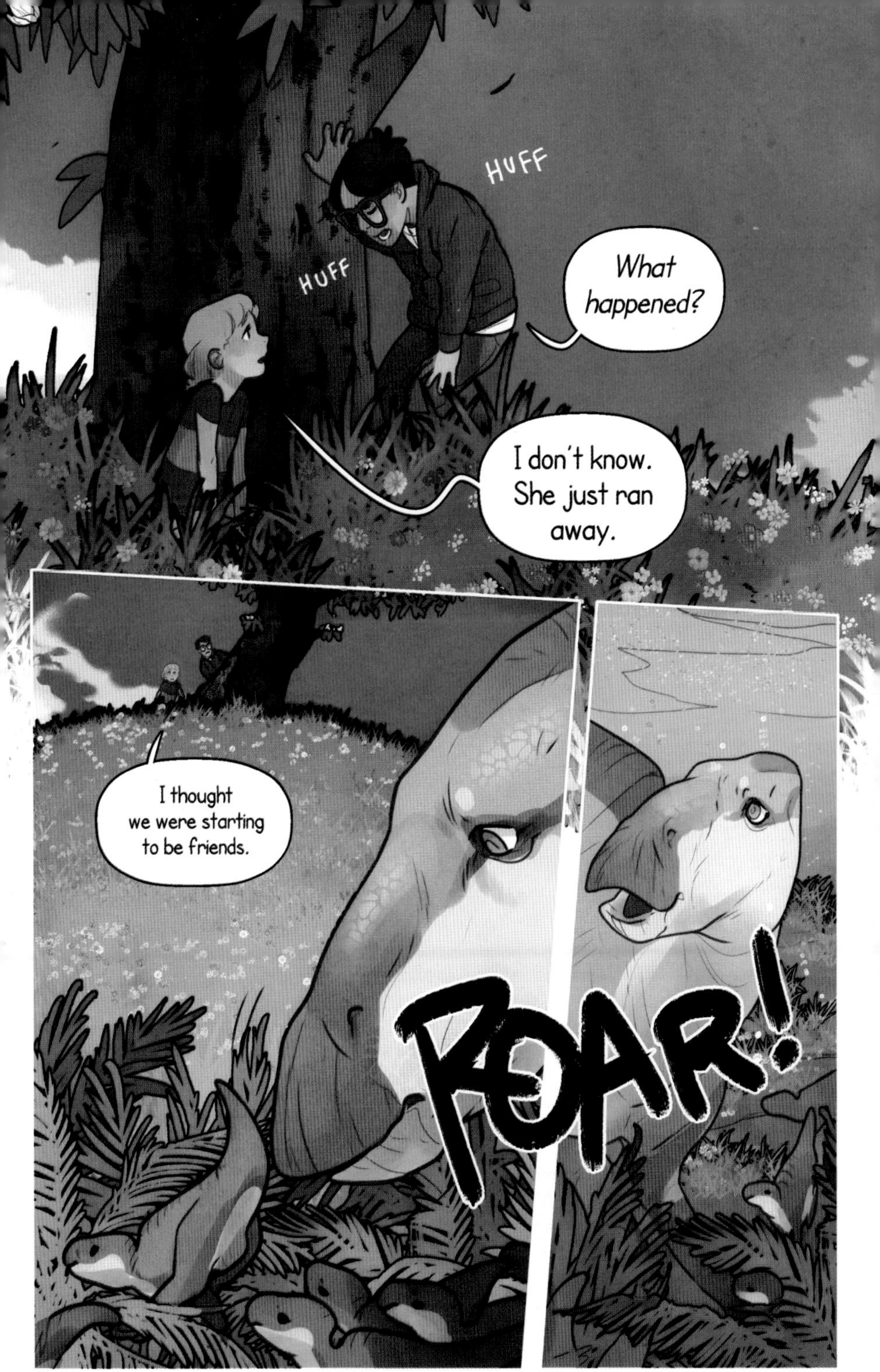
HUFF
HUFF
What happened?
I don't know. She just ran away.
I thought we were starting to be friends.
ROAR!

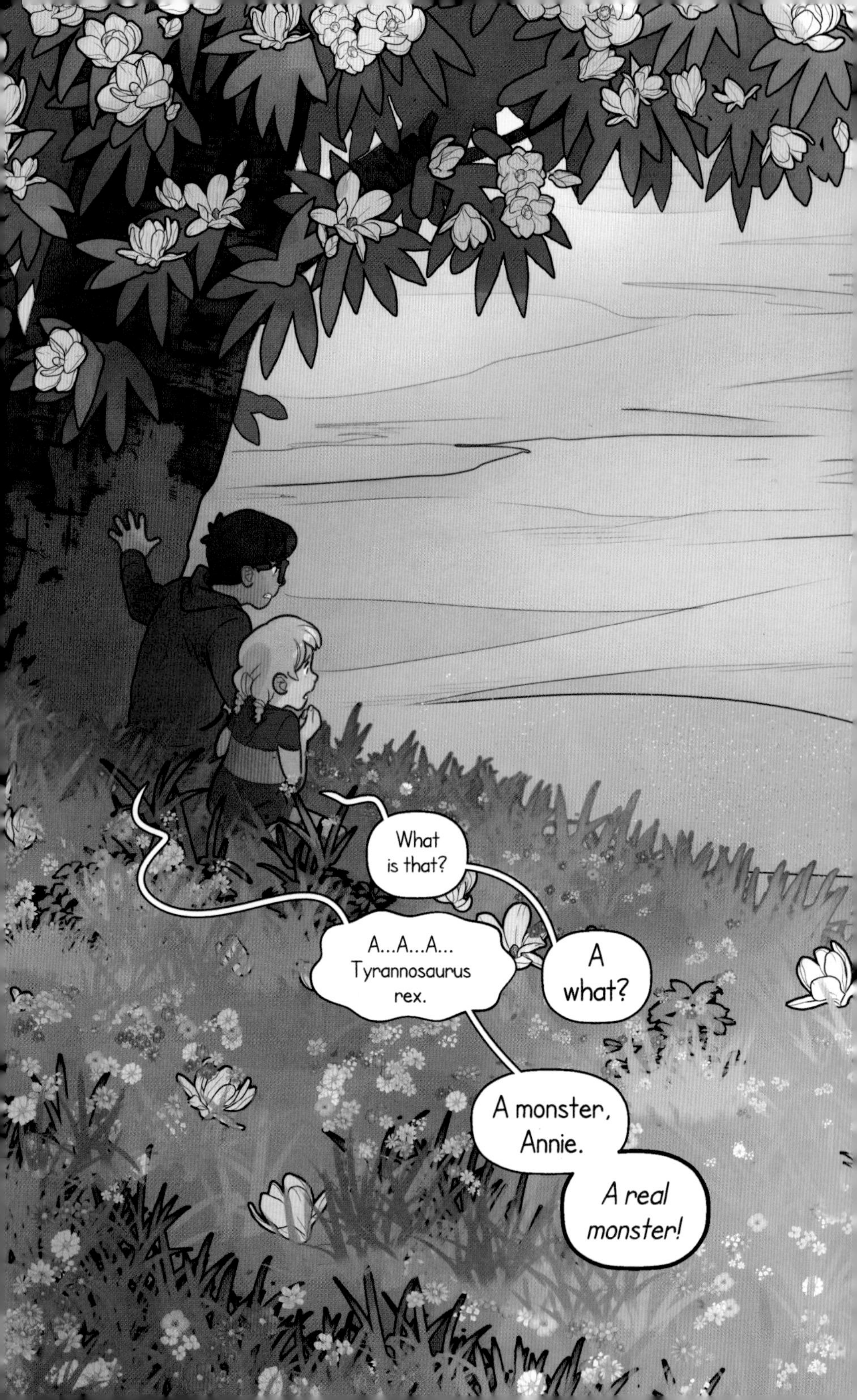
What is that?
A...A...A... Tyrannosaurus rex.
A what?
A monster, Annie.
A real monster!

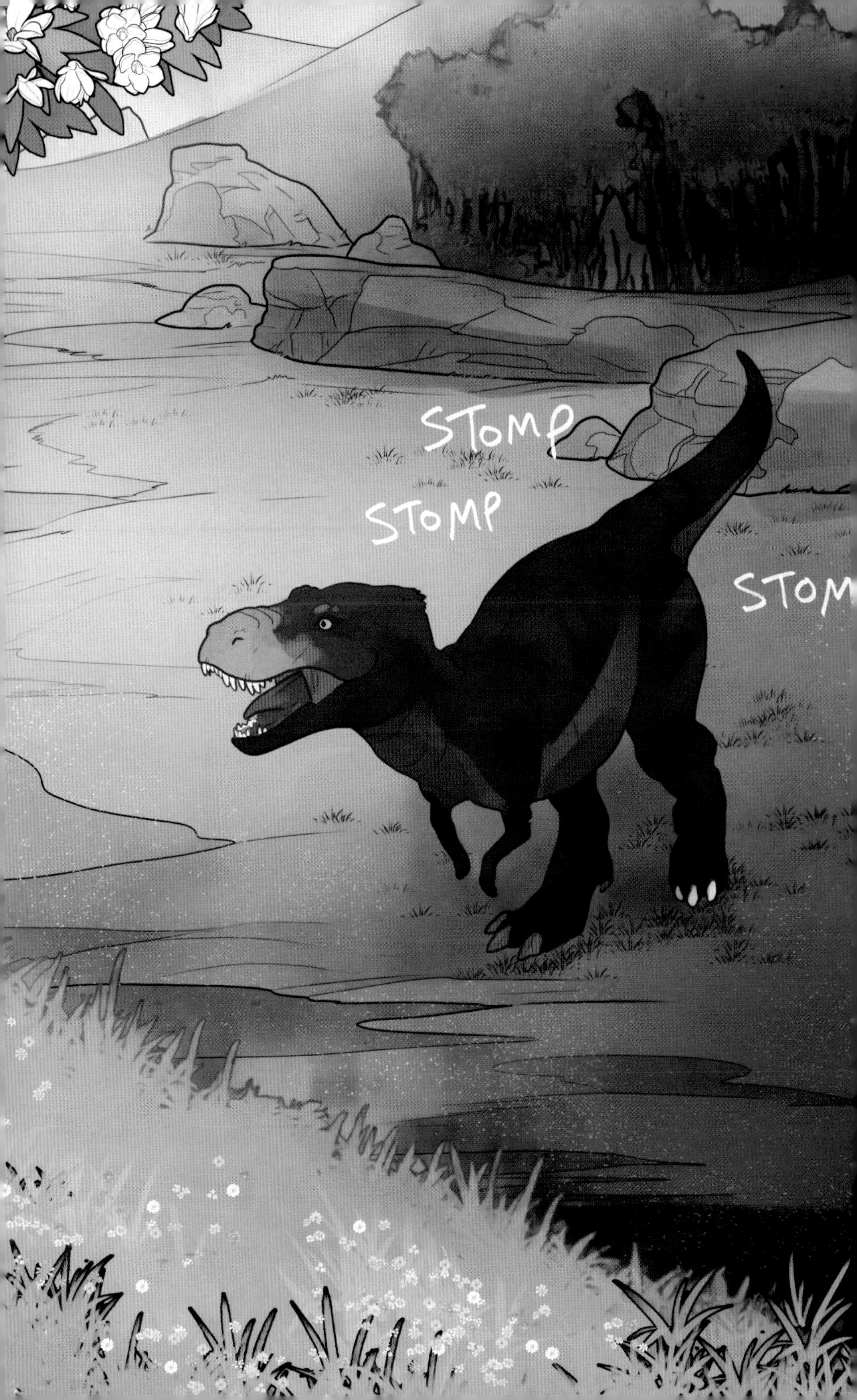
STOMP
STOMP
STOM

CHAPTER SEVEN
Ready, Set, Go!

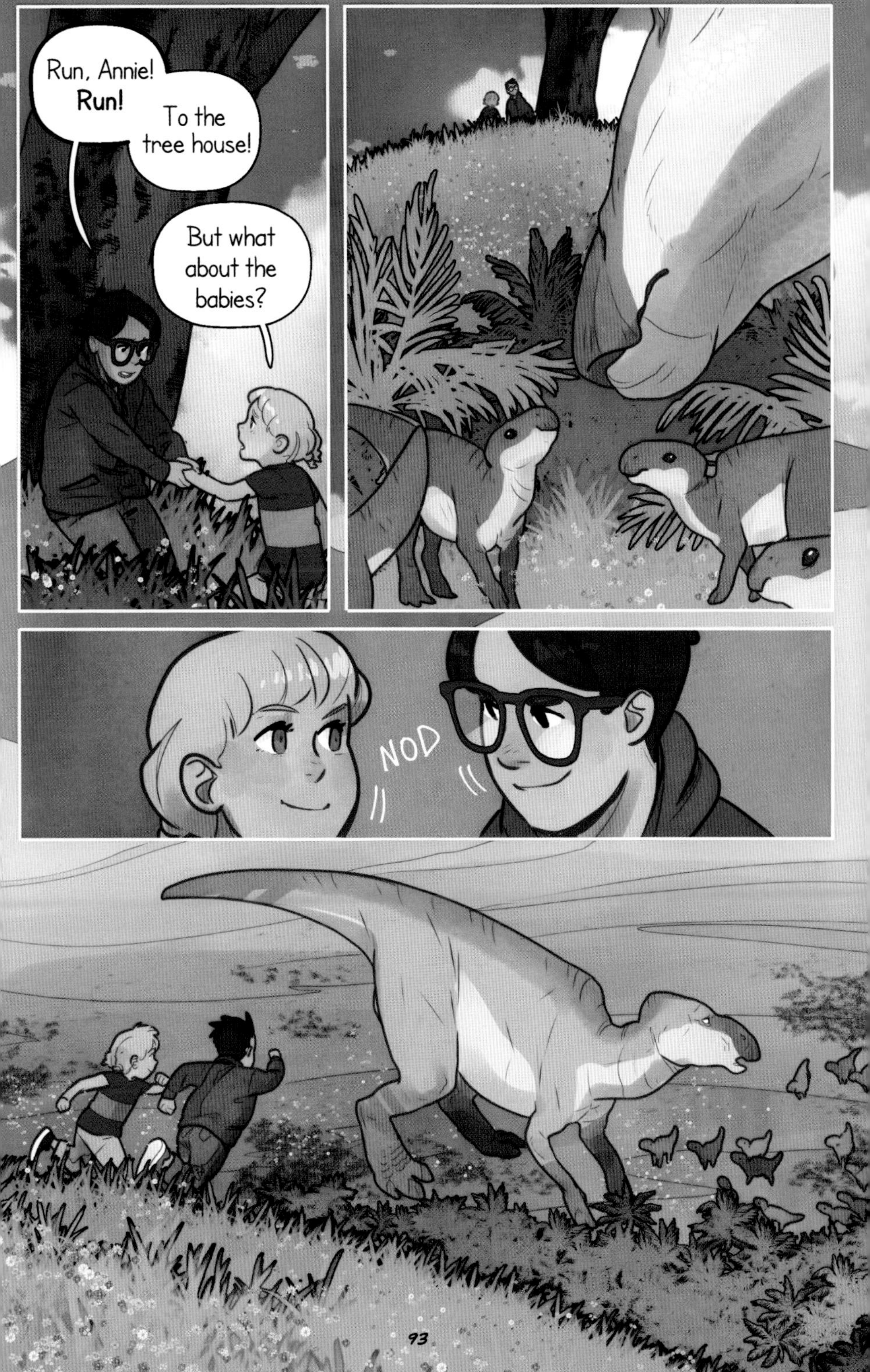
Run, Annie!
Run!
To the tree house!
But what about the babies?
NOD

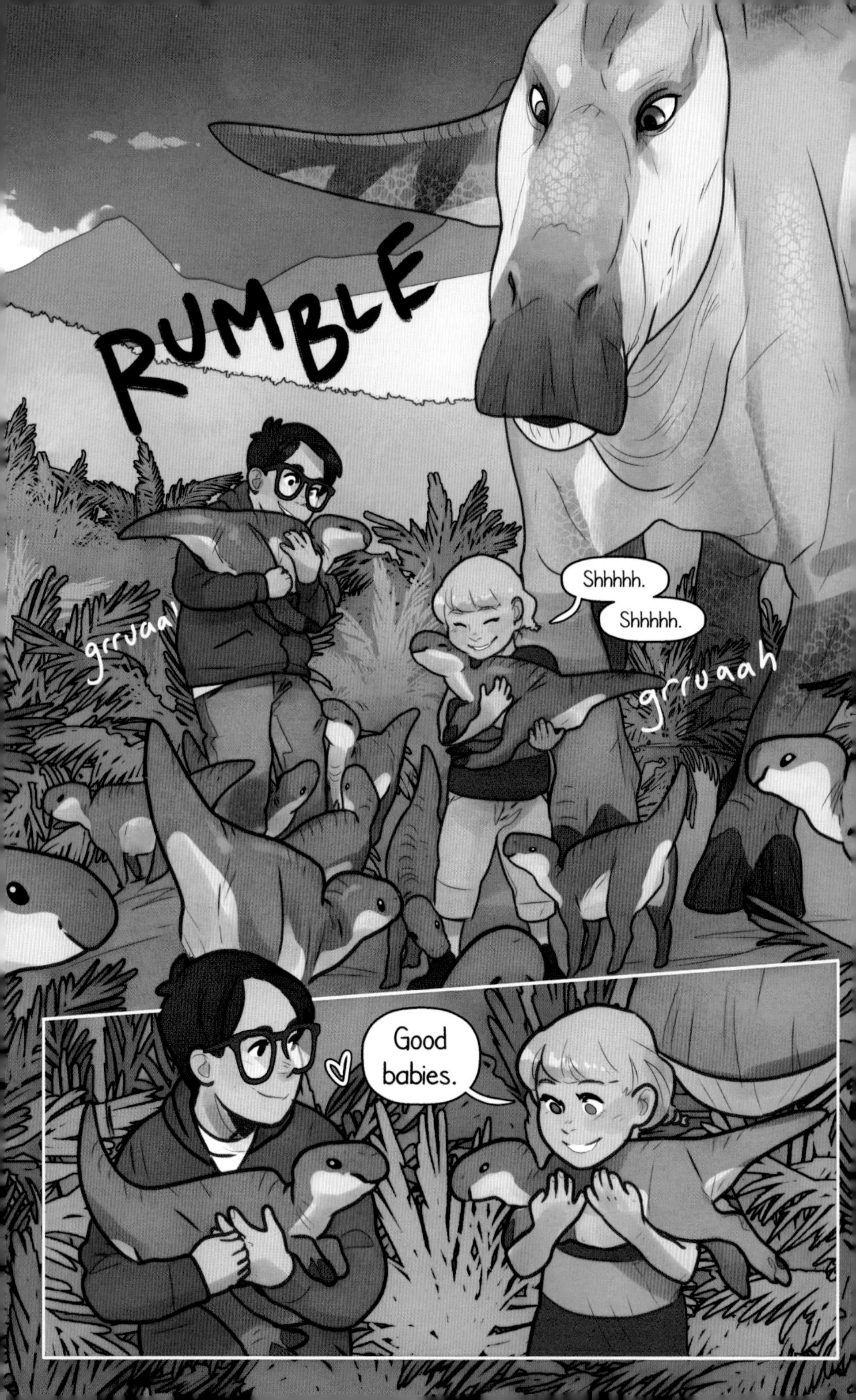
RUMBLE
grruaa
Shhhhh.
Shhhhh.
grruaah
Good babies.

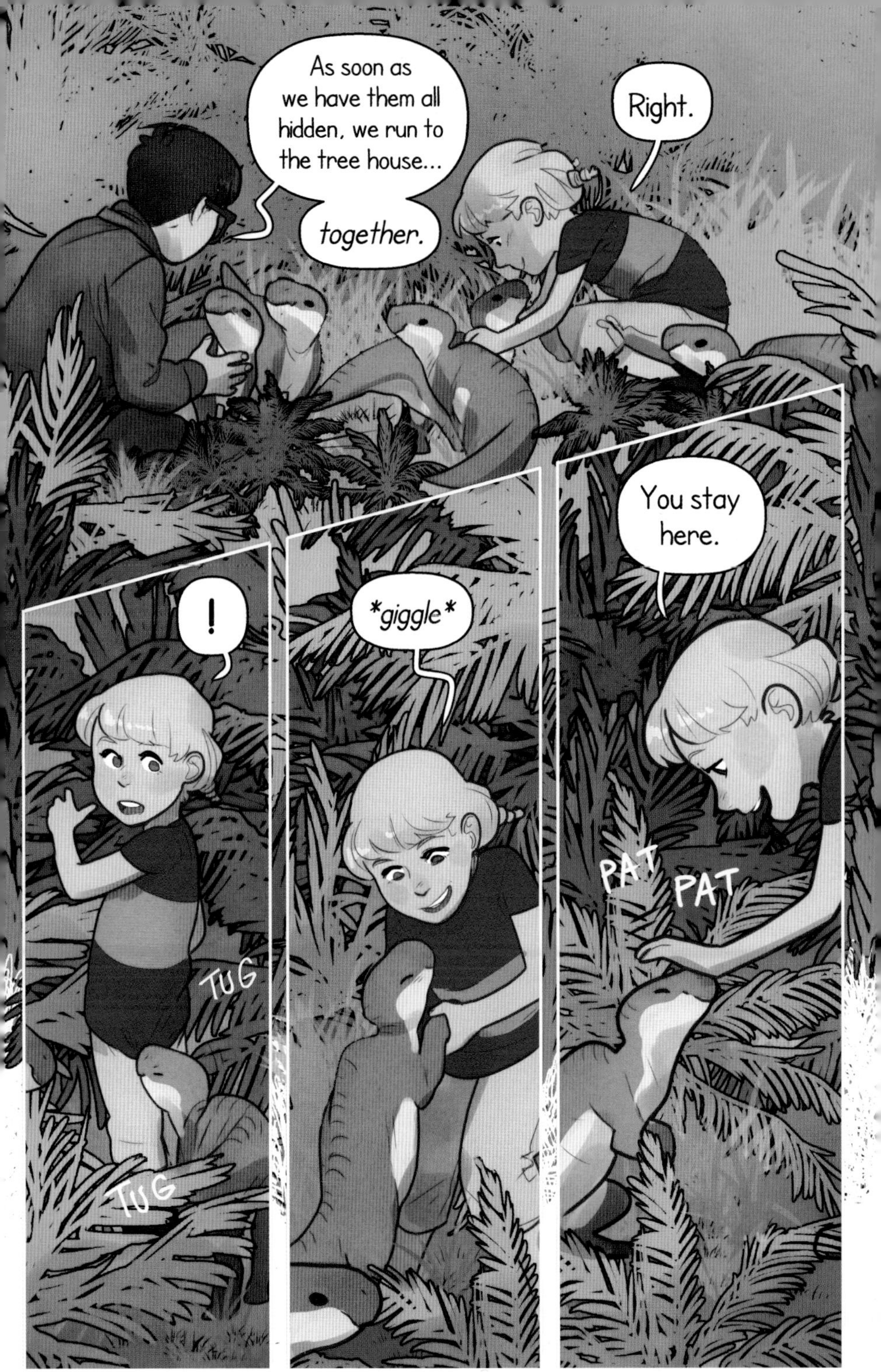
As soon as we have them all hidden, we run to the tree house...
together.
Right.
!
TUG
TUG
giggle
You stay here.
PAT
PAT

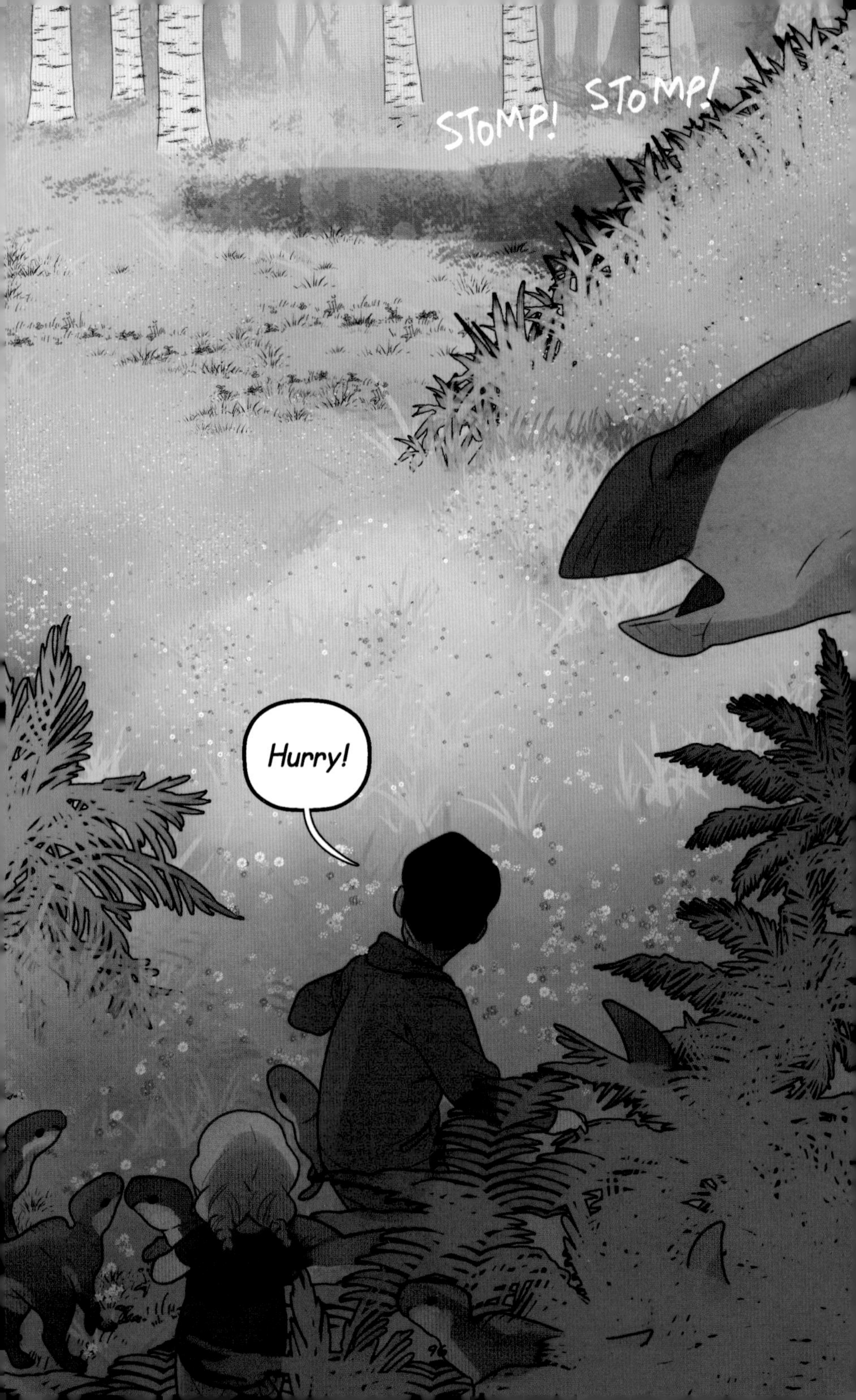
STOMP! STOMP!
Hurry!

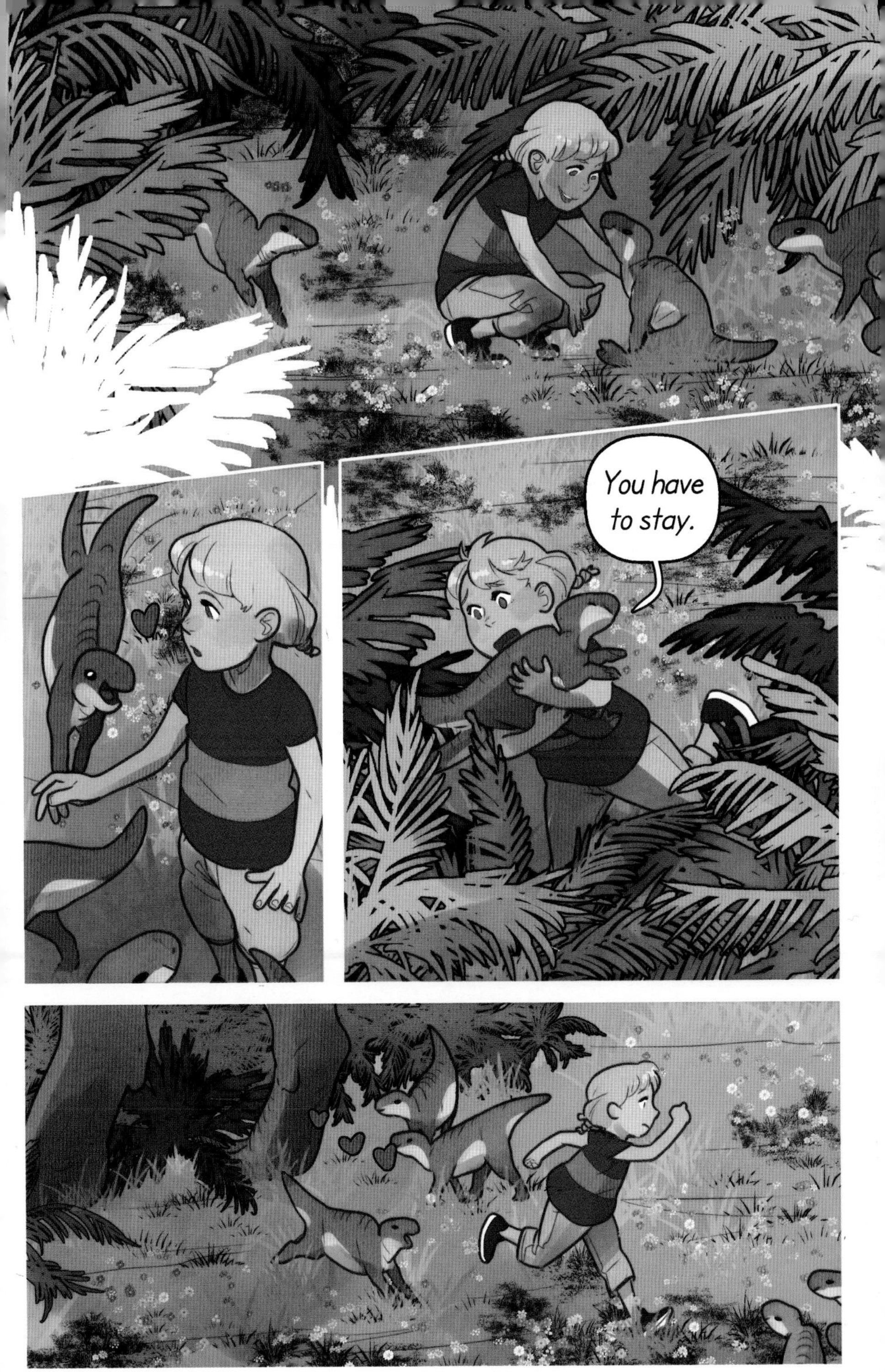
You have to stay.

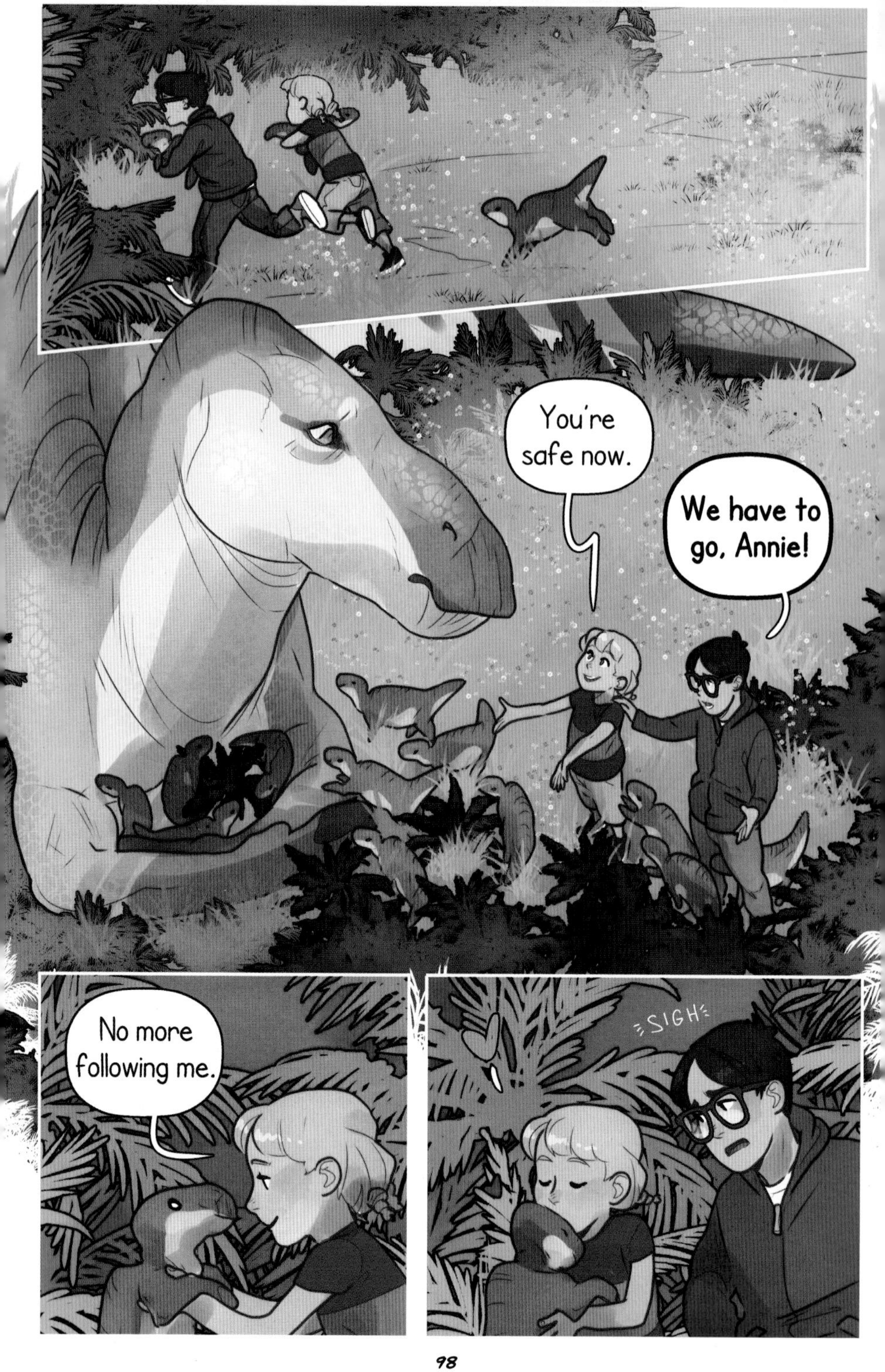
You're safe now.
We have to go, Annie!
No more following me.
SIGH

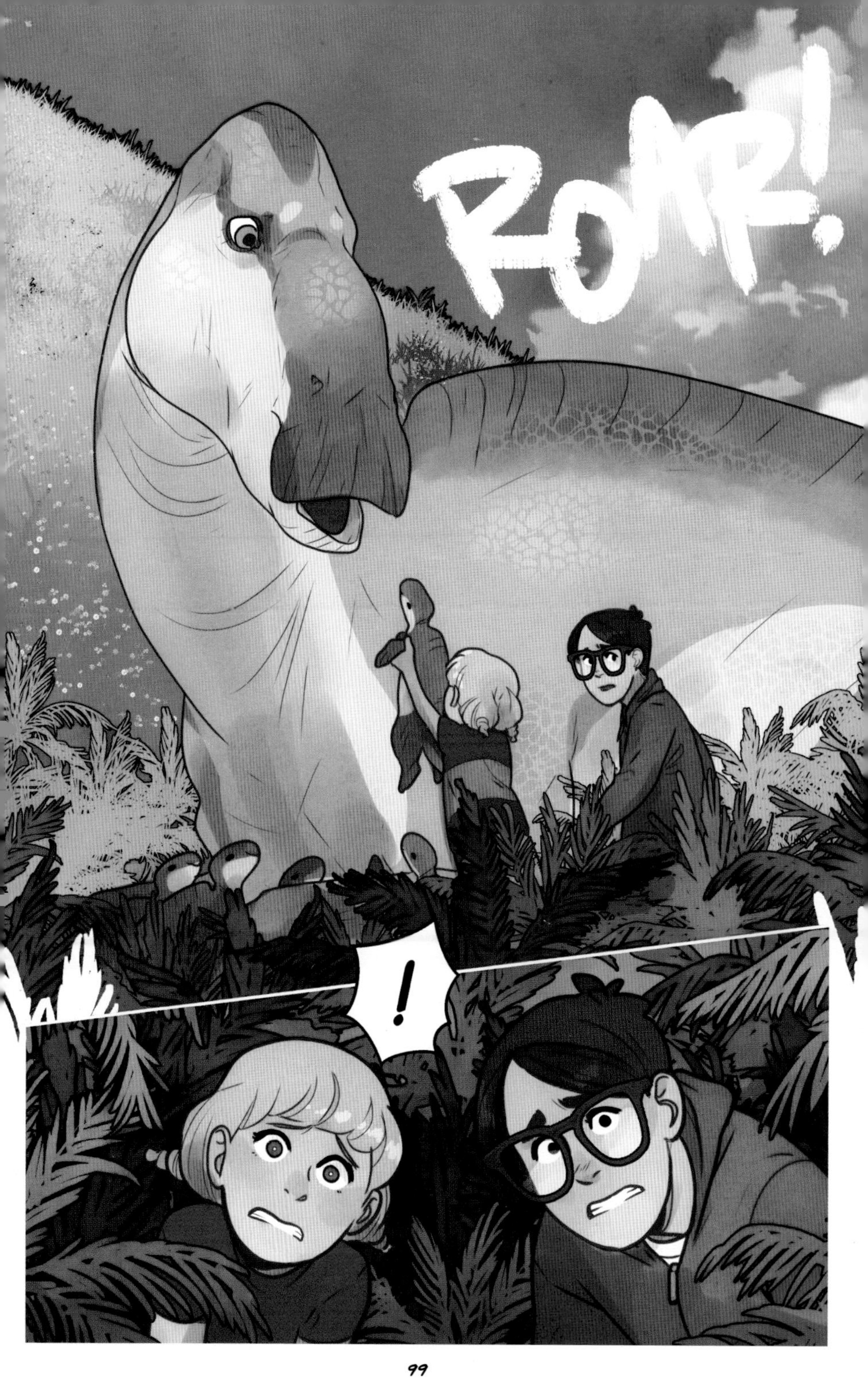
ROAR!
!

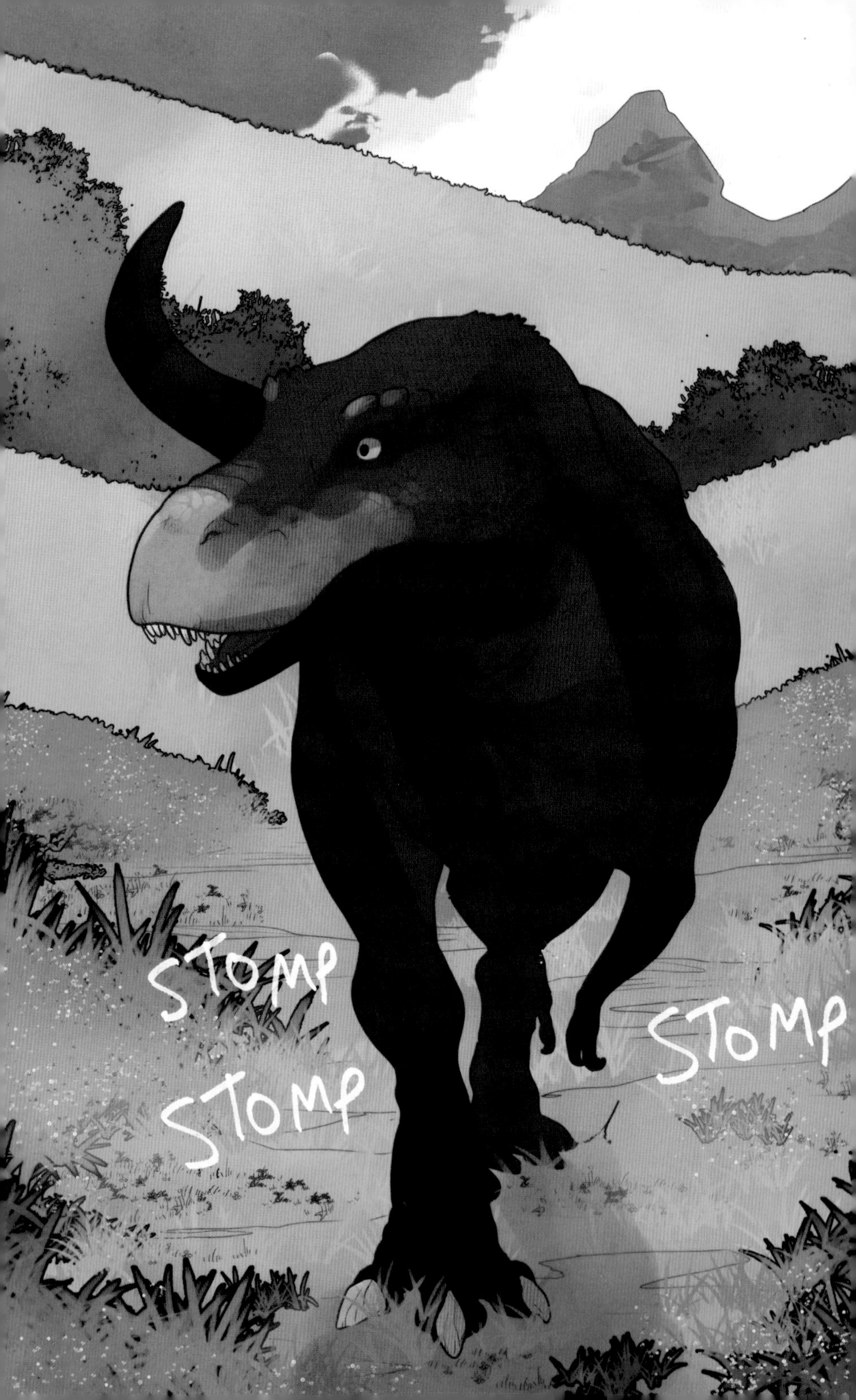
STOMP
STOMP
STOMP

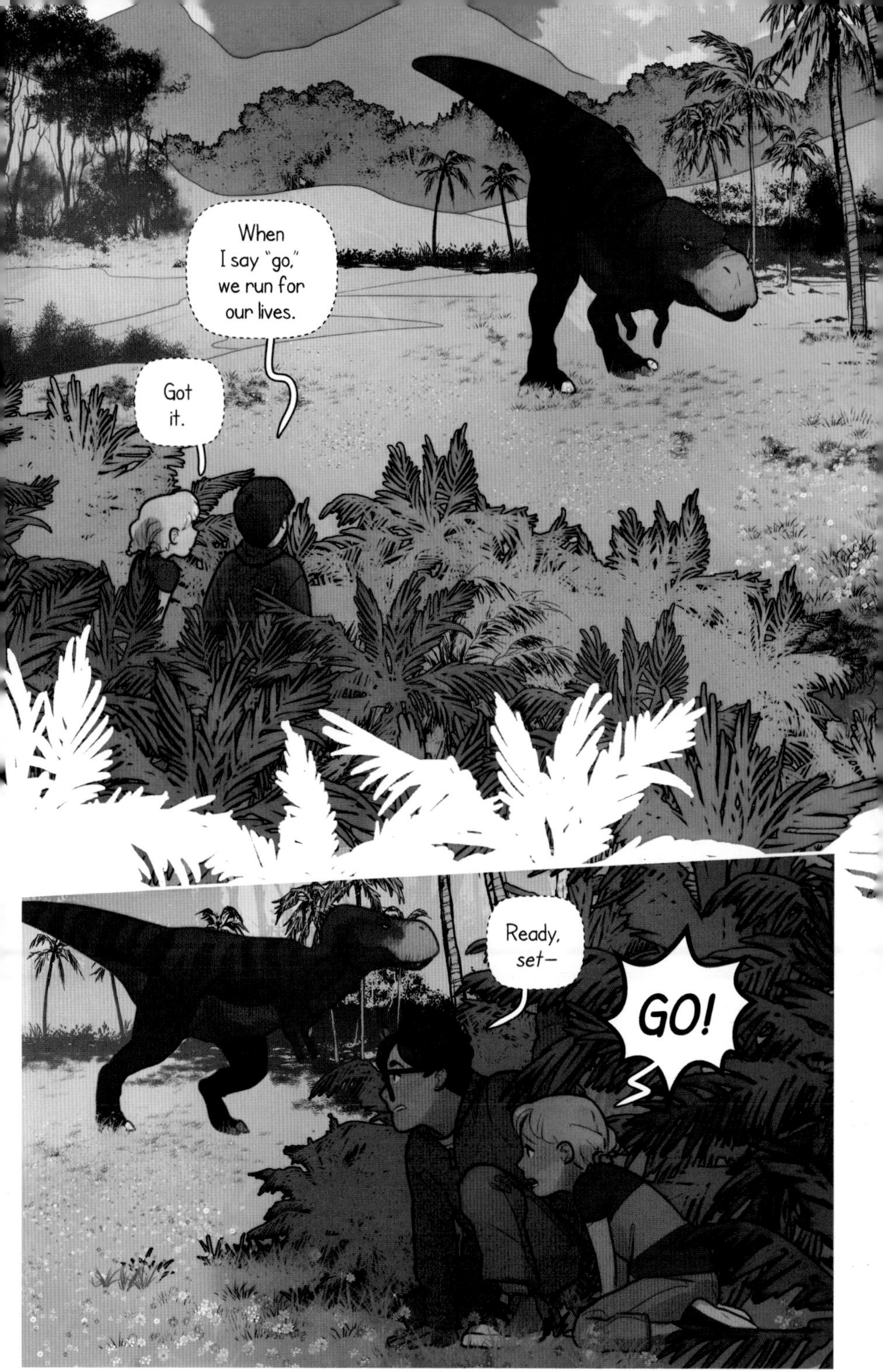
When I say "go," we run for our lives.
Got it.
Ready, set—
GO!

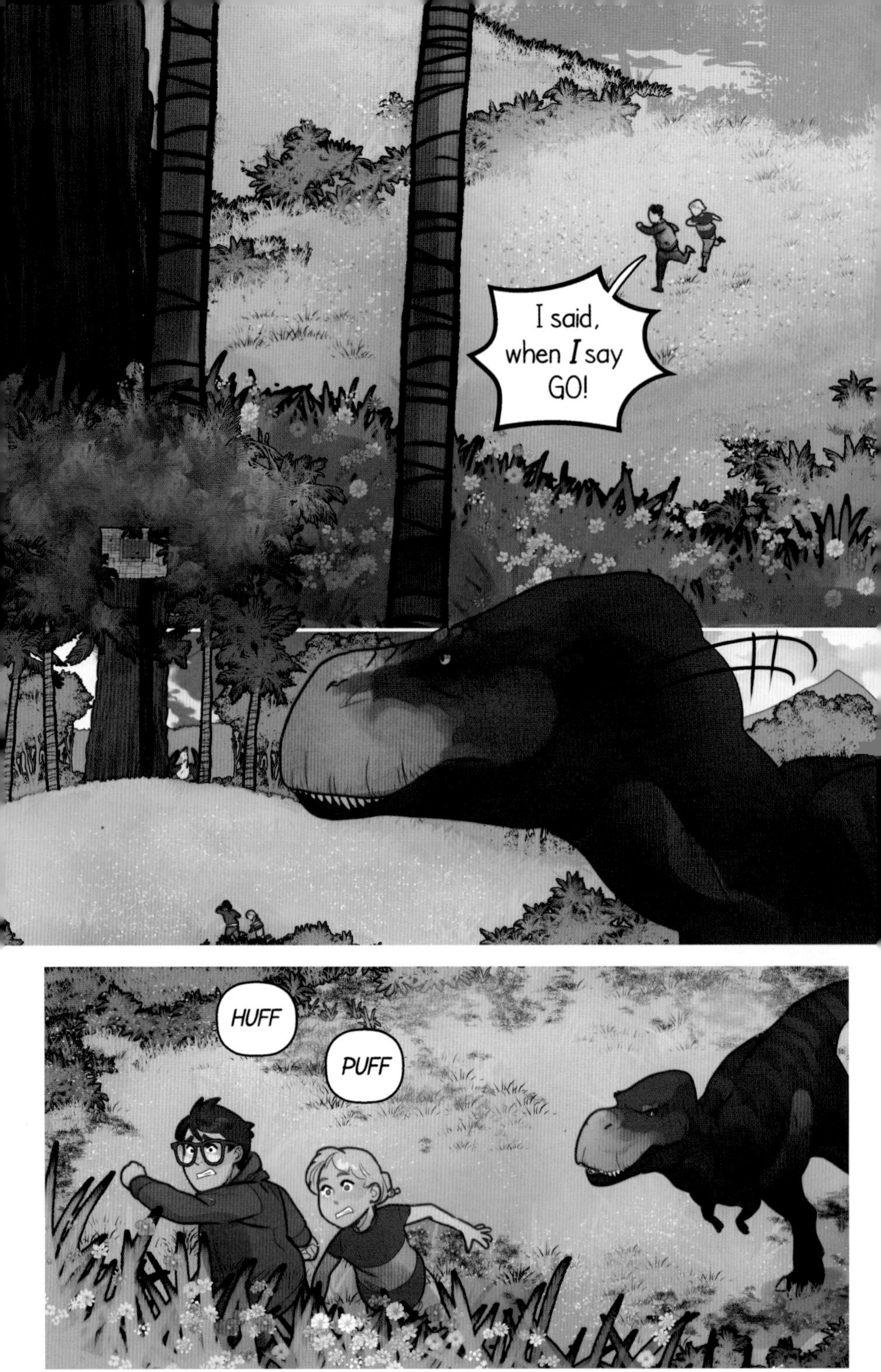
I said, when *I* say GO!
HUFF
PUFF

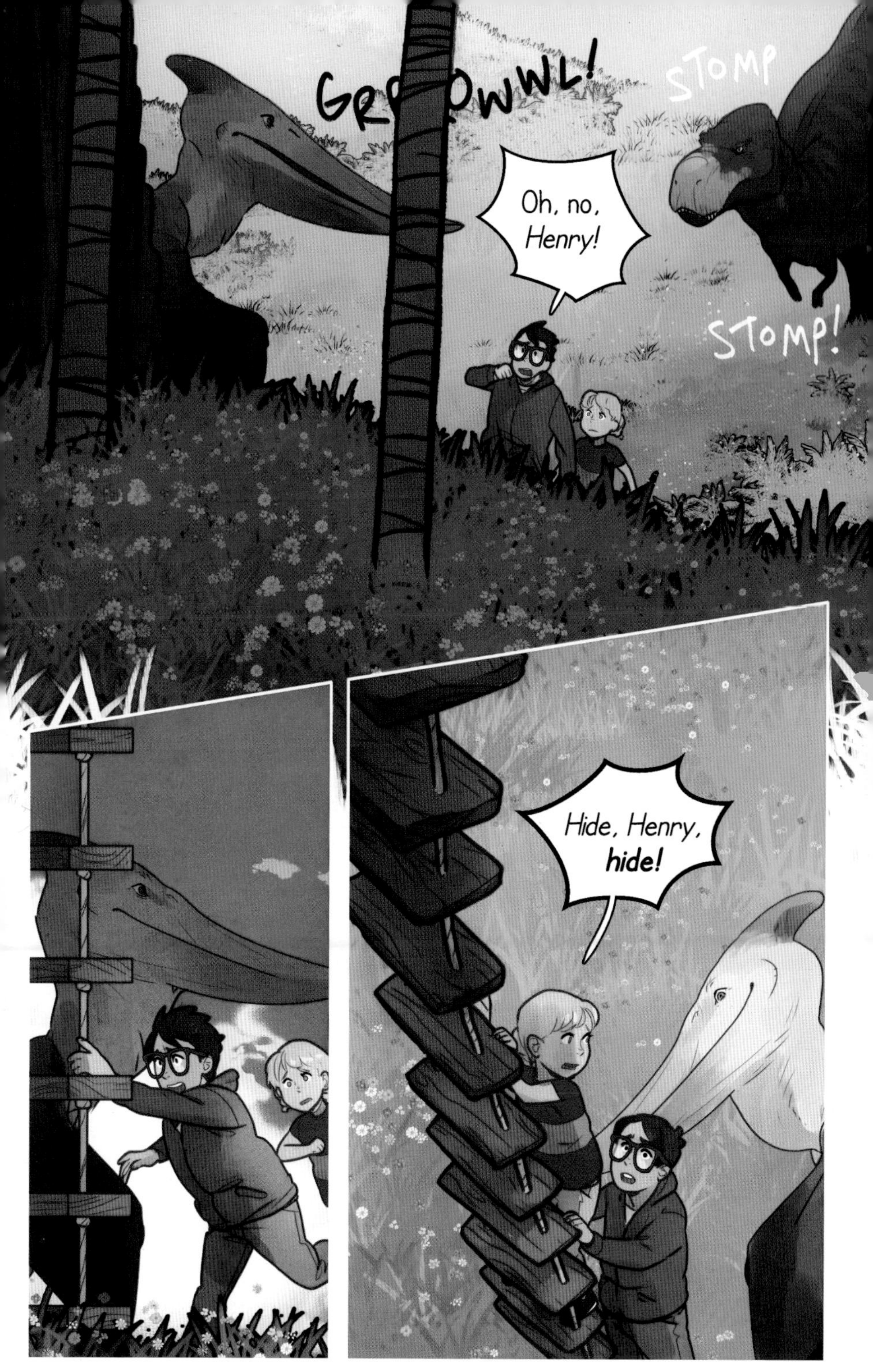
GROWWL!
STOMP
Oh, no, Henry!
STOMP!
Hide, Henry, hide!

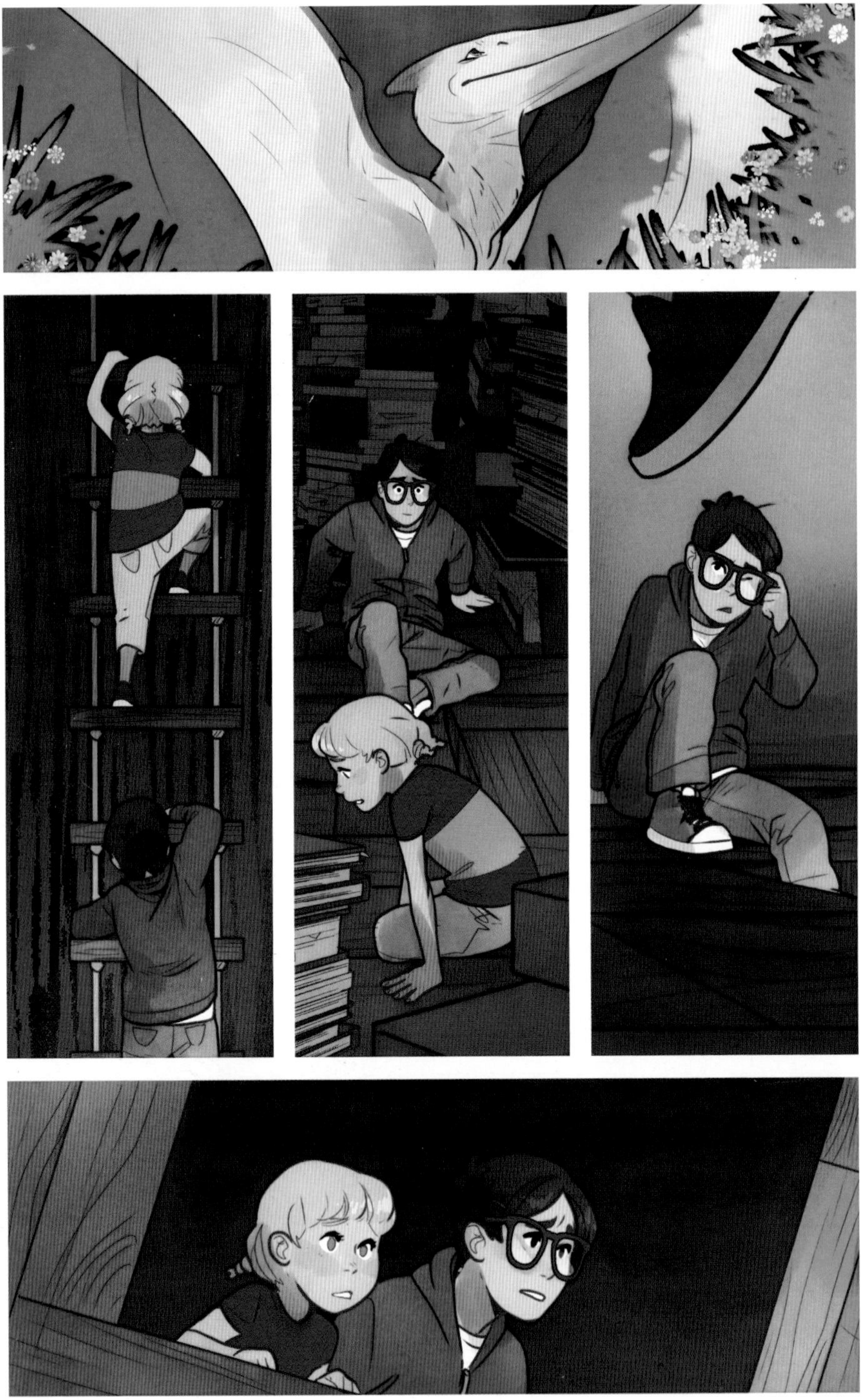

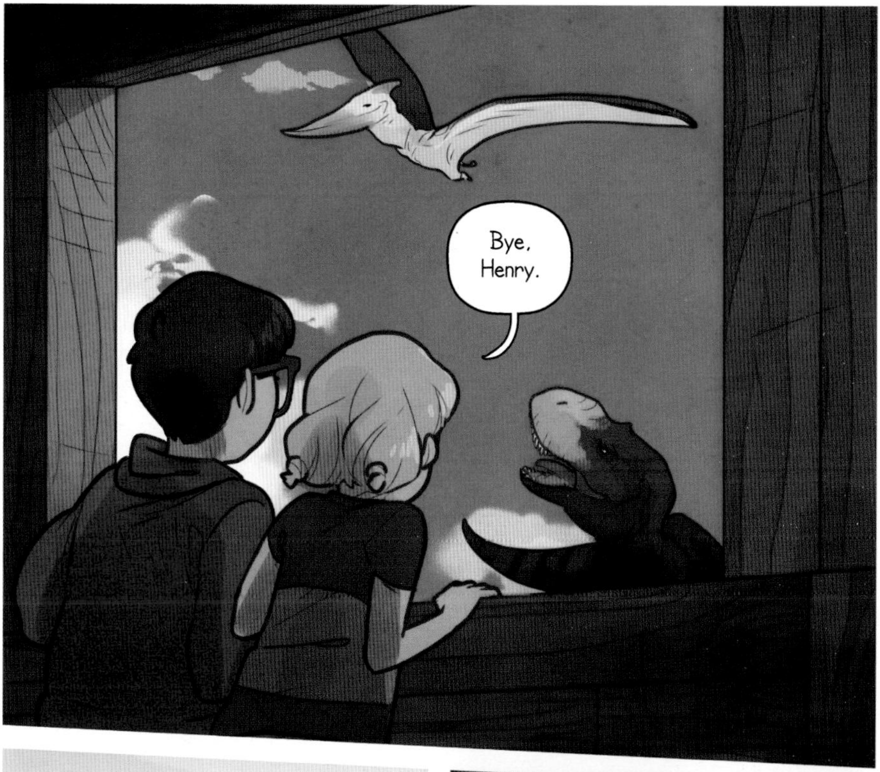
Bye, Henry.

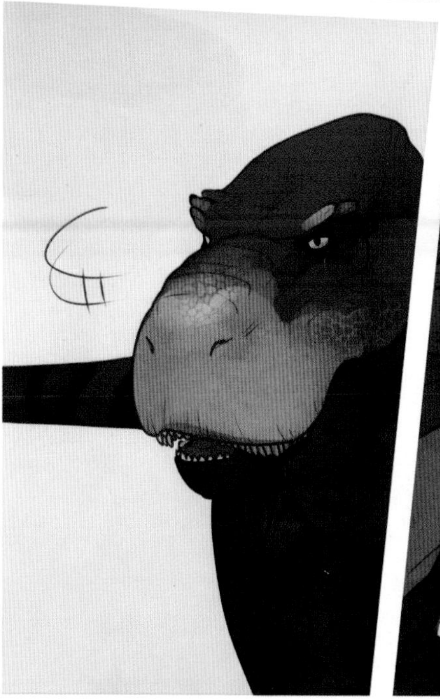

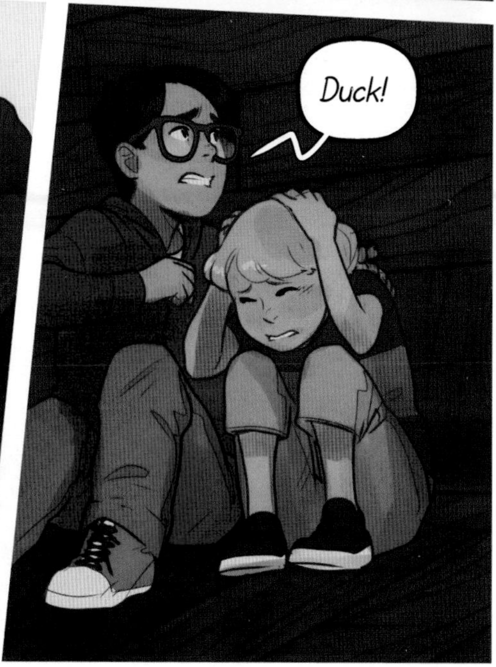
Duck!

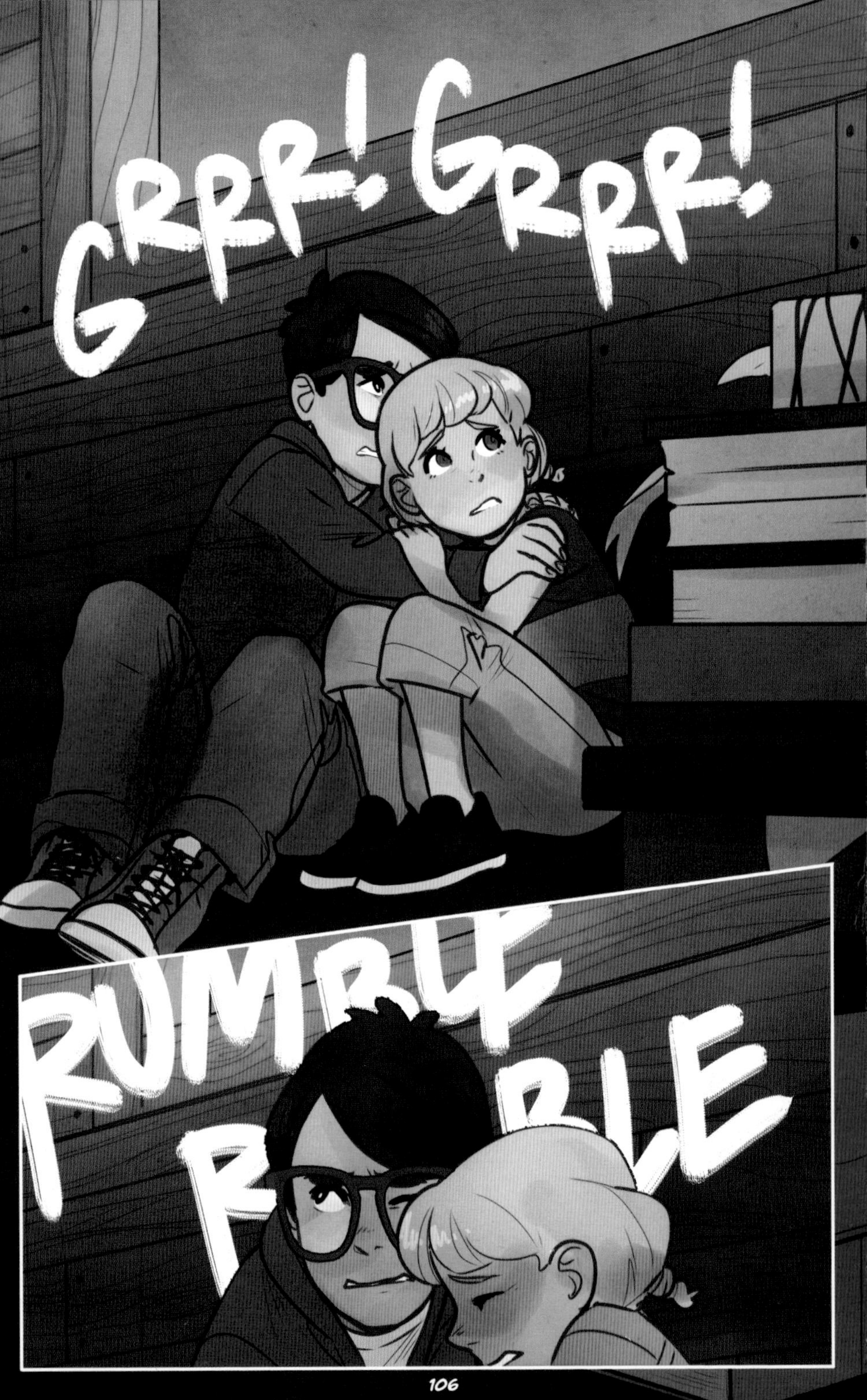
GRRR! GRRR!
RUMBLE

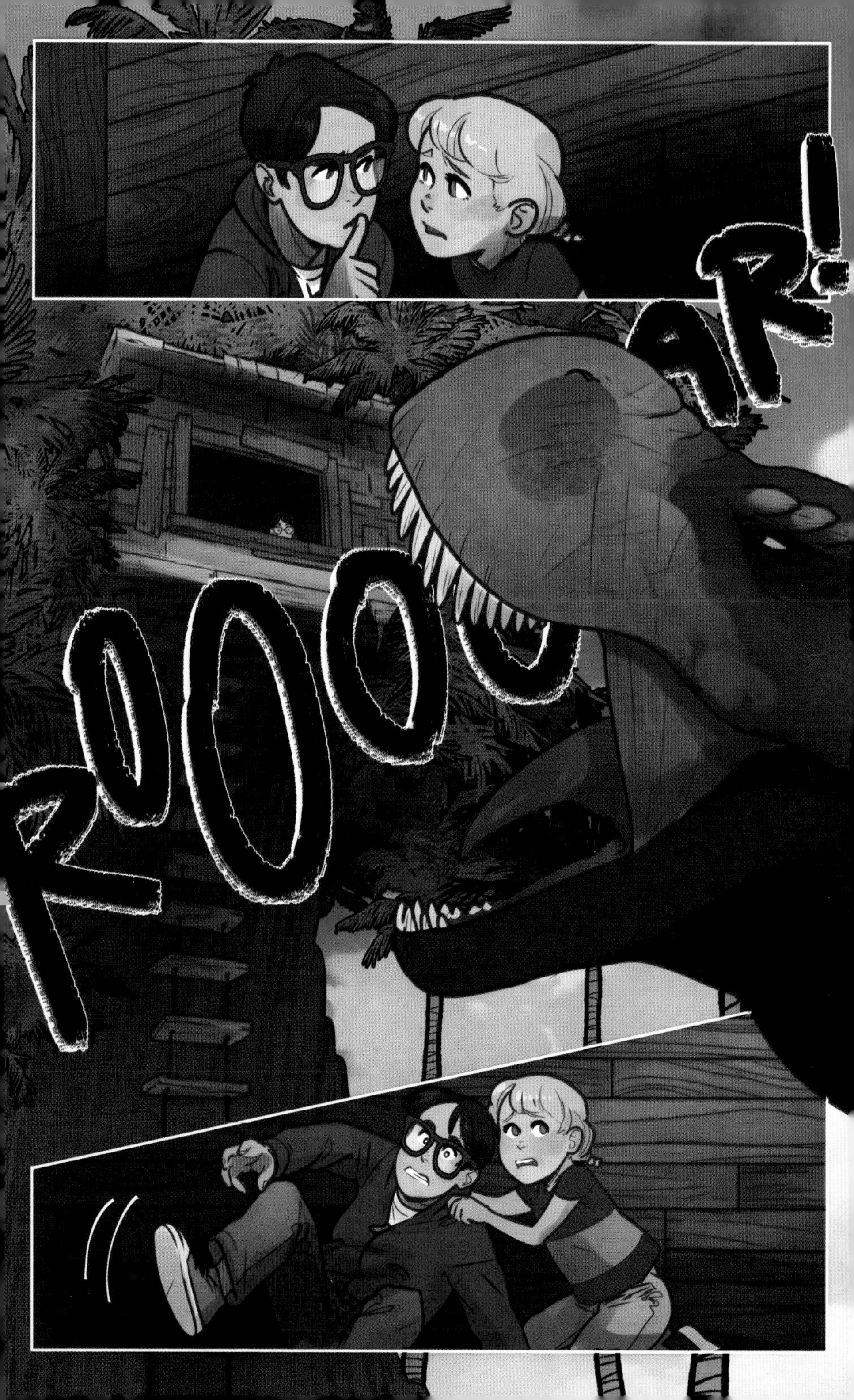
ROOOOAR!

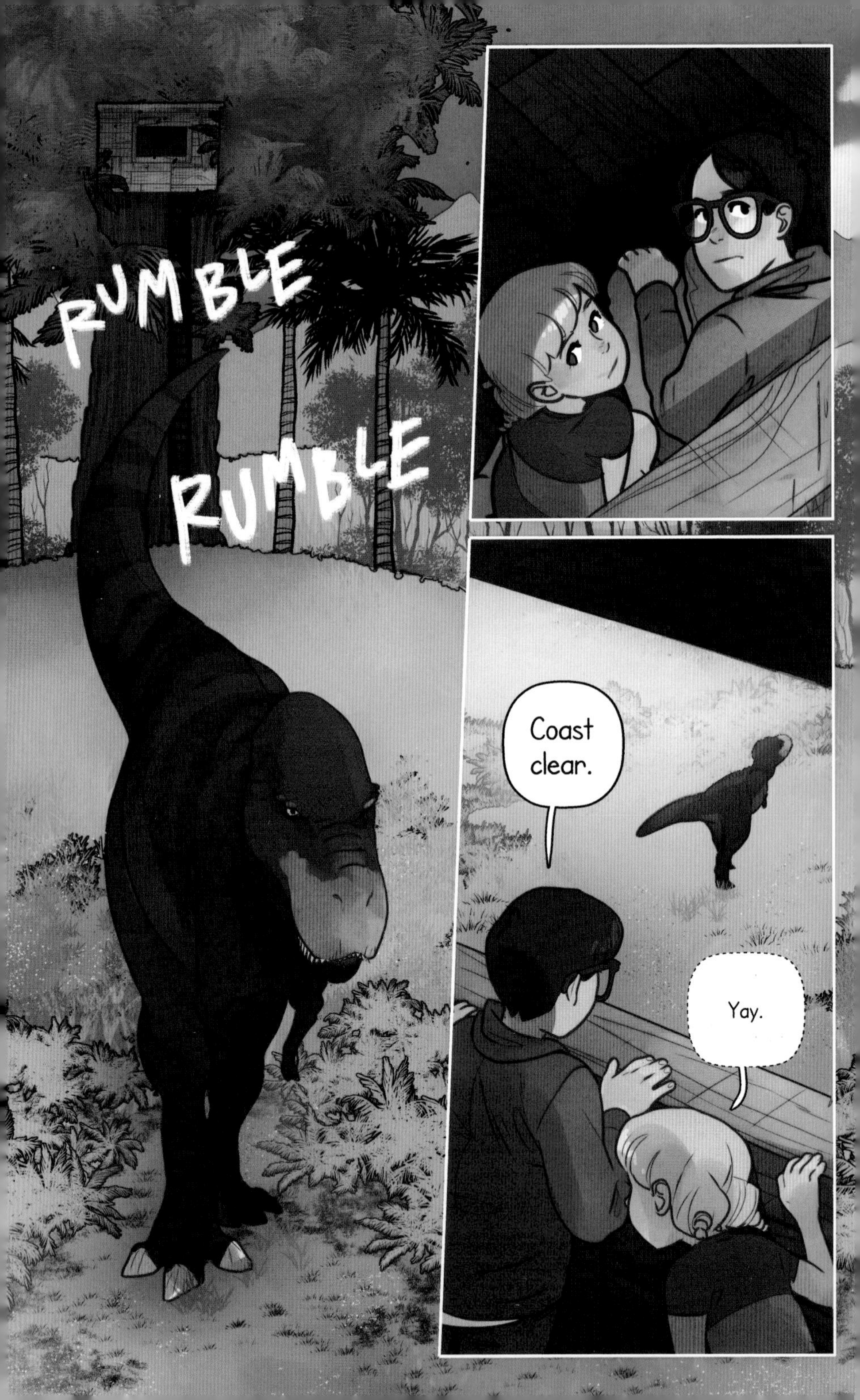
RUMBLE
RUMBLE
Coast clear.
Yay.

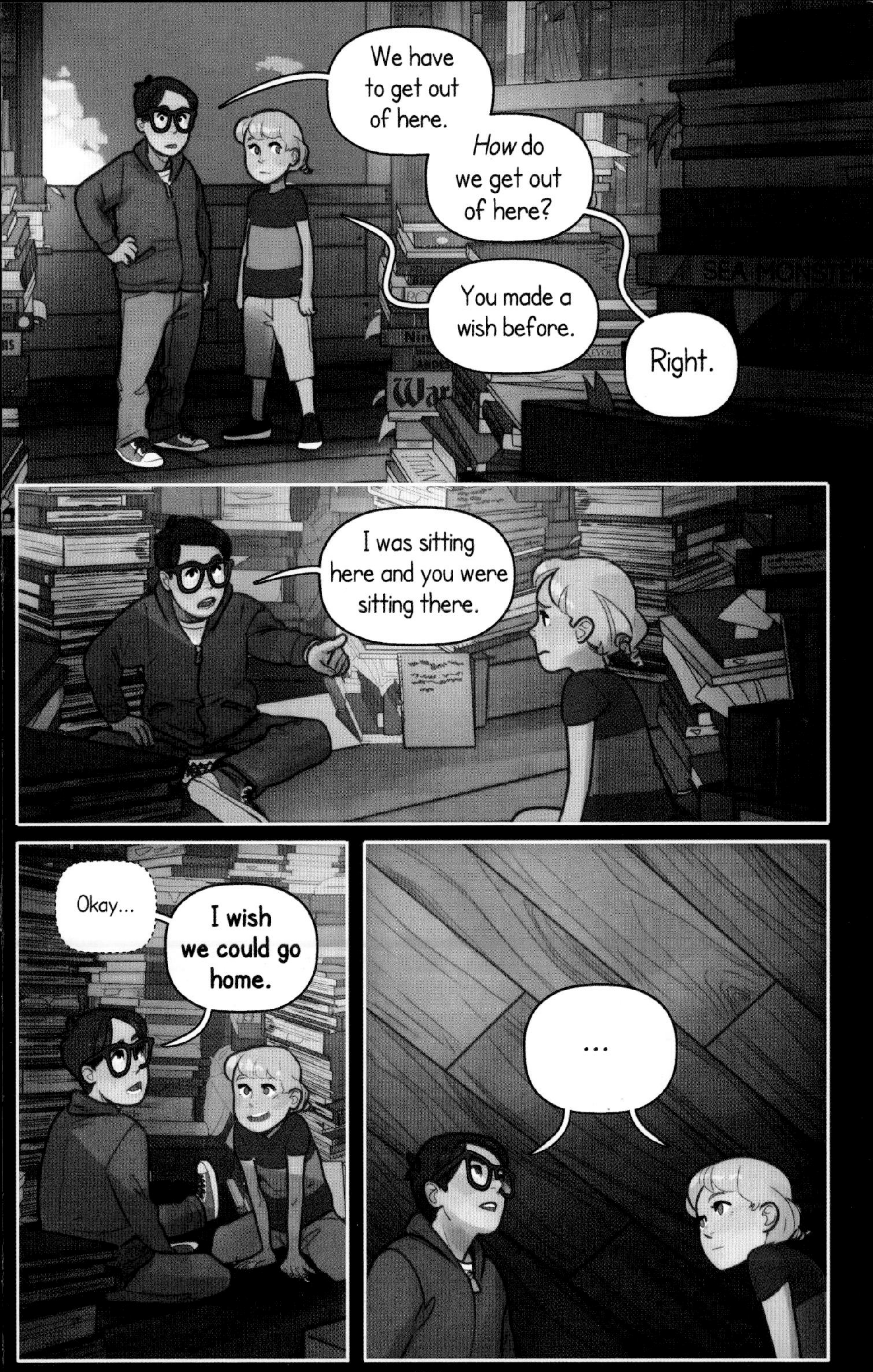
We have to get out of here.
How do we get out of here?
You made a wish before.
Right.
I was sitting here and you were sitting there.
Okay...
I wish we could go home.
...

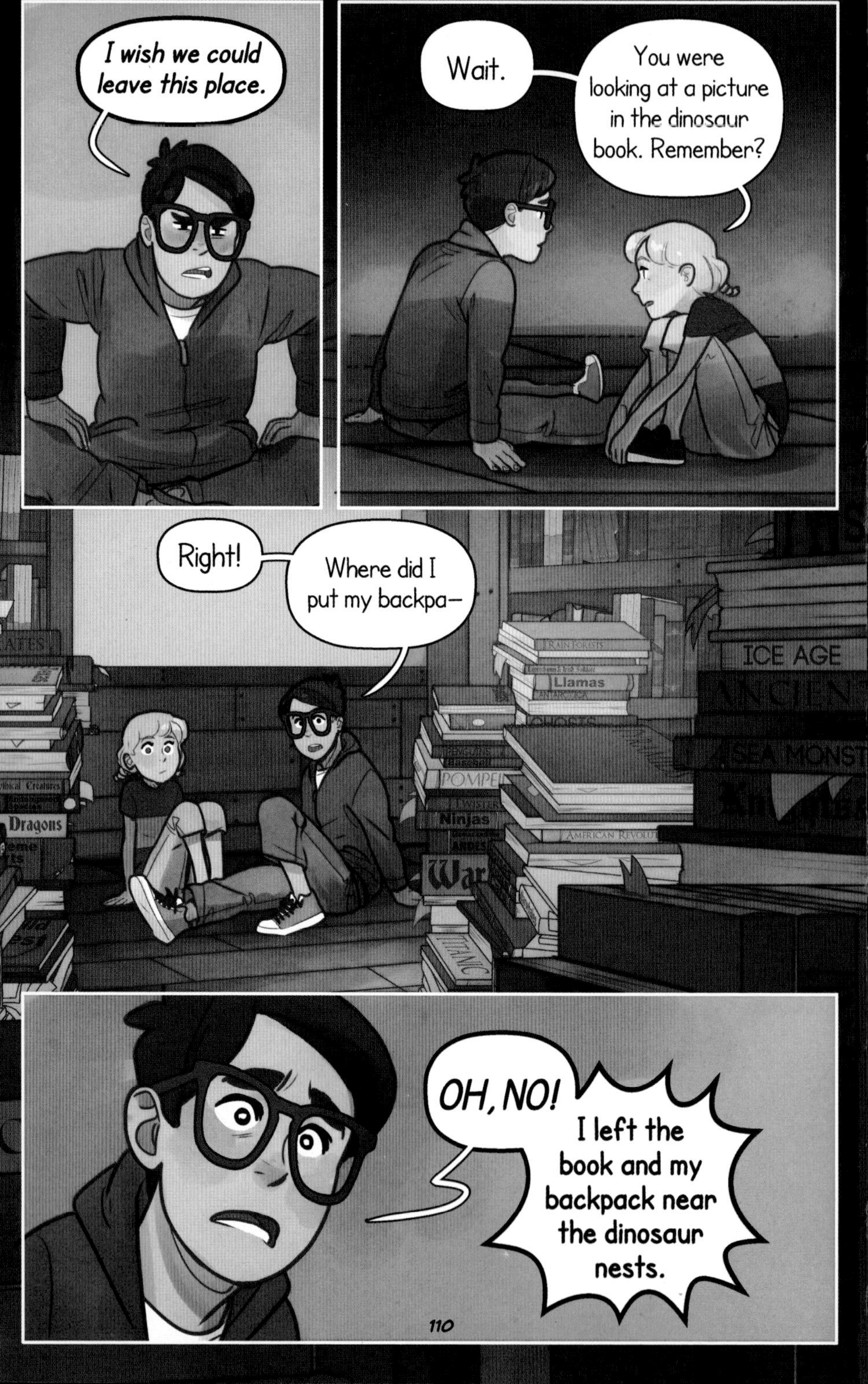
I wish we could leave this place.
Wait.
You were looking at a picture in the dinosaur book. Remember?
Right!
Where did I put my backpa—
ICE AGE
OH, NO!
I left the book and my backpack near the dinosaur nests.

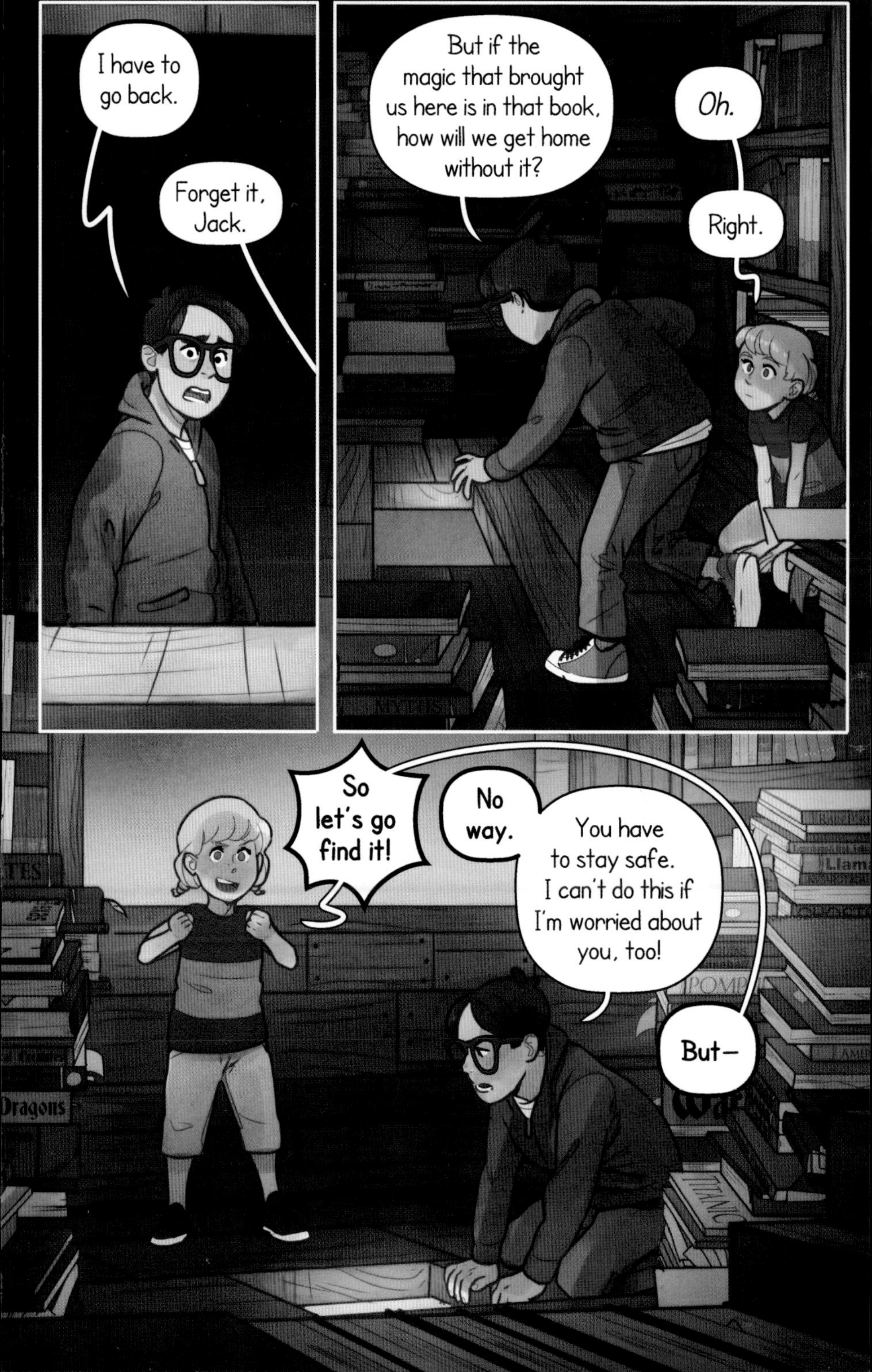
I have to go back.
Forget it, Jack.
But if the magic that brought us here is in that book, how will we get home without it?
Oh.
Right.
So let's go find it!
No way.
You have to stay safe. I can't do this if I'm worried about you, too!
But—

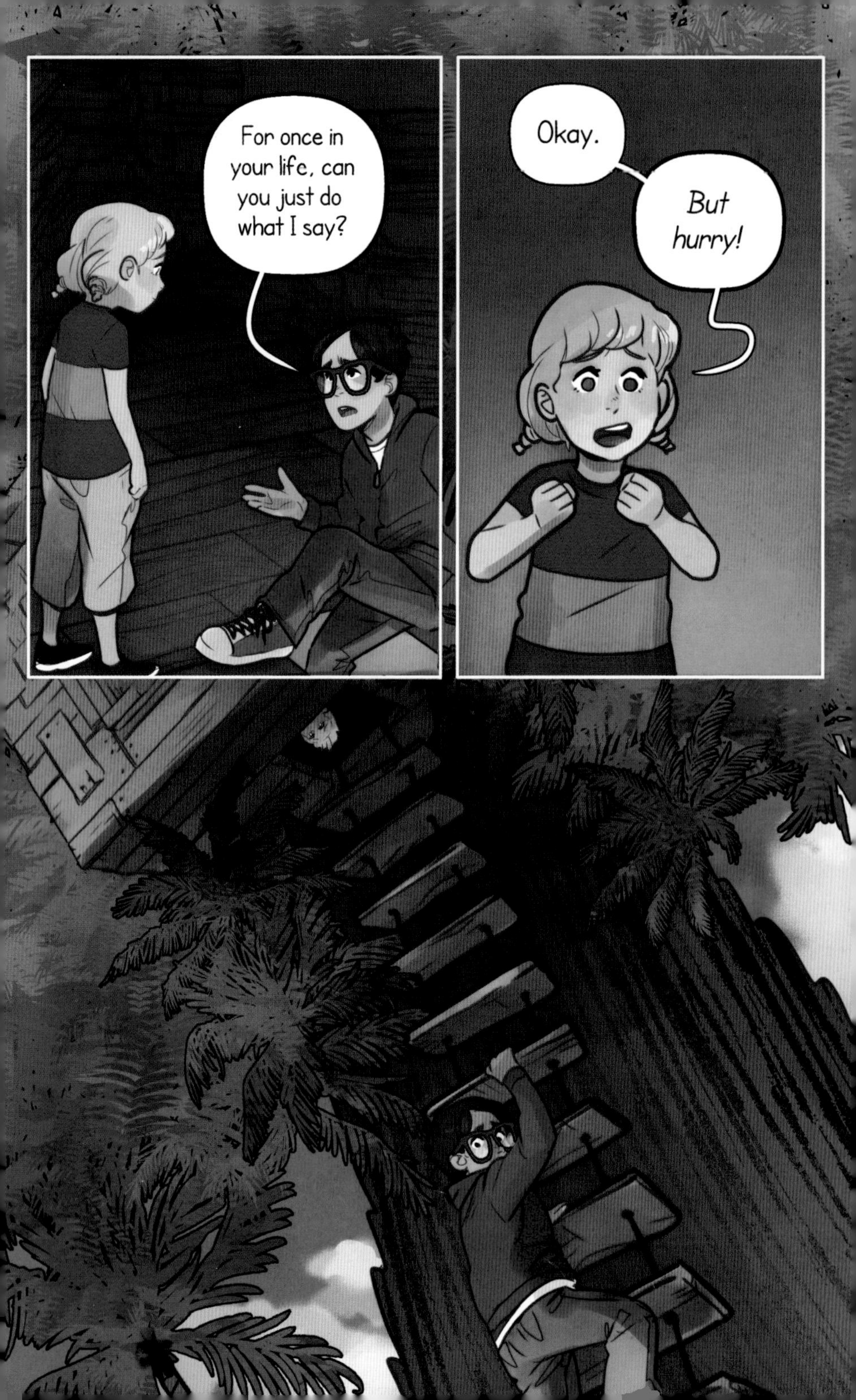
For once in your life, can you just do what I say?
Okay.
But hurry!

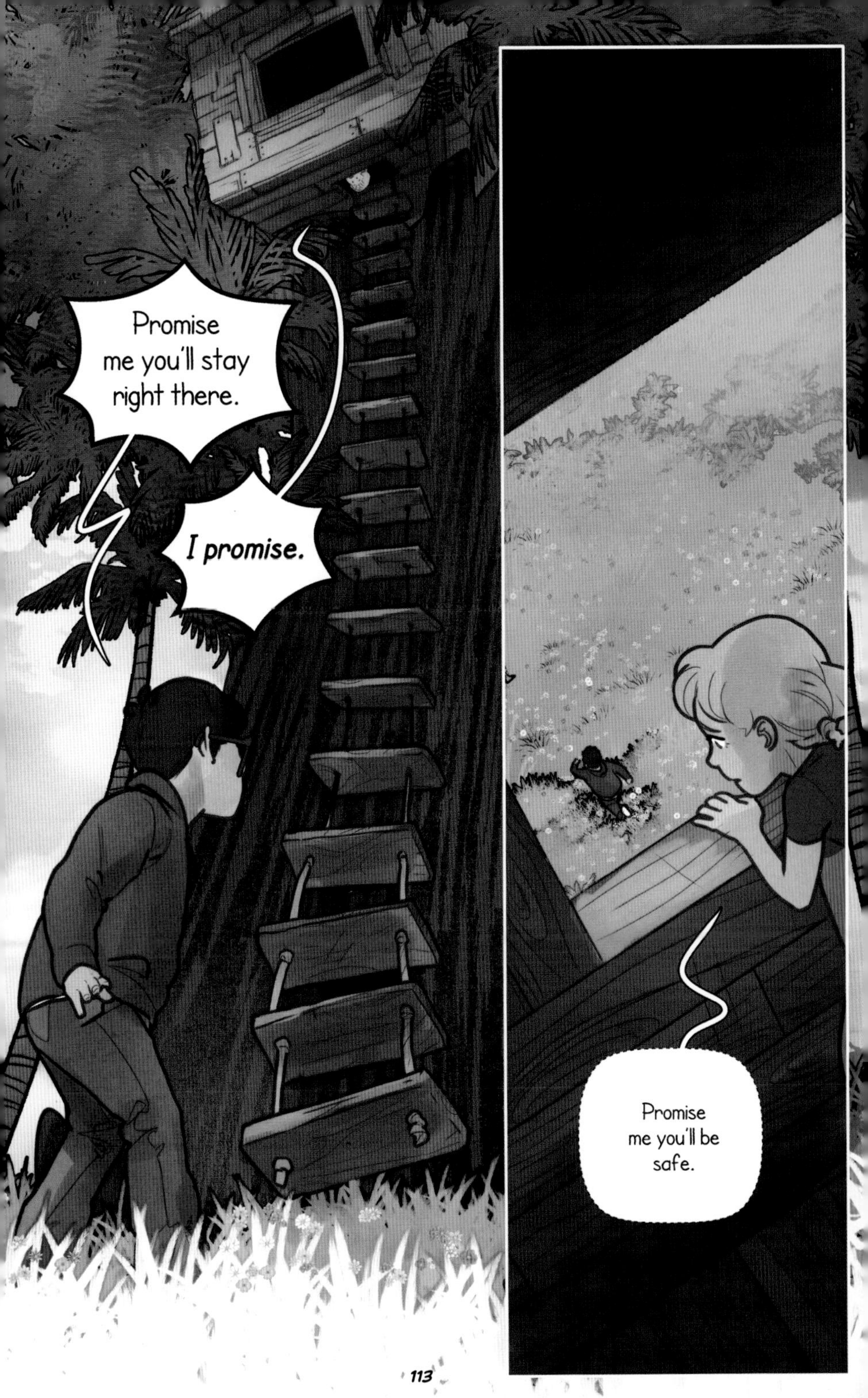
Promise me you'll stay right there.
I promise.
Promise me you'll be safe.

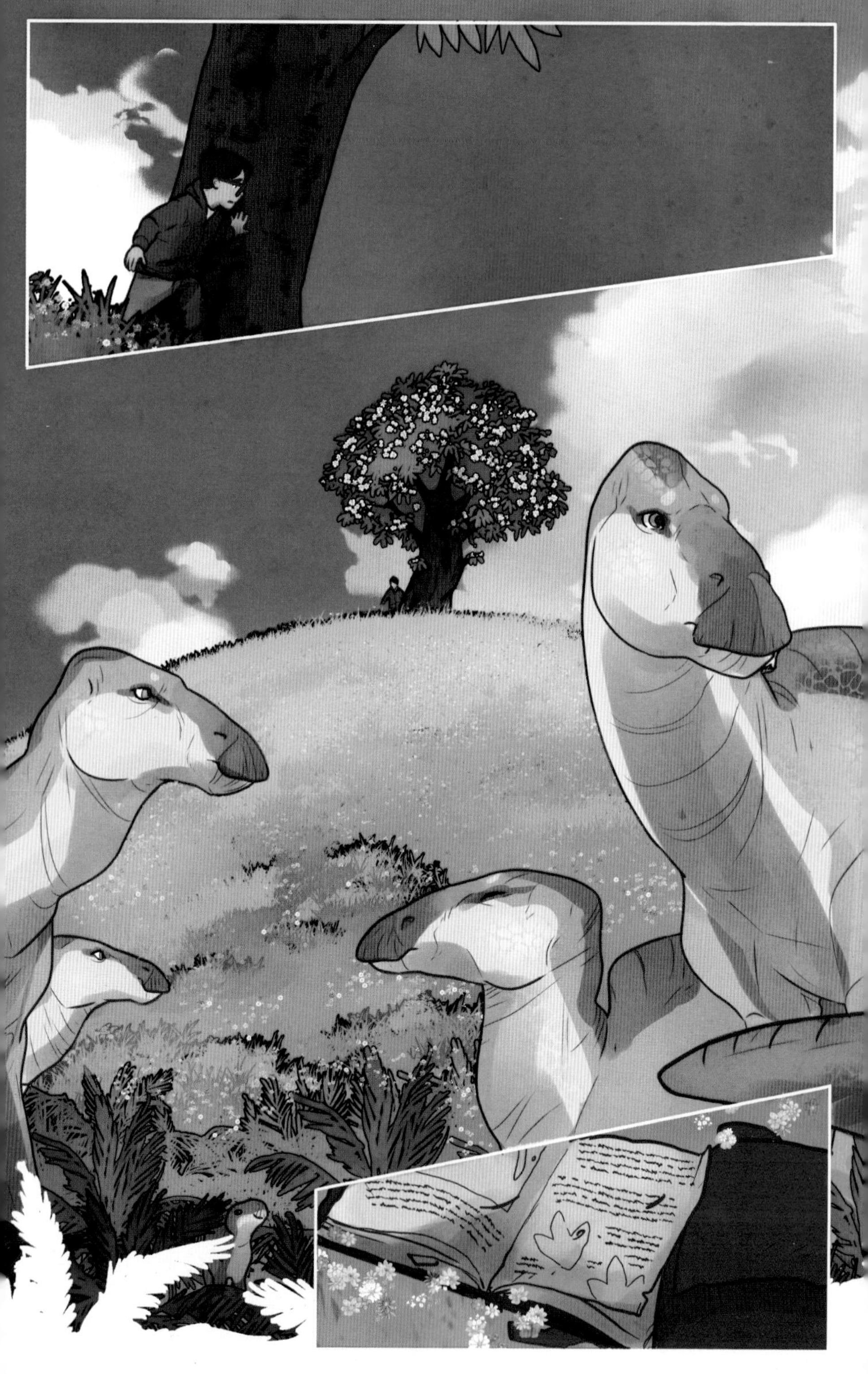

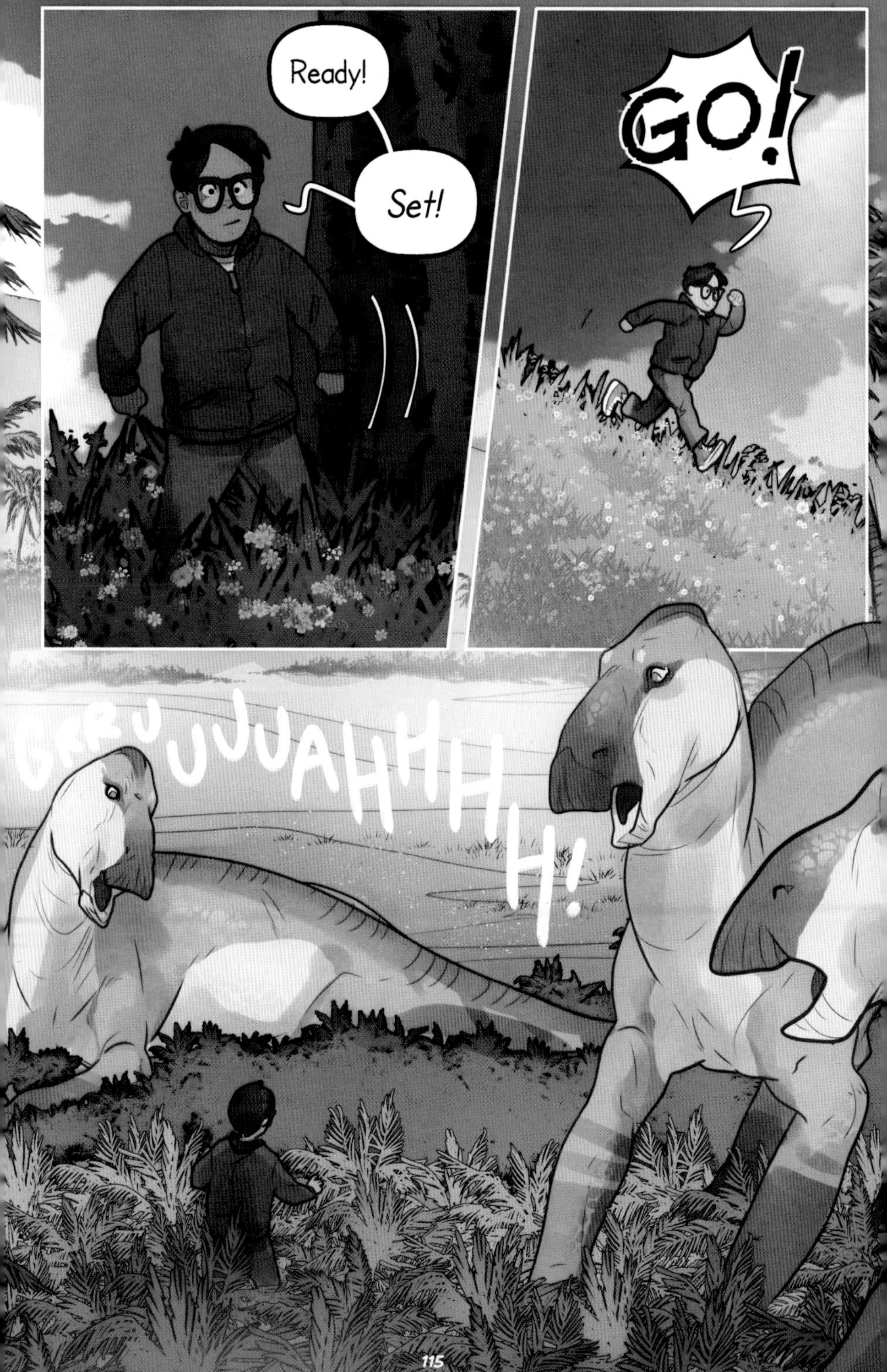
Ready!
Set!
GO!
GRRUUUUAHHHHH!

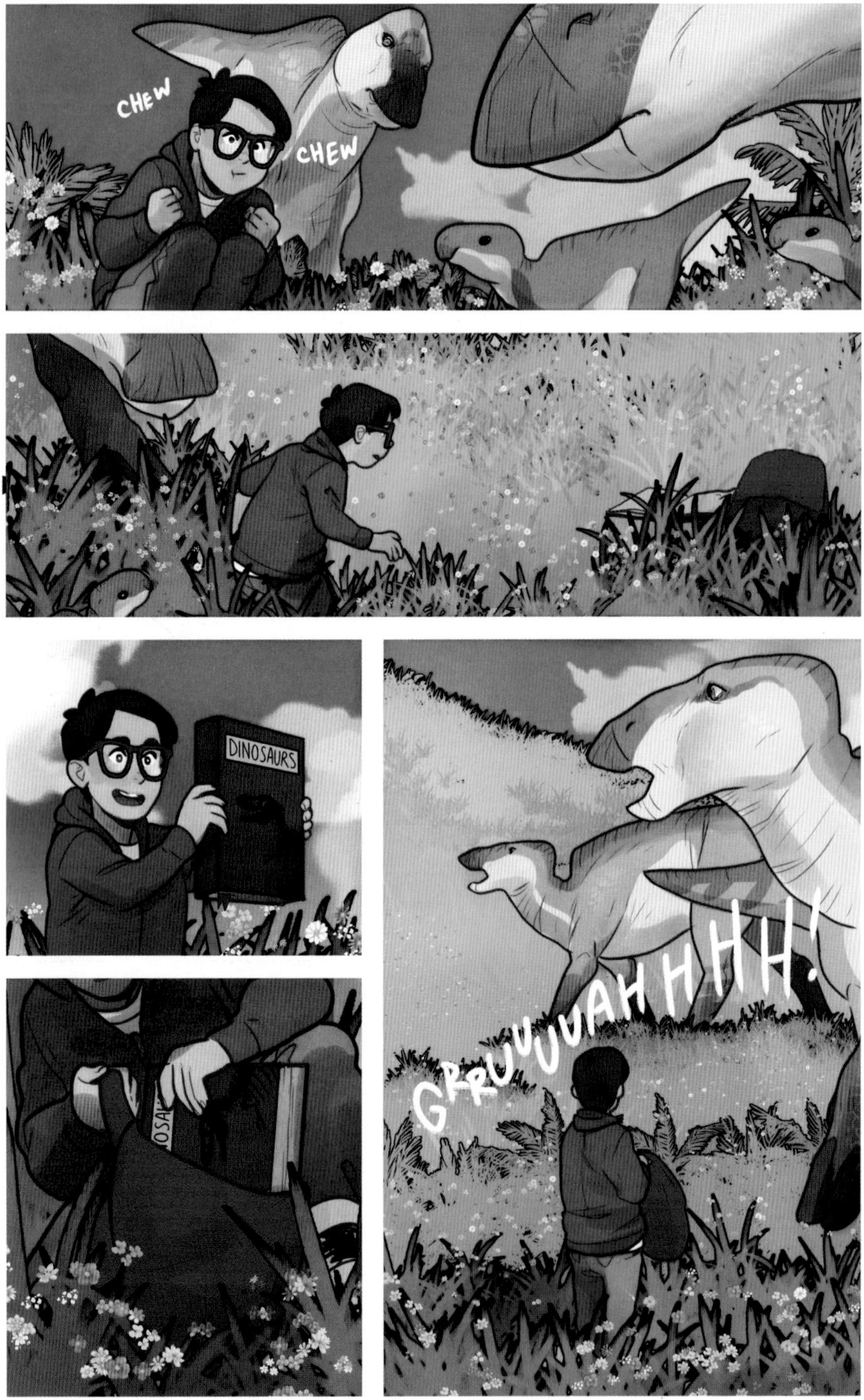
CHEW
CHEW
DINOSAURS
GRRUUUUAHHHH!

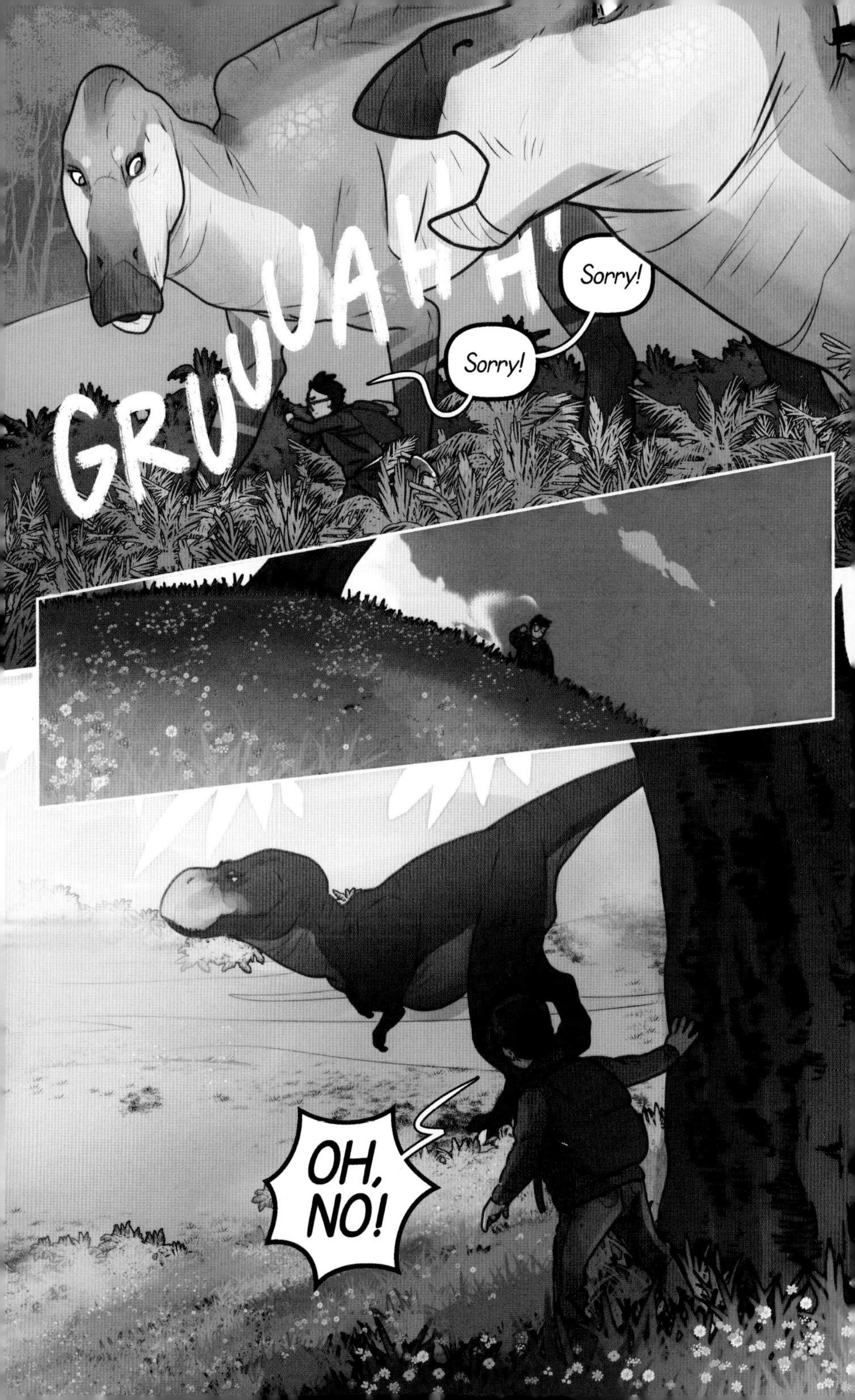
GRUUUAHH!
Sorry!
Sorry!
OH, NO!

CHAPTER EIGHT
A Giant Shadow

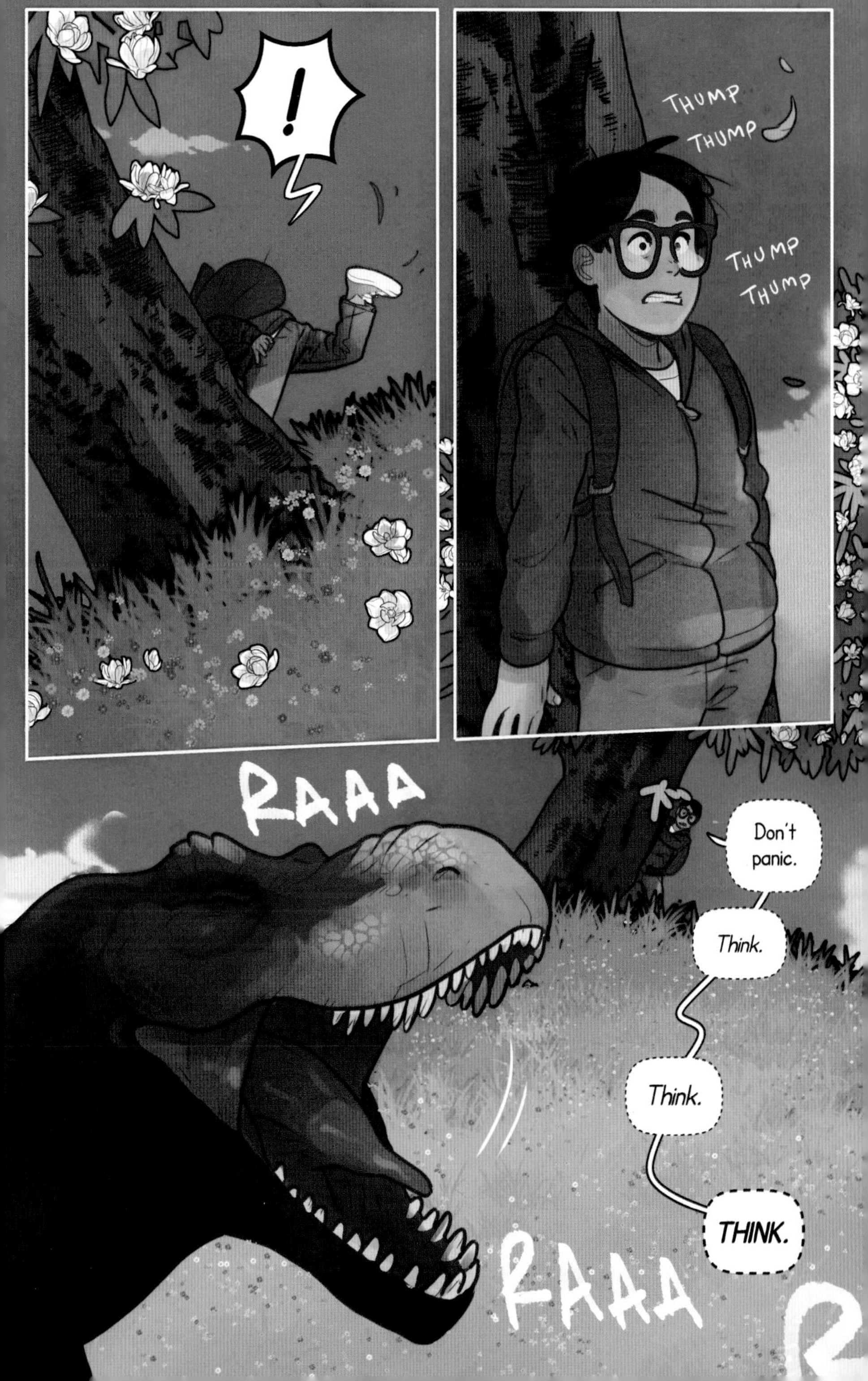
!
THUMP
THUMP
THUMP
THUMP
RAAA
Don't panic.
Think.
Think.
THINK.
RAAA

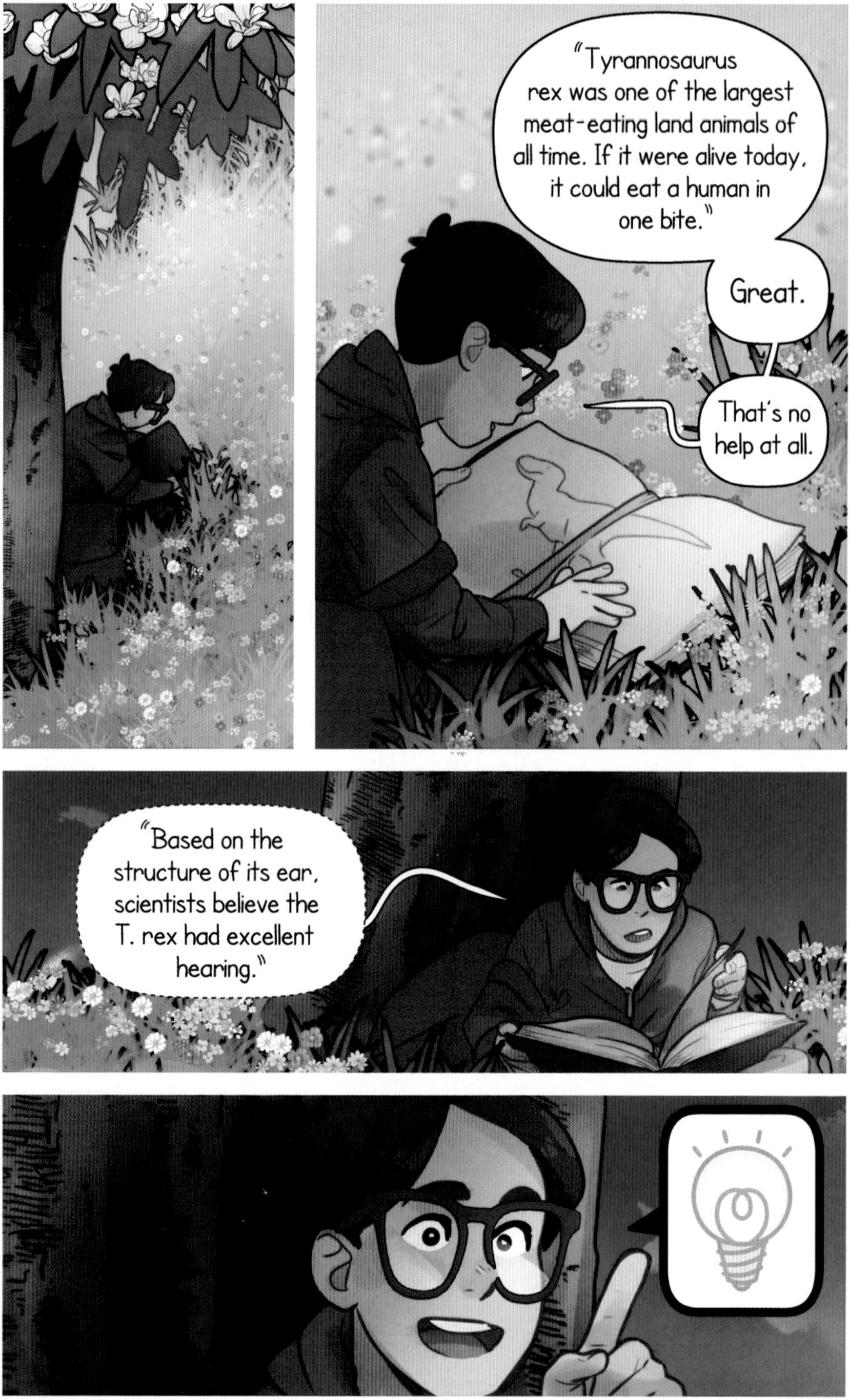
"Tyrannosaurus rex was one of the largest meat-eating land animals of all time. If it were alive today, it could eat a human in one bite."
Great.
That's no help at all.
"Based on the structure of its ear, scientists believe the T. rex had excellent hearing."

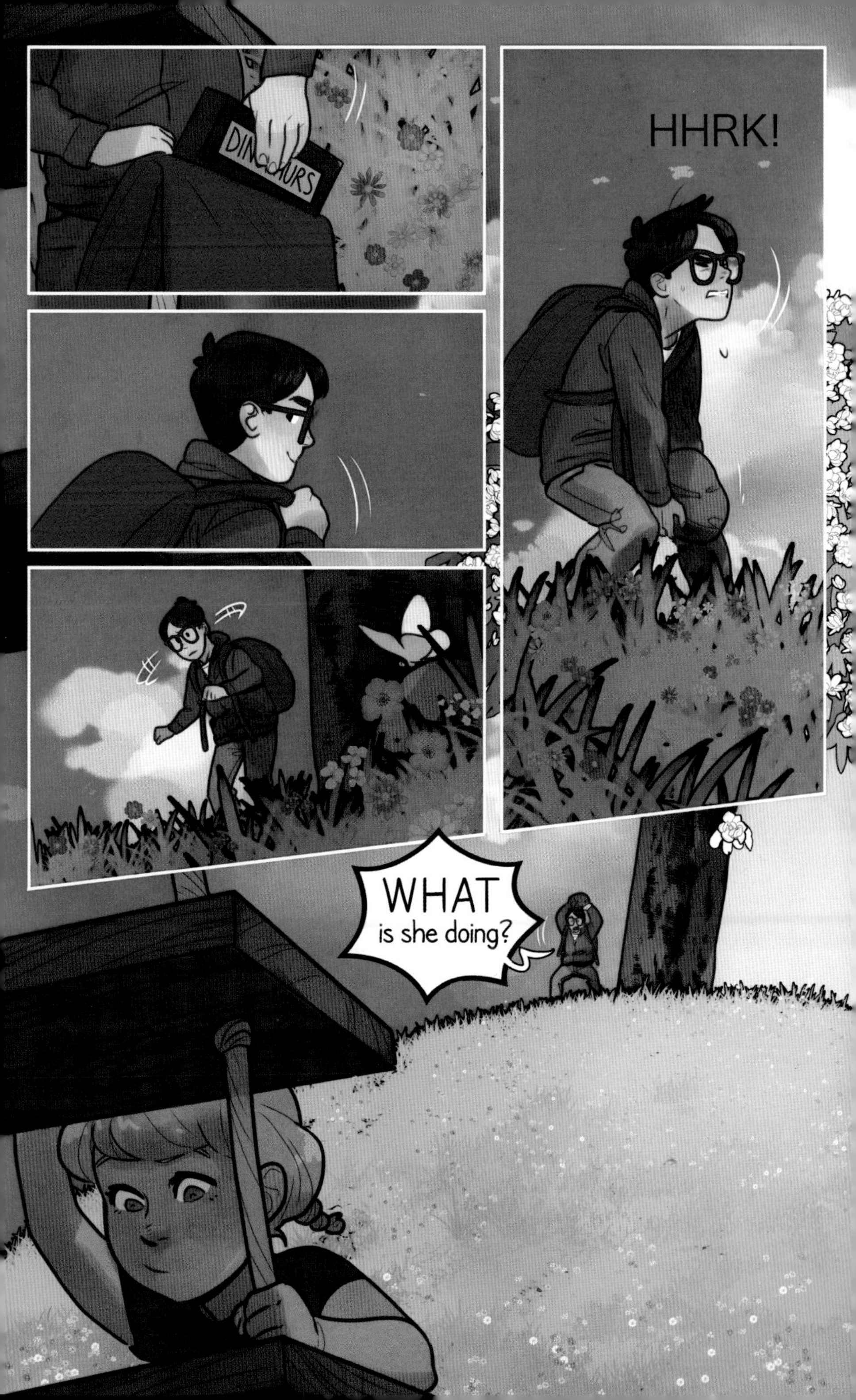
DINOSAURS
HHRK!
WHAT is she doing?

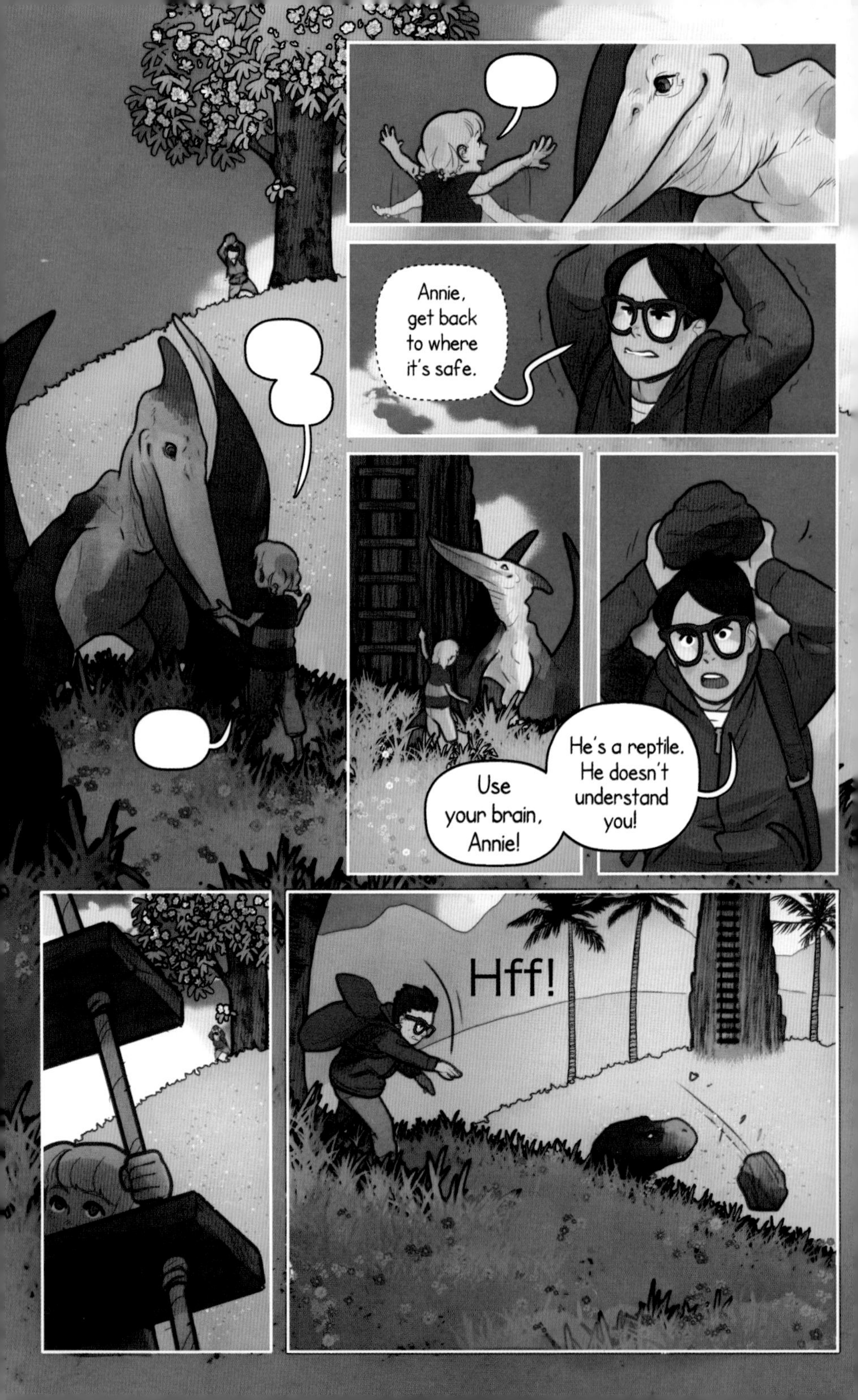
Annie, get back to where it's safe.
He's a reptile. He doesn't understand you!
Use your brain, Annie!
Hff!

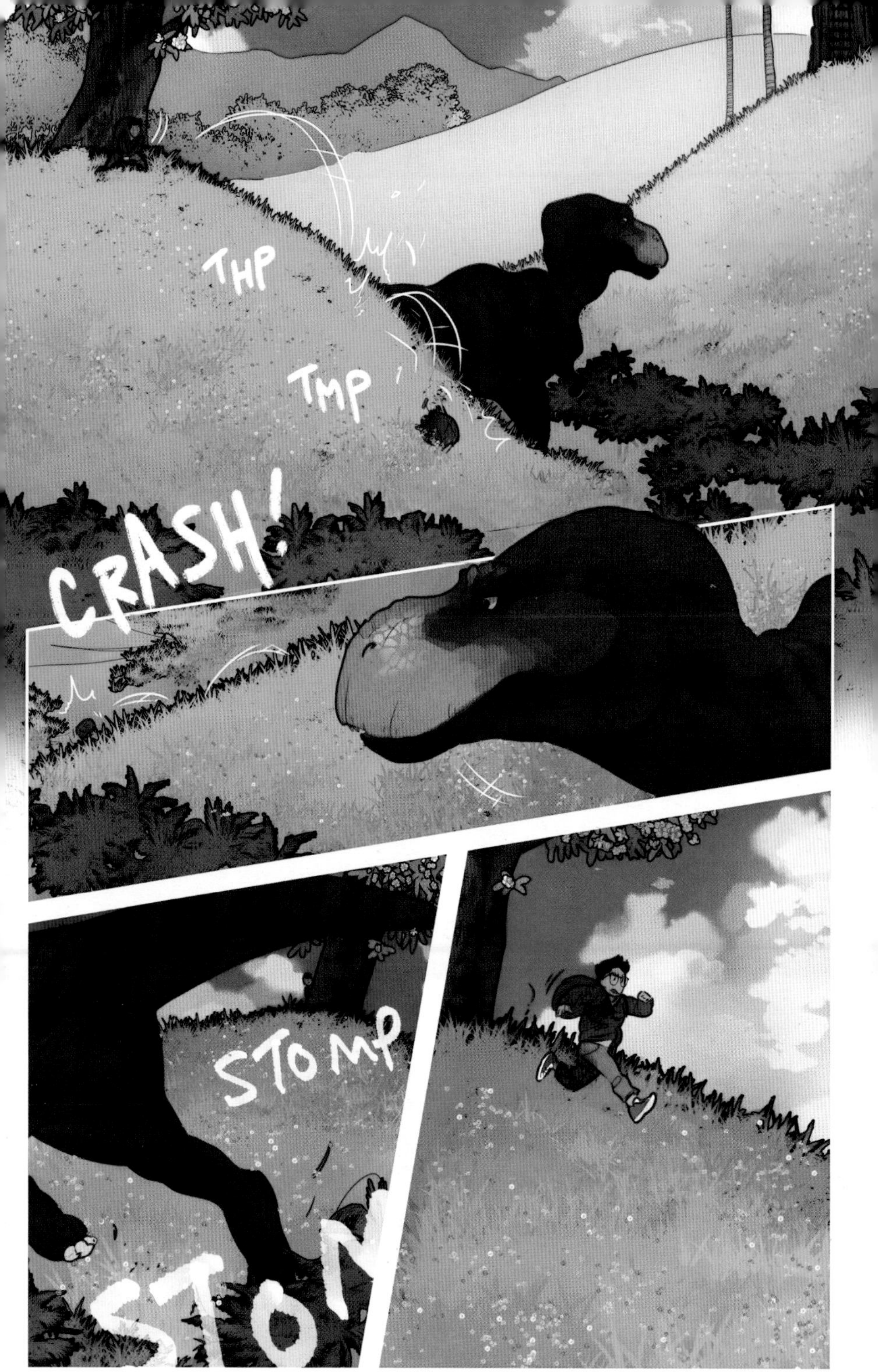
THP
TMP
CRASH!
STOMP
STOM

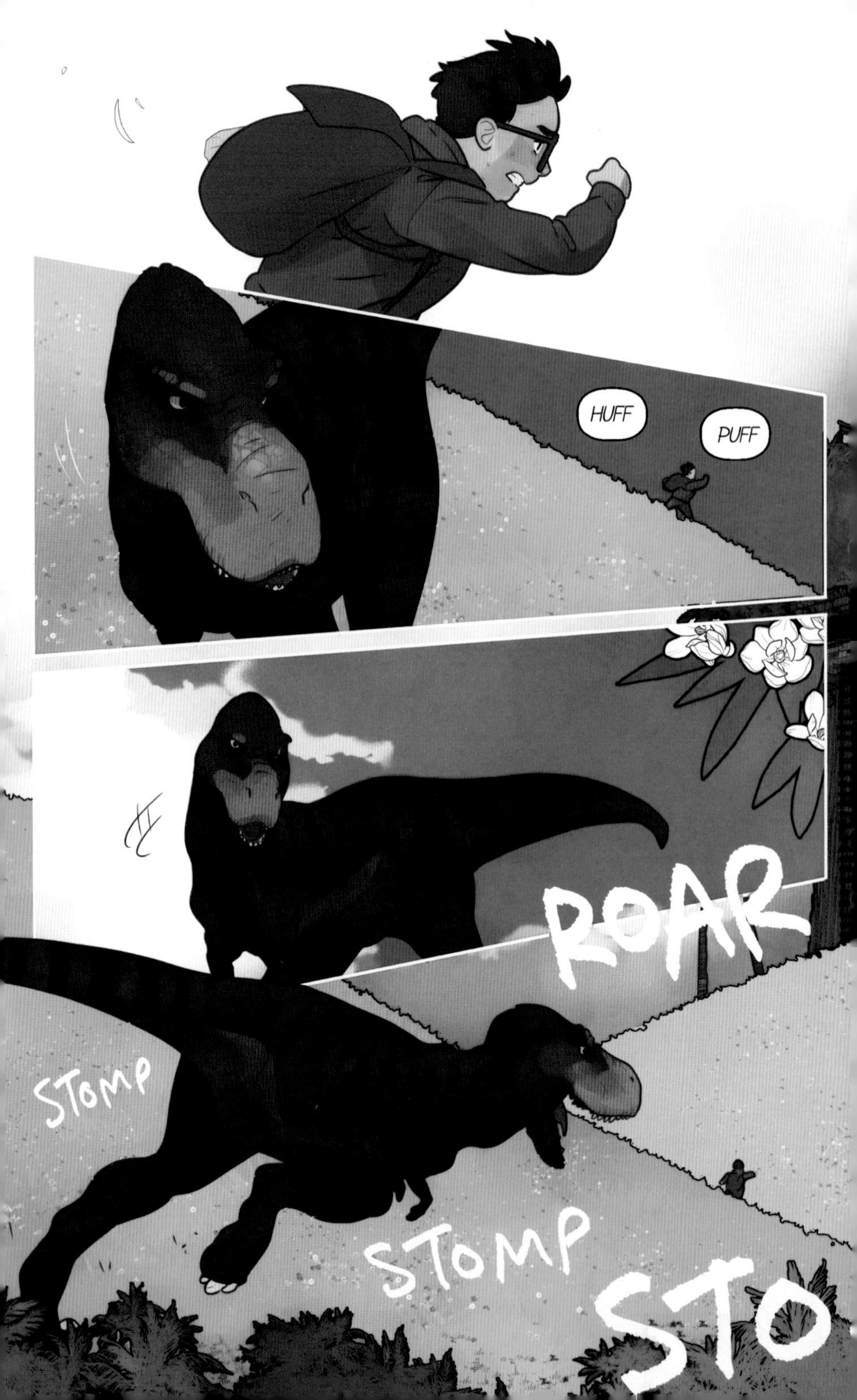
HUFF
PUFF
ROAR
STOMP
STOMP
STO

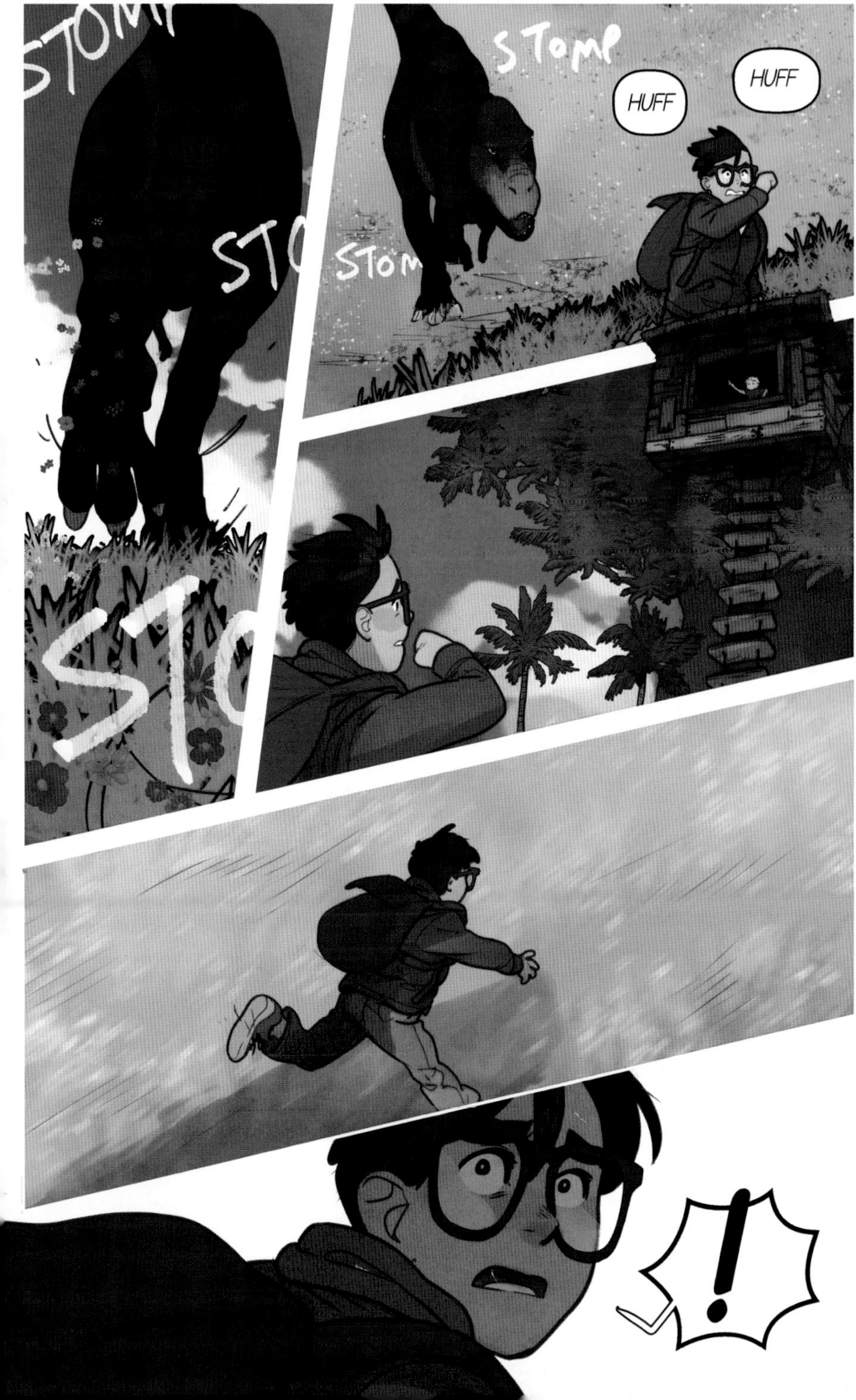
STOMP
HUFF
HUFF
!

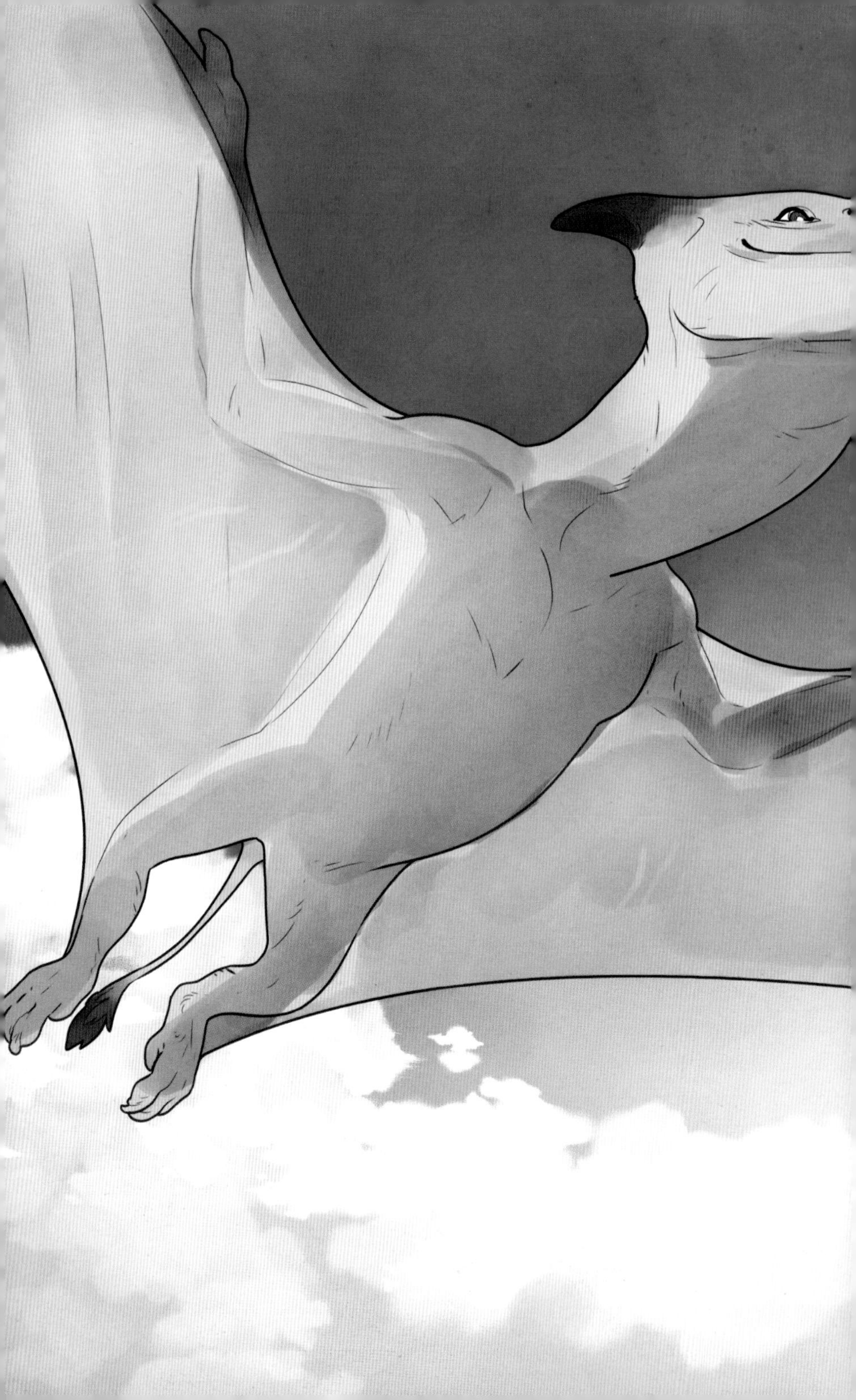

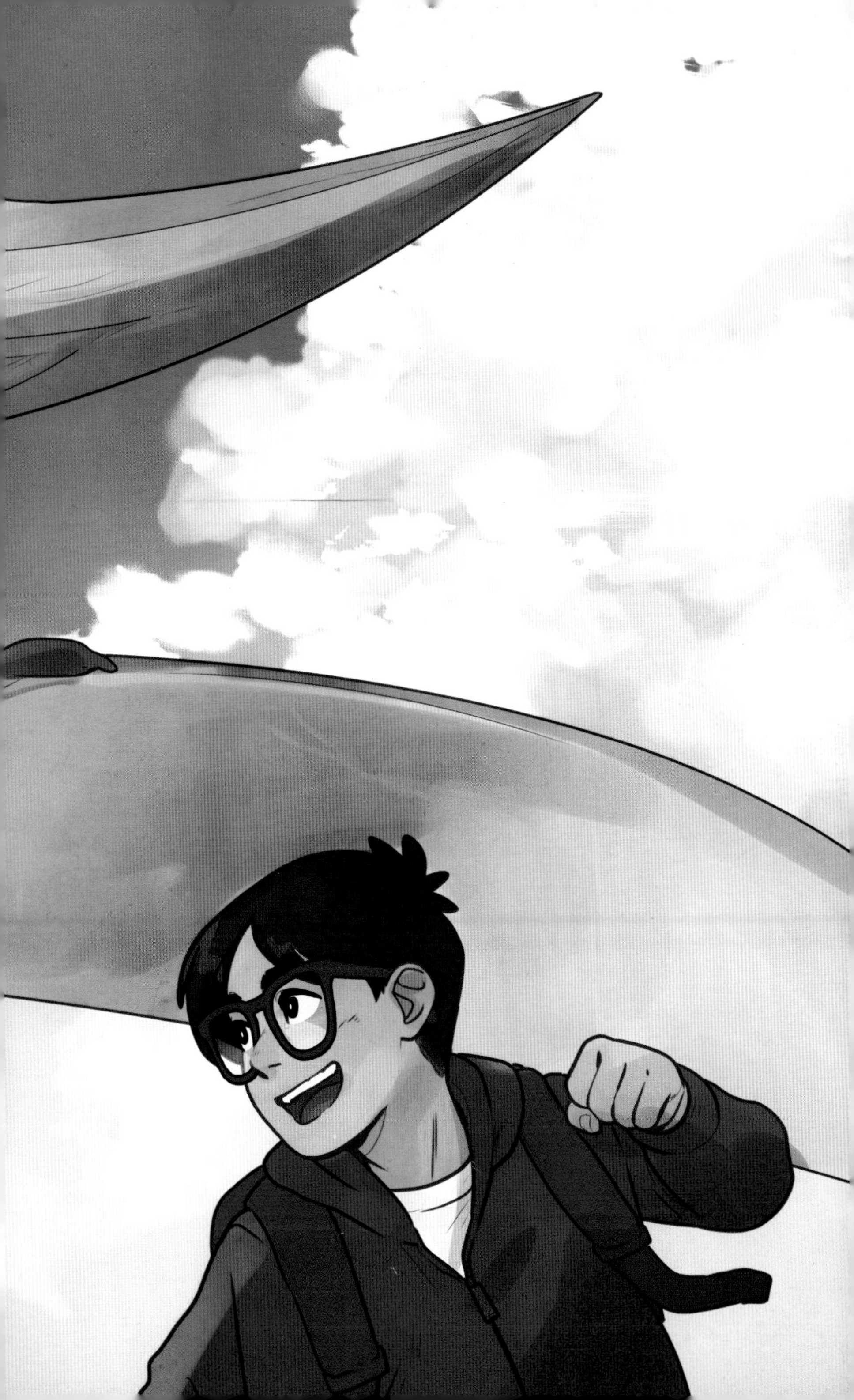

CHAPTER NINE

The Amazing Ride

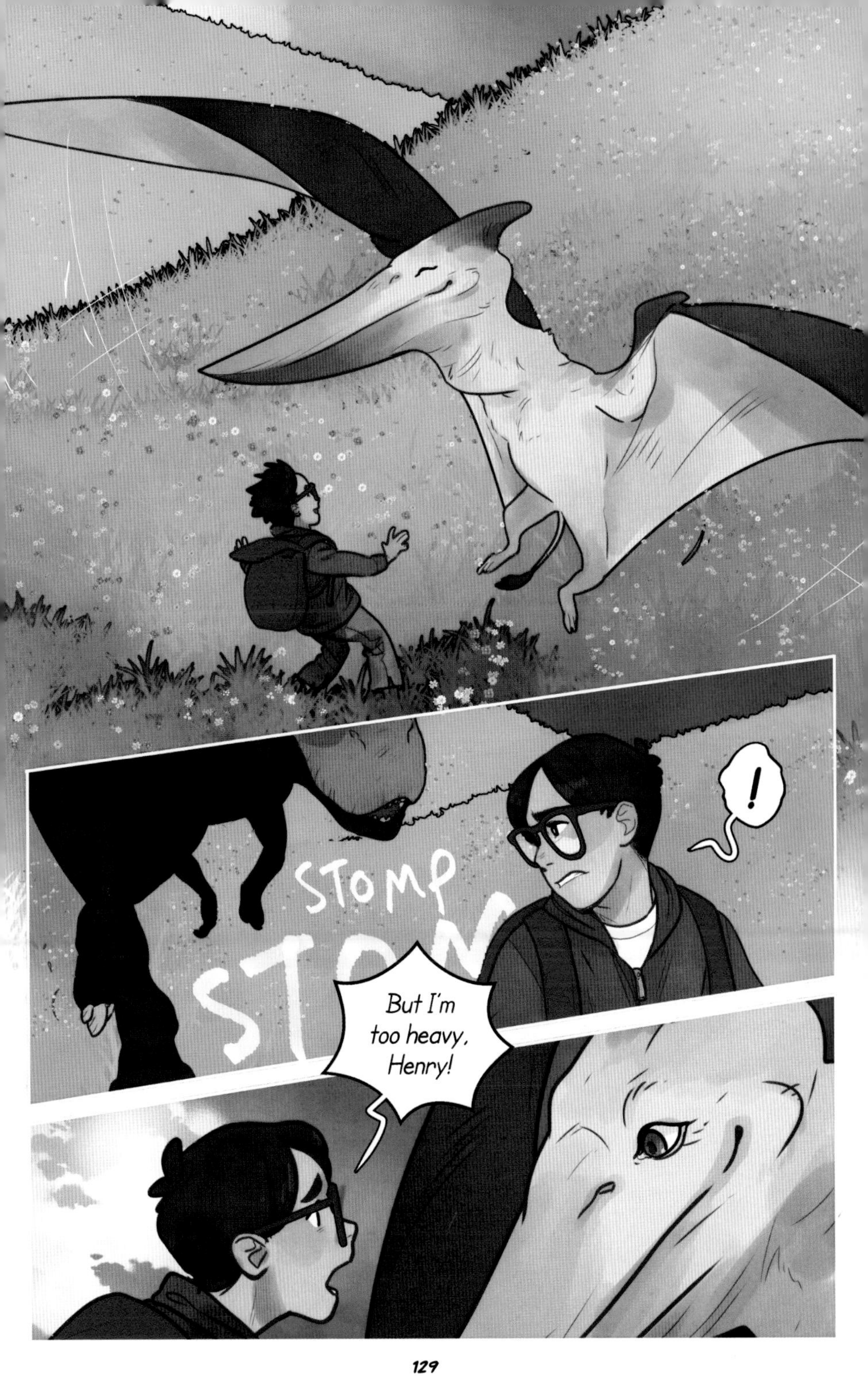
!
STOMP
STOM
But I'm too heavy, Henry!

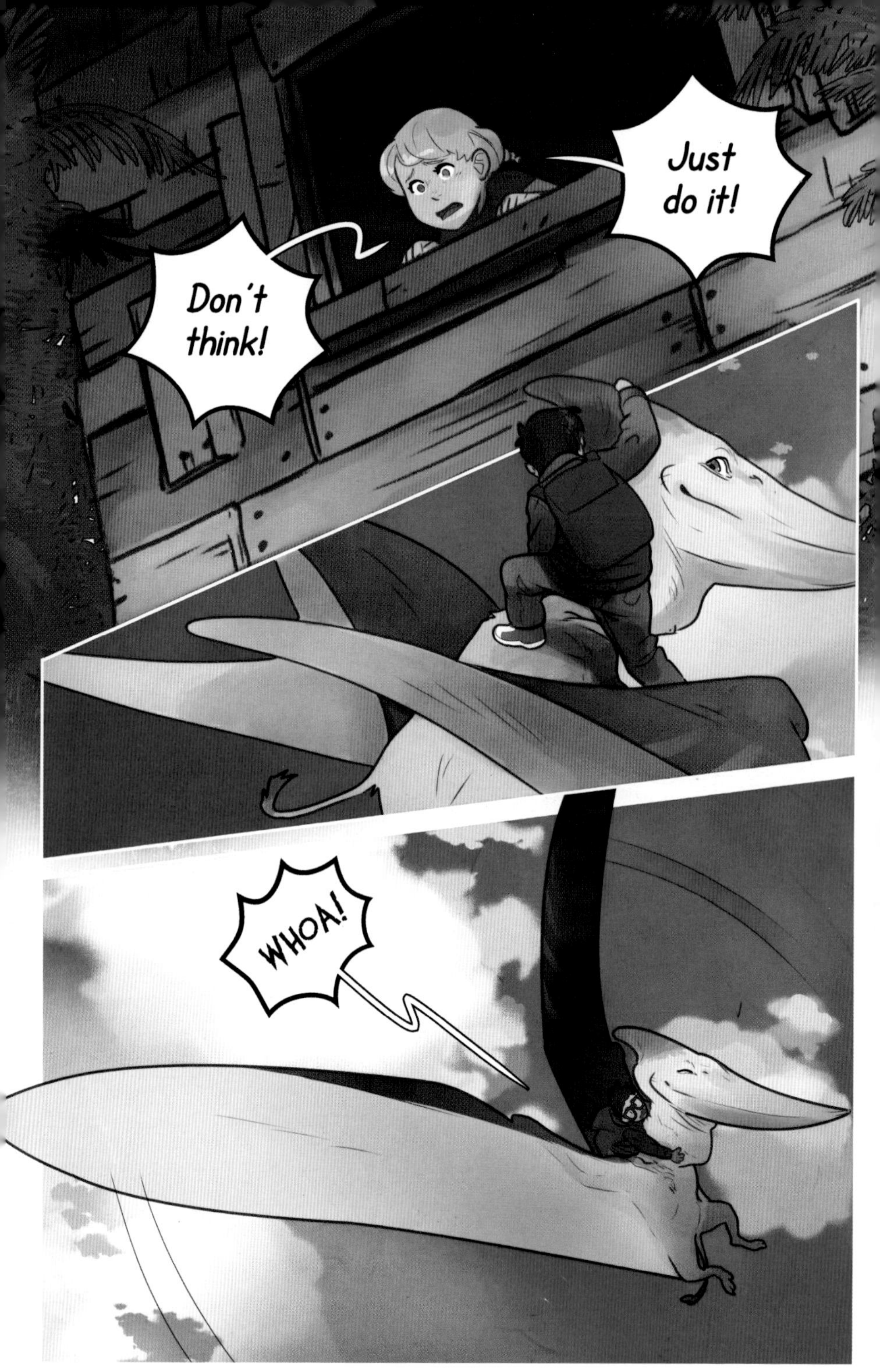
Don't think!
Just do it!
WHOA!

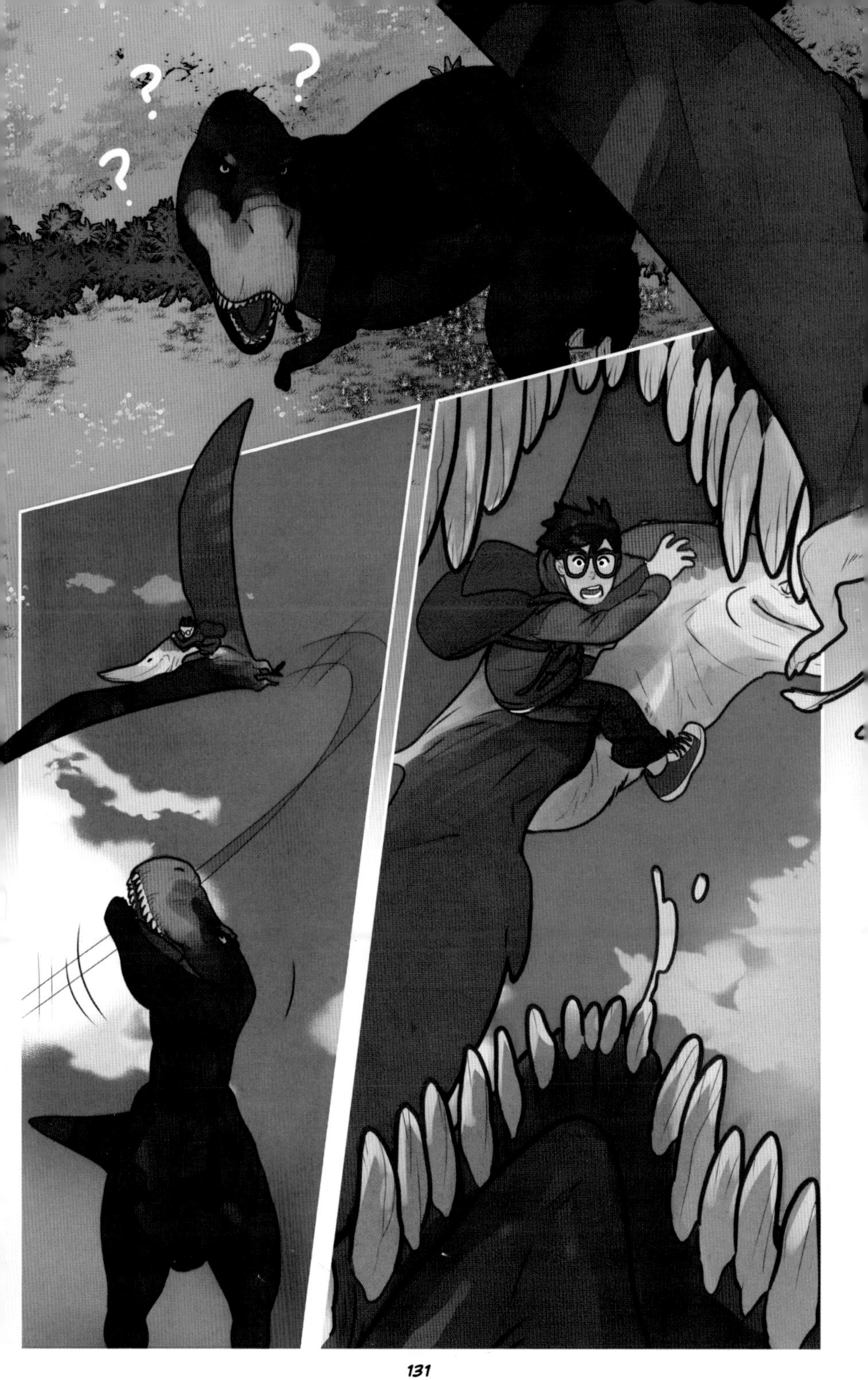
?
?
?

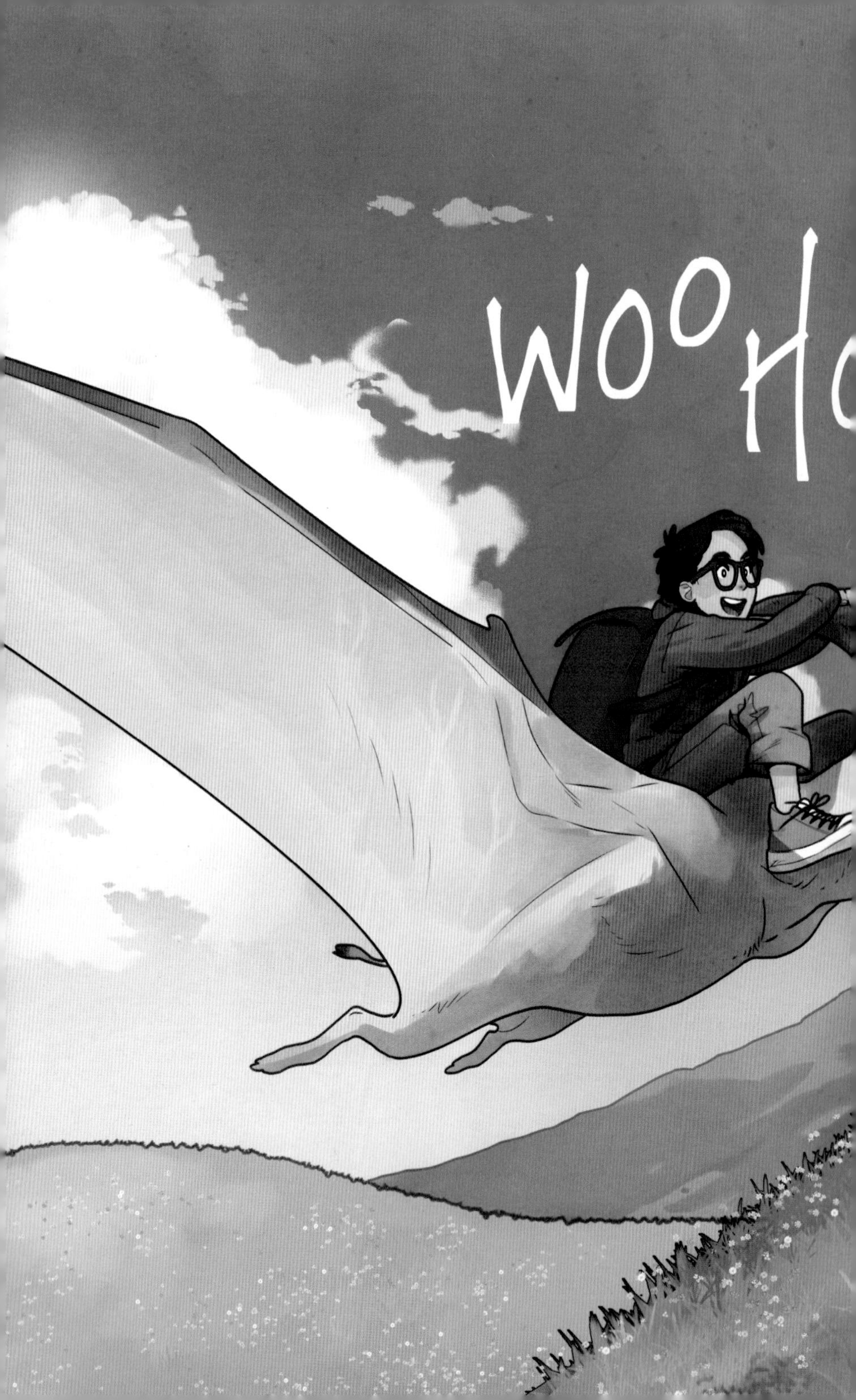
WOO HO

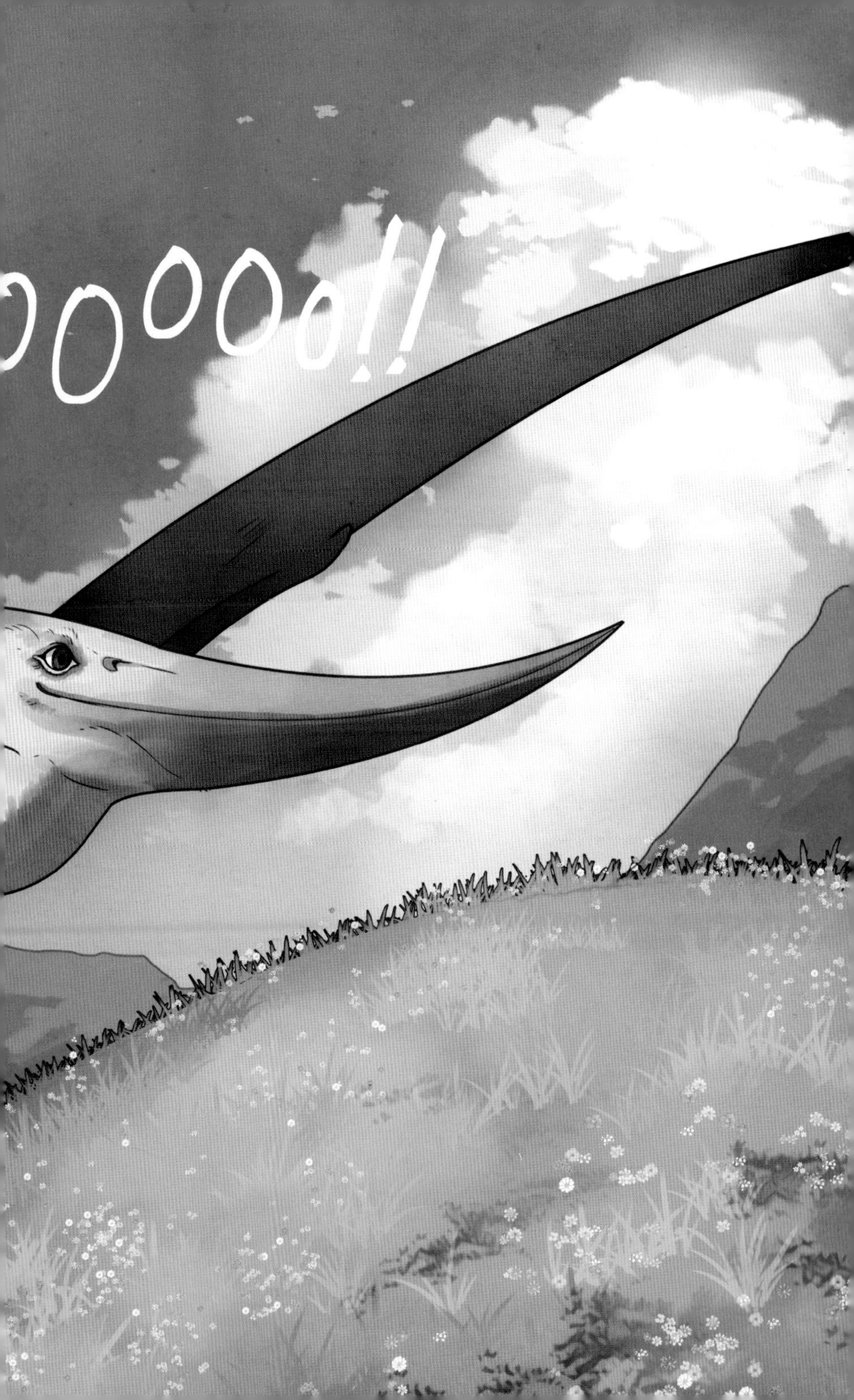
OOOOO!!

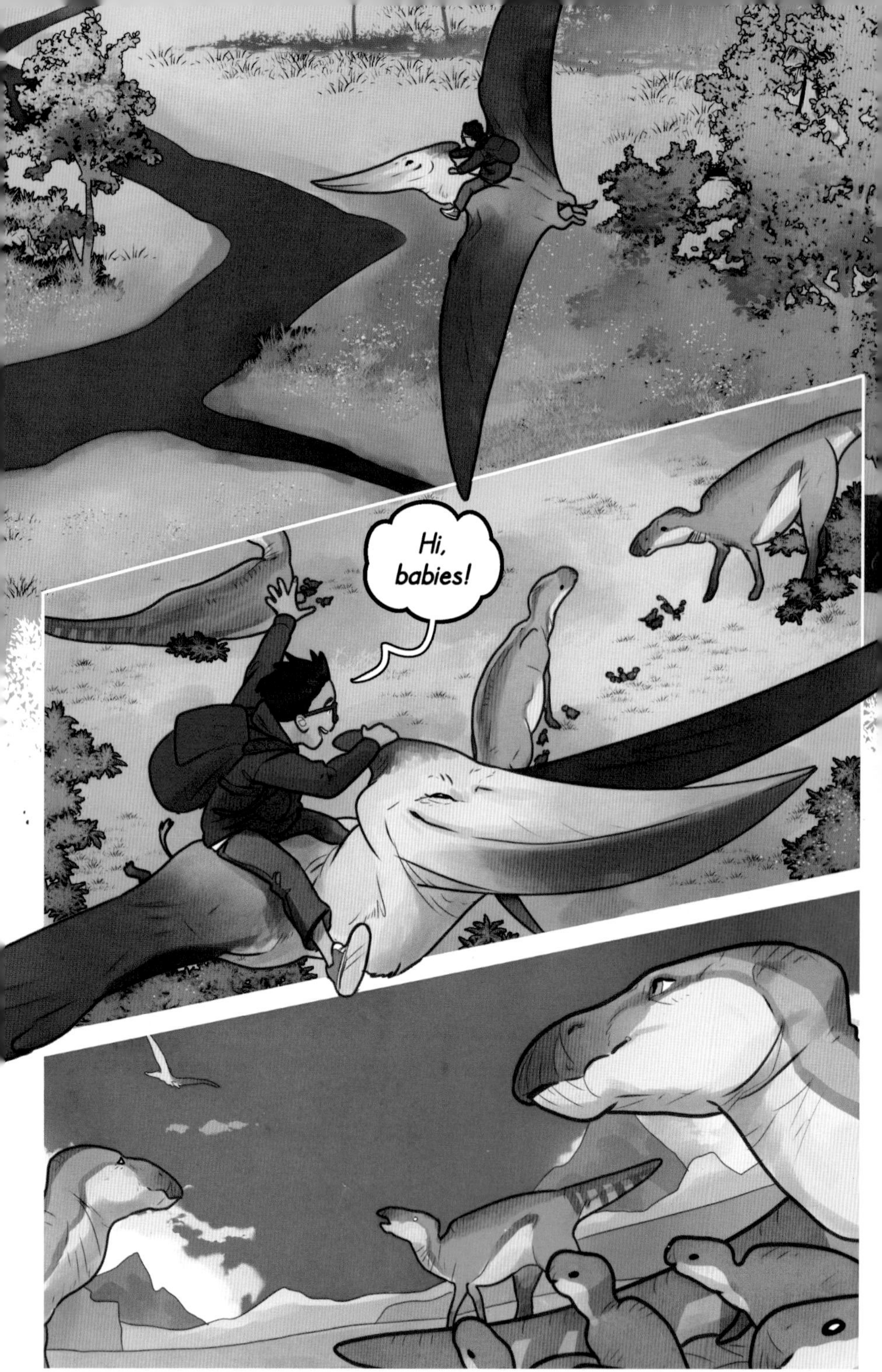
Hi, babies!

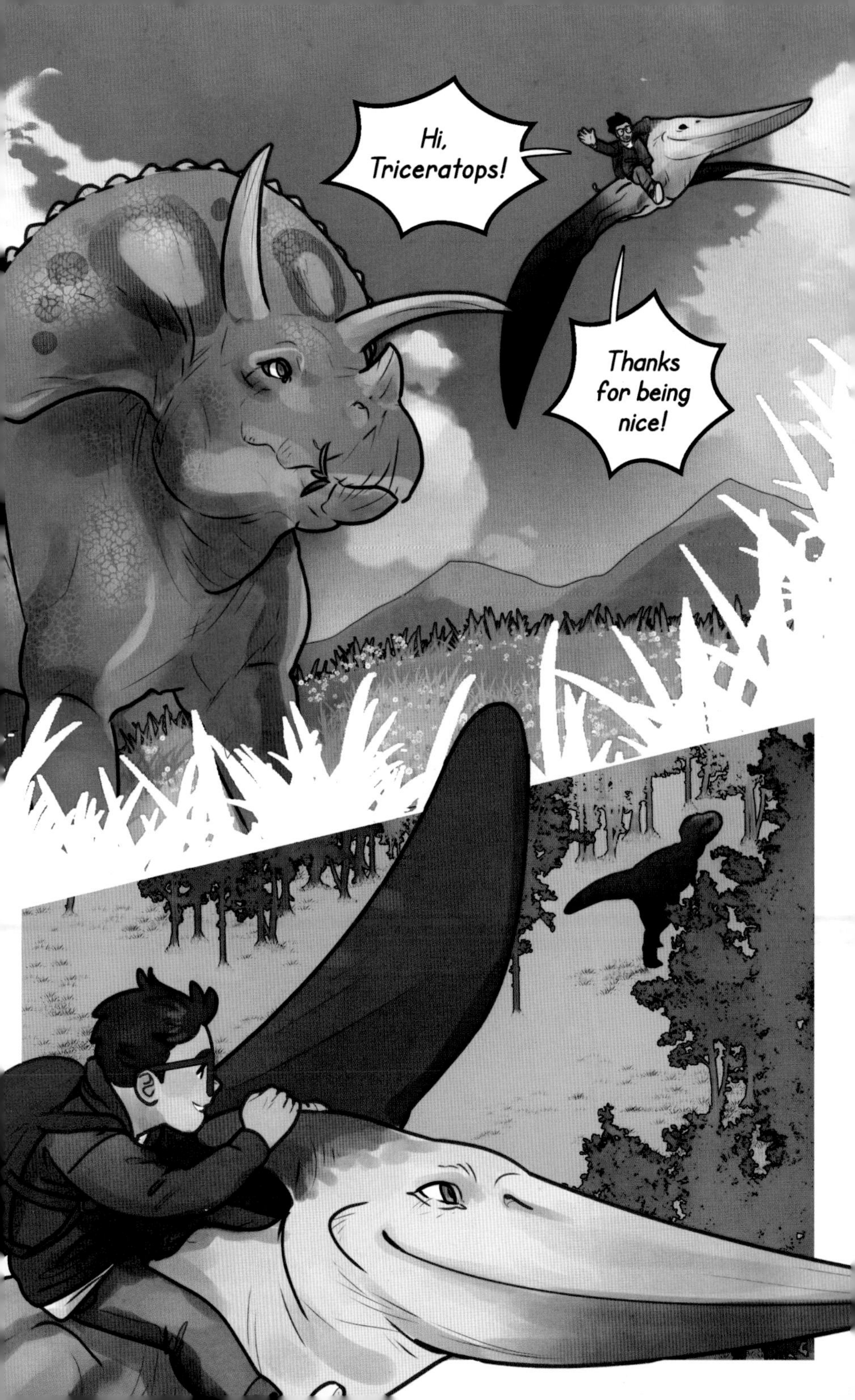
Hi, Triceratops!
Thanks for being nice!

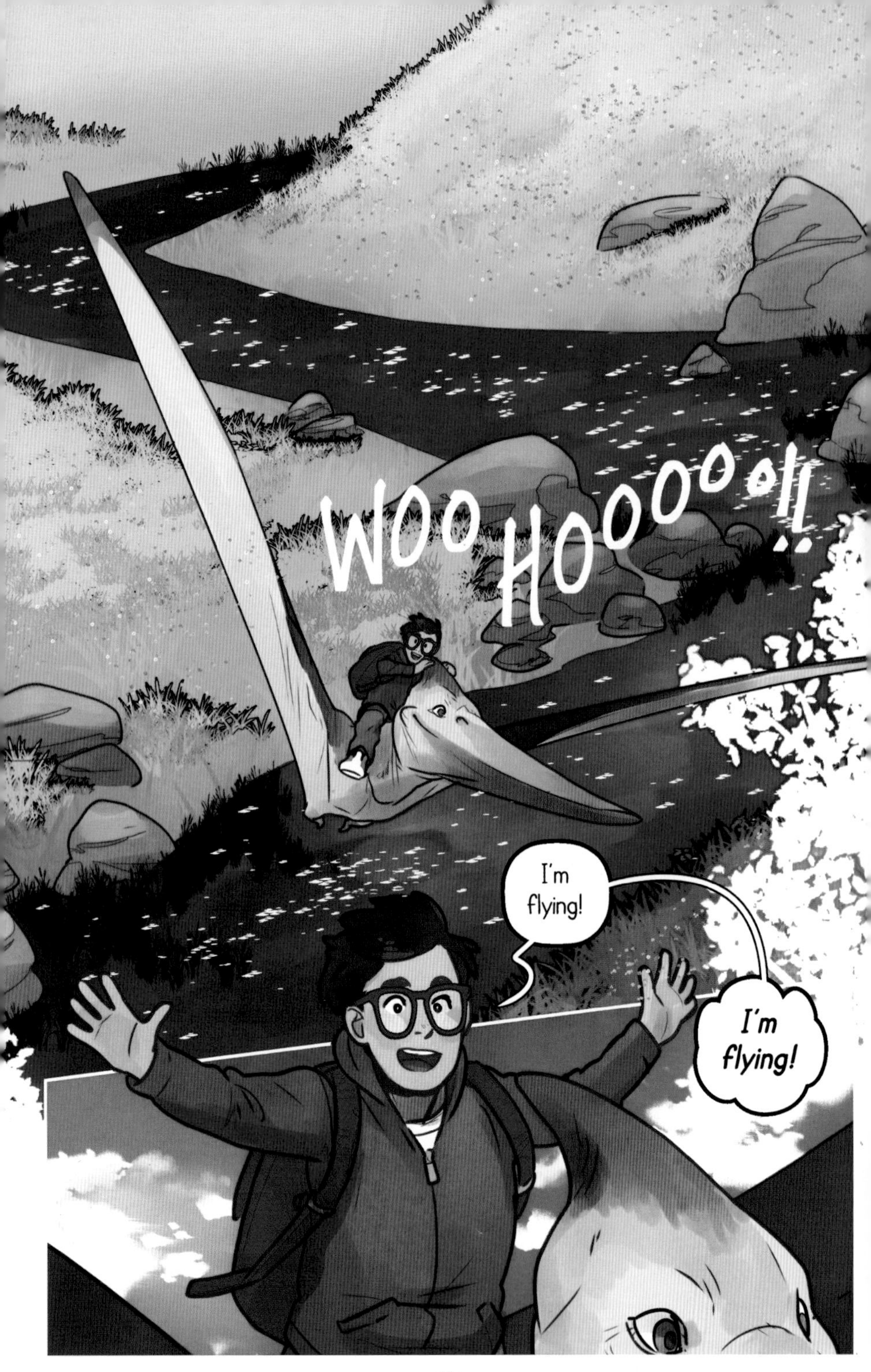
WOO HOOOOO!!
I'm flying!
I'm flying!

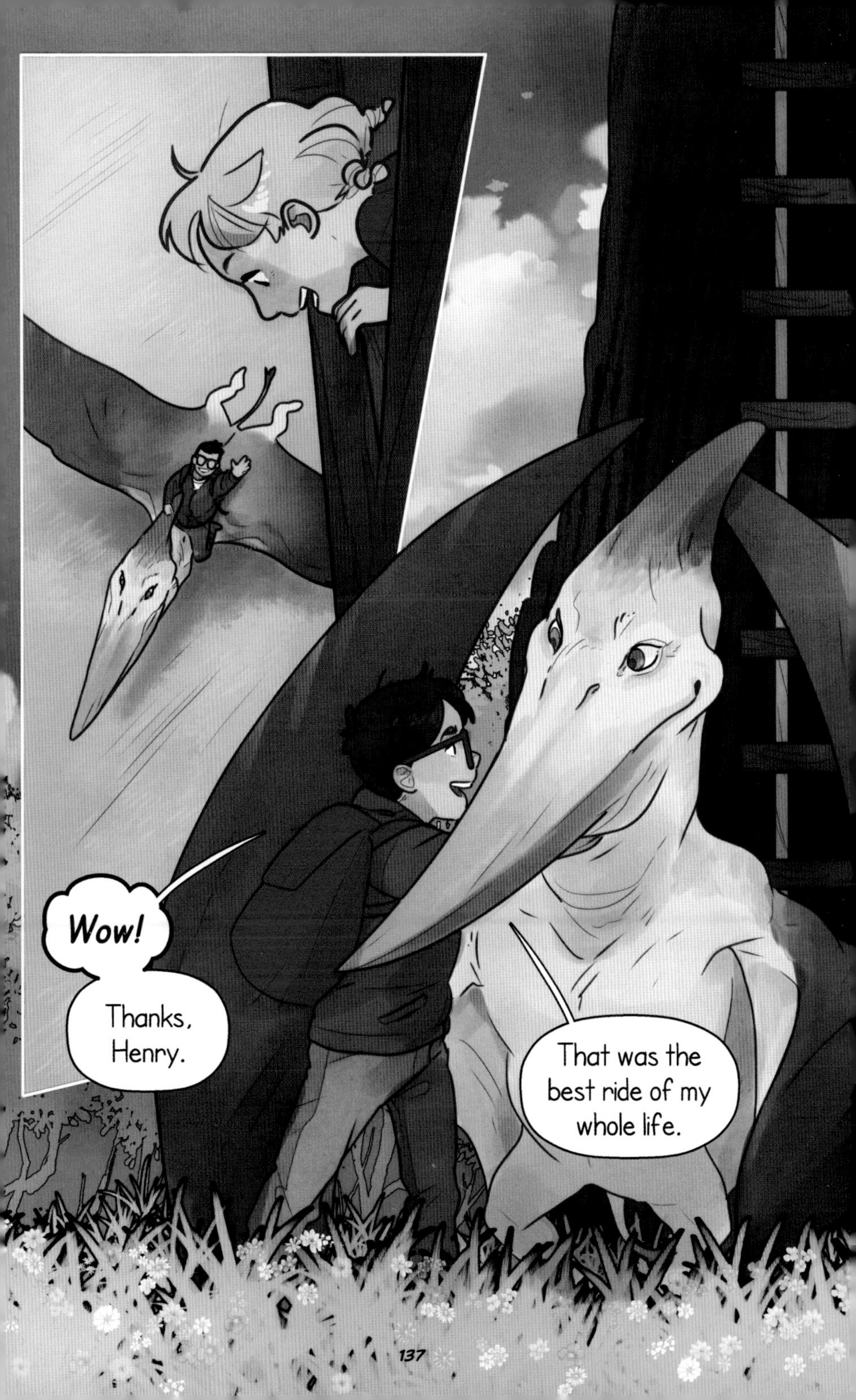
Wow!
Thanks, Henry.
That was the best ride of my whole life.

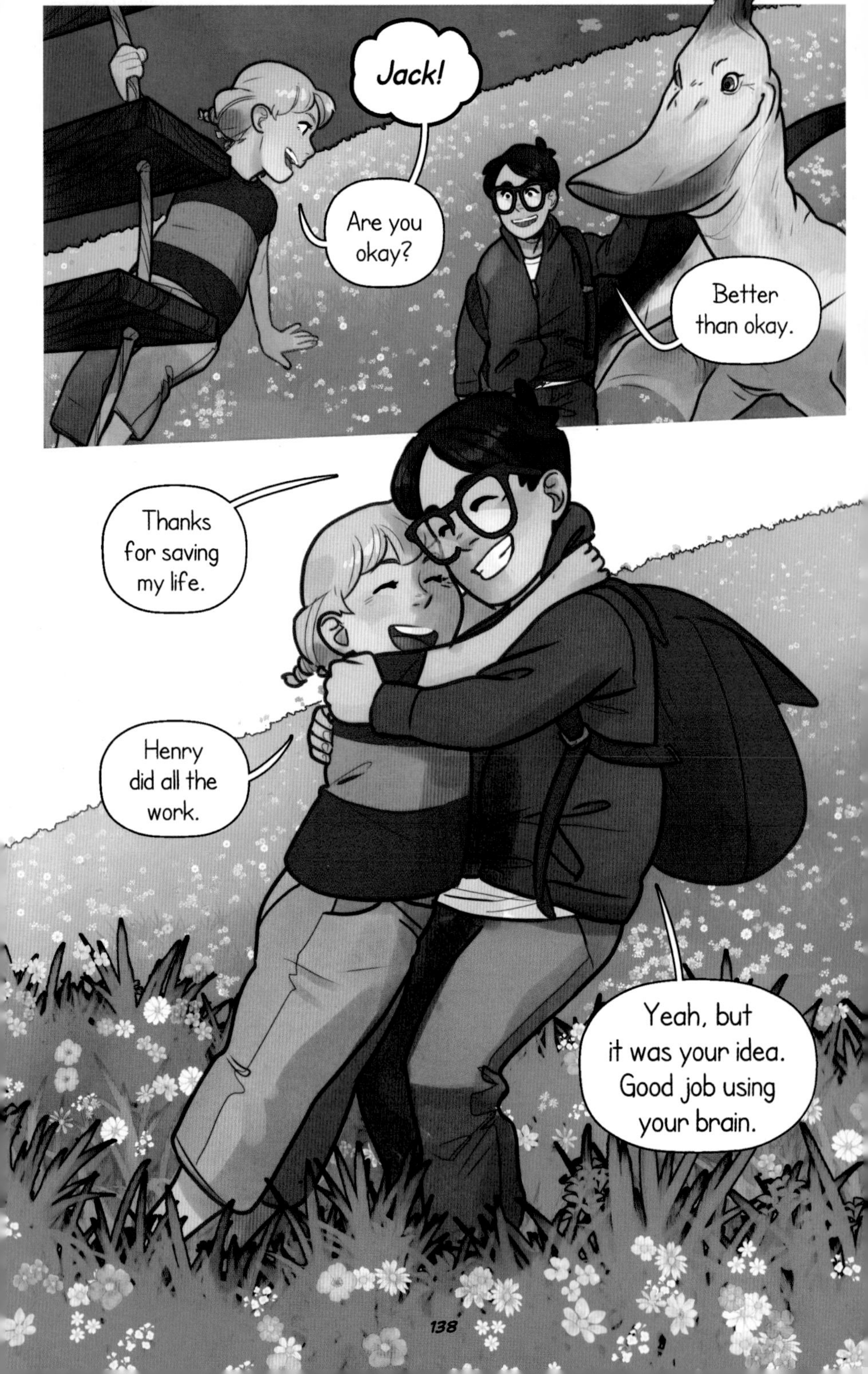
Jack!
Are you okay?
Better than okay.
Thanks for saving my life.
Henry did all the work.
Yeah, but it was your idea. Good job using your brain.

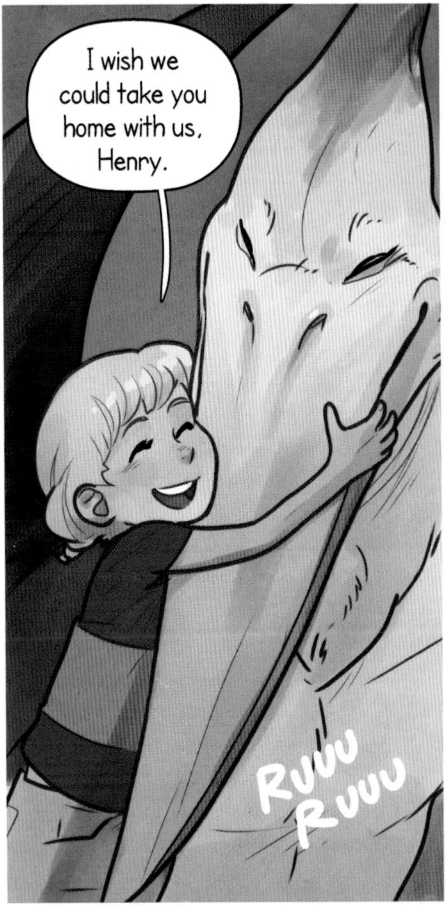
I wish we could take you home with us, Henry.
RUUU RUUU

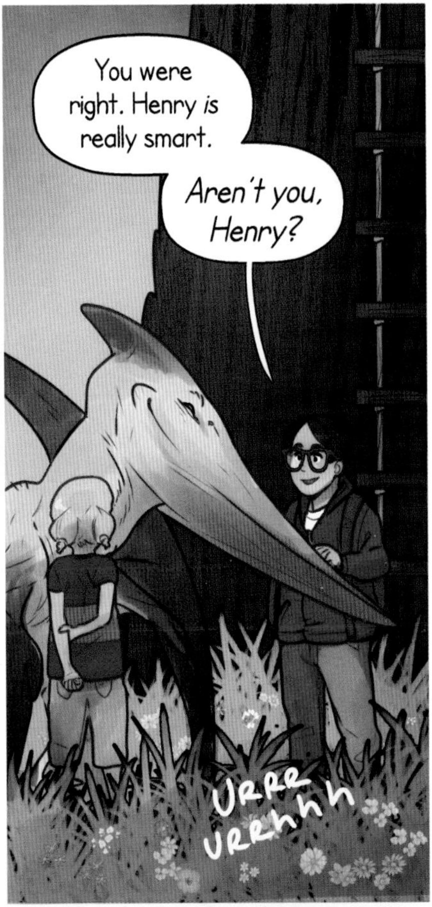
You were right. Henry *is* really smart.
Aren't you, Henry?
URRR URRhhh

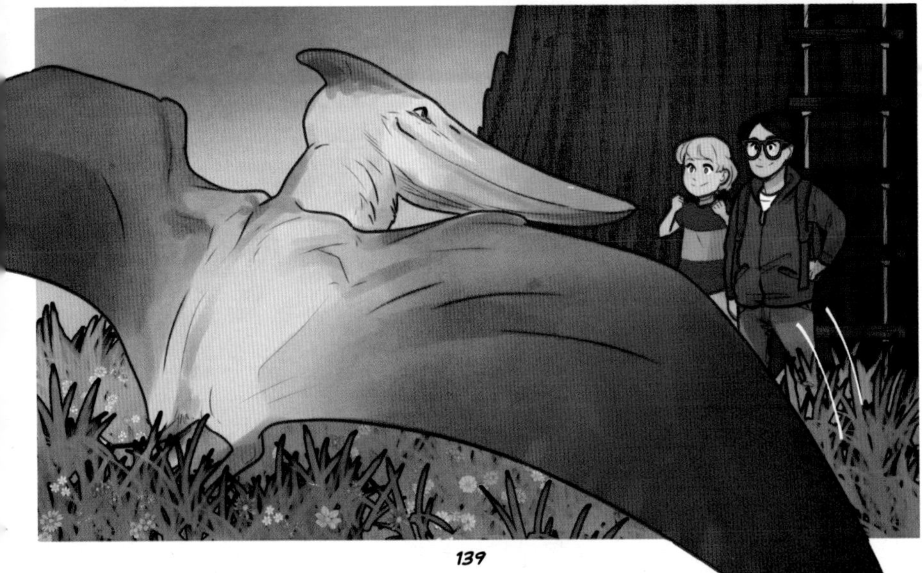

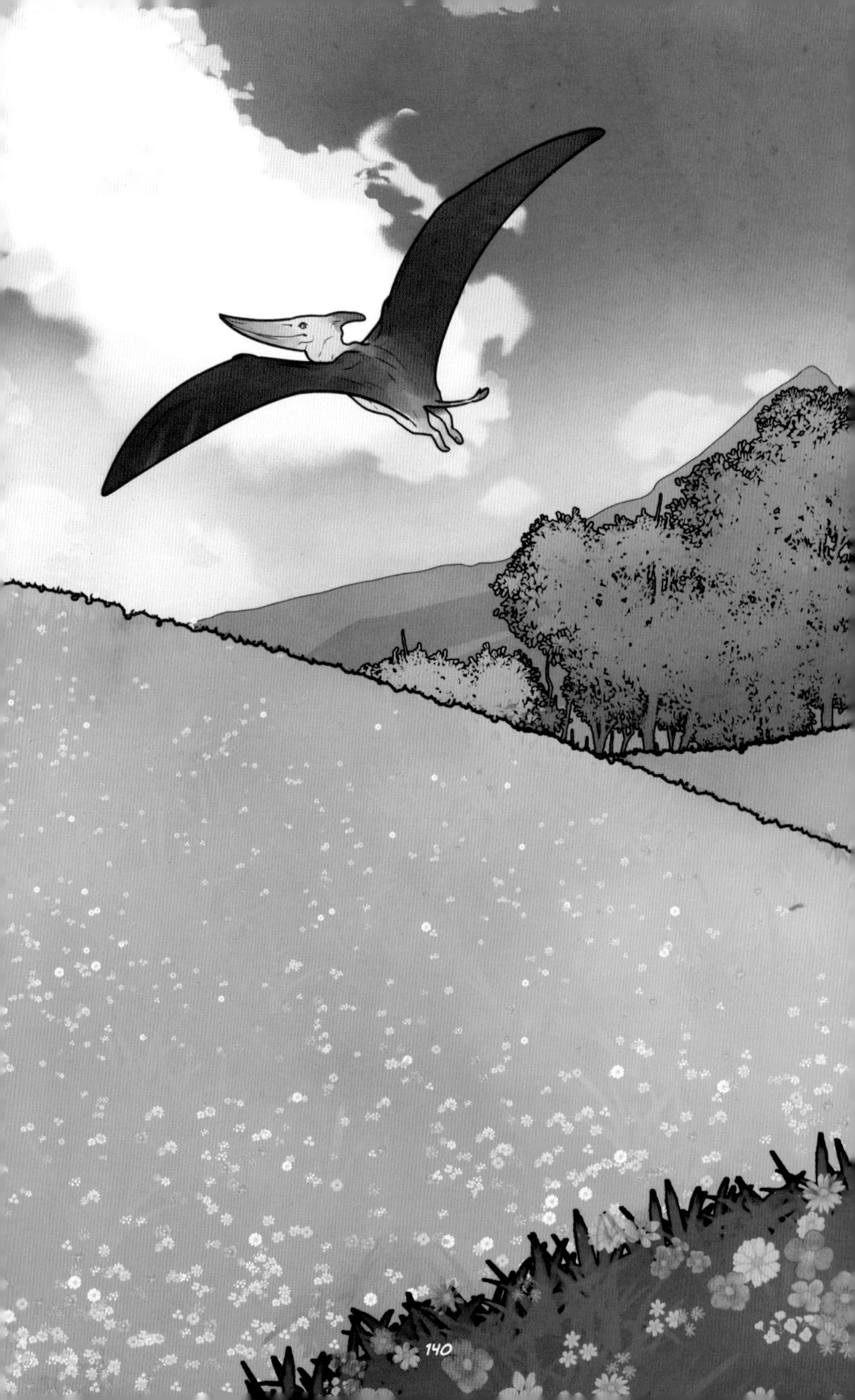

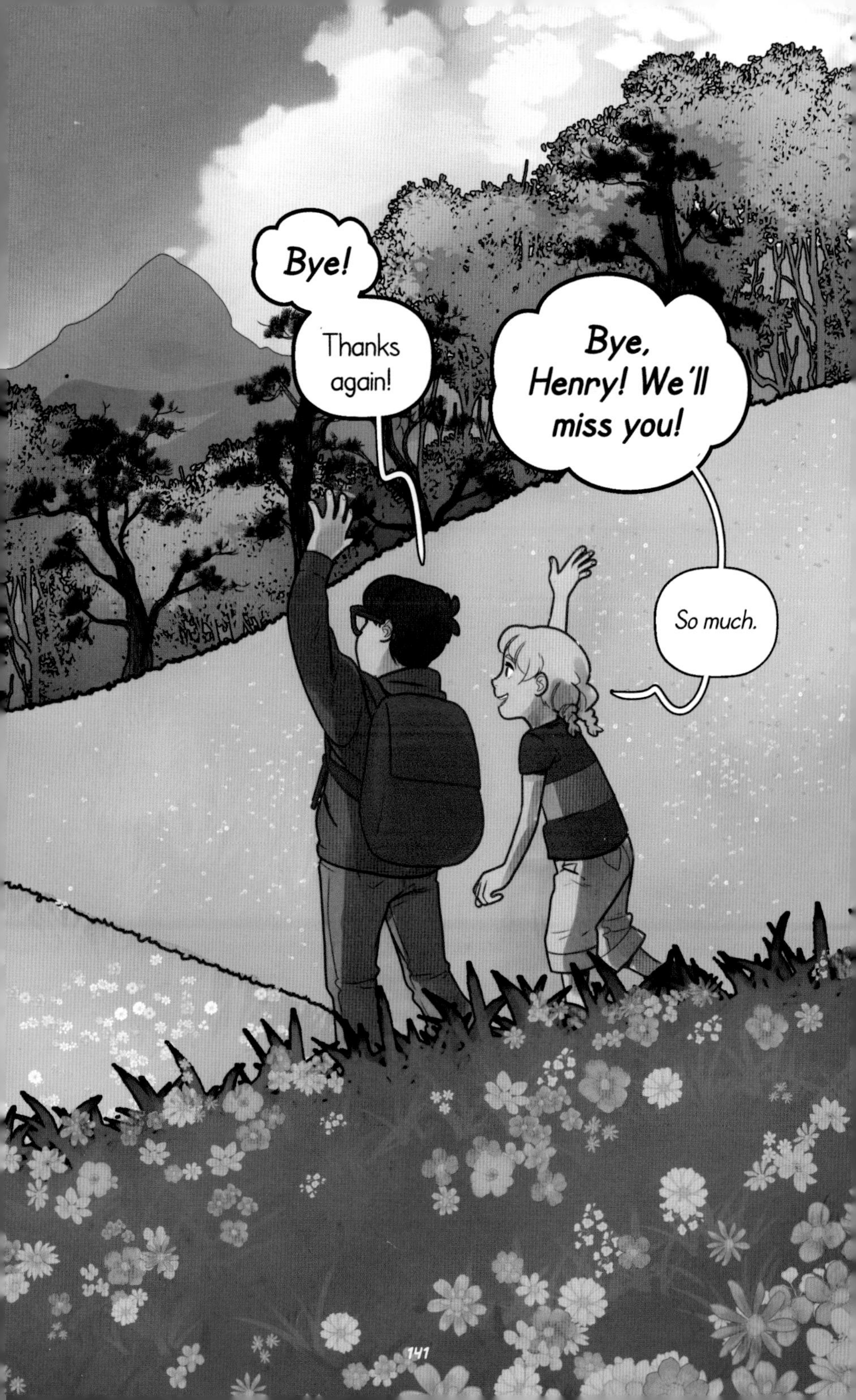
Bye!
Thanks again!
Bye, Henry! We'll miss you!
So much.

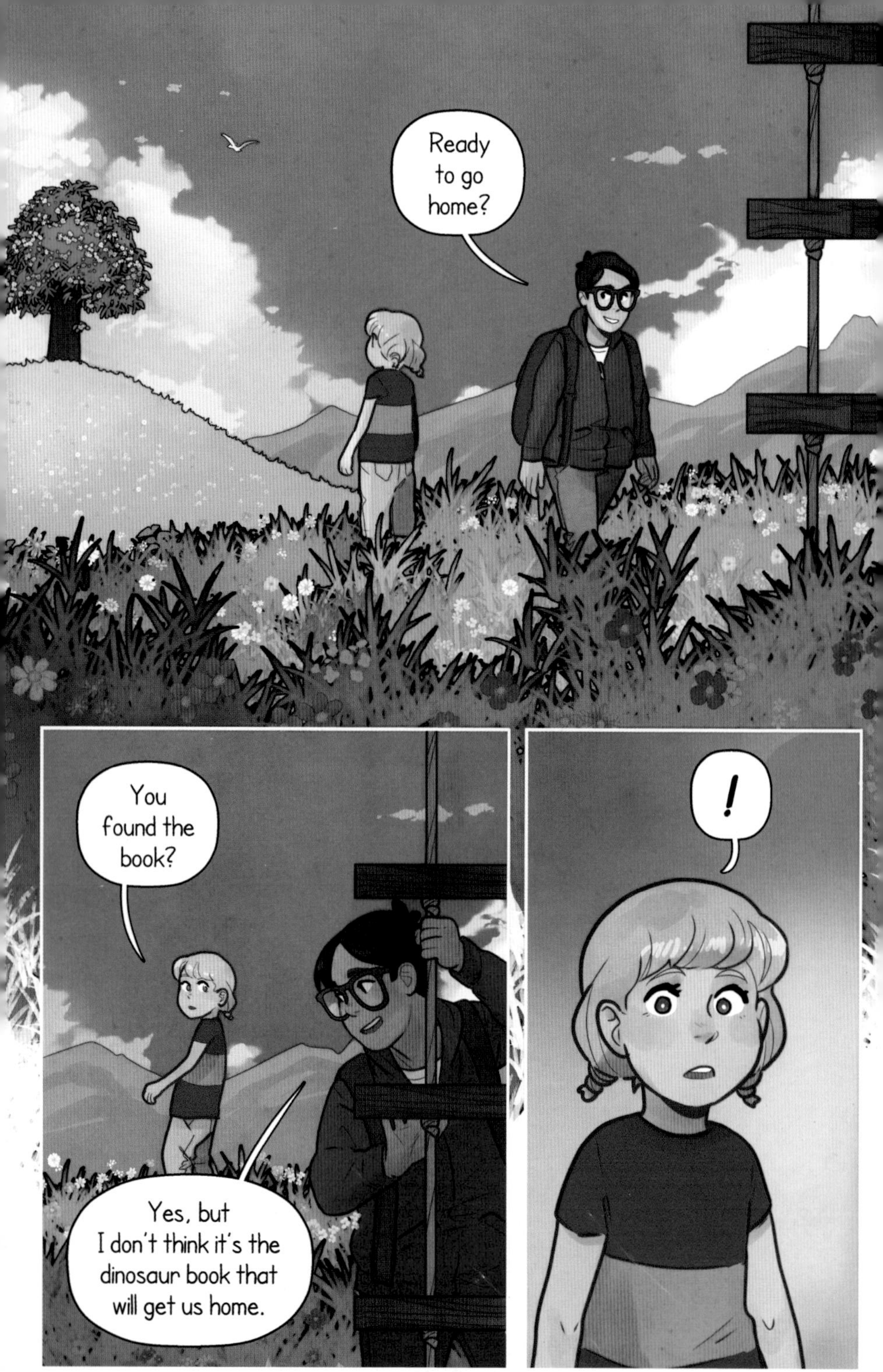
Ready to go home?
You found the book?
Yes, but I don't think it's the dinosaur book that will get us home.
!

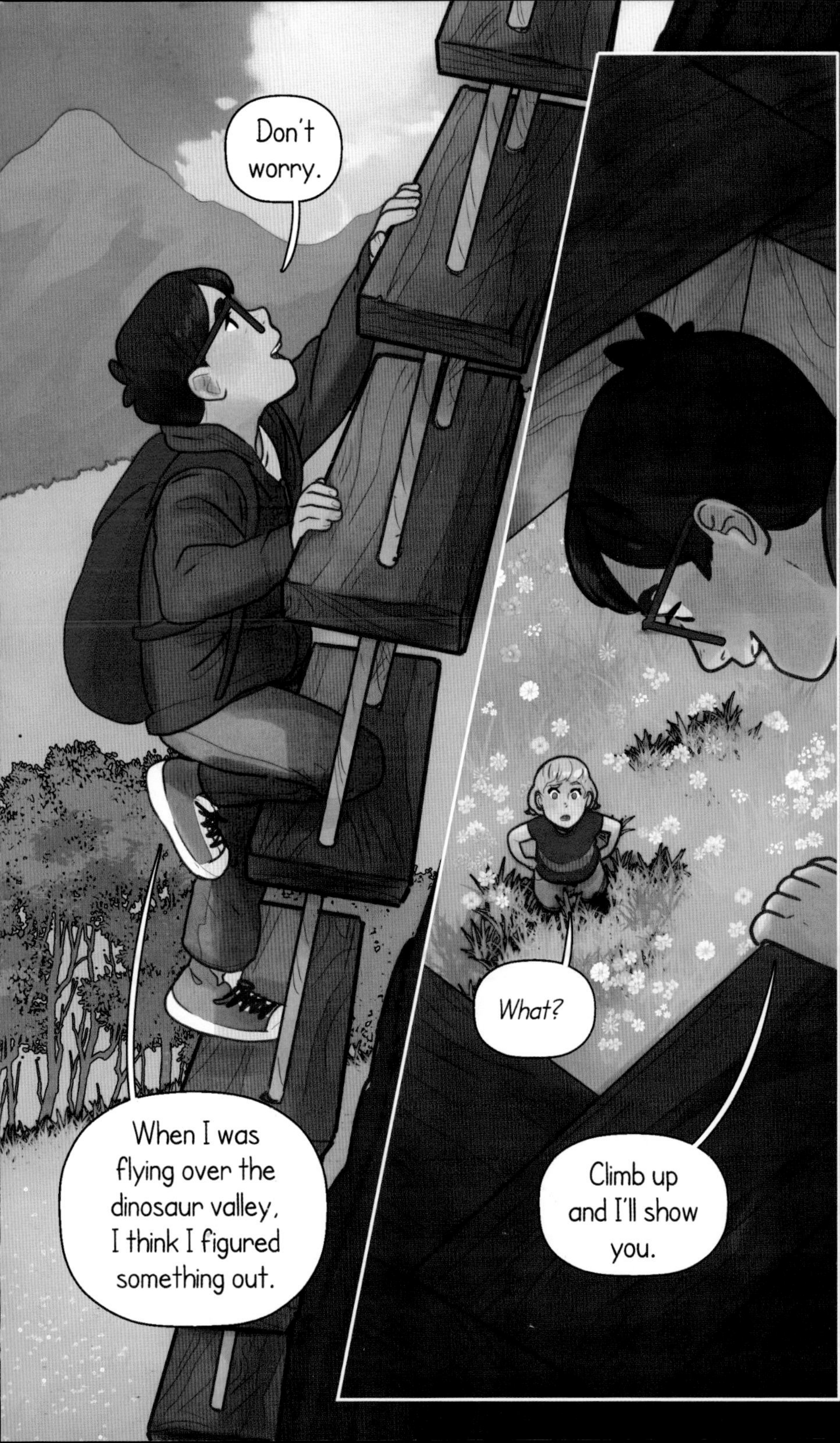
Don't worry.
When I was flying over the dinosaur valley, I think I figured something out.
What?
Climb up and I'll show you.

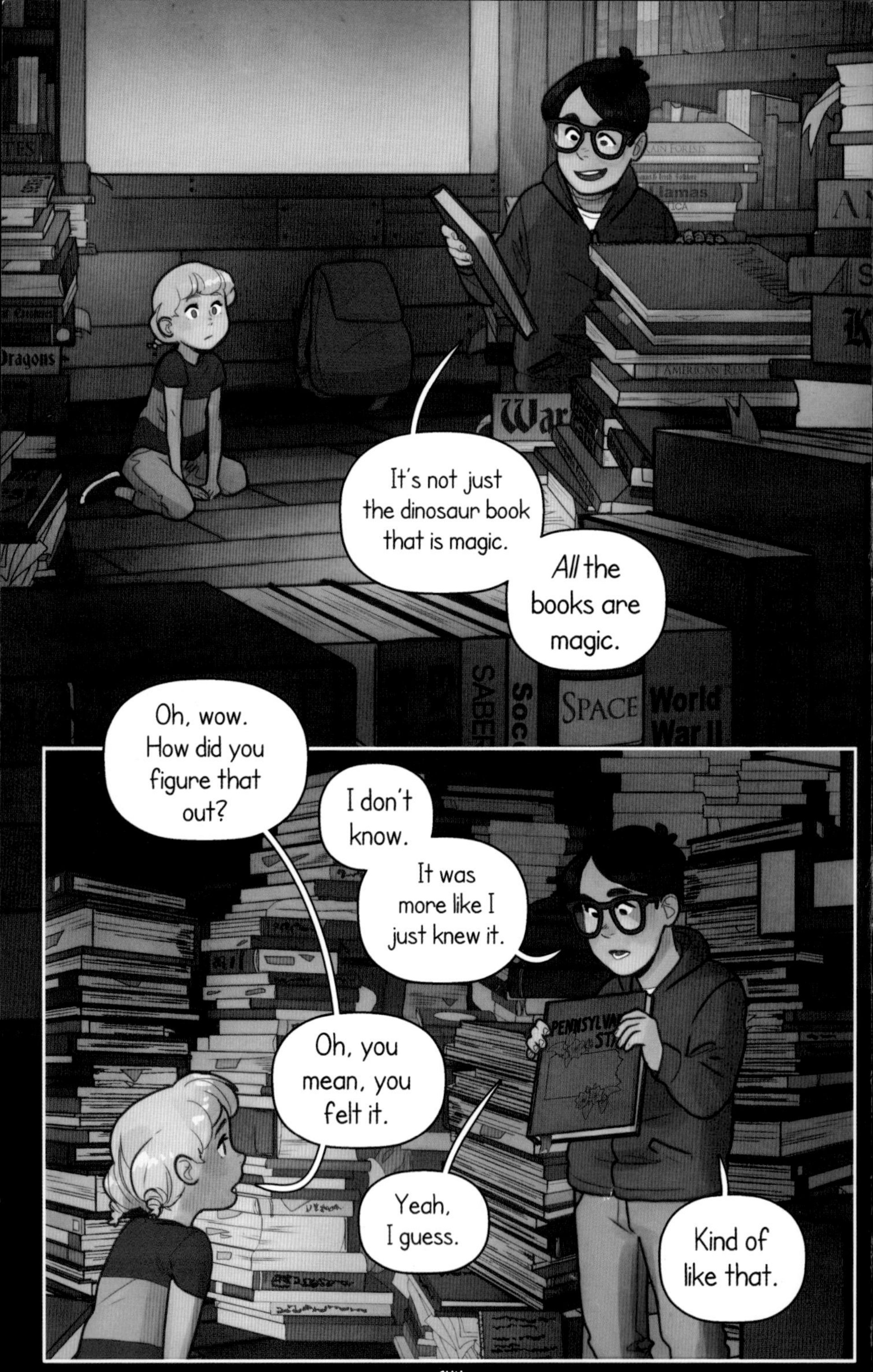
It's not just the dinosaur book that is magic.
All the books are magic.
Oh, wow. How did you figure that out?
I don't know.
It was more like I just knew it.
Oh, you mean, you felt it.
Yeah, I guess.
Kind of like that.

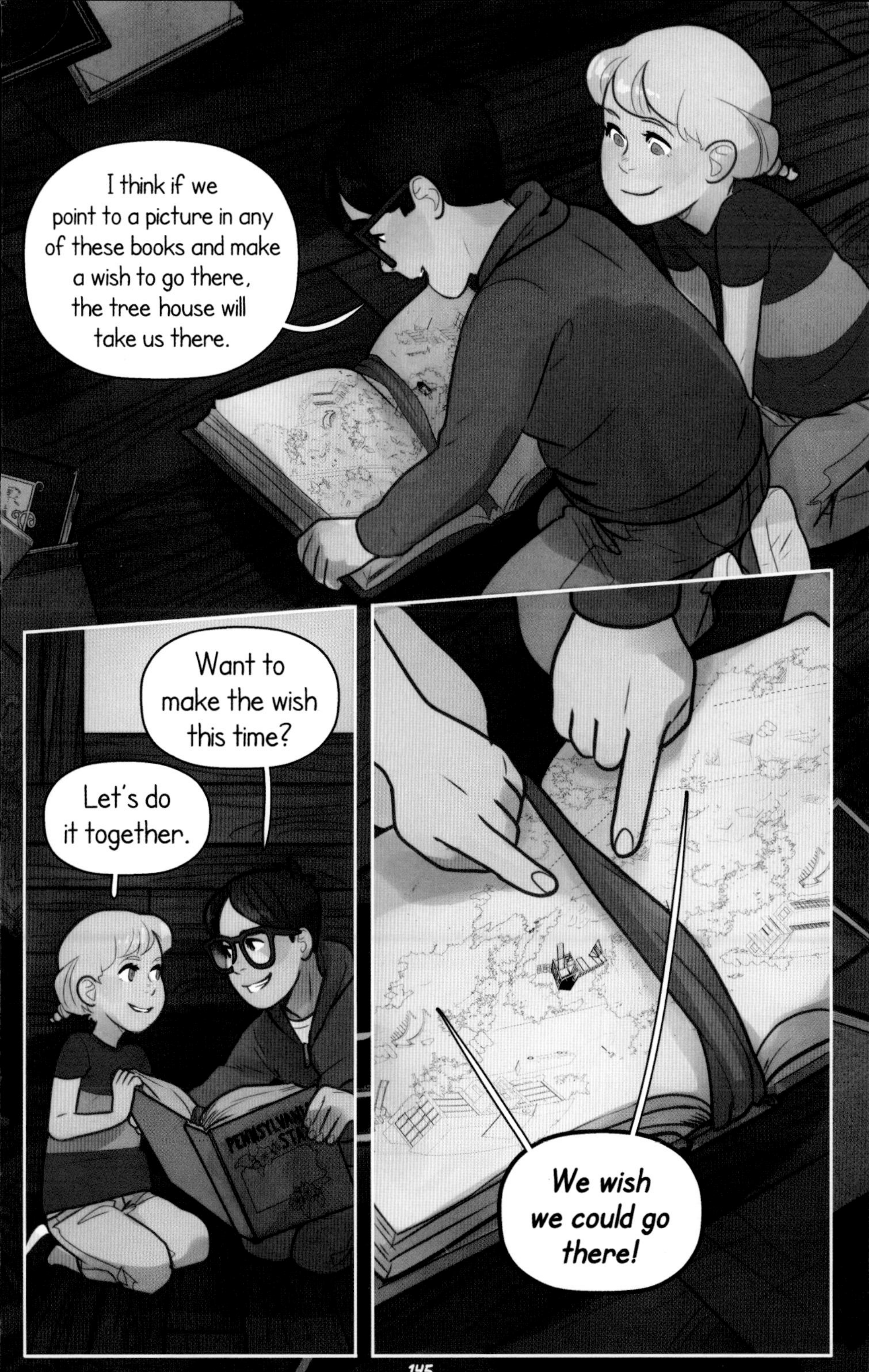
I think if we point to a picture in any of these books and make a wish to go there, the tree house will take us there.
Want to make the wish this time?
Let's do it together.
We wish we could go there!

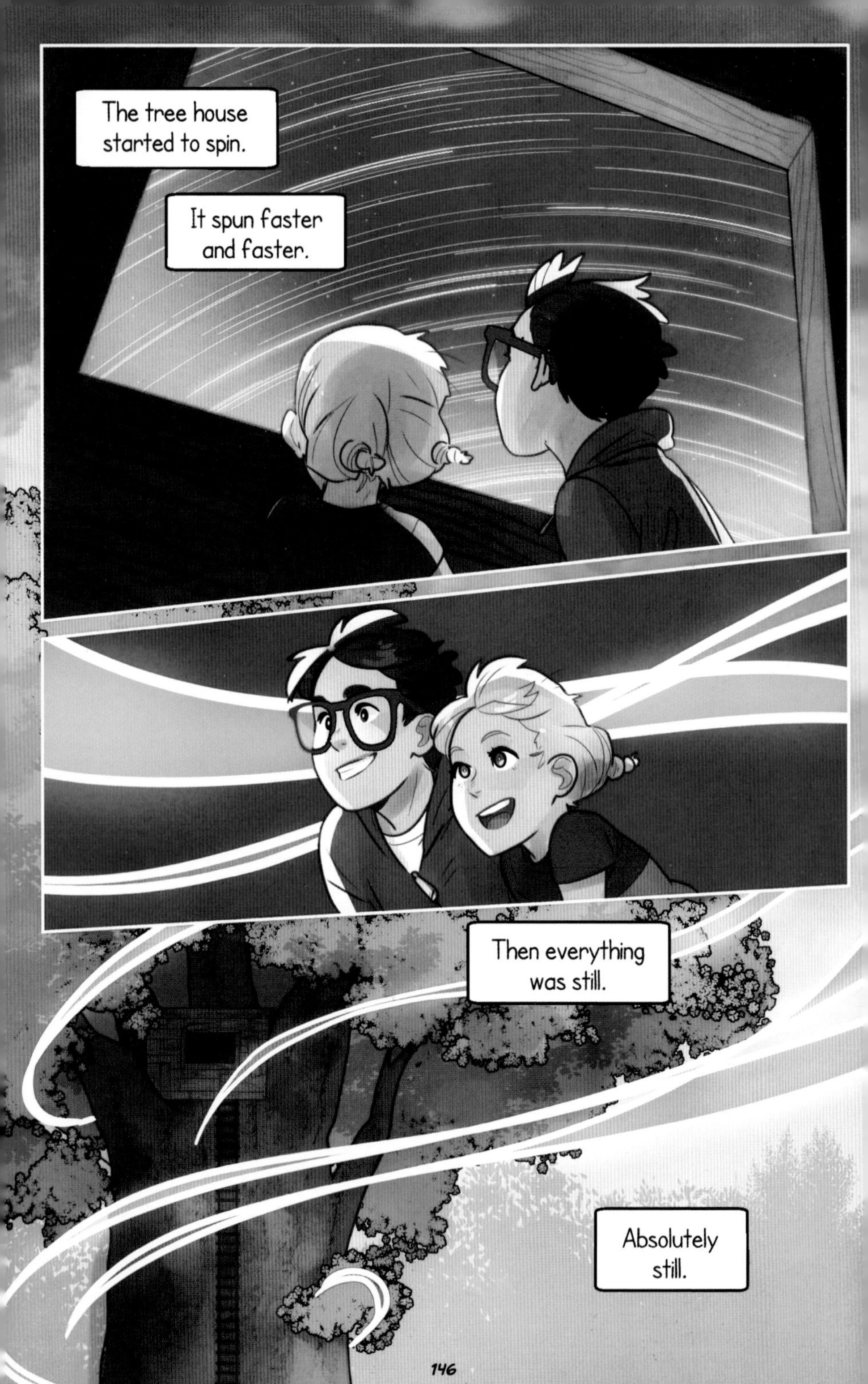
The tree house started to spin.
It spun faster and faster.
Then everything was still.
Absolutely still.

CHAPTER TEN

Home Before Dark

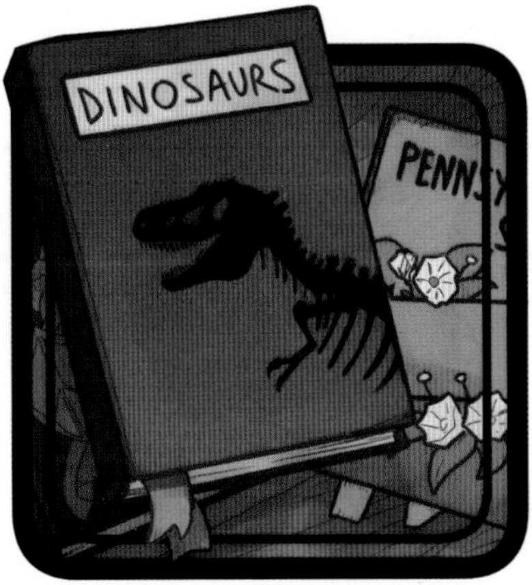
DINOSAURS
PENN

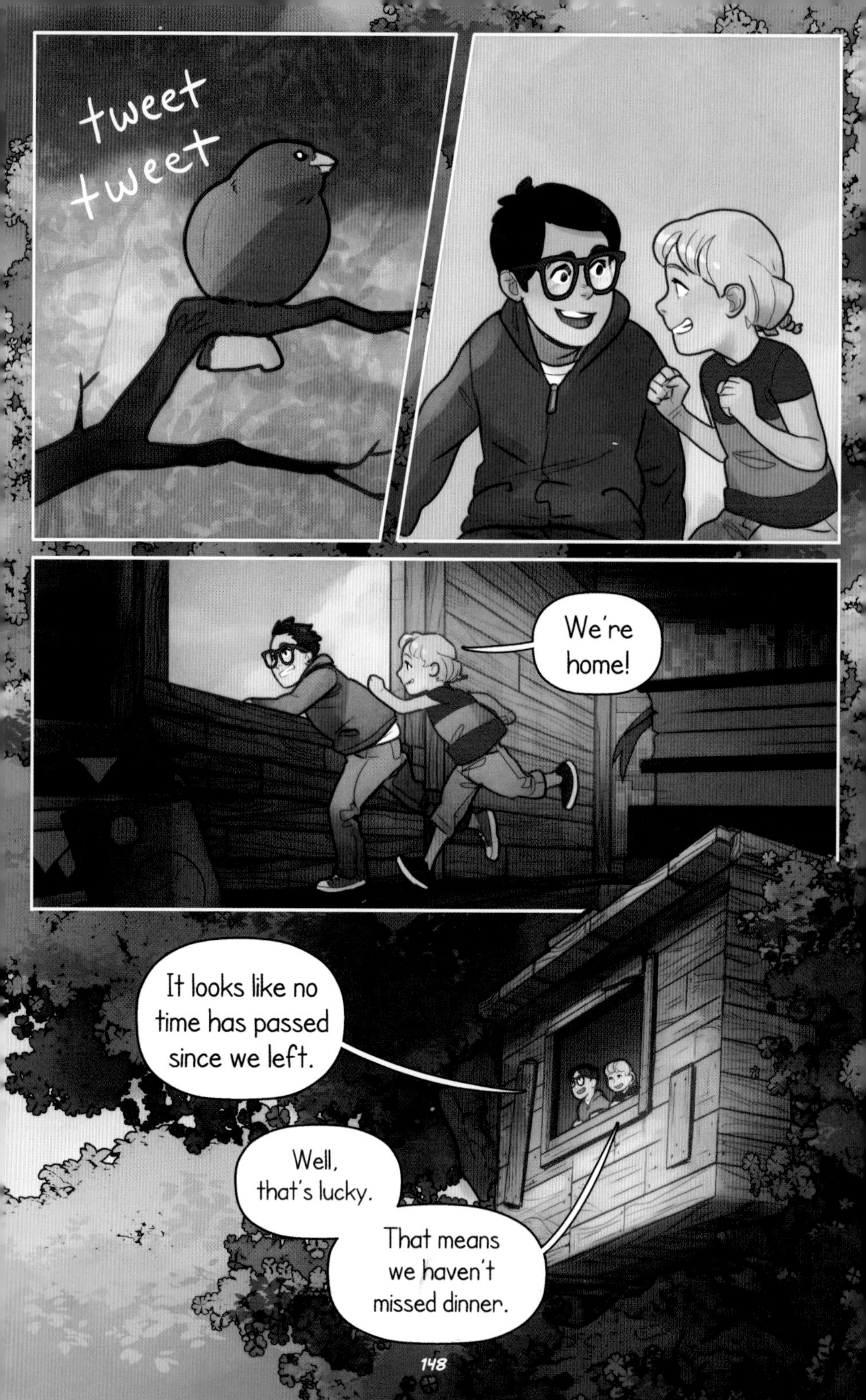
tweet
tweet
We're home!
It looks like no time has passed since we left.
Well, that's lucky.
That means we haven't missed dinner.

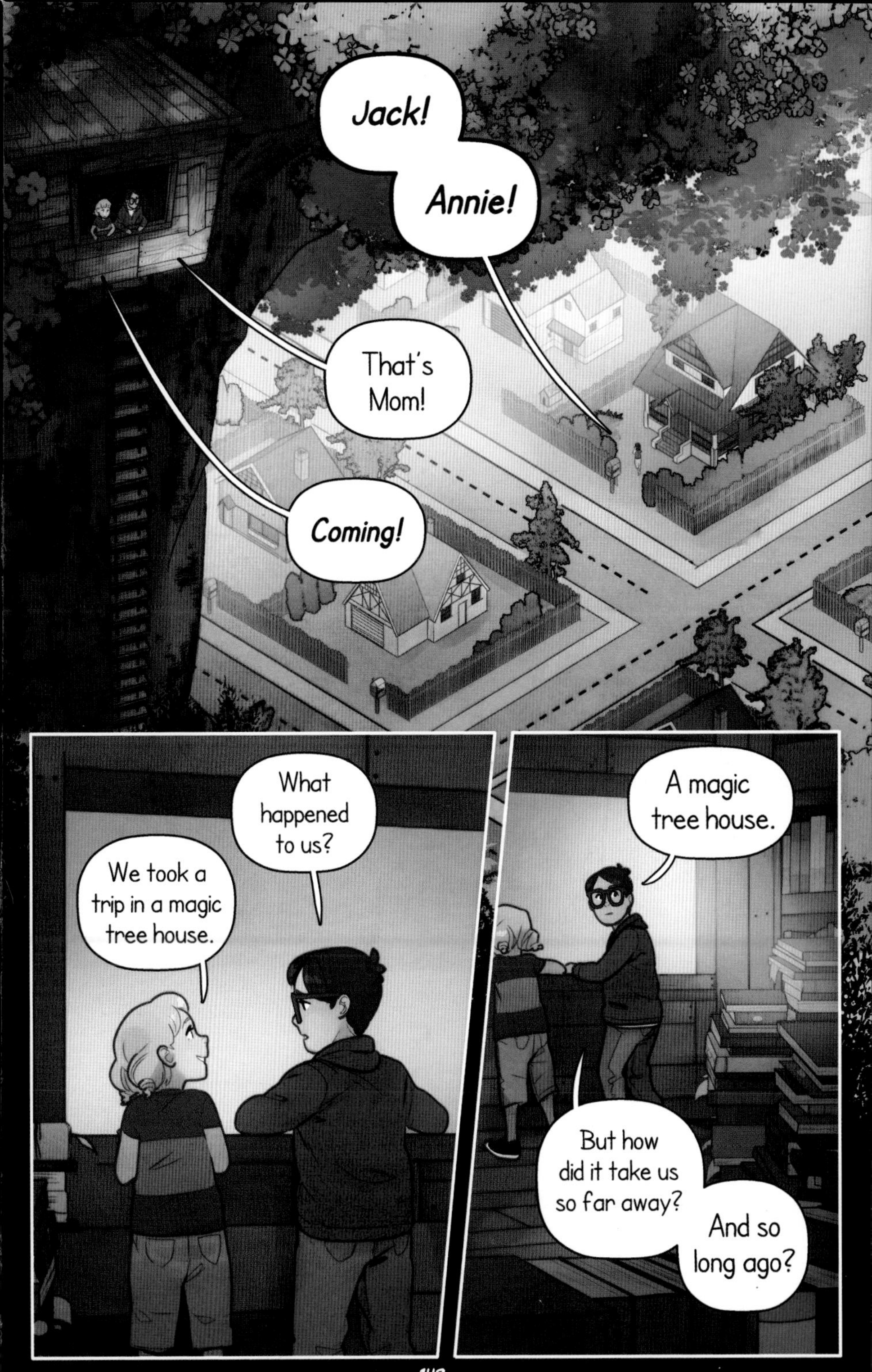
Jack!
Annie!
That's Mom!
Coming!
What happened to us?
We took a trip in a magic tree house.
A magic tree house.
But how did it take us so far away?
And so long ago?

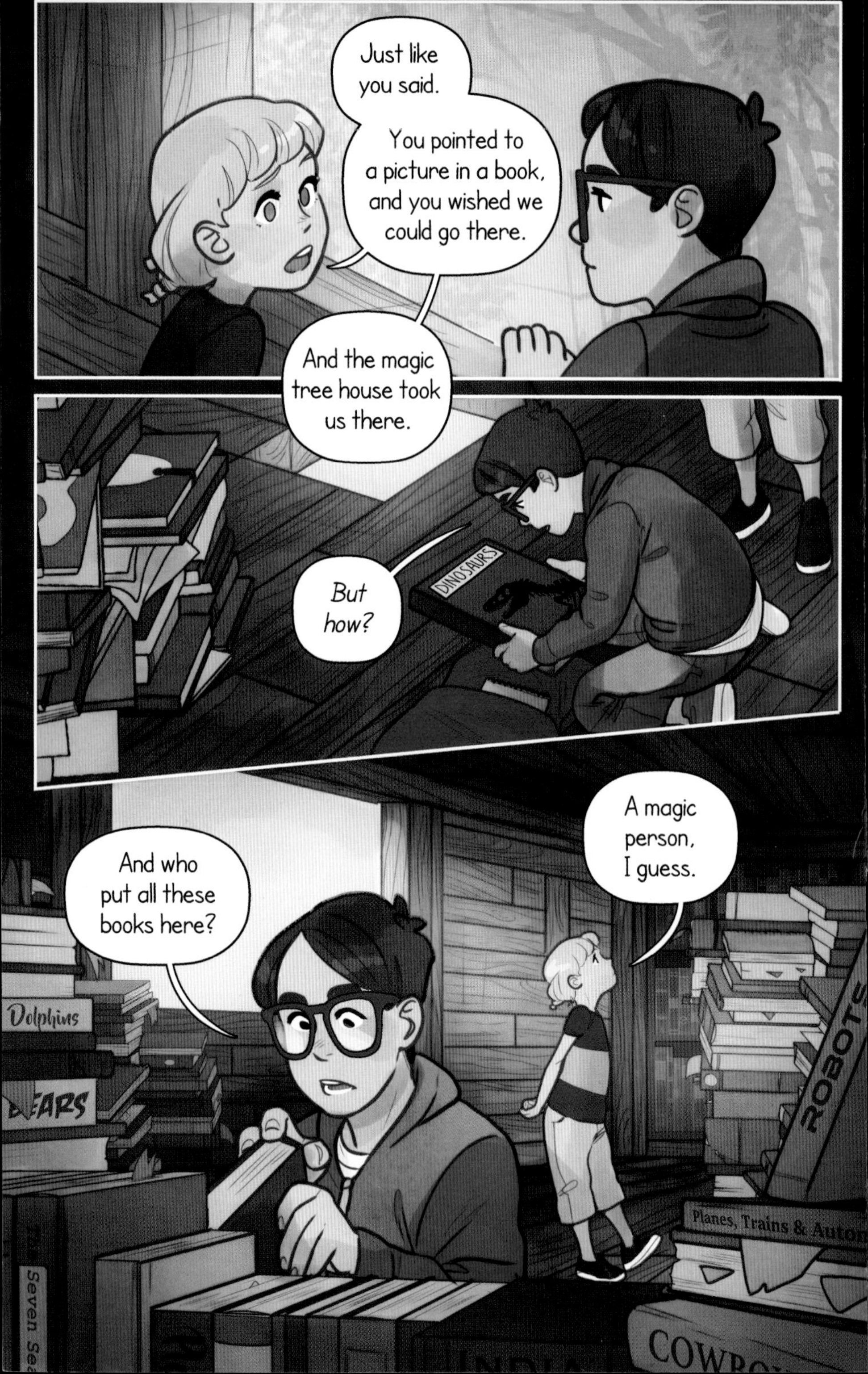
Just like you said.
You pointed to a picture in a book, and you wished we could go there.
And the magic tree house took us there.
DINOSAURS
But how?
And who put all these books here?
A magic person, I guess.
Dolphins
ROBOTS

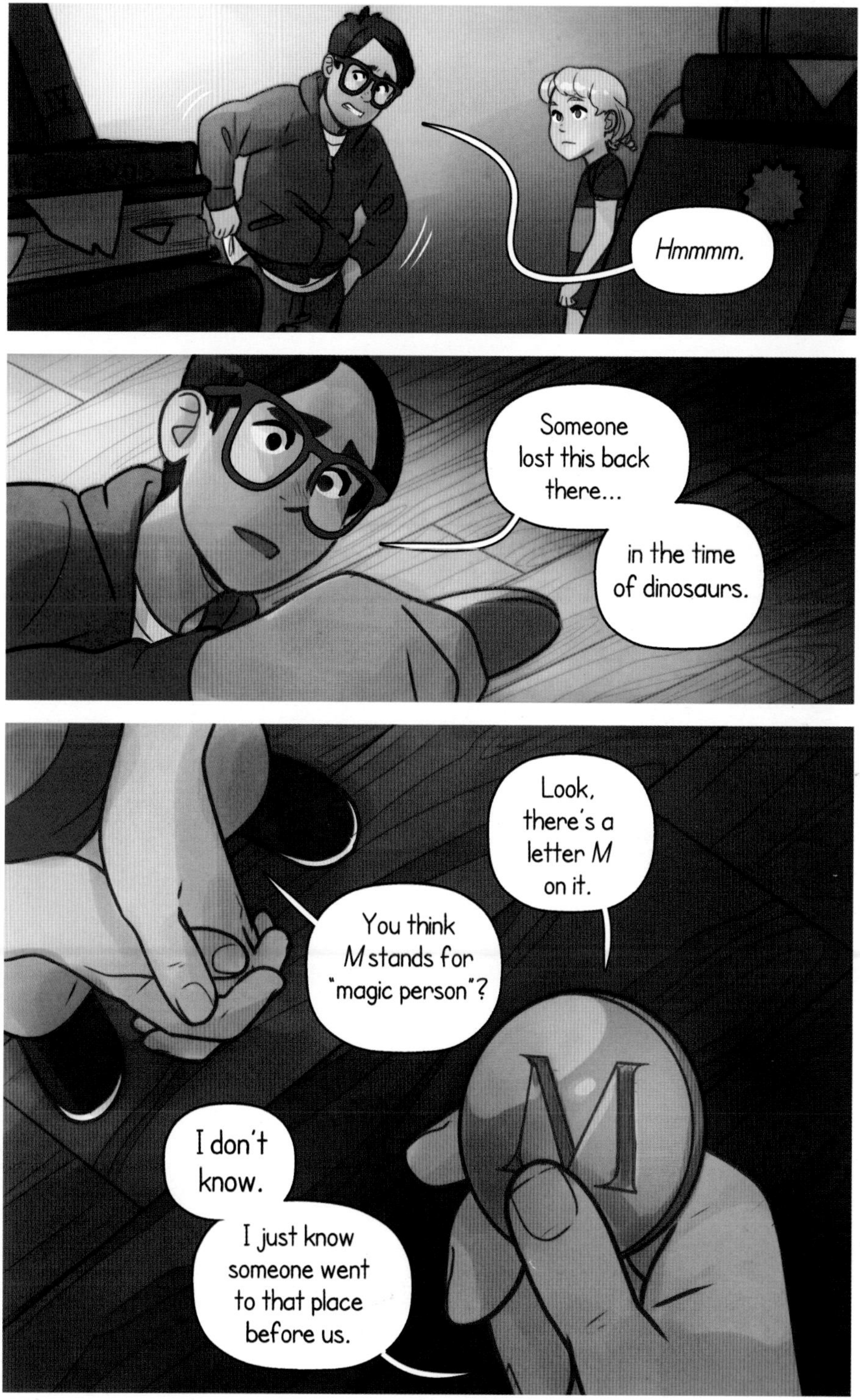
Hmmmm.
Someone lost this back there...
in the time of dinosaurs.
Look, there's a letter M on it.
You think M stands for "magic person"?
M
I don't know.
I just know someone went to that place before us.

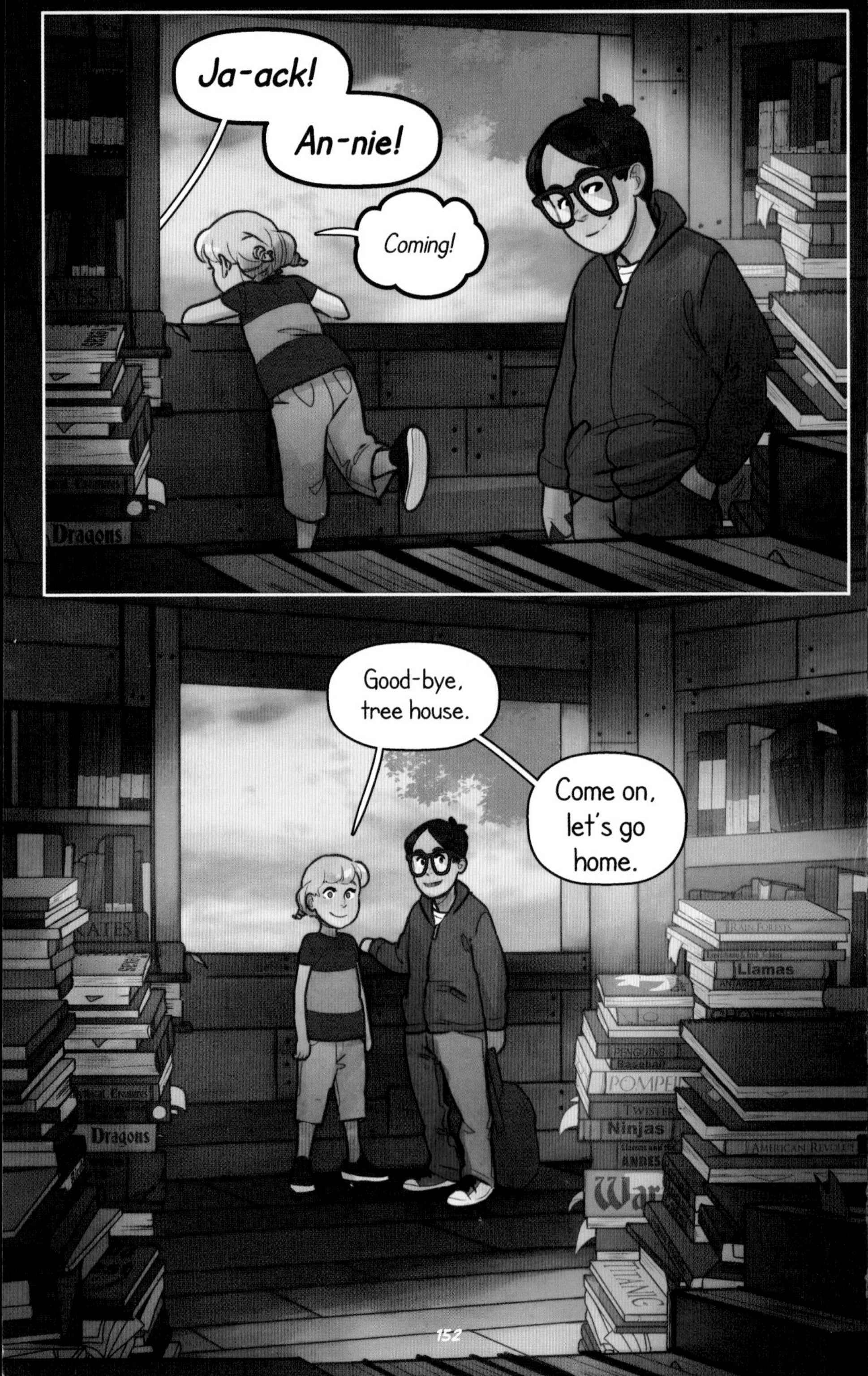
Ja-ack!
An-nie!
Coming!
Dragons
Good-bye, tree house.
Come on, let's go home.
Llamas
Ninjas
Dragons

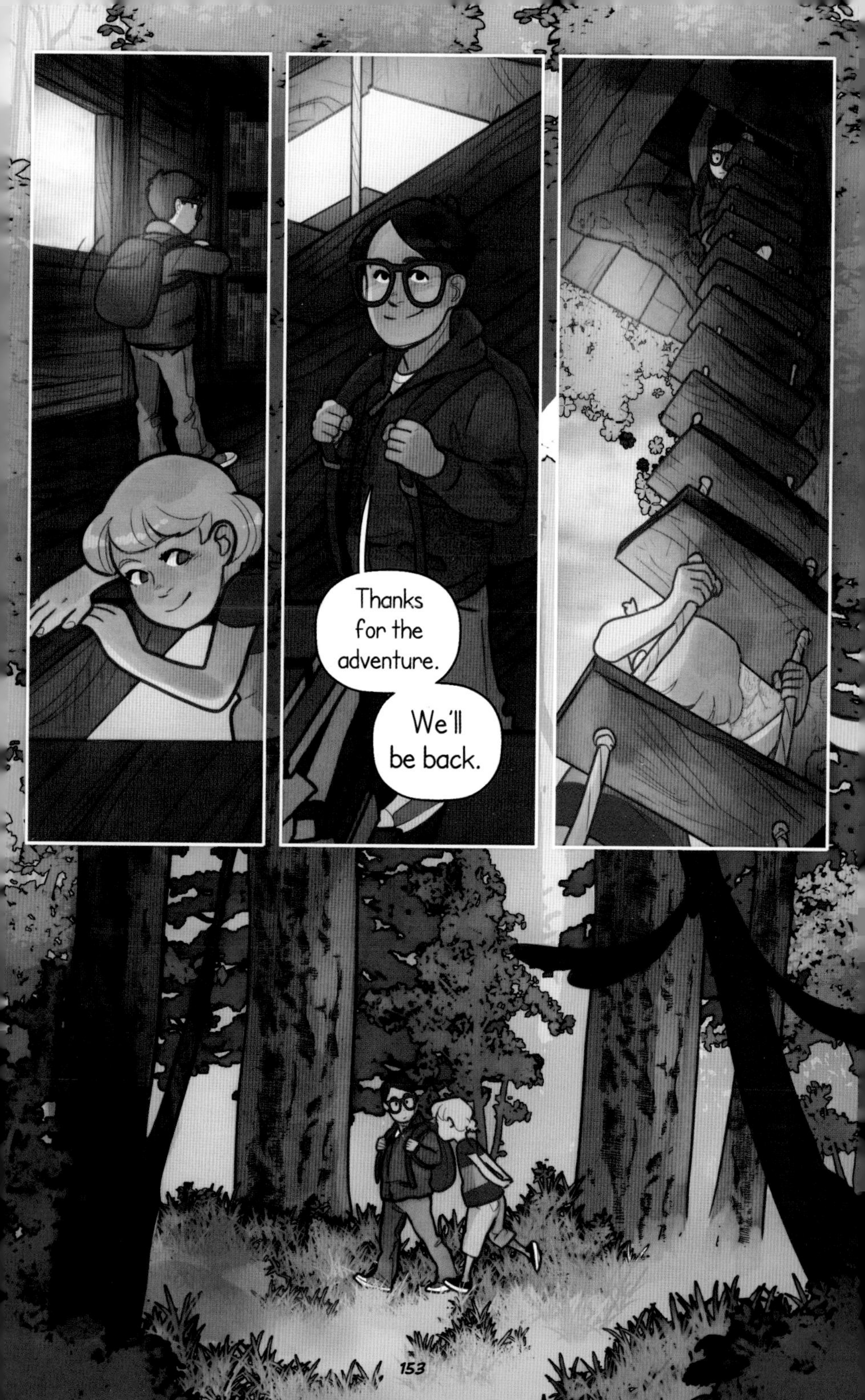
Thanks for the adventure.
We'll be back.

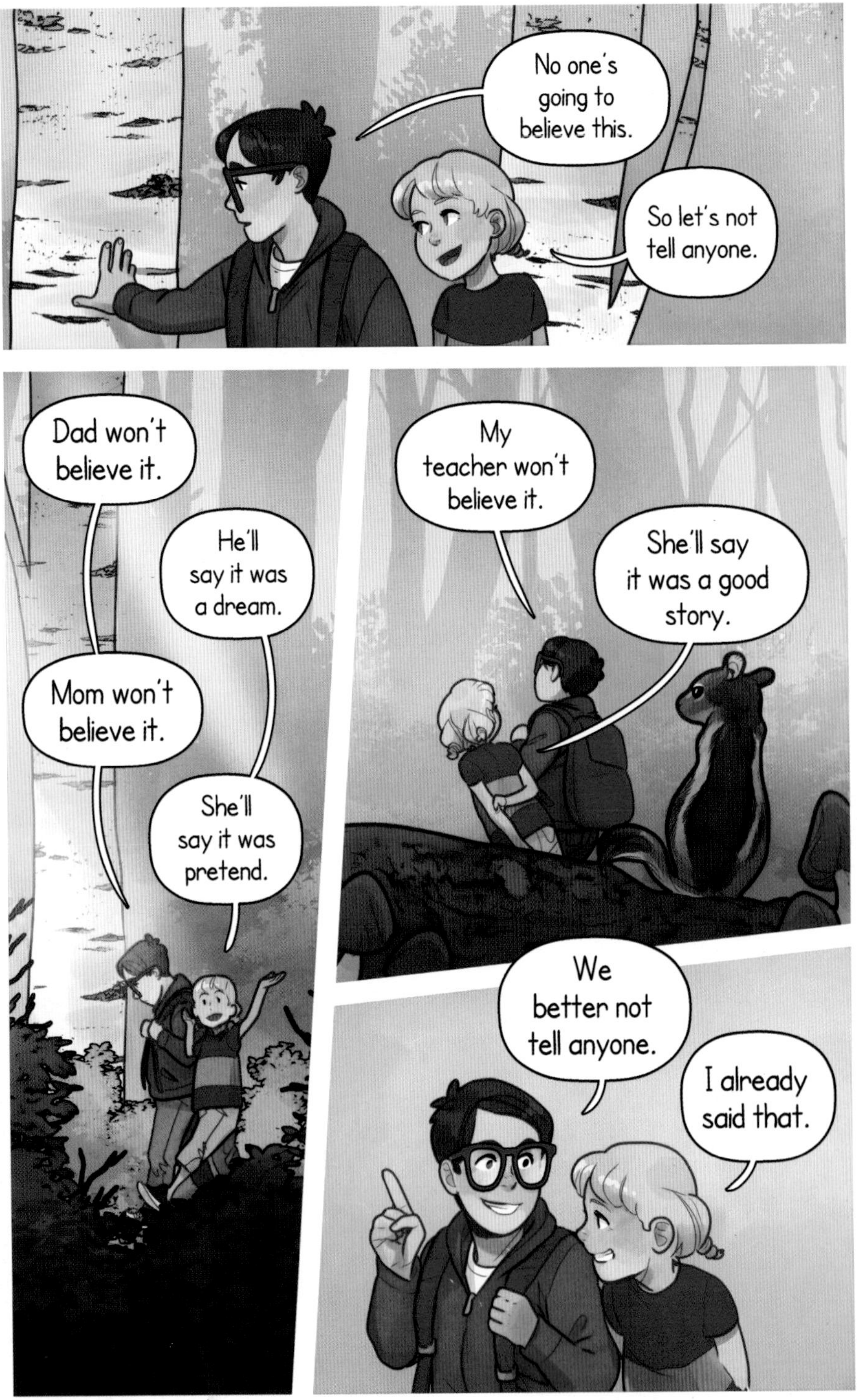
No one's going to believe this.
So let's not tell anyone.
Dad won't believe it.
He'll say it was a dream.
Mom won't believe it.
She'll say it was pretend.
My teacher won't believe it.
She'll say it was a good story.
We better not tell anyone.
I already said that.

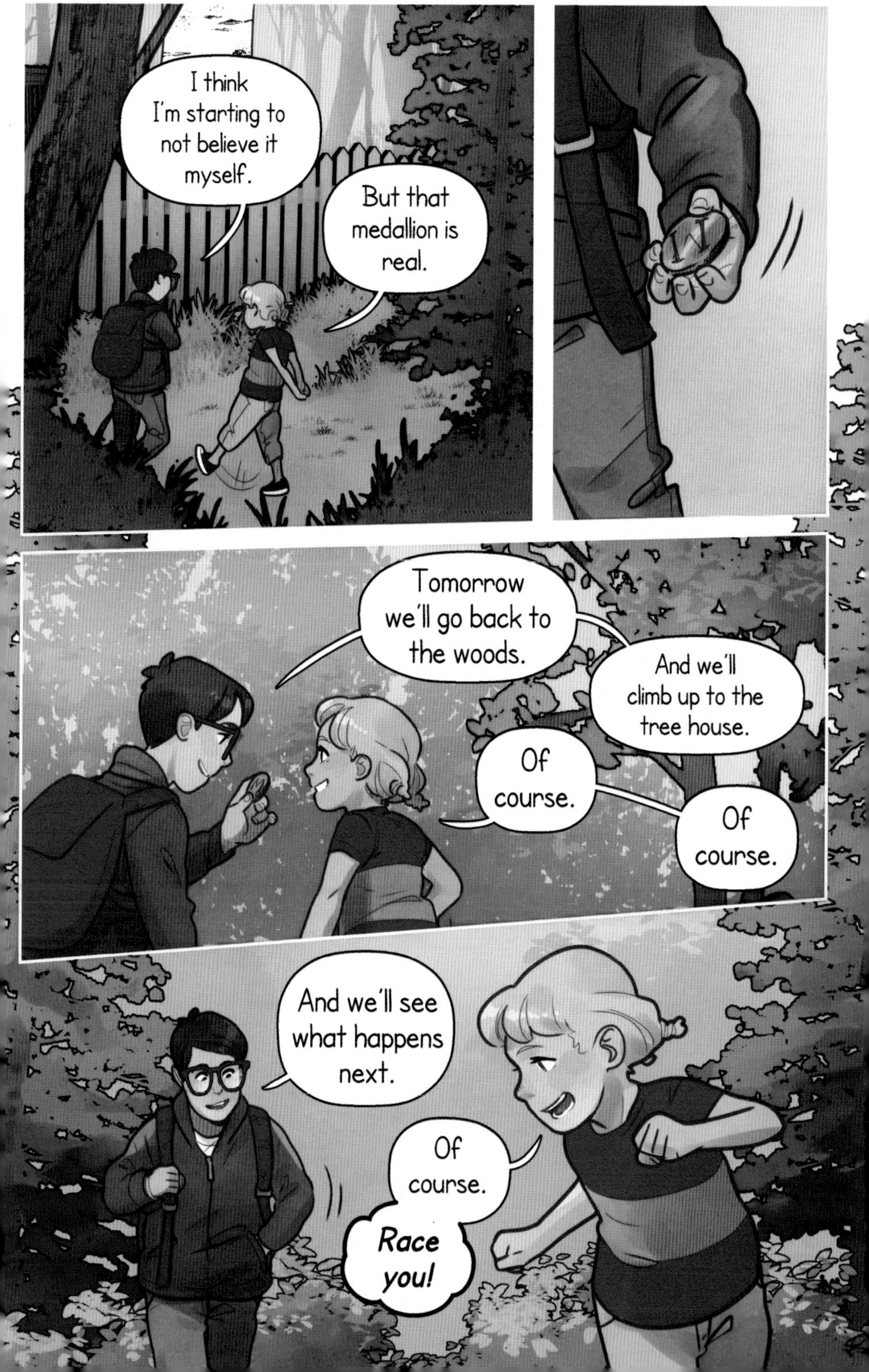
I think I'm starting to not believe it myself.
But that medallion is real.
Tomorrow we'll go back to the woods.
And we'll climb up to the tree house.
Of course.
Of course.
And we'll see what happens next.
Of course.
Race you!

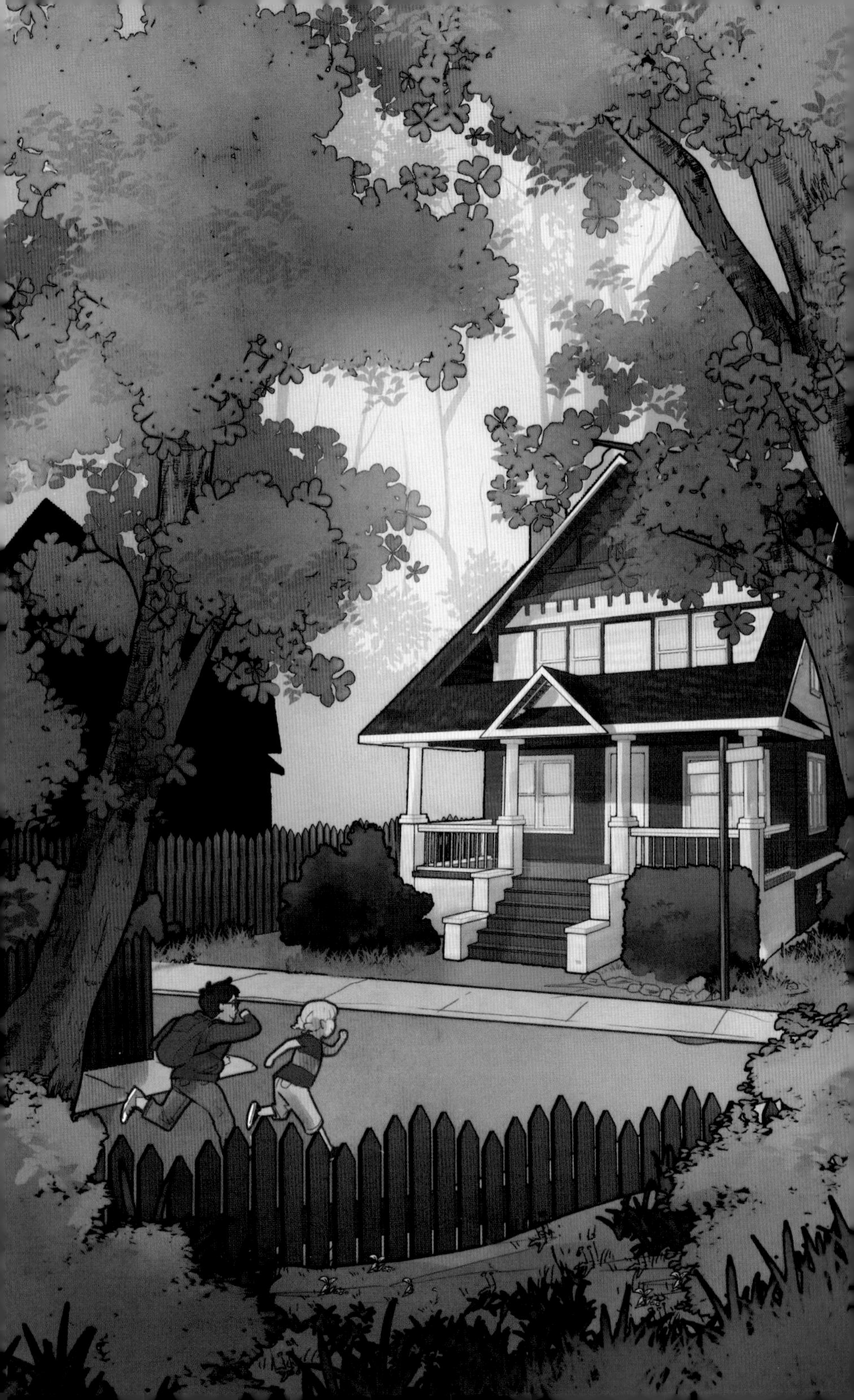

Don't miss the next adventure
in the magic tree house when Jack and Annie
are whisked away to the Middle Ages!

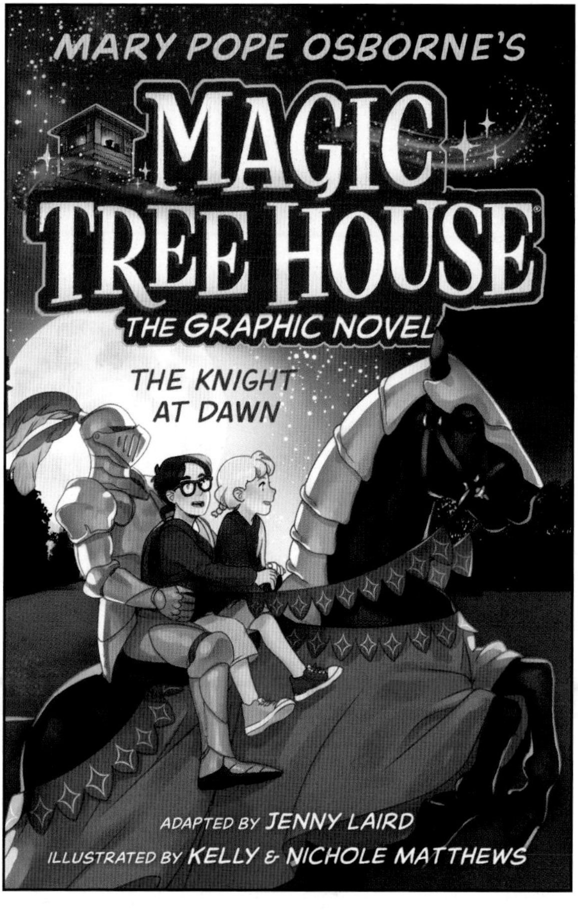
MARY POPE OSBORNE'S
MAGIC TREE HOUSE
THE GRAPHIC NOVEL
THE KNIGHT AT DAWN
ADAPTED BY JENNY LAIRD
ILLUSTRATED BY KELLY & NICHOLE MATTHEWS

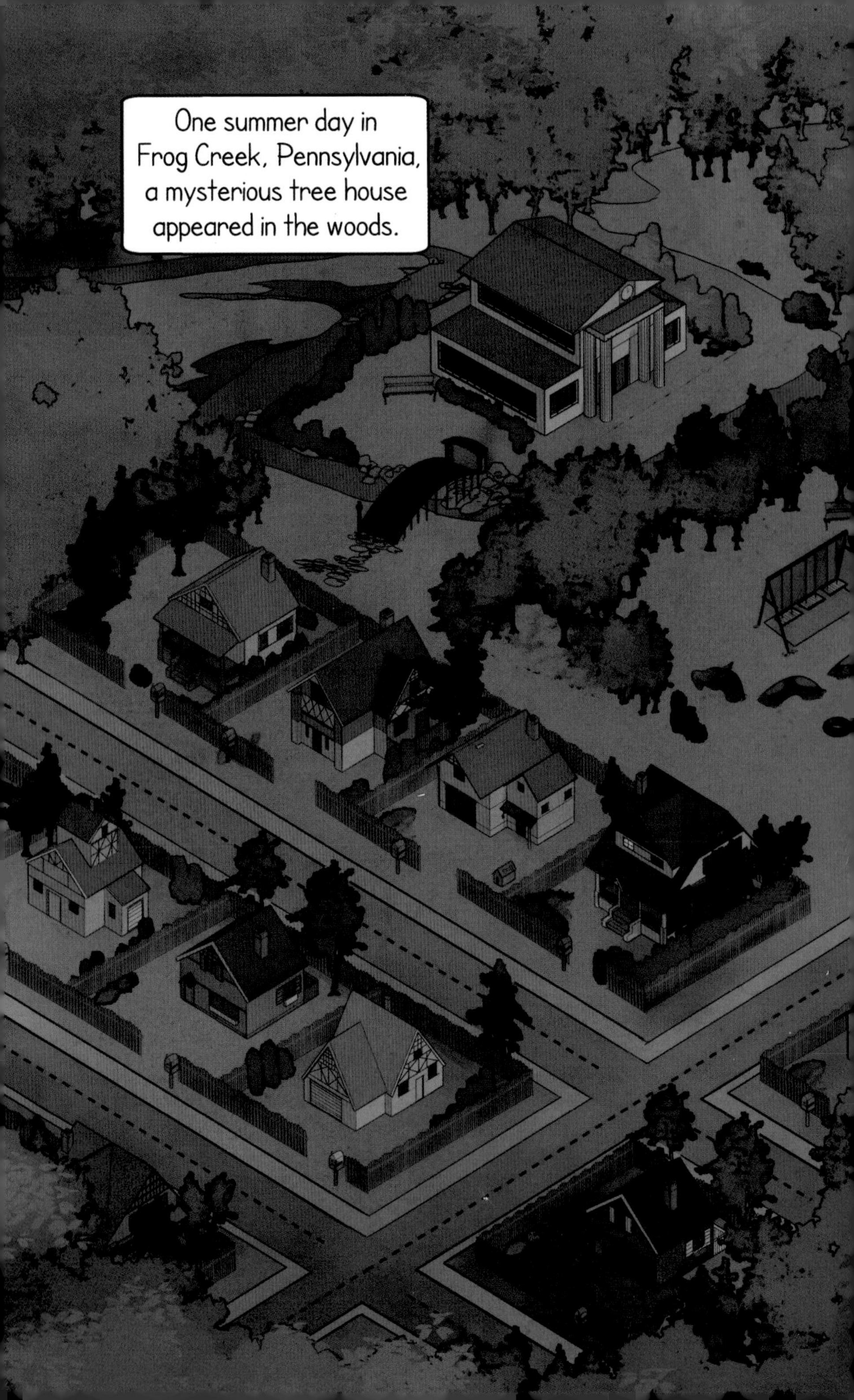
One summer day in Frog Creek, Pennsylvania, a mysterious tree house appeared in the woods.

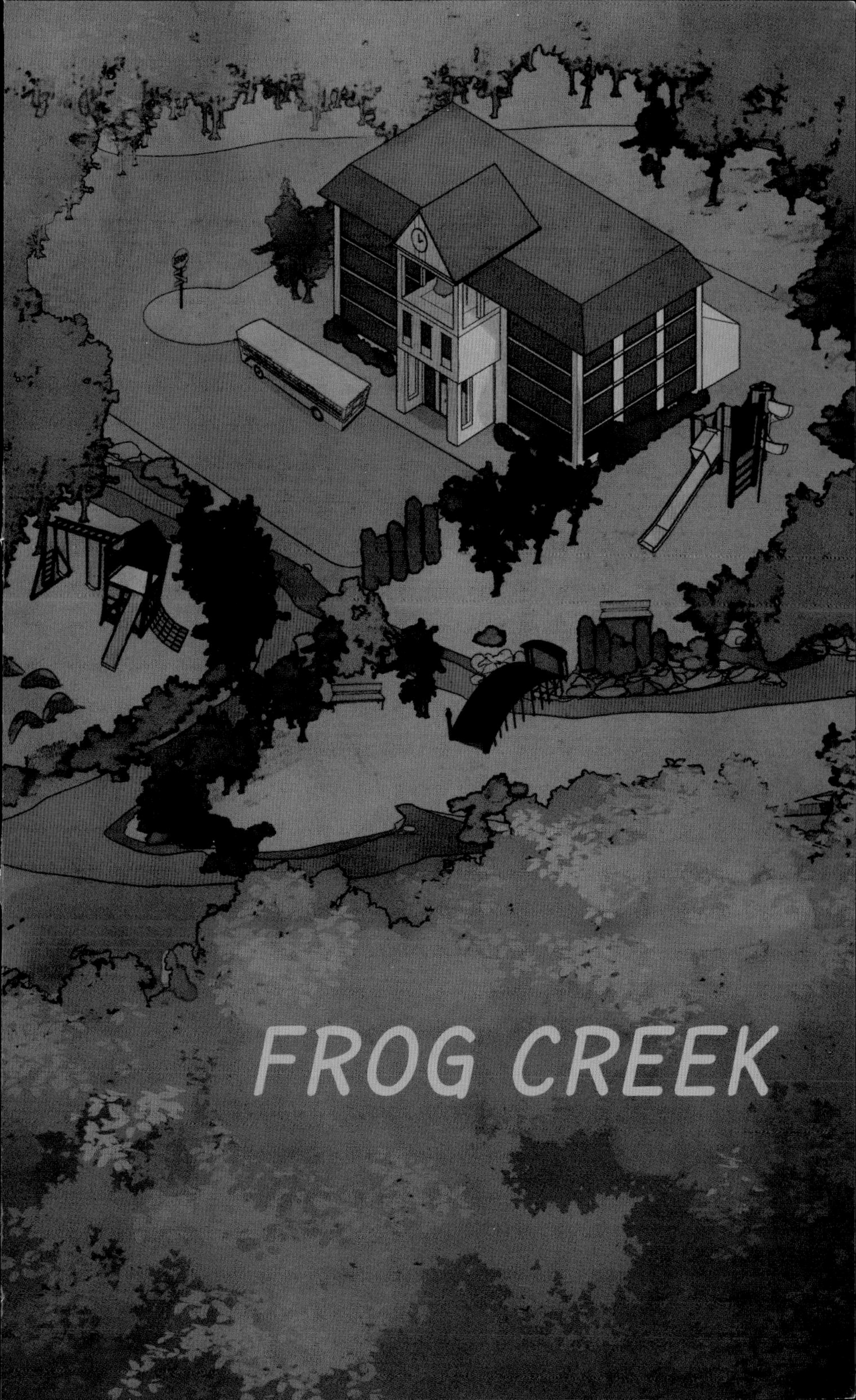
FROG CREEK

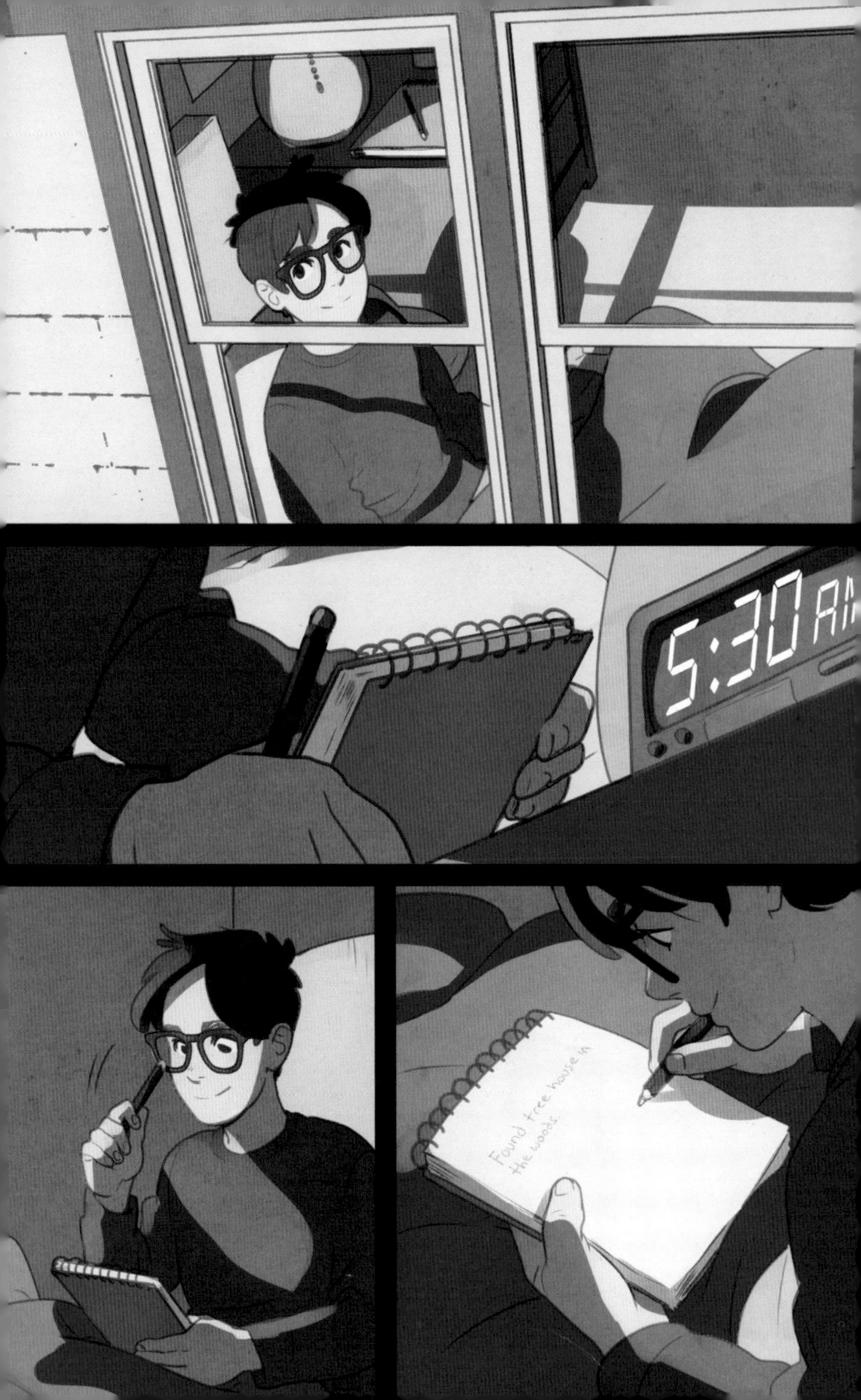
5:30
Found tree house in the woods

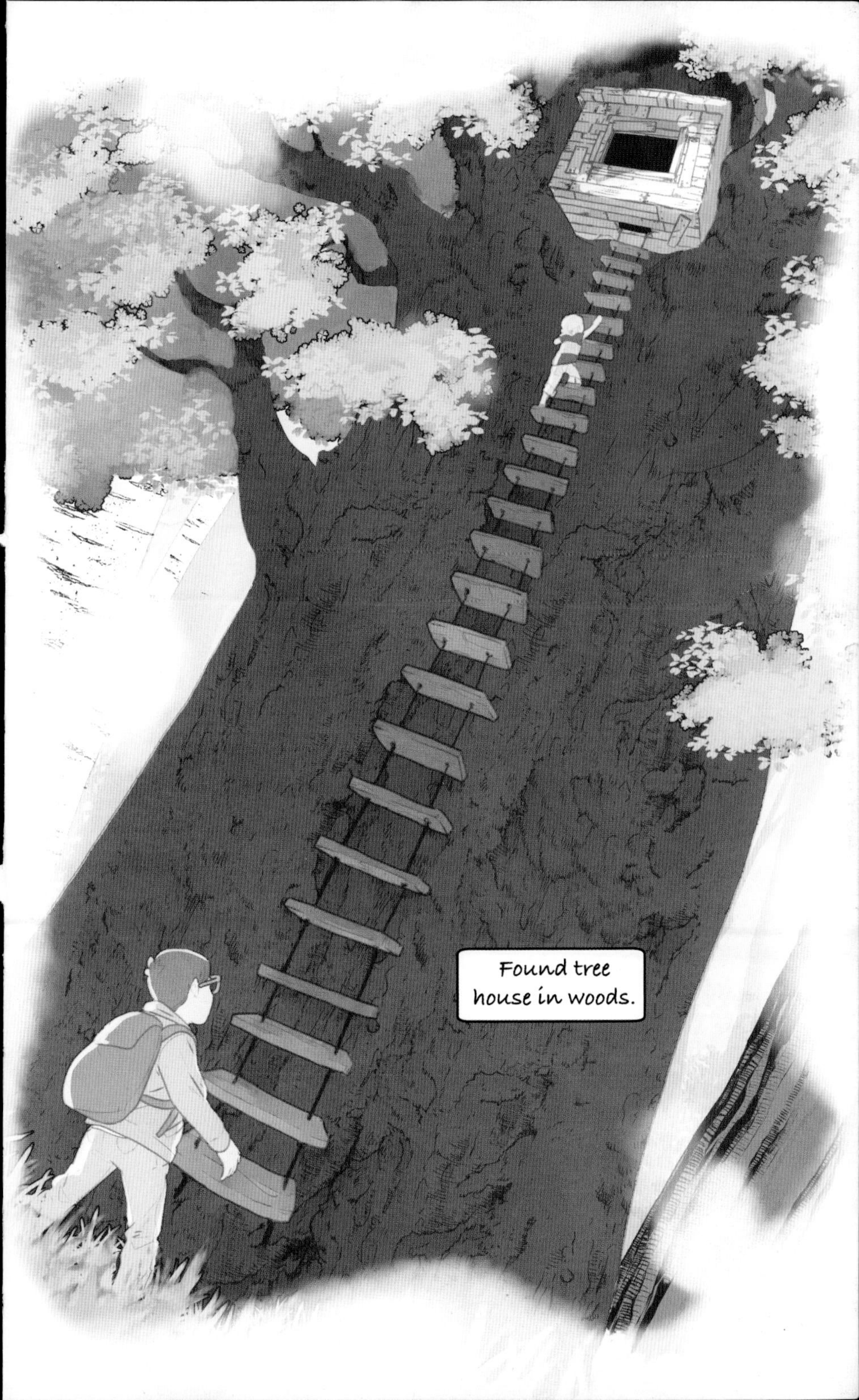
Found tree
house in woods.

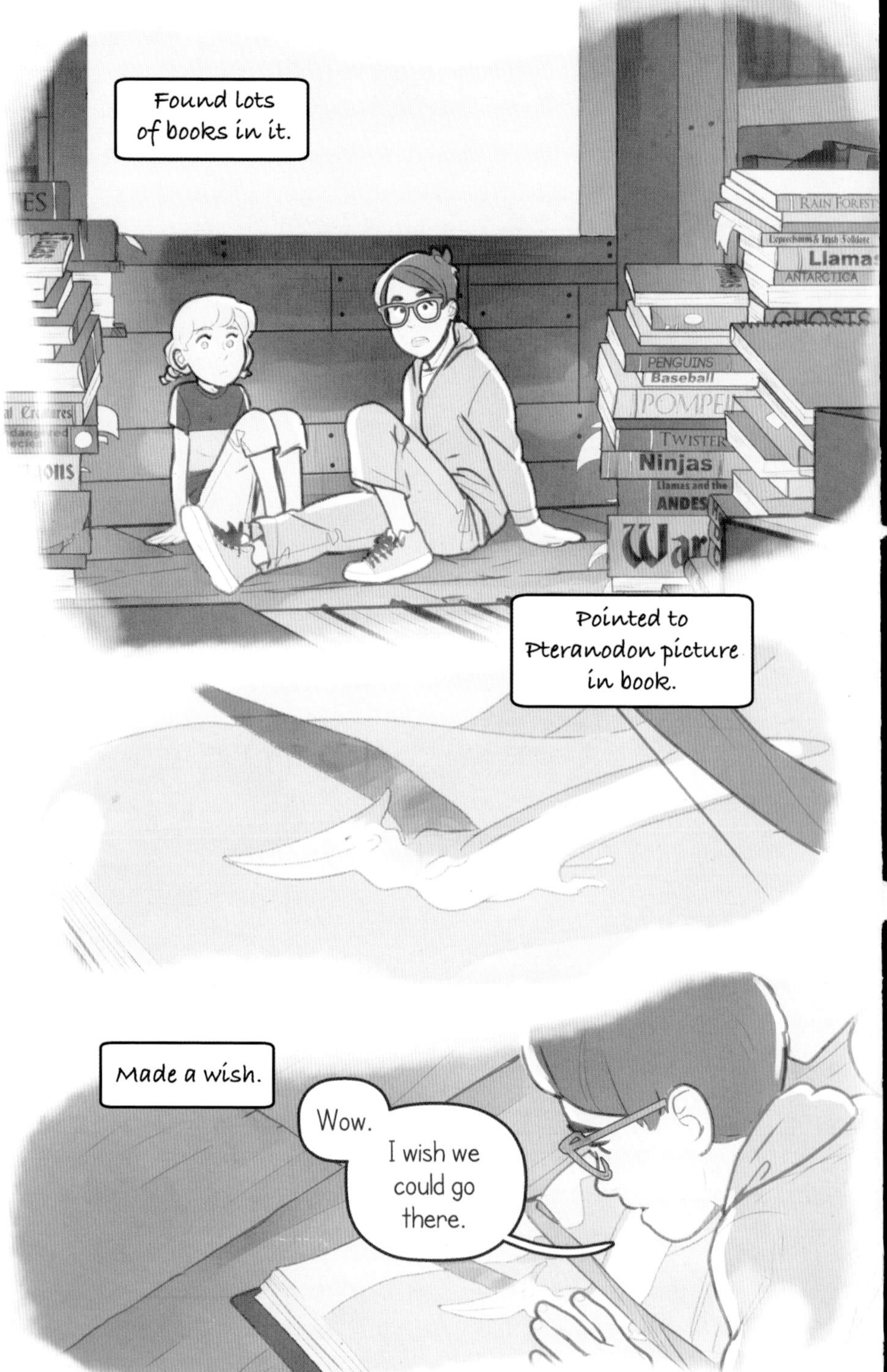
Found lots of books in it.
Leprechauns & Irish Folklore
Llamas
ANTARCTICA
GHOSTS
PENGUINS
Baseball
POMPEII
TWISTER
Ninjas
Llamas and the ANDES
War
Pointed to Pteranodon picture in book.
Made a wish.
Wow.
I wish we could go there.

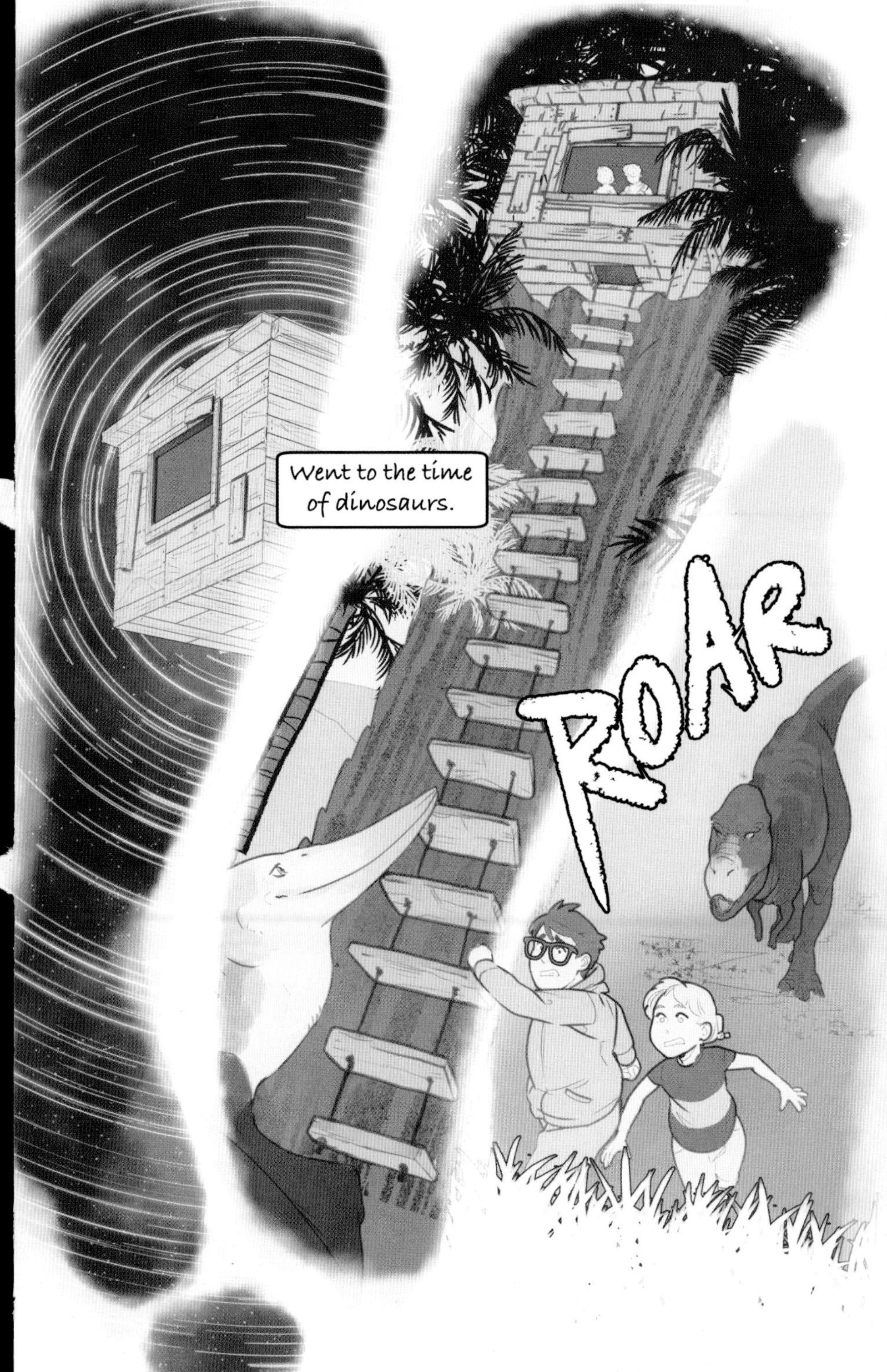
Went to the time of dinosaurs.
ROAR

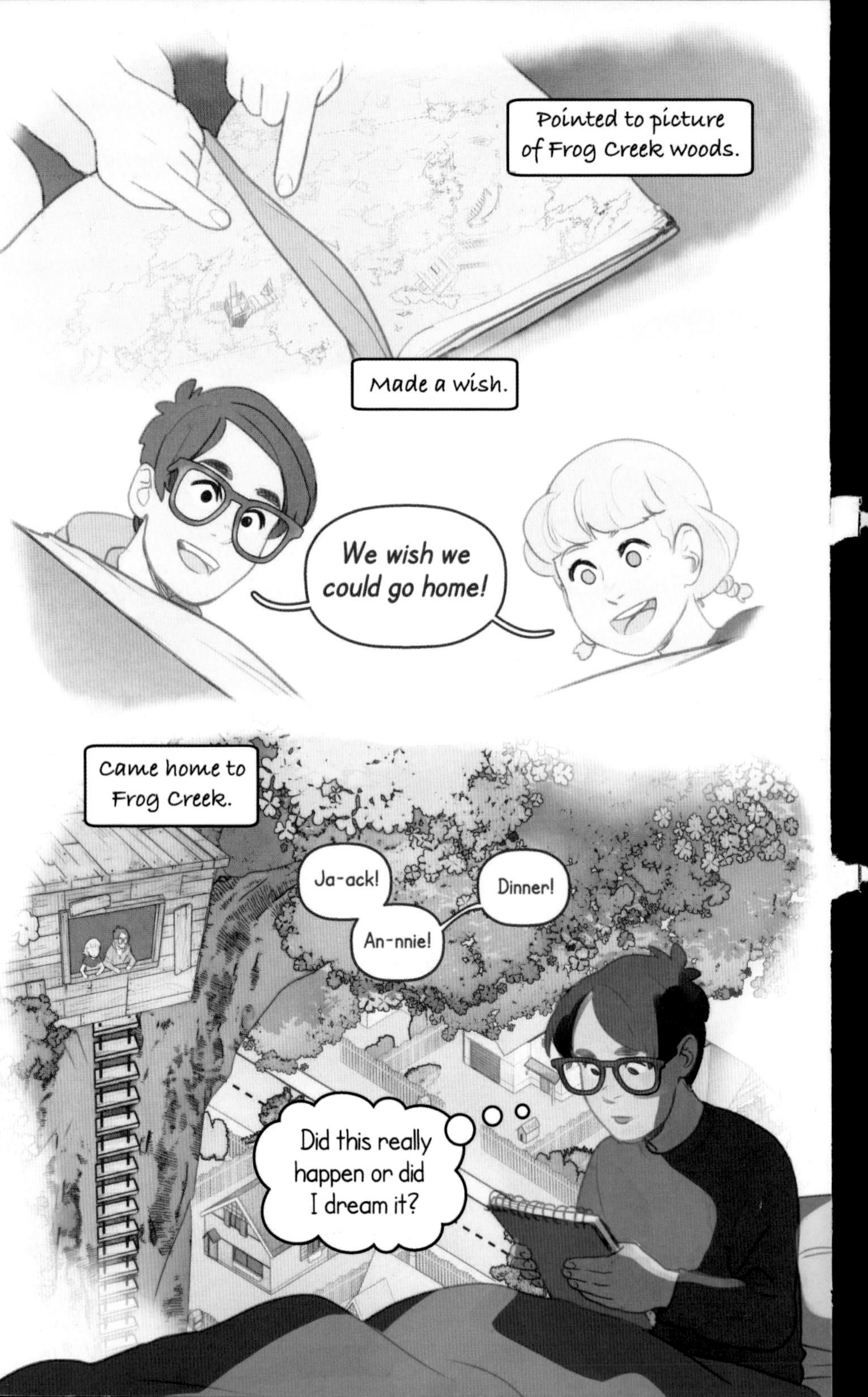
Pointed to picture of Frog Creek woods.
Made a wish.
We wish we could go home!
Came home to Frog Creek.
Ja-ack!
An-nnie!
Dinner!
Did this really happen or did I dream it?

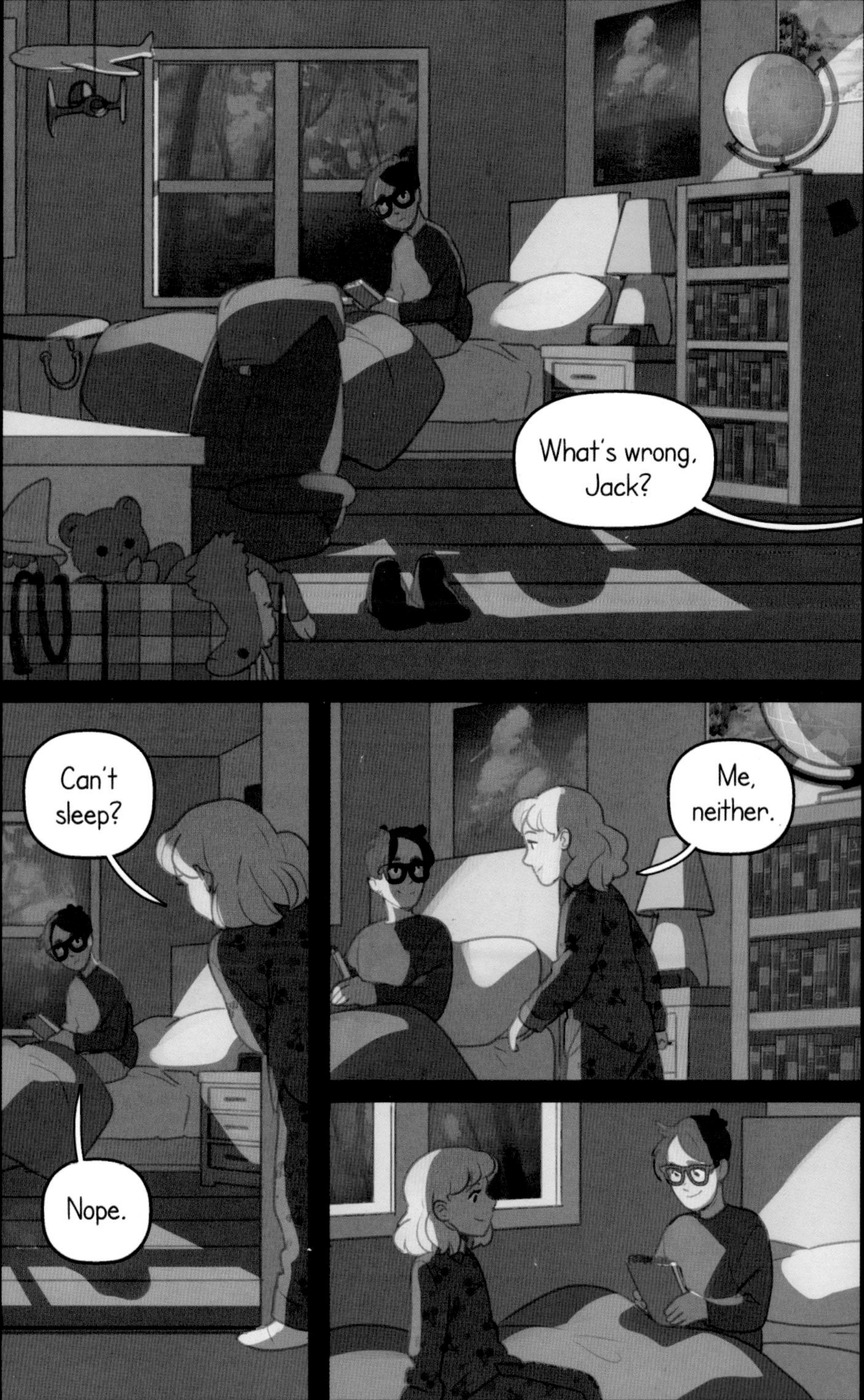
What's wrong, Jack?
Can't sleep?
Nope.
Me, neither.

LET THE MAGIC TREE HOUSE® WHISK YOU AWAY!

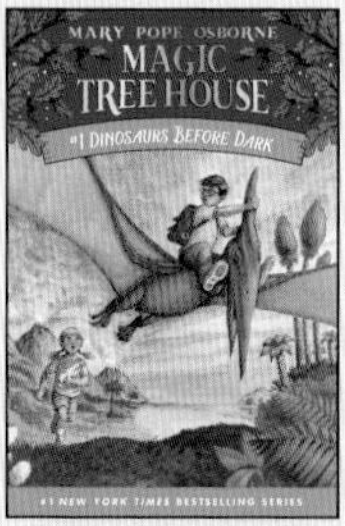
MARY POPE OSBORNE
MAGIC TREE HOUSE
#1 Dinosaurs Before Dark
#1 NEW YORK TIMES BESTSELLING SERIES

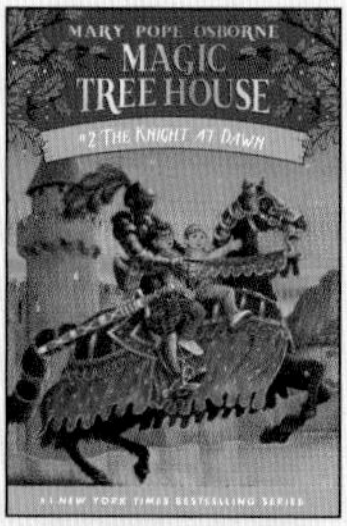
MARY POPE OSBORNE
MAGIC TREE HOUSE
#2 The Knight at Dawn
#1 NEW YORK TIMES BESTSELLING SERIES

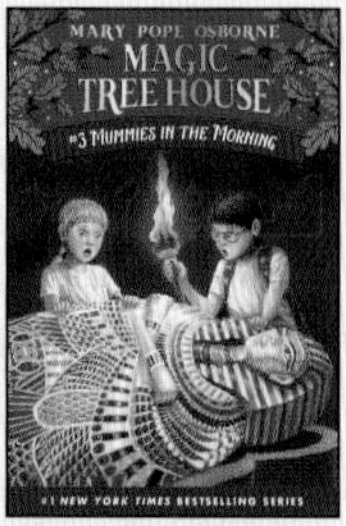
MARY POPE OSBORNE
MAGIC TREE HOUSE
#3 Mummies in the Morning
#1 NEW YORK TIMES BESTSELLING SERIES

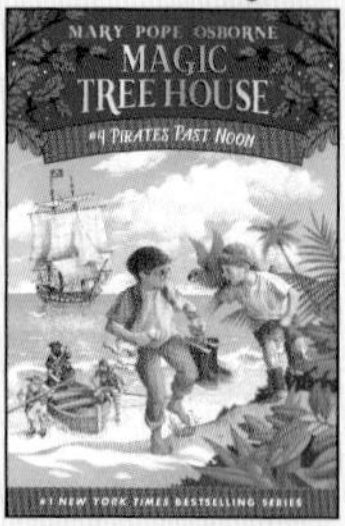
MARY POPE OSBORNE
MAGIC TREE HOUSE
#4 Pirates Past Noon
#1 NEW YORK TIMES BESTSELLING SERIES

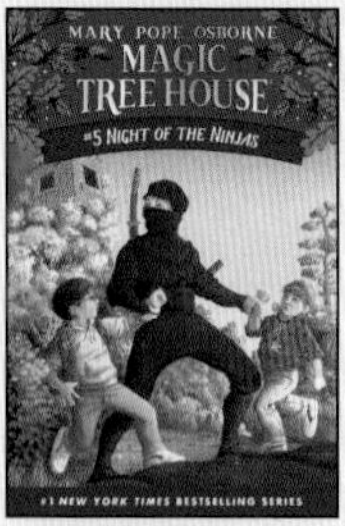
MARY POPE OSBORNE
MAGIC TREE HOUSE
#5 Night of the Ninjas
#1 NEW YORK TIMES BESTSELLING SERIES

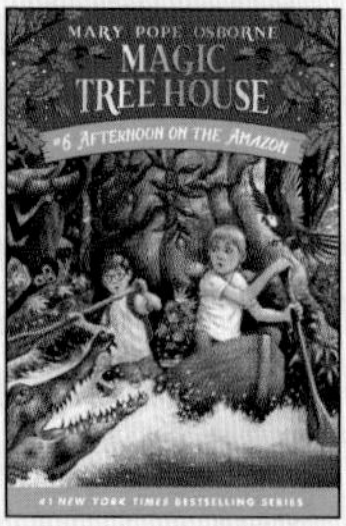
MARY POPE OSBORNE
MAGIC TREE HOUSE
#6 Afternoon on the Amazon
#1 NEW YORK TIMES BESTSELLING SERIES

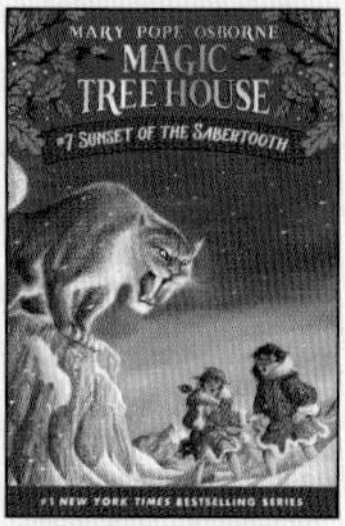
MARY POPE OSBORNE
MAGIC TREE HOUSE
#7 Sunset of the Sabertooth
#1 NEW YORK TIMES BESTSELLING SERIES

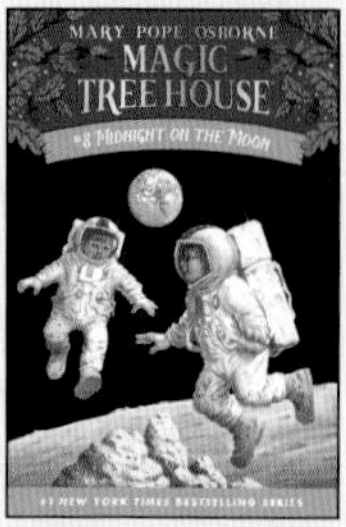
MARY POPE OSBORNE
MAGIC TREE HOUSE
#8 Midnight on the Moon
#1 NEW YORK TIMES BESTSELLING SERIES

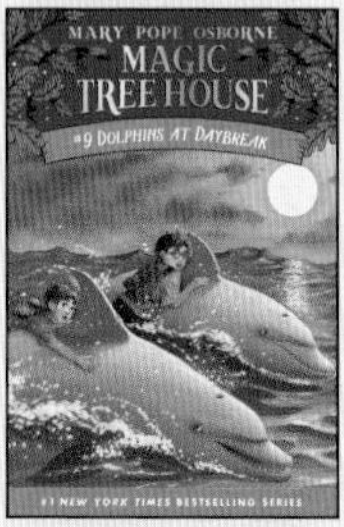
MARY POPE OSBORNE
MAGIC TREE HOUSE
#9 Dolphins at Daybreak
#1 NEW YORK TIMES BESTSELLING SERIES

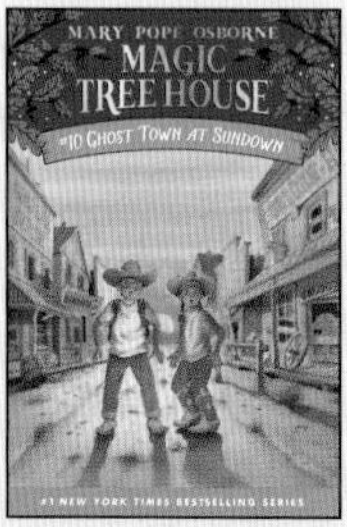
MARY POPE OSBORNE
MAGIC TREE HOUSE
#10 Ghost Town at Sundown
#1 NEW YORK TIMES BESTSELLING SERIES

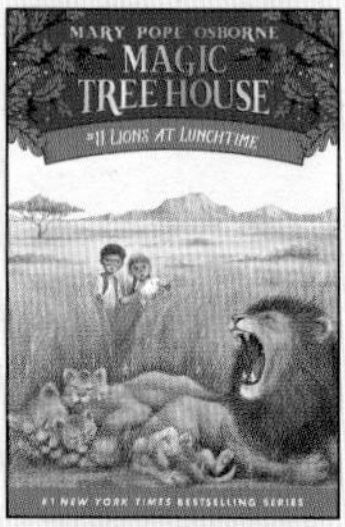
MARY POPE OSBORNE
MAGIC TREE HOUSE
#11 Lions at Lunchtime
#1 NEW YORK TIMES BESTSELLING SERIES

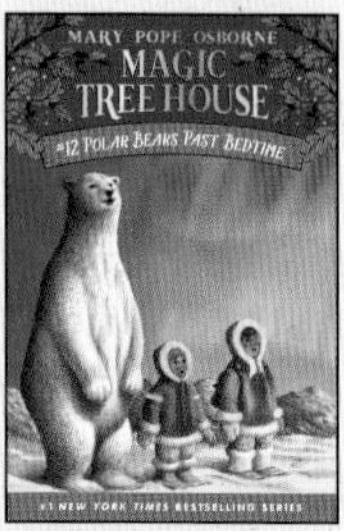
MARY POPE OSBORNE
MAGIC TREE HOUSE
#12 Polar Bears Past Bedtime
#1 NEW YORK TIMES BESTSELLING SERIES

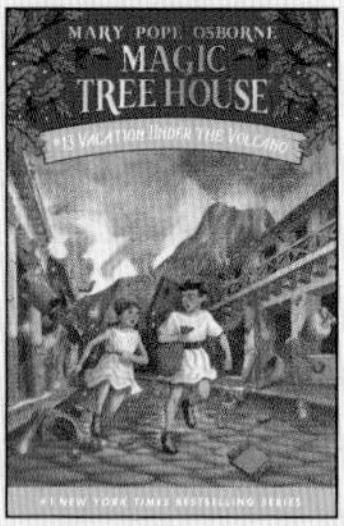
MARY POPE OSBORNE
MAGIC TREE HOUSE
#13 Vacation Under the Volcano
#1 NEW YORK TIMES BESTSELLING SERIES

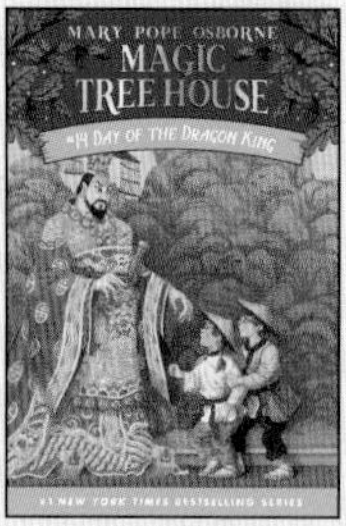
MARY POPE OSBORNE
MAGIC TREE HOUSE
#14 Day of the Dragon King
#1 NEW YORK TIMES BESTSELLING SERIES

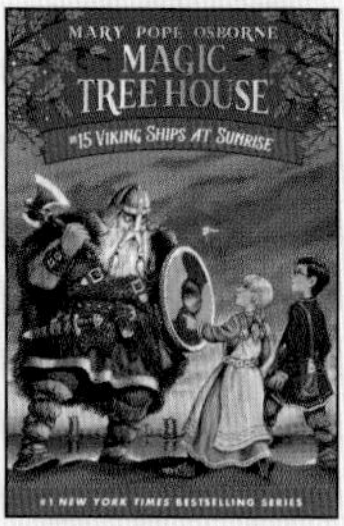
MARY POPE OSBORNE
MAGIC TREE HOUSE
#15 Viking Ships at Sunrise
#1 NEW YORK TIMES BESTSELLING SERIES

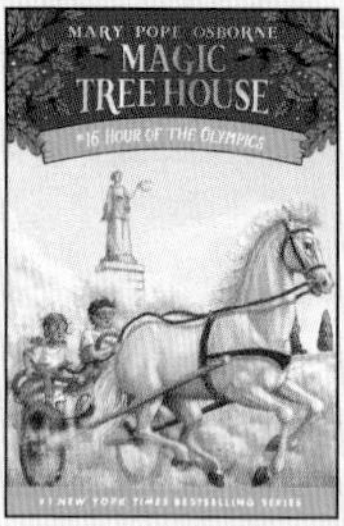
MARY POPE OSBORNE
MAGIC TREE HOUSE
#16 Hour of the Olympics
#1 NEW YORK TIMES BESTSELLING SERIES

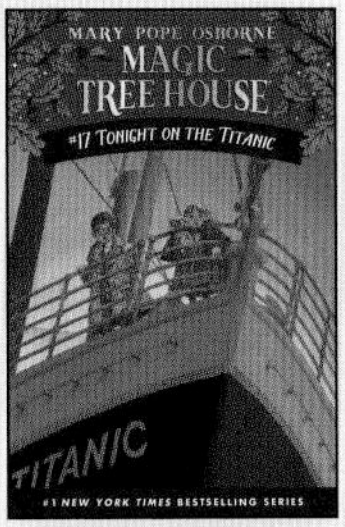
MARY POPE OSBORNE
MAGIC TREE HOUSE
#17 Tonight on the Titanic
TITANIC
#1 NEW YORK TIMES BESTSELLING SERIES
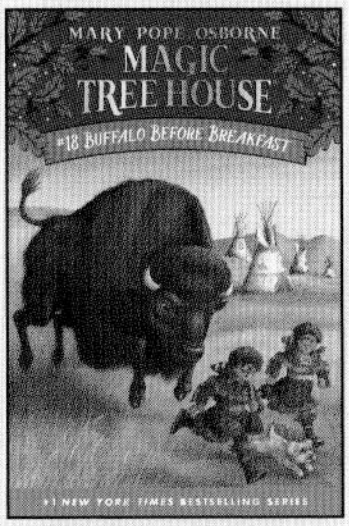
MARY POPE OSBORNE
MAGIC TREE HOUSE
#18 Buffalo Before Breakfast
#1 NEW YORK TIMES BESTSELLING SERIES
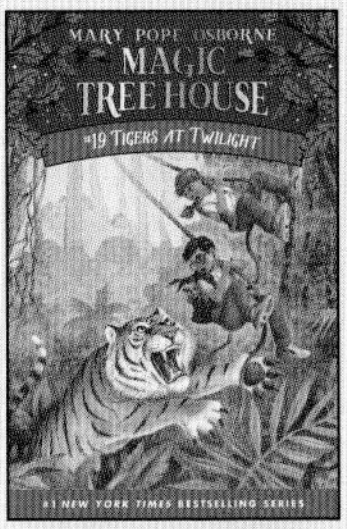
MARY POPE OSBORNE
MAGIC TREE HOUSE
#19 Tigers at Twilight
#1 NEW YORK TIMES BESTSELLING SERIES
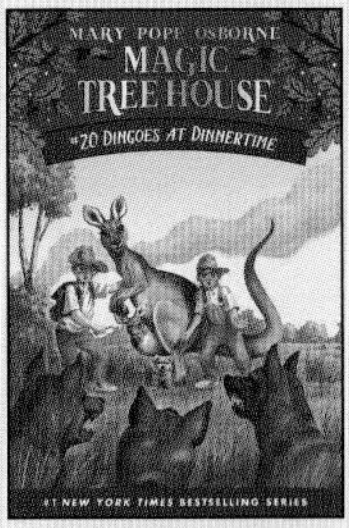
MARY POPE OSBORNE
MAGIC TREE HOUSE
#20 Dingoes at Dinnertime
#1 NEW YORK TIMES BESTSELLING SERIES
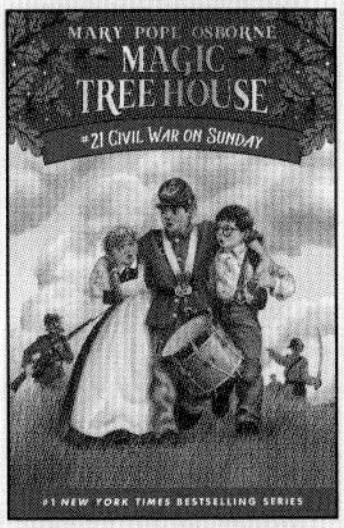
MARY POPE OSBORNE
MAGIC TREE HOUSE
#21 Civil War on Sunday
#1 NEW YORK TIMES BESTSELLING SERIES
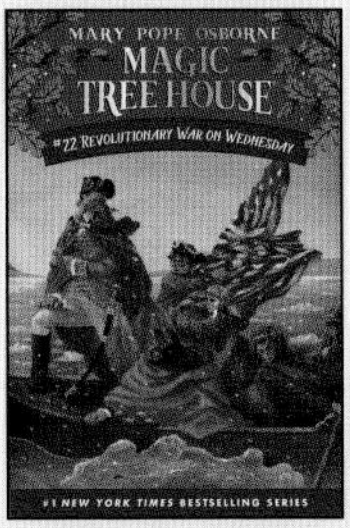
MARY POPE OSBORNE
MAGIC TREE HOUSE
#22 Revolutionary War on Wednesday
#1 NEW YORK TIMES BESTSELLING SERIES
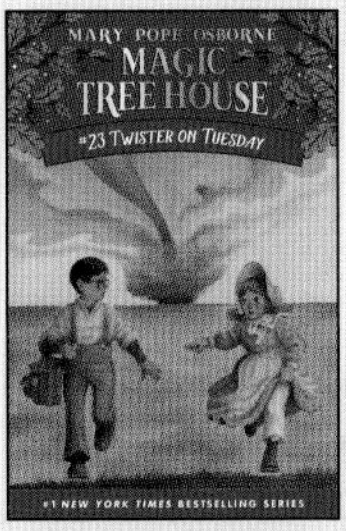
MARY POPE OSBORNE
MAGIC TREE HOUSE
#23 Twister on Tuesday
#1 NEW YORK TIMES BESTSELLING SERIES
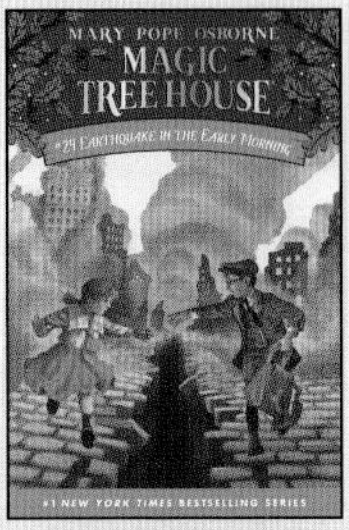
MARY POPE OSBORNE
MAGIC TREE HOUSE
#24 Earthquake in the Early Morning
#1 NEW YORK TIMES BESTSELLING SERIES
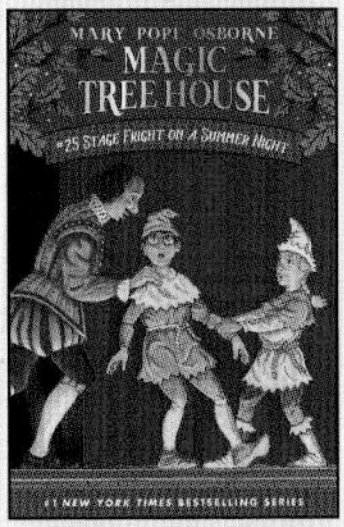
MARY POPE OSBORNE
MAGIC TREE HOUSE
#25 Stage Fright on a Summer Night
#1 NEW YORK TIMES BESTSELLING SERIES
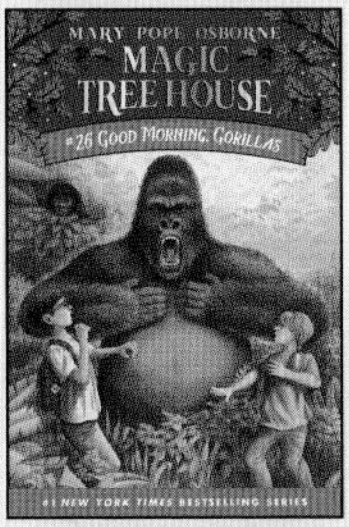
MARY POPE OSBORNE
MAGIC TREE HOUSE
#26 Good Morning, Gorillas
#1 NEW YORK TIMES BESTSELLING SERIES
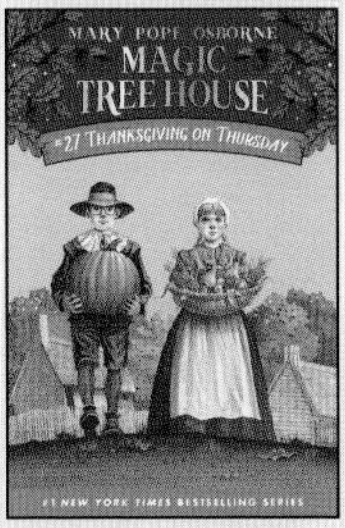
MARY POPE OSBORNE
MAGIC TREE HOUSE
#27 Thanksgiving on Thursday
#1 NEW YORK TIMES BESTSELLING SERIES
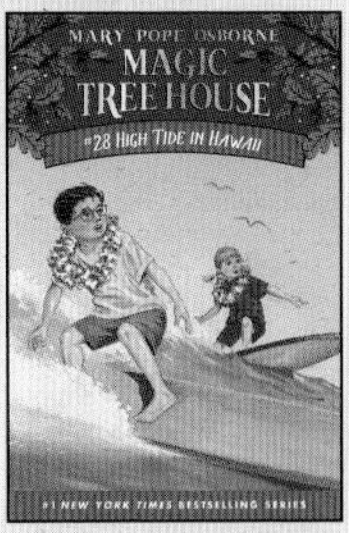
MARY POPE OSBORNE
MAGIC TREE HOUSE
#28 High Tide in Hawaii
#1 NEW YORK TIMES BESTSELLING SERIES
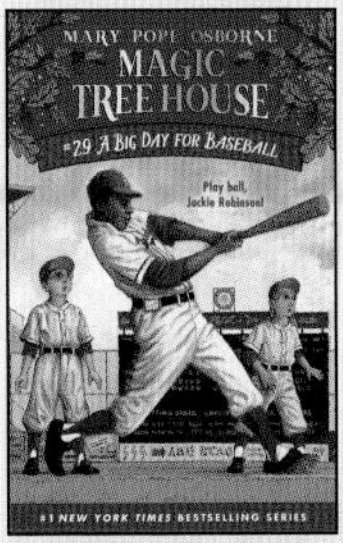
MARY POPE OSBORNE
MAGIC TREE HOUSE
#29 A Big Day for Baseball
Play ball, Jackie Robinson!
#1 NEW YORK TIMES BESTSELLING SERIES
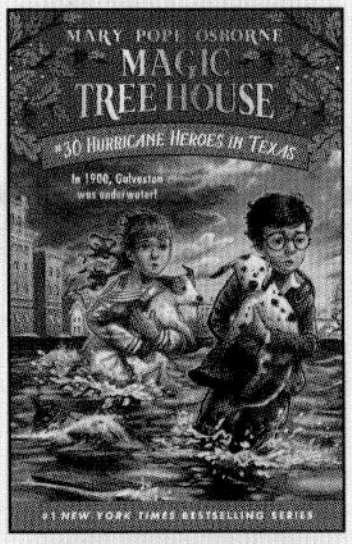
MARY POPE OSBORNE
MAGIC TREE HOUSE
#30 Hurricane Heroes in Texas
In 1900, Galveston was underwater!
#1 NEW YORK TIMES BESTSELLING SERIES
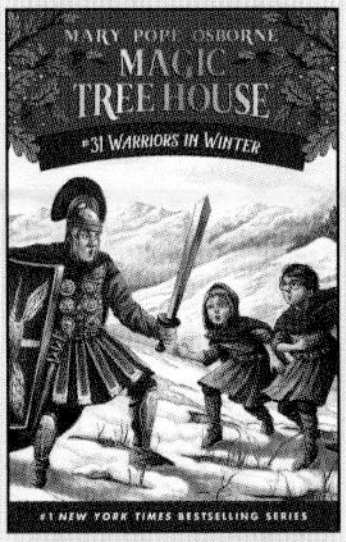
MARY POPE OSBORNE
MAGIC TREE HOUSE
#31 Warriors in Winter
#1 NEW YORK TIMES BESTSELLING SERIES
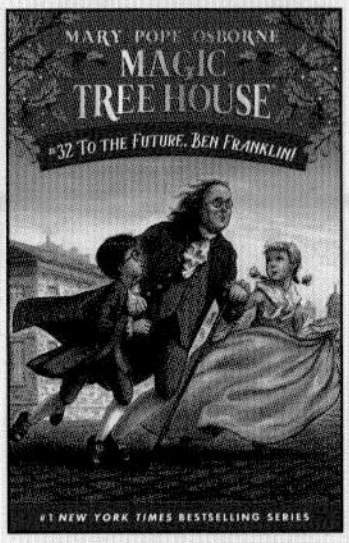
MARY POPE OSBORNE
MAGIC TREE HOUSE
#32 To the Future, Ben Franklin!
#1 NEW YORK TIMES BESTSELLING SERIES
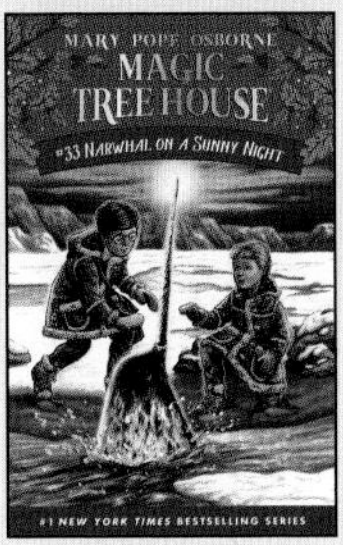
MARY POPE OSBORNE
MAGIC TREE HOUSE
#33 Narwhal on a Sunny Night
#1 NEW YORK TIMES BESTSELLING SERIES
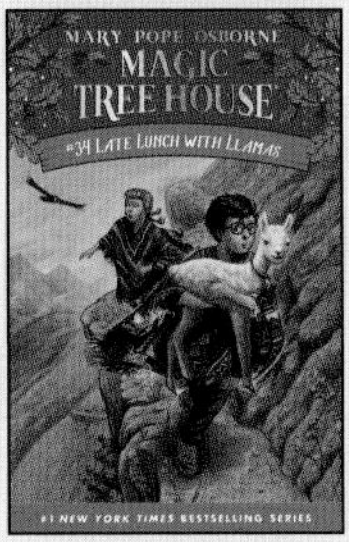
MARY POPE OSBORNE
MAGIC TREE HOUSE
#34 Late Lunch with Llamas
#1 NEW YORK TIMES BESTSELLING SERIES
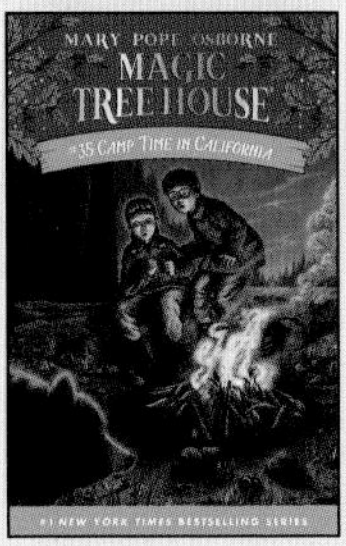
MARY POPE OSBORNE
MAGIC TREE HOUSE
#35 Camp Time in California
#1 NEW YORK TIMES BESTSELLING SERIES

Read all the novels in the #1 bestselling chapter book series of all time!

TRACK THE FACTS WITH JACK & ANNIE!

MAGIC TREE HOUSE FACT TRACKER
Dinosaurs

A NONFICTION COMPANION TO MAGIC TREE HOUSE #1: Dinosaurs Before Dark

Will Osborne and Mary Pope Osborne

MAGIC TREE HOUSE FACT TRACKER
Knights and Castles

A NONFICTION COMPANION TO MAGIC TREE HOUSE #2: The Knight at Dawn

Will Osborne and Mary Pope Osborne

MAGIC TREE HOUSE FACT TRACKER
Mummies and Pyramids

Will Osborne and Mary Pope Osborne

MAGIC TREE HOUSE FACT TRACKER
Pirates

Will Osborne and Mary Pope Osborne

MAGIC TREE HOUSE FACT TRACKER
Rain Forests

Will Osborne and Mary Pope Osborne

MAGIC TREE HOUSE FACT TRACKER
Space

Will Osborne and Mary Pope Osborne

MAGIC TREE HOUSE FACT TRACKER
Titanic

Will Osborne and Mary Pope Osborne

MAGIC TREE HOUSE FACT TRACKER
Twisters and Other Terrible Storms

Will Osborne and Mary Pope Osborne

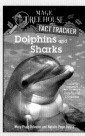

MAGIC TREE HOUSE FACT TRACKER
Dolphins and Sharks

Mary Pope Osborne and Natalie Pope Boyce

MAGIC TREE HOUSE FACT TRACKER
Ancient Greece and the Olympics

Mary Pope Osborne and Natalie Pope Boyce

MAGIC TREE HOUSE FACT TRACKER
American Revolution

Mary Pope Osborne and Natalie Pope Boyce

MAGIC TREE HOUSE FACT TRACKER
Sabertooths and the Ice Age

Mary Pope Osborne and Natalie Pope Boyce

MAGIC TREE HOUSE FACT TRACKER
Pilgrims

Mary Pope Osborne and Natalie Pope Boyce

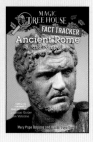

MAGIC TREE HOUSE FACT TRACKER
Ancient Rome and Pompeii

Mary Pope Osborne and Natalie Pope Boyce

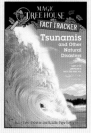

MAGIC TREE HOUSE FACT TRACKER
Tsunamis and Other Natural Disasters

Mary Pope Osborne and Natalie Pope Boyce

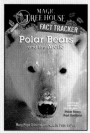

MAGIC TREE HOUSE FACT TRACKER
Polar Bears and the Arctic

Mary Pope Osborne and Natalie Pope Boyce

MAGIC TREE HOUSE FACT TRACKER
Sea Monsters

Mary Pope Osborne and Natalie Pope Boyce

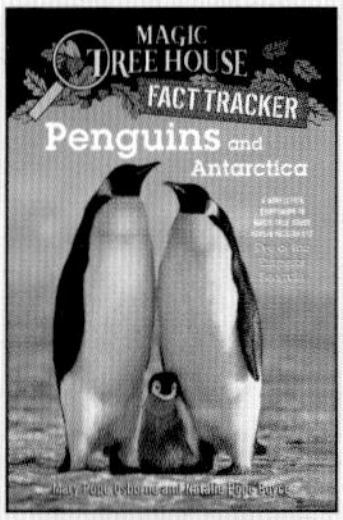
MAGIC TREE HOUSE
FACT TRACKER
Penguins and Antarctica
Mary Pope Osborne and Natalie Pope Boyce
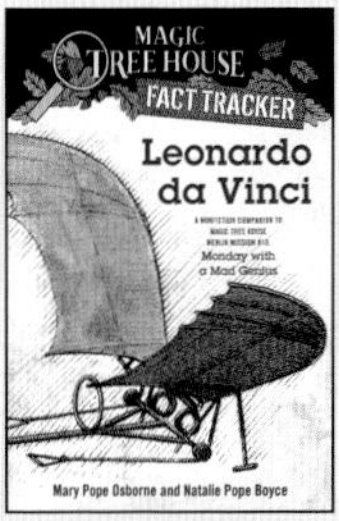
MAGIC TREE HOUSE
FACT TRACKER
Leonardo da Vinci
Monday with a Mad Genius
Mary Pope Osborne and Natalie Pope Boyce
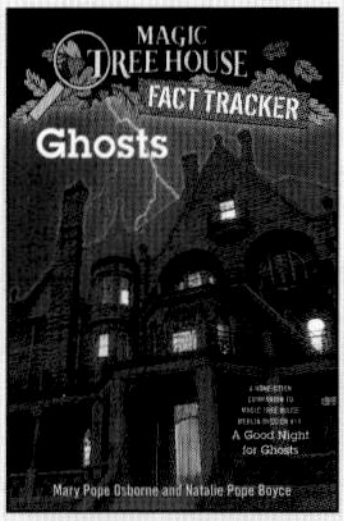
MAGIC TREE HOUSE
FACT TRACKER
Ghosts
A Good Night for Ghosts
Mary Pope Osborne and Natalie Pope Boyce
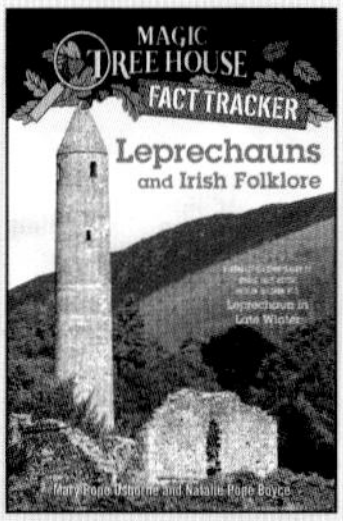
MAGIC TREE HOUSE
FACT TRACKER
Leprechauns and Irish Folklore
Mary Pope Osborne and Natalie Pope Boyce
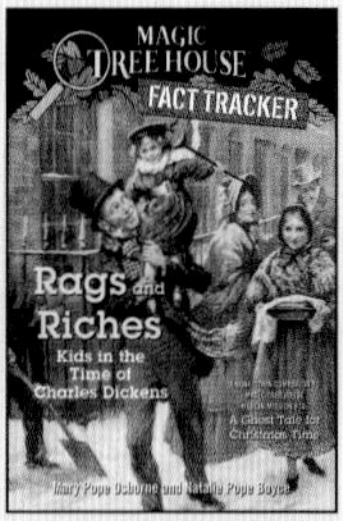
MAGIC TREE HOUSE
FACT TRACKER
Rags and Riches
Kids in the Time of Charles Dickens
Mary Pope Osborne and Natalie Pope Boyce
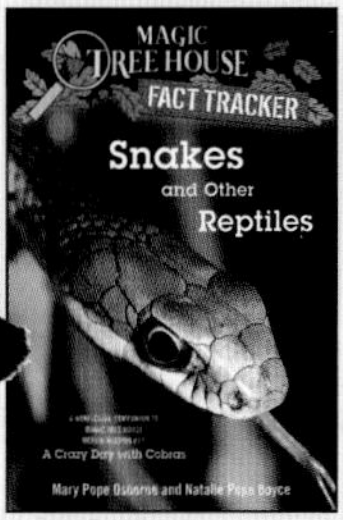
MAGIC TREE HOUSE
FACT TRACKER
Snakes and Other Reptiles
A Crazy Day with Cobras
Mary Pope Osborne and Natalie Pope Boyce
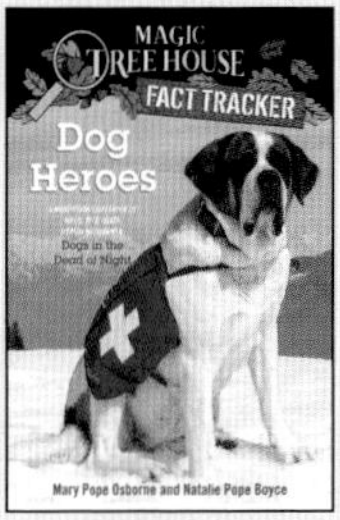
MAGIC TREE HOUSE
FACT TRACKER
Dog Heroes
Mary Pope Osborne and Natalie Pope Boyce
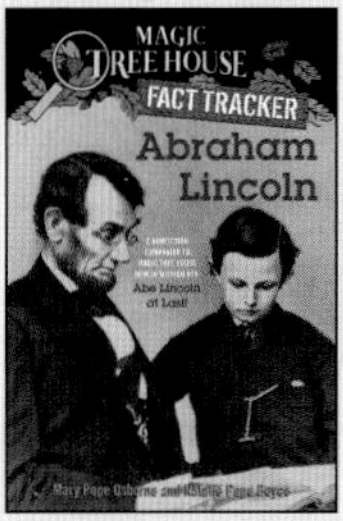
MAGIC TREE HOUSE
FACT TRACKER
Abraham Lincoln
Abe Lincoln at Last!
Mary Pope Osborne and Natalie Pope Boyce
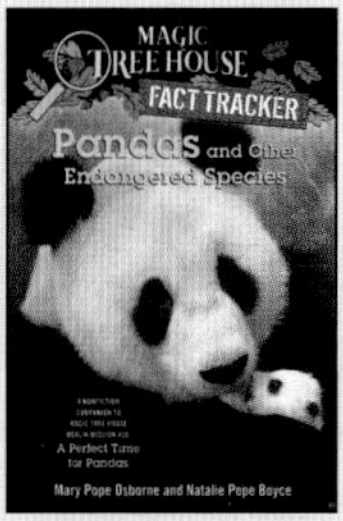
MAGIC TREE HOUSE
FACT TRACKER
Pandas and Other Endangered Species
A Perfect Time for Pandas
Mary Pope Osborne and Natalie Pope Boyce
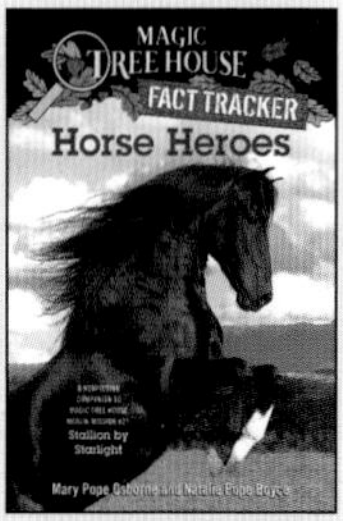
MAGIC TREE HOUSE
FACT TRACKER
Horse Heroes
Stallion by Starlight
Mary Pope Osborne and Natalie Pope Boyce
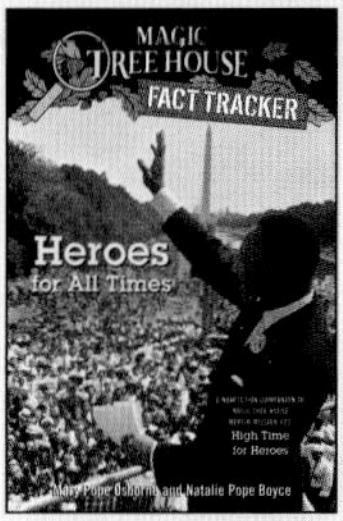
MAGIC TREE HOUSE
FACT TRACKER
Heroes for All Times
High Time for Heroes
Mary Pope Osborne and Natalie Pope Boyce
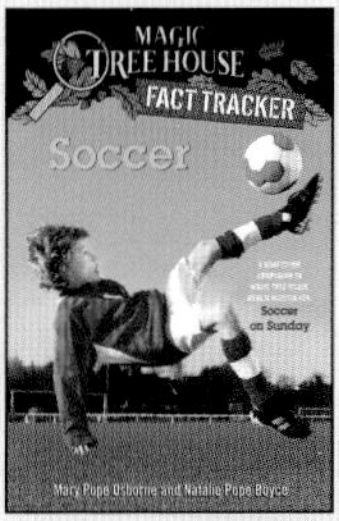
MAGIC TREE HOUSE
FACT TRACKER
Soccer
Soccer on Sunday
Mary Pope Osborne and Natalie Pope Boyce
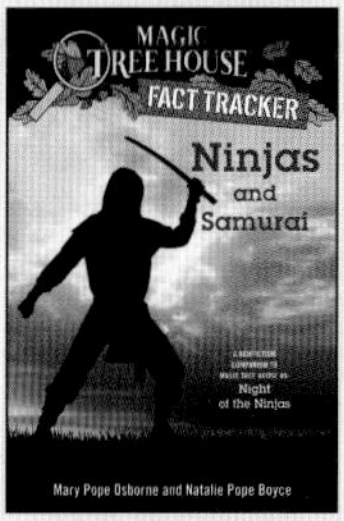
MAGIC TREE HOUSE
FACT TRACKER
Ninjas and Samurai
Night of the Ninjas
Mary Pope Osborne and Natalie Pope Boyce
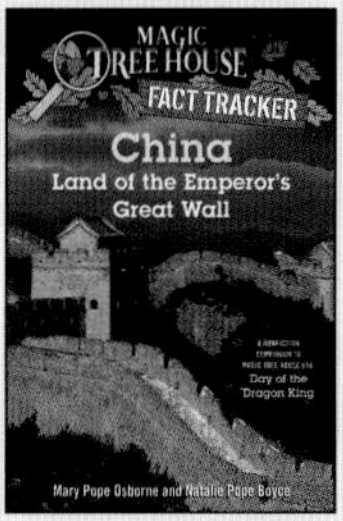
MAGIC TREE HOUSE
FACT TRACKER
China
Land of the Emperor's Great Wall
Day of the Dragon King
Mary Pope Osborne and Natalie Pope Boyce
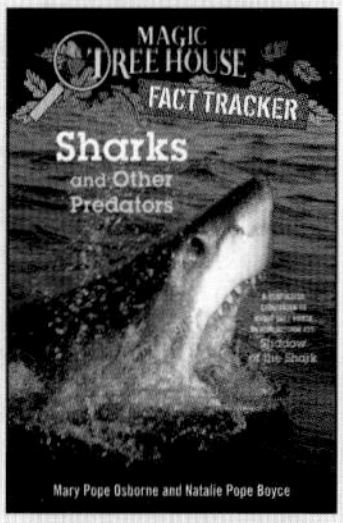
MAGIC TREE HOUSE
FACT TRACKER
Sharks and Other Predators
Shadow of the Shark
Mary Pope Osborne and Natalie Pope Boyce
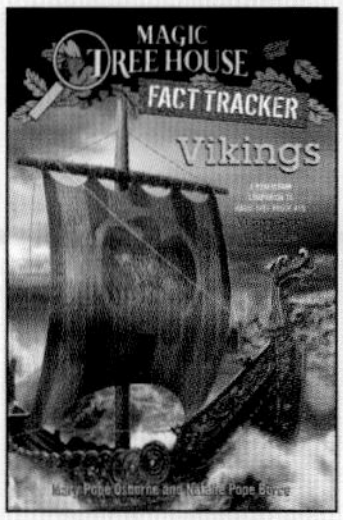
MAGIC TREE HOUSE
FACT TRACKER
Vikings
Mary Pope Osborne and Natalie Pope Boyce
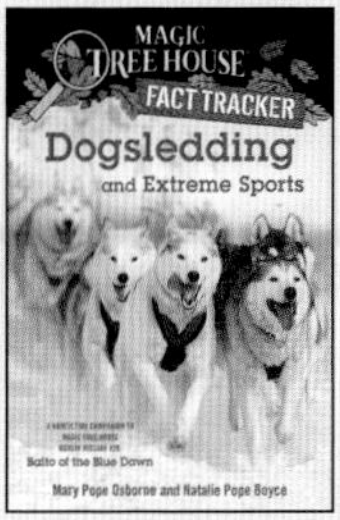
MAGIC TREE HOUSE
FACT TRACKER
Dogsledding and Extreme Sports
Balto of the Blue Dawn
Mary Pope Osborne and Natalie Pope Boyce
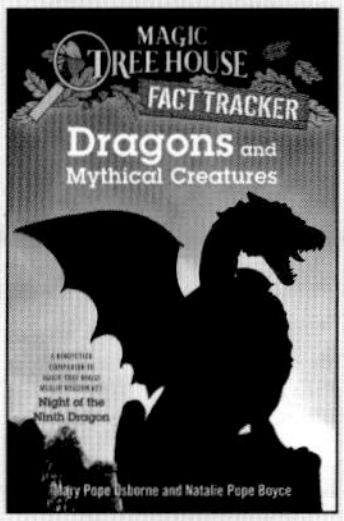
MAGIC TREE HOUSE
FACT TRACKER
Dragons and Mythical Creatures
Night of the Ninth Dragon
Mary Pope Osborne and Natalie Pope Boyce
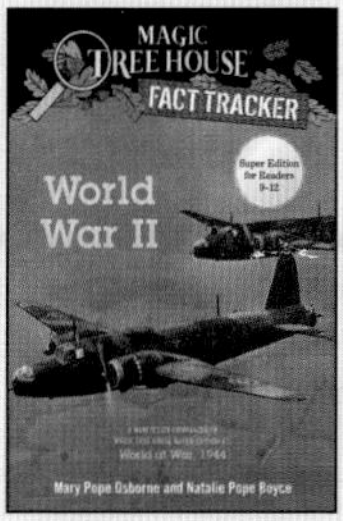
MAGIC TREE HOUSE
FACT TRACKER
World War II
Super Edition for Readers 9-12
World at War, 1944
Mary Pope Osborne and Natalie Pope Boyce
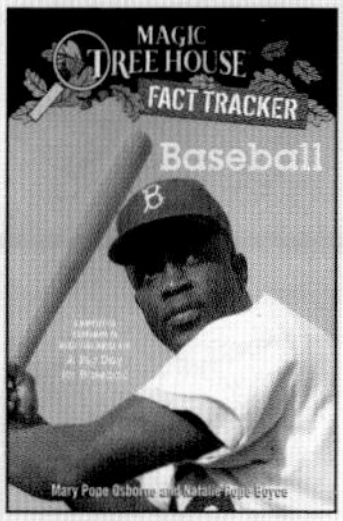
MAGIC TREE HOUSE
FACT TRACKER
Baseball
A Big Day for Baseball
Mary Pope Osborne and Natalie Pope Boyce
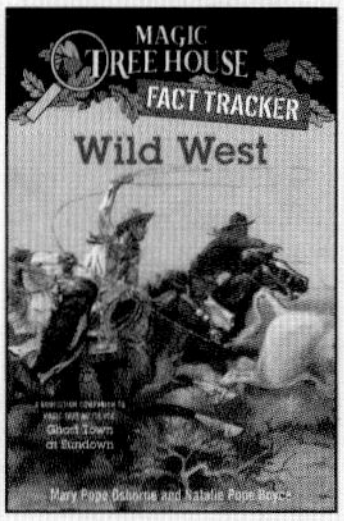
MAGIC TREE HOUSE
FACT TRACKER
Wild West
Ghost Town at Sundown
Mary Pope Osborne and Natalie Pope Boyce
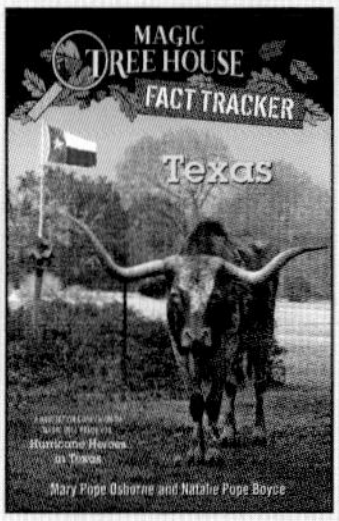
MAGIC TREE HOUSE
FACT TRACKER
Texas
Hurricane Heroes in Texas
Mary Pope Osborne and Natalie Pope Boyce
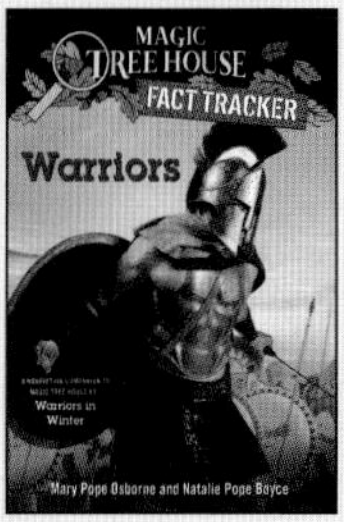
MAGIC TREE HOUSE
FACT TRACKER
Warriors
Warriors in Winter
Mary Pope Osborne and Natalie Pope Boyce
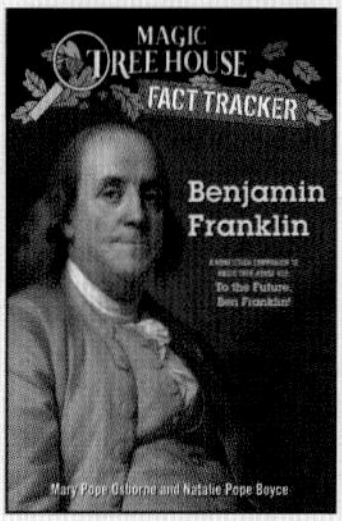
MAGIC TREE HOUSE
FACT TRACKER
Benjamin Franklin
To the Future, Ben Franklin!
Mary Pope Osborne and Natalie Pope Boyce
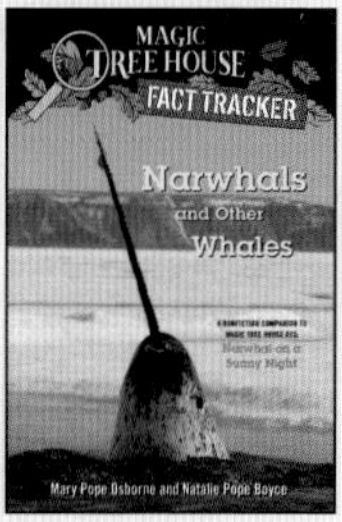
MAGIC TREE HOUSE
FACT TRACKER
Narwhals and Other Whales
Narwhal on a Sunny Night
Mary Pope Osborne and Natalie Pope Boyce

MARY POPE OSBORNE is the author of many novels, picture books, story collections, and nonfiction books. Her #1 *New York Times* bestselling Magic Tree House® series has been translated into numerous languages around the world. Highly recommended by parents and educators everywhere, the series introduces young readers to different cultures and times, as well as to the world's legacy of ancient myth and storytelling.

JENNY LAIRD is an award-winning playwright. She collaborates with Will Osborne and Randy Courts on creating musical theater adaptations of the Magic Tree House® series for both national and international audiences. Their work also includes shows for young performers, available through Music Theatre International's Broadway Junior® Collection. Currently the team is working on a Magic Tree House® animated television series.

KELLY & NICHOLE MATTHEWS are twin sisters and a comic-art team. They get to do their dream job every day, drawing comics for a living. They've worked with Boom Studios!, Archaia, the Jim Henson Company, Hiveworks, and now Random House!